TWO … ELM
CREEK …
IN ON…
HOL…

Christmas QUILT

JENNIFER CHIAVERINI

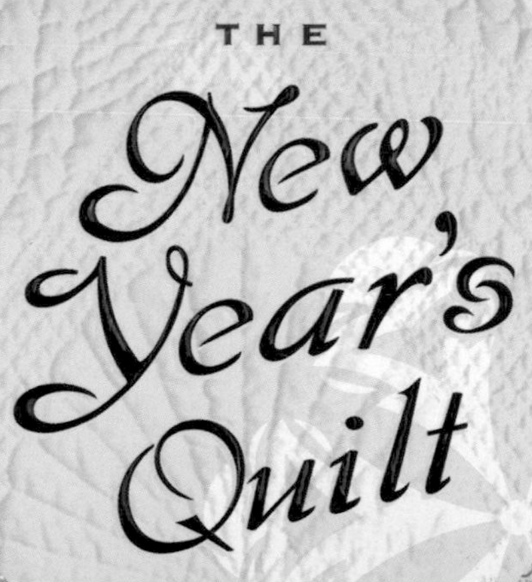

$7.99 U.S.
$8.99 CAN.

New York Times bestselling author Jennifer Chiaverini's Elm Creek Quilts novels are "warm and wise" (*South Cheatham Advocate,* TN). . . . Enjoy these two wonderful holiday tales from her acclaimed series!

The Christmas Quilt

"A charming story of love and family."

—*Library Journal* (starred review)

"This redemptive novel beautifully [celebrates] the strength of women, sisterhood, and friendship. Wrap this one up for a cherished friend."

—*The Virginian-Pilot*

"This captivating story unfolds at a perfect pace."

—*Star-Telegram* (Ft. Worth, TX)

"Stylish and satisfying . . . a wonderful holiday mix of family legacy, reconciliation, and shared experiences."

—*Tucson Citizen*

"A book that can be enjoyed in an evening, savored over hot chocolate and shared with any quilters you know."

—*Winston-Salem Journal*

"The perfect Christmas story. . . . Read this book and feel the glow."

—*The Kingston Observer* (MA)

The New Year's Quilt

"Chiaverini's stitches are sound."

—*Publishers Weekly*

Books by Jennifer Chiaverini

The Winding Ways Quilt

The Quilter's Homecoming

Circle of Quilters

The New Year's Quilt

The Christmas Quilt

The Sugar Camp Quilt

The Master Quilter

The Quilter's Legacy

The Runaway Quilt

The Cross-Country Quilters

Round Robin

The Quilter's Apprentice

Elm Creek Quilts: Quilt Projects Inspired by the Elm Creek Quilts Novels

Return to Elm Creek: More Quilt Projects Inspired by the Elm Creek Quilts Novels

An Elm Creek Quilts Sampler

An Elm Creek Quilts Album

The Christmas Quilt

★

The New Year's Quilt

Two Elm Creek Quilts novels

JENNIFER CHIAVERINI

POCKET BOOKS
New York · London · Toronto · Sydney

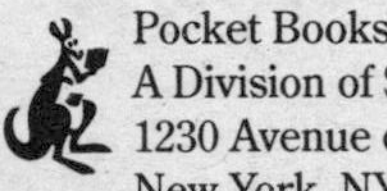

Pocket Books
A Division of Simon & Schuster, Inc.
1230 Avenue of the Americas
New York, NY 10020

First Pocket Books paperback edition November 2008

POCKET and colophon are registered trademarks of Simon & Schuster, Inc.

For information about special discounts for bulk purchases, please contact Simon & Schuster Special Sales at 1-800-456-6798 or business@simonandschuster.com.

Cover art and design: Honi Werner

Manufactured in the United States of America

10 9 8 7 6 5 4 3 2 1

ISBN-13: 978-1-4391-0025-7
ISBN-10: 1-4391-0025-X

These titles were originally published individually by Simon & Schuster.

Contents

The Christmas Quilt 1

The New Year's Quilt 225

The Christmas Quilt

★

To my grandparents,
Virginia and Edward Riechman

"I give you simply the joy and hope of the season."

—Gerda Bergstrom

Chapter One

SYLVIA'S CHILDHOOD HOME was so full of memories it was a wonder there was any room for furniture. As the December days grew colder and the nights longer, the bygone years seemed to encroach ever more insistently into the present—vexing Sylvia day and night with their persistence. She imagined spirits of Christmases past crowding the halls, arguing over favorite chairs by the fire, looking about Elm Creek Manor, and shaking their heads in dismay over how she had let the place go. She would earn a small fortune if she could charge them rent, but regrettably, the spirits offered only longing whispers and mournful sighs. Nothing would appease them save an old-fashioned Bergstrom family Christmas, with all the trappings of the holiday, every beloved tradition fulfilled to the letter.

If Sylvia addressed the spirits—which she would not do, she was seventy-six but not quite ready to speak aloud to an empty room, thank you very much—she would warn them that they were bound to be disappointed. As much as Sylvia missed the Christmas joys of her youth, the Bergstroms were gone, every last one of them save Sylvia herself, and their traditions had passed on with them. Besides, Sylvia had a plan whose success depended upon this being the dullest, least festive, and most yawn-inducing Christmas in the history of Elm Creek Manor.

Her young friend Sarah McClure laughed off Sylvia's warnings of a dreary Christmas in their remote central

Pennsylvania home. "Excitement is precisely what I'm trying to avoid," explained Sarah as she sewed three quilted stockings to hang before the fireplace in the library. "Christmas at my mother's house would be interesting, but for all the wrong reasons."

Exasperated, Sylvia strengthened her resolve to bring about reconciliation between Sarah and her mother. After all, Sarah had promised to try. A year and a half earlier, Sylvia had returned to Elm Creek Manor after a fifty-year absence, the sole heir to the Bergstrom estate upon the death of her estranged sister, Claudia. She had intended to sell it, but with Sarah's help, she made peace with her past and realized that she could never sell her beloved family home. The question remained, however, of how to restore life and happiness to the manor, which was much too large for one old woman living alone. Sarah had devised an ingenious solution, combining their love for quilting with their need for community by turning the Bergstrom estate into a summer retreat for quilters. As Sylvia and Sarah negotiated their business agreement, Sylvia, in repayment for all Sarah had done to help Sylvia reconcile with estranged loved ones, decided to add a clause that would encourage Sarah to mend fences in her own life.

"I don't know what kind of conflict stands between you and your mother," Sylvia had said, "but you must promise me you'll talk to her and do your best to resolve it. Don't be a stubborn fool like me and let grudges smolder and relationships die."

The unexpected request had clearly caught Sarah by surprise. "I don't think you know how difficult that will be."

"I don't pretend to know, but I can guess. I don't expect miracles. All I ask is that you learn from my mistakes and try."

Sarah had hesitated so long before making her reply that Sylvia had feared she would refuse and that their agreement to create Elm Creek Quilt Camp would fall through, but at last, Sarah agreed. Sylvia took her at her word and both women devoted themselves to the creation of Elm Creek Quilts. They worked so hard that first year to realize their vision that Sylvia could excuse Sarah's failure to make good on her promise. They were so busy, working fourteen-hour days or more with the help of Sarah's husband, Matt, and their talented staff of quilting teachers, that Sarah had no time to visit her mother and resolve their differences. But then camp ended for the summer, and still Sarah did little more than call her mother for a brief chat every other week. When she announced her intention to spend the holidays at Elm Creek Manor, Sylvia realized that Sarah would put off fulfilling her promise forever if she could get away with it. Since voiding their agreement was out of the question—Elm Creek Quilts had enriched Sylvia's life too much for her to throw it all away—she must see to it that her condition was fulfilled.

Sylvia figured there was no better time than Christmas to seek peace within a family, but Sarah could hardly reconcile with her mother from a hundred miles away. Somehow Sylvia would have to persuade Sarah that she would have a much merrier Christmas in her own childhood home, with a mother who loved her even if they did not always get along. Unfortunately, Sarah wasn't buying. Instead of seeking a happier holiday elsewhere, she had become determined to force a Merry Christmas upon Sylvia whether she wanted one or not.

If Sylvia had her way, she would observe Christmas as she had every season since abandoning her family estate for a modest home in Sewickley, Pennsylvania—church services in the morning, a Christmas concert on the radio after, perhaps dinner later at the home of a persistent friend who refused to heed Sylvia's firm assurances that she did not mind spending the holidays alone. It had always sufficed, and she had woken every December 26 relieved that she had made it through another Christmas without a fuss, without too many wistful reminiscences of holidays long past. But it had been much easier to ignore the whispers of memory from a distance. Now that she had returned home, she found herself longing to heed their call.

And if she didn't know better, she might suspect that Sarah knew how close she was to giving in, so often did she tempt her to abandon her plans for an unremarkable Christmas.

"Sylvia?" Sarah called from the hallway, moments before she appeared in the doorway to the kitchen where Sylvia was preparing a cup of tea. "Are you busy?"

Sylvia stirred honey into her tea. "I was just about to settle down with a good book."

"Then you have time to help me find the Christmas decorations."

"I already told you where to look." Sylvia carried her cup into the west sitting room, her favorite place to read or quilt. Sunlight streamed in through the windows shut tight against the cold. Through the bare branches of the stately elms outside, she glimpsed the bright red of the barn on the other side of Elm Creek, which was a slash of gray-blue cutting through the white crust of snow.

"You told me the decorations are in the attic. If you can't be more specific than that, it will be Easter before I find them."

Sylvia shrugged, lifted her book from where it lay facedown on her chair, and seated herself. "Perhaps you shouldn't bother then."

"Honestly, Sylvia," admonished Sarah. "It's the morning of Christmas Eve. If we don't decorate today, what's the point?"

"You're right. Why don't we forgo decorations this year? We'll have to take them down in a few days anyway. It hardly seems worth the effort."

Sarah stared at her in disbelief. "I half expected you to wrap that up with a 'Bah, humbug!'"

Sylvia slipped on her glasses, which hung from a fine silver chain around her neck. "I am neither a Scrooge nor a Grinch, thank you, but I have kept a quiet Christmas since before you were born. I warned you time and time again. If you wanted a more festive holiday, you and Matthew should have accepted your mother's invitation. I imagine her decorations are lovely."

Sarah frowned as she usually did whenever Sylvia brought up her mother. "My mother invited me, not Matt."

"Is that so? I assumed your husband was included implicitly. Husbands usually are for this sort of thing."

"You've never met my mother or you'd know better than to assume Matt's included unless she mentions him by name. She still hopes our wedding was a bad dream and she'll wake up one morning to find me engaged to my boyfriend from freshman year at Penn State."

Sylvia was certain Sarah was exaggerating. Matthew was a fine young man, and Sylvia could not imagine how Sarah's mother could possibly disapprove of their marriage as vehemently as Sarah claimed. "But what of your agreement to alternate visits between your side of the family and Matthew's? Since you spent last Christmas with his father, your mother was quite reasonable to expect you would visit her this year."

"We could have." Sarah sat down in the chair opposite Sylvia's. "Except that we wanted to have Christmas here, with you."

"Christmas is a time for family."

"You know you're like family to us. Elm Creek Manor is our home now. We couldn't bear to leave you in this big house all alone at Christmas time."

Sylvia feigned indifference and turned a page, although she had not read a word of it. "Don't lay the burden of your decision at my feet. I managed just fine last year."

"If we had known we were leaving you here by yourself, we would have stayed. You told us you were going to invite Agnes for Christmas dinner."

"My sister-in-law was out of town visiting one of her daughters."

"Yes, which you'd known since Thanksgiving but neglected to mention. Would you please put down that book and talk to me?"

Sylvia closed the book, marking her page with a finger, and peered at Sarah over the rims of her glasses. "Very well, young lady. I'm listening."

Sarah regarded her with fond exasperation. "You keep suggesting that if Matt and I wanted a festive Christmas, we should have gone somewhere else. I don't understand why we can't celebrate a Merry Christmas here, with you."

Privately, Sylvia acknowledged that Sarah had good reason to be puzzled. After all, they had so much worth celebrating: Sylvia's return to the family estate, the successful first year of Elm Creek Quilt Camp, new friends, and a future bright with possibilities. If anyone ought to be dancing about with a "Merry Christmas" on her lips, it should be Sylvia.

"I'm too old to make such a fuss," she said. "Christmas is for children."

She could tell from Sarah's expression that she had done little to dampen her young friend's enthusiasm. "Then long live childhood," Sarah declared. Sylvia sighed and opened her book again, but Sarah reached over and closed it. "You must have some Bergstrom family Christmas traditions you'd like to revive."

It was true; the Bergstroms had passed down many lovely Christmas traditions through the generations. The week before Christmas, the best cooks in the family would labor in the kitchen, turning out the most delicious treats—cookies, gingerbread, and strudel from her great-grandfather's sister's secret recipe. Delicious aromas of spices and baking once filled Elm Creek Manor at Christmastime, mingling with the scents of pine and holly and cinnamon. Every member of the family helped trim the stairways and mantels with freshly cut boughs, but only the most recently married couple was allowed to select the family Christmas tree. Before the south wing of the manor was constructed, the Christmas tree was displayed in the front parlor, but in later years it occupied the ballroom. They adorned the tree with the accumulated treasures of three generations—ceramic figurines from Germany, sparkling crystal teardrops from New York City, carved wooden angels with woolen hair from Italy. The children's favorite ornament was an eight-pointed glass star. Its red points with gold tips shone in the candlelight, casting flashes of brilliant color from floor to ceiling. On

Christmas Eve, an adult would hide the star somewhere in the manor and send the children searching. The lucky child who found the star would win a prize, a small toy or bag of candy, and would be lifted high to place the star on the top of the tree. Twice Sylvia had found the star, but after her brother learned to walk, she always let him find it. Her sister had never found the star without the help of a kindly uncle whispering in her ear.

There was so much more, of course—memories crowded in of church services, music, stories, friends, and laughter. Yes, the Bergstroms had enjoyed many wonderful holiday traditions, but Sylvia did not think she could bear seeing them restored by well-meaning youngsters who could not truly understand their significance, especially if it meant that Sarah would postpone for yet another year a visit home for Christmas.

Undaunted by Sylvia's silence, Sarah persisted. "You can't be too old to sit back and enjoy Christmas decorations."

Sylvia sighed. There seemed little point in preventing her. "Of course not."

Sarah took her hands. "Then keep me company in the attic while I look for the decorations. We have to put up a little tinsel and holly or Santa will think we've forgotten him."

Sarah insisted Sylvia precede her up the narrow, creaking attic steps—the better to break her fall should she stumble, Sylvia supposed. She shivered in the chilly darkness as Sarah stepped around her toward the center of the space. With a tug on the pull cord, pale light from the single, bare bulb spilled down, illuminating a circle of floorboards. Stacks of trunks, cartons, and old furniture cast deep shadows in the corners beyond the reach of the light.

To Sylvia's right lay the older west wing of the manor, the original home of the Bergstrom family, built in the middle of the nineteenth century by the first Bergstroms to immigrate to America from Germany. Directly before her stretched the south wing, added when her father was a boy. In the attic, the seams joining the original house and the addition were more evident than on the first three stories, the color of the walls subtly different, the floor not quite even. Little visible evidence betrayed that fact, as the belongings of four generations of her family covered nearly every square foot of floor space.

Sarah surveyed the attic with satisfaction, in all likelihood congratulating herself for finally persuading Sylvia upstairs. "Well? Where should we begin?"

Sylvia hadn't the faintest idea. Since returning from her self-imposed exile, she had visited the attic as infrequently as possible. She had not sought out the boxes of Christmas trimmings in more than fifty years.

"Over this way, I suppose," Sylvia told Sarah, gesturing toward what she guessed was the general location of two trunks, one green and one blue, and one sturdy carton. At first she stood aside and let Sarah do the work, but soon she began to feel foolish and impatient standing idle, so she joined in the search.

"I think I've found something," called Sarah from the other side of the trap door. Sylvia watched as she dragged a long rectangular box into the open, her wavy brown hair falling onto her face. The box, embellished with a forest of green pines, announced in red ink, "Festive Christmas Tree." Smaller black print identified the product as, "Evergleam. Made in Manitowoc, Wisconsin, U.S.A."

"I've never seen that before," said Sylvia, dusting off her hands and coming closer for a better look. Sarah opened one end of the box, reached inside, and with some effort pulled out a handful of what appeared to be wood shavings as shiny as tinfoil.

"It's one of those aluminum Christmas trees," said Sarah, delighted. "My grandmother used to have one."

"Mine didn't," said Sylvia dryly, imagining her father's mother recoiling in horror at the very thought. "This must be one of Claudia's more recent contributions to the estate. It reflects her taste."

"Oh, don't be so hard on her. These were the height of fashion once." Sylvia tugged until more of the atrocious foil tree emerged from the box.

"Hmph. If you say so."

"Would you mind if I set it up in my room?"

"If your husband can bear it, you may do whatever you like." Sylvia quickly amended, "As long as you promise to keep it out of my sight."

"I wonder if it came with one of those rotating colored floodlights like my grandmother had." Sarah disappeared behind an old wardrobe, her voice momentarily replaced by the sound of boxes scuffing across the floor. "Wait a minute. Sylvia? What color did you say those trunks were?"

"One was blue and one green." Sylvia picked her way through the clutter to join Sarah, who was removing a paint-spattered drop cloth from the top of a dusty forest green trunk with brass fastenings. "My word. You found it."

"Here's the other one," said Sarah, beaming up at Sylvia in triumph, resting her hand on a blue trunk. "The carton must be nearby."

"One would think so. There," said Sylvia. She could not help but be pleased to see them. Claudia had sold off so many things in Sylvia's absence that she had prepared herself for the possibility that they would not have found the trunks in the attic. The Bergstroms' old ornaments and trims probably had no more than sentimental value, but Sylvia would not have put it past Claudia to part with them for pocket change.

She tried to talk Sarah into waiting until her husband came home to carry the trunks and carton downstairs, but Sarah insisted upon doing it herself. It took four trips, but Sarah managed with Sylvia doing little more to help than barking anxious directions when her young friend seemed likely to tumble down the stairwell. After the last was settled three floors down in the foyer, Sarah barely paused to catch her breath before throwing back the lid of the blue trunk. Sylvia looked on warily, wondering if her sister had replaced their family heirlooms with thin aluminum varieties, but she relaxed at the sight of the green-and-red tartan tablecloth and a garland of gold beads. One familiar treasure after another—a wooden nativity set her grandfather had carved, eight personalized Christmas stockings, a china angel blowing a brass horn, the family Christmas tree ornaments—emerged from the trunk looking exactly as they had when she last packed them away, as if they had not been disturbed in more than fifty years.

Was it possible that her sister had never opened the boxes in all that time?

As Sarah turned to the second trunk, Sylvia sat down on the floor beside her, marveling over each item as Sarah passed them to her. Her brother's nutcracker, dressed in the bright red coat of a soldier, a sword in his fist. The wooden music box shaped like a sleigh full of toys that played "God Rest Ye Merry, Gentlemen" when the key was wound. The paper angels she and Claudia had made in Sunday school. A wreath made of pinecones she and her mother had gathered in the forest along Elm Creek. The memory of a snowy afternoon flooded her—the sound of her mother's laughter, the crisp winter air nipping her cheeks—and she clutched the wreath so tightly that brittle pieces broke off in her fingers.

She gasped and set the wreath on the floor. Sarah glanced over her shoulder, her expression darkening with concern. "Are you all right?"

"I'm fine." Sylvia shifted on the floor so that Sarah would think discomfort rather than grief had provoked her. She forced a smile. "Well. You should have plenty of decorations to work with, don't you agree?"

"Enough for the entire manor, but before I get started, I want to see what's in those other two boxes."

"Two?" Sylvia checked, and sure enough, two cartons sat on the marble floor just beyond the trunks. "Goodness. If I had paid more attention I could have saved you that last trip upstairs. I said two trunks and one carton, remember?"

Sarah shrugged, returning her attention to the contents of the green trunk. "I know, but I peeked inside and saw some Christmasy colors, so I brought them both down. Maybe Claudia added to the collection while you were away."

Judging by the metal tree her sister had acquired, Sylvia certainly hoped not. She went to the nearest carton and pulled open the flaps. There she discovered more familiar decorations—candlesticks, china teacups and saucers encircled with pictures of holly leaves and berries, the jolly Santa Claus cookie jar Great-Aunt Lucinda kept filled with lebkuchen, anisplätzchen, and zimtsterne from St. Nicholas Day through the Feast of the Three Kings. She sorted through the carton, each discovery rekindling a long-neglected memory until it was almost too much for her to continue. When she finished, she scanned the items Sarah had laid out on the floor as she emptied the trunks. Nothing seemed to be missing except for the ruby star for the top of the tree, which had been lost long ago—but what, then, filled the last box?

"Perhaps you should open that one," said Sylvia, less than enthusiastic at the prospect of discovering more of her sister's garish purchases.

Sarah dusted off her hands and opened the last carton. "Good news. I told you I didn't waste a trip to the attic. It's more Christmas stuff."

"What's the bad news?"

"There is no bad news. Come and see for yourself." Sarah grinned over her shoulder at Sylvia, amused by her wariness. "I'm sure you'll like it. It's fabric, not foil."

A memory tickled the back of Sylvia's mind, but as soon as she peered inside the box, the memory struck with the full force of a blow. "Oh, my goodness."

"What is it?"

Sylvia sank to her knees beside the box, overwhelmed by the sensation of discovery and loss. She had never forgotten the Christmas Quilt, nor had she ever expected to see it again. Begun by her Great-Aunt Lucinda when Sylvia was very young, the unfinished quilt had been taken up and worked upon by a succession of Bergstrom women—among them, Sylvia herself. From what she could see of the folded bundle of patchwork and appliqué, not a single stitch had been added since she last worked upon it. And yet every intricate Feathered Star block, every graceful appliquéd cluster of holly leaves and berries had been tucked away as neatly as if a conscientious quiltmaker had had every intention of completing her masterpiece. Even the scraps of fabric had been sorted according to color—greens here, reds there, golds and creams in their own separate piles. The Christmas Quilt had been abandoned, but it had not been discarded.

Had Claudia intended to finish it herself one day, only to find that it evoked too many painful memories? She had borne no children, so she could not have meant to leave it for a member of the next generation to finish, as their great-aunt and mother had, each in her turn. She certainly could not have been saving the quilt for Sylvia's homecoming.

How many Christmases had her sister spent in Elm Creek Manor, alone and longing, haunted by memories of more joyful times long past?

"Sylvia?" Sarah placed a hand upon Sylvia's, concerned. "What's wrong?"

"Oh, you know how it is with me every time you insist upon poking around in this old place." Sylvia patted Sarah's hand and sighed. For Sarah it was great fun, a trip back in time into the history of Elm Creek Manor. For Sylvia it was something else entirely. "Whenever we stumble upon some old artifact from Bergstrom family history, I'm reminded of how I failed my ancestors by walking out, by allowing everything they spent their lives building to fall apart."

"You left, but you also returned," Sarah reminded her, as she always did. "Elm Creek Manor still stands, and you brought life back to it. Your family would be proud."

"Astonished, yes. Proud?" Sylvia shook her head. "I'm not so certain."

Sarah smiled, understanding her perfectly. "Granted, they probably never imagined the manor as a quilters' retreat, but everything you've told me about them suggests they valued art and education and community. Isn't that what Elm Creek Quilts stands for?"

Sylvia considered. "Perhaps you're right."

"I know I'm right." Sarah reached into the box and took out a folded bundle of patchwork. "You never mentioned a long-lost Christmas quilt." She unfolded the fabric and discovered that instead of a finished quilt top, she held only a strip of Log Cabin blocks sewn together and wrapped around a small stack of additional blocks. "Oh. It's a UFO."

"It is indeed an Unfinished Fabric Object, and destined to remain so." Sylvia removed the next carefully folded bundle, and felt a twist of painful longing in her heart upon recognizing her mother's handiwork, the perfect appliqué stitches that were her trademark. "My great-aunt Lucinda began this quilt before I was born. It became something of a family joke. Every November she would take it from her sewing basket and declare that this year she would finish it in time for Christmas morning. Of course she never did, and once the holidays passed, she would lose interest in it and pack it away. I understand her point; who thinks about Christmas projects in April? But without fail, when Thanksgiving rolled around, she'd get in a Christmas mood again and pick up where she left off." Sylvia nodded to a thin stack of green-and-red Feathered Star blocks as Sarah removed them from the box. "She made those. Her original design called for twenty, if I remember correctly, but I don't believe she ever made more than six."

"And then she switched to Variable Stars?" guessed Sarah, glancing inside the box at what remained.

"Good heavens, no. Lucinda wouldn't have resorted to something so simple after devoting years to these Feathered Stars." With a sniff, Sylvia dismissed the blocks remaining within the carton. "Claudia pieced the Variable Stars when she took it upon herself to finish the quilt. Before my sister got her hands on it, my mother appliquéd these holly wreaths." Sylvia remembered all too well the day her mother had set the quilt aside, and why. Years later, Sylvia tried to finish what the other women of her family had begun, thinking, wrongly, that her Log Cabin blocks would pull the disparate pieces together. "I'm afraid what you see here amounts to nothing more than good intentions gone awry. Or rather, gone nowhere."

Sarah's glance took in the different sections of the quilt. "We could finish it."

Sylvia snapped out a laugh. "I don't think so."

"Why not? We've finished other quilts together. My sampler, the memorial quilt Claudia and Agnes made from your husband's clothes—"

"That's different. Those quilts were begun in special circumstances."

"And this quilt wasn't?"

"Well—" Sylvia fumbled for an excuse. "We won't have time to quilt, dear. Have you forgotten? We have Christmas decorations to put up."

Sarah regarded her skeptically. "Not twenty minutes ago you insisted that there was no reason to decorate for Christmas, and now it's more important than working on this quilt?"

"I suppose I've come around to your way of thinking. I believe you underestimate how long it takes to decorate such a large house. Then there's Christmas dinner to make, and church services in the morning, and I have gifts for you and Matthew. By the time we get to the quilt, you'll find that Christmas is over and you won't feel like working on it anymore, just like my great-aunt Lucinda."

"All the more reason to work on it now, while I'm full of Christmas cheer."

Sylvia indicated the trunks and cartons and decorations Sarah had spread out on the floor. "So you intend to leave the foyer in this state, after dragging those heavy trunks down from the attic?"

Sarah surveyed the mess guiltily. "I suppose I should tidy up first."

"I can take care of it myself if you need the time to pack—"

"Sylvia, for the last time, I'm not going to my mother's for Christmas."

"Well, don't expect me to help you with that quilt when we both know you ought to be in a car on your way to Uniontown," said Sylvia, finally out of patience. She knew that the moment Sarah decided to finish that quilt, she had dealt Sylvia's plan a staggering blow. And time was running out.

Sarah returned the pieces of the Christmas Quilt to the box, but the affectionate pat she gave Great-Aunt Lucinda's Feathered Stars told Sylvia they wouldn't remain set aside for long. As Sylvia suspected she would, the young woman also declared that since the decorations were already down from the attic and out of the boxes and trunks, it made more sense to put them up than to put them away. Sylvia decided to leave her to it, so she returned to the west sitting room and her book, and the cup of tea that had long since grown cold.

Exasperated, she went to the kitchen to put the kettle on, shaking her head at Sarah's irrepressibility. Now Sarah had a decorating plan and a quilt to keep her in the manor. Once that young lady caught hold of a fanciful idea, she would not let go until it sent her soaring off into the clouds as if it were the tail of some enormous kite. She always managed to latch on to some grand scheme. Creating a quilt camp, for example. Or convincing a bitter old woman to take a second chance on life.

Then again, compared to what Sarah had already accomplished, finishing a quilt that had daunted several more experienced quilters might prove to be a simple matter.

The kettle whistled and sent up a thin jet of white steam. Sylvia poured and waited for the tea to steep, lost in thought. From down the hall, faint music drifted to her ear. Curious, she quickly stirred honey into her cup and carried it back to the foyer. Sarah had accomplished little in the way of tidying up, but she had hung wreaths on the two tall double doors of the manor's front entrance and had strung garlands along the grand oak staircase. In the corner she had plugged in her CD player, which was responsible for the strains of "White Christmas" that had beckoned Sylvia from the kitchen.

"Things are shaping up nicely here," remarked Sylvia, looking about the foyer.

Sarah glanced up from sorting through a box of ornaments and smiled. "Later I'll call Matt on his cell phone and ask him to bring home a Christmas tree from the lot at the mall."

"Nonsense. I won't have him pay ten dollars a foot for a tree when we have plenty to choose from right here on the estate. Besides, you're supposed to bring in the tree together."

"He *is* a landscape architect. If he can tend an orchard I'm sure he can pick out a Christmas tree."

"I'm not questioning his qualifications, but in my family we always . . ."

When she did not continue, Sarah prompted, "You always what?"

"We always . . . saved our money for more important things and cut down a tree from our own woods. But you and Matthew may do whatever you like."

"So you won't mind having a Christmas tree?"

"Not as long as you sweep up the fallen needles."

"It's a deal." Sarah gave the ornaments one last admiring look, rose, and made a show of checking her watch. "Ten o'clock. I think it's time for a quilting break."

"But you just started."

In reply, Sarah simply picked up the box holding the pieces of the Christmas Quilt.

Clutching her teacup, Sylvia trailed after Sarah, down the hall and through the kitchen to the west sitting room. Frowning, Sylvia sat down in her favorite chair by the window and picked up her book, studiously ignoring Sarah as she spread out the various sections of the incomplete quilt on the sofa and the rug. The younger woman studied the Bergstrom women's handiwork for several minutes in silence before she spoke. "I think we have enough for a complete quilt right here."

Sylvia closed her book. "Don't be ridiculous. It couldn't possibly be that easy or one of us would have done it years ago."

Sarah peered closely at the patchwork and appliqué, considering. "Maybe it took an objective outsider to see the possibilities."

"Young lady, I've been quilting much longer than you

have. A person can stitch together any two pieces of fabric in any haphazard way they choose and call it a quilt, but unless you've lowered your standards, I expect you to strive for something that also pleases the eye. That simply isn't possible with what you see here. You don't have enough of any one of the blocks for a complete quilt, and yet you don't have enough variety for an attractive sampler."

"No, look," said Sarah, rearranging two of the appliquéd holly plumes so that they flanked one of Claudia's Variable Stars. "This could be the center of the quilt. We could set the Feathered Star blocks around them, kind of like a rectangle with the other Variable Stars in the corners. The Feathered Star blocks will be the focus of the quilt, which is perfect because they're so beautifully made."

"Indeed they are," said Sylvia, proud of her great-aunt. "You could always leave out my sister's Variable Stars rather than risk ruining the quilt. Accuracy was never her strong suit. Some of those blocks don't look to be true squares."

"I wouldn't dream of leaving Claudia out of a family quilt. I'm sure her blocks are accurate enough."

Sylvia was far less certain, and she could cite a wealth of evidence to support her assessment of Claudia's piecing skills, but she did not feel like arguing—and, she reminded herself, it did not matter to her whether this quilt would ever be finished. So she settled back down with her book and her now lukewarm cup of tea, but after reading a few lines, Sarah's shuffling of blocks and patches drew her attention. She had arranged Great-Aunt Lucinda's six Feathered Star blocks in an elongated ring—two on one side, two on the other, and one on each end. Sylvia had to admit the placement would complement the exquisite blocks. Lucinda had pieced all of her quilts by hand and was as precise and exacting in her sewing as she was generous and forgiving in every other aspect of her life. She was Sylvia's grandfather's youngest sister, the baby of their family, and perhaps that was why the others teased her so affectionately about her repeated failures to complete the Christmas Quilt. In Sylvia's earliest childhood memories, Lucinda always appeared as a patient and reassuring figure, calm and wise—and old, although in hindsight Sylvia realized she was probably not yet fifty when she set aside the Christmas Quilt for the last time.

In fair weather Lucinda enjoyed sewing on the front veranda, but the approach of autumn beckoned her inside to the front parlor, which looked out upon the veranda and the broad, sweeping lawn that separated the house from the forest. Sylvia, who had not yet learned to quilt, often watched her aunt drawing templates for a new quilt with a freshly sharpened pencil, carefully tracing their shapes on the wrong side of brightly colored fabrics, and cutting out the pieces with brisk snips of her shears. Sylvia hung on to the arm of her chair as she sewed, watching and pestering Lucinda with questions as she stitched four small, cream-colored triangles to a larger octagon cut from cheerful red fabric. Eager to help, she paired green triangles with white so they would be ready for her great-aunt's needle. Sylvia admired the intricate blocks, which she thought resembled green snowflakes with red tips. As the fifth Feathered Star took shape, Sylvia begged Lucinda to teach her how to make one. "I will teach you to quilt someday," promised Lucinda, "but this pattern is too difficult for a little girl's first project. Let's make a Log Cabin quilt instead."

"When?" persisted Sylvia. "When can we start?"

With a nod, Lucinda indicated the Feathered Star pieces spread on her lap. "After I finish my Christmas Quilt, we will begin yours."

Thrilled, Sylvia raced off to tell her older sister the news, secretly pleased when Claudia tossed her brown curls and declared that she was too busy helping Mother to quilt with Great-Aunt Lucinda, a sure sign that she was sick with jealousy. Then Claudia added, "Everyone says she'll never finish that quilt, anyway."

"She will so," snapped Sylvia and marched back to the parlor to help. She had heard the teasing remarks, too, but they had never been a cause for worry until now.

To Sylvia's relief, her great-aunt kept up an industrious pace and showed no signs of abandoning her quilt. As Christmas approached, Sylvia forgot her worries in the excitement of the season. She and Claudia were both chosen to participate in the Christmas pageant at school—Claudia as an angel, Sylvia as a lamb. Between rehearsing for the pageant and practicing with the children's choir at church, helping Grandma with the baking and secretly working on Christmas gifts for the family, Sylvia had little time to spare for observing the Christmas Quilt. Still, Great-Aunt Lucinda made good progress despite Sylvia's absence from her side every hour of the day. Although she did take time away from her sewing to bake Christmas cookies, she always returned to her Feathered Stars by evening. Sylvia's quilting lessons would surely begin before the end of winter.

The approach of Christmas brought visitors to Elm Creek Manor, friends and relatives from near and far. Best of all was the day Sylvia's beloved second cousin Elizabeth returned, accompanied by her parents. For the past five summers, she had come to Elm Creek Manor to help care for the children and, as she said, "enjoy the fresh country air." Sometimes she went riding with a boy her age from a neighboring farm, but except for those annoying interruptions, she was Sylvia's nearly constant companion, favorite playmate, and most trusted confidante. Sylvia could not help but adore her; Elizabeth was kind and funny and smart and beautiful—all the things Sylvia hoped to be when she grew up.

Elizabeth was barely in the door before Sylvia was tugging off her coat and seizing her hand to lead her off on some secret adventure. Elizabeth laughingly obliged, shaking snow from her hair and handing off her mittens to her mother, but she seemed distracted and quiet. When Sylvia asked her what was wrong, Elizabeth looked surprised. "Nothing," she said. "Everything is wonderful." Then she tickled Sylvia and acted like the old Elizabeth so convincingly that Sylvia decided to believe her.

Great-Aunt Lucinda finished her fifth Feathered Star block on the morning of Christmas Eve. "Only fifteen more to go," she told Sylvia at breakfast, and Sylvia's heart sank in despair. So many blocks stood between her and her lessons! But she brightened up when Elizabeth came to the table, breathless and apologizing for her tardiness, her long golden hair tied back in a grosgrain ribbon the color of the winter sky. Sylvia had a ribbon almost the exact same hue, and if Elizabeth helped Sylvia fix her hair the same way, they could be twins—except that Sylvia's hair was dark brown.

After breakfast, Uncle William and his wife went out to find the Christmas tree, sent on their way with teasing and laughter and strange remarks from the other grown-ups that Sylvia suspected she only partially understood.

The couple had been married less than a year, and Sylvia overheard her grandmother say that it would be a very bad sign if they were gone more than two hours.

"It will be a far worse sign if they're back within thirty minutes," Sylvia's father replied. The uncles grinned and the aunts nodded thoughtfully. Sylvia looked around at the faces of her family, puzzled. If they found a perfect tree right away and brought it home as quickly as they could cut it down, what could be wrong with that? They could begin trimming the tree sooner, and Sylvia couldn't wait. The previous day, she and Claudia had helped Elizabeth and their grandmother unpack the two trunks of Christmas ornaments. They'd had a wonderful time admiring their favorite pieces, singing carols, and munching on Great-Aunt Lucinda's lebkuchen still warm from the oven—until a cousin appeared in the doorway and called Elizabeth away to meet a visitor. Elizabeth rushed off with barely a word of good-bye, but Sylvia had not minded until dinnertime, when she discovered that the visitor was that man Elizabeth used to go riding with in the summers, and that he had taken the seat beside Elizabeth Sylvia usually reserved for herself. She scowled at him from across the table, but he merely smiled pleasantly back, so he was obviously not smart enough to understand when someone was angry with him.

The newlyweds returned with a tree not quite two hours after they had departed. "That's just about right," Sylvia's grandmother told Lucinda as they trailed after the rest of the family to the ballroom, where the tree would be raised. Her voice was so soft that Sylvia knew she was not meant to overhear. "Any sooner and I'd worry that she wouldn't be strong enough for him."

"William can be stubborn," said Lucinda. "I suspect

he gave in quickly rather than displease his lovely bride. That contrary behavior can't possibly last. We'll see how long it takes them next year, and whether they're still speaking when they return home."

"*If* they'll be eligible to choose the tree next year," said Grandmother archly. "I suspect they may not be allowed a second turn."

The women exchanged knowing smiles and disappeared into the ballroom. Sylvia stopped in the foyer, frowning as she mulled over their words. Why shouldn't Uncle William and his wife be allowed to pick the tree again? There wasn't anything wrong with the one they had chosen. Was Great-Aunt Lucinda jealous because she had never been allowed a turn? Sylvia searched her memory but could not recall any other time when her great-aunt had seemed envious. Well, if Great-Aunt Lucinda wanted to pick the Christmas tree, she would just have to get married. That's what the rules said, and Sylvia strongly disapproved of anyone—even Great-Aunt Lucinda—thinking she could simply toss out the family's rules when it suited.

Noise and laughter beckoned her from her worries, and she hurried into the ballroom rather than miss all the fun. As young and old adorned the branches of Uncle William's tree with their favorite ornaments, Great-Aunt Lucinda told them stories of long-ago Christmases when her mother, Sylvia's great-grandmother Anneke, was a little girl in Germany. Sylvia was surprised to learn that her great-grandmother had not been allowed to help decorate the Christmas tree. "None of the children were," explained Great-Aunt Lucinda. "The adults of the family decorated the tree while the children waited in another room. On Christmas Eve, her mother would ring a bell and all the children would come running in to admire the tree and eat delicious treats—cookies and nuts and fruits. My mother and the other girls and boys would search the branches of the tree, and whoever found the lucky pickle would win a prize."

"A pickle?" said Sylvia. "How did a pickle get in their tree?"

"Not a real pickle, dear. A glass pickle, an ornament. Her mother or father would hide it there before the children came in." Great-Aunt Lucinda paused thoughtfully. "I suppose that's where our tradition of hiding the Christmas star came from."

"Did Santa bring her presents?" asked Claudia.

"Not on Christmas," said Lucinda. "Of course you know that Santa Claus is really St. Nicholas, and that we celebrate his day on December 6. On the night before, Great-Grandmother Anneke and her brothers and sisters would each leave a shoe by the fireplace, just as you children hang stockings. If they had been good children all year, when they woke in the morning, they would find their shoes filled with candy, nuts, and fruit. If they had been naughty, they might find coal or twigs. One year, my uncle found an onion. I always wondered what he had done to deserve that."

"But we get St. Nicholas Day and Christmas," said Sylvia. It didn't seem fair that her great-grandmother had not.

"You are very lucky children," Great-Aunt Lucinda pronounced. "You're fortunate in another regard, too. In your great-grandmother's day, St. Nicholas traveled with a helper named Knecht Ruprecht. He carried St. Nicholas's bag of treats for him, and it was he who went up and down the chimneys filling the children's shoes. But he also carried a sack and a stick. He used the stick to beat the naughty little children, and if a child was very,

very bad, Knecht Ruprecht would stuff him in the sack and carry him off, never to see his family again."

Sylvia shivered.

"Aunt Lucinda, you're frightening the children," said Sylvia's mother.

"Why should these children be scared?" protested Great-Aunt Lucinda. She looked around the circle of worried young faces, brow furrowing in concern. "None of you children were naughty this year, were you?"

The children shook their heads fervently, but as they did, Sylvia thought of the times she had argued with her sister, disobeyed her parents, and taken cookies from Great-Aunt Lucinda's cookie jar without permission. She hoped Knecht Ruprecht had stayed behind in Germany with the pickle trees.

"Perhaps a less alarming story, Aunt Lucinda?" prompted Sylvia's mother.

Great-Aunt Lucinda played along. "Did I ever tell you children about the Bergstroms' first Christmas in America?"

They shook their heads.

"I've been remiss, then." She composed her thoughts for a moment. "Your great-grandfather, Hans, arrived in America several years before Anneke and Gerda—Hans's sister—but their first Christmas together wasn't until 1856. The stone house that we now know as the west wing of the manor wouldn't be built for another two years, so for a time they lived in a log cabin on the land they called Elm Creek Farm. Hans and Anneke were newlyweds, and Anneke was determined to make their first Christmas one to remember, as grand an affair as she would have put on had she been a hausfrau in Berlin, the city of her birth.

"As you can imagine, this was not easily done. The

Bergstroms were recent immigrants living in a small cabin in the middle of rural Pennsylvania. They had the land, some livestock, and the stores of their first harvest, but none of the comforts we enjoy today. Anneke wanted a goose for Christmas dinner, but there were none to be had. She wanted to give her new husband a gift that befitted her love for him, but the shops in town had nothing suitable that she could afford."

"And no pickles for the trees?" asked Sylvia.

"Not a single pickle," said Great-Aunt Lucinda. "On Christmas Eve, Gerda discovered Anneke digging through the steamer trunk she had brought over from Germany. Anneke confessed that she was searching for a Christmas gift for Hans, but she had found nothing worthy of him. 'What will he think of me,' lamented Anneke, 'if I have no gift for him on Christmas morning?'

"'Do you think my brother loves you for the things you give him?' asked Gerda. 'Give him the gift of your heart and your company, and he will want nothing more.'

"'But I've already given him those,' said Anneke.

"'Then he already has his heart's desire.'

"Anneke seemed comforted by this, but not completely satisfied. So late that night, after everyone else had gone to bed, she wrote Hans a letter telling him how much she loved him and how much she looked forward to their future together. On Christmas morning, she gave him the letter. He read it in silence, and when he finished, he hugged her and told her it was the greatest present he had ever received."

"Did Hans get her anything?" asked Claudia.

Great-Aunt Lucinda considered. "I suppose he did, but the story doesn't say. I do know what Gerda gave Hans and Anneke, though. She had traded with a neighbor for two shiny, red, perfect apples, and as she gave one to her brother and one to her sister-in-law, she said, 'I give you simply the joy and hope of the season.'"

At this the grown-ups nodded and murmured in approval, but Sylvia frowned. "She gave them apples?"

"They were more than just apples," said Great-Aunt Lucinda. "Think of the sweetness of the fruit and the promise in the seeds. In that simple gift, Gerda was expressing how joyful her life was with Hans and Anneke, and how full of blessings their future would be."

Claudia looked dubious. "They were just apples."

"They were not just apples," said Great-Aunt Lucinda firmly. "They were expressions of her love and hopes, simply and eloquently presented. Don't you see? You can give someone all the riches of the world, but it is an empty gesture if you withhold the gift of yourself."

"I think that's beyond their understanding," said Uncle William with a grin. "They're awfully young for such philosophizing."

"Perhaps." Great-Aunt Lucinda looked around the circle of young, curious faces until her gaze settled on Sylvia. "If they don't understand today, someday they will."

Sylvia longed to show Lucinda that she understood, but she was not sure that she did. An apple didn't seem like much of a present to her, but maybe back in the olden days, apples were considered wonderful gifts. Maybe, she thought suddenly, Hans and Anneke had planted the seeds of the apples Gerda had given them. Maybe those very seeds grew into the orchard their family tended and enjoyed today. If that were true, Gerda had indeed given Hans and Anneke the joy and hope of the season—and continued to give it, with every harvest, to their descendants.

When the tree decorating was almost finished, Grandmother entrusted Elizabeth, her namesake, with the task of hiding the glass star somewhere in the manor. Sylvia hoped Elizabeth would give her a secret clue to help her find the star before the others, but a few minutes later, Elizabeth slipped back into the room, whispered close to her grandmother's ear, and smiled equally warmly at all her young cousins. If anything, her gaze lingered longest on her friend, that man from the neighboring farm, who had reappeared while the family was setting the tree in its stand and showed no sign of leaving anytime soon. With dismay, Sylvia realized that she would probably lose her favorite seat at the dinner table two nights in a row.

Lost in this new troublesome concern, she did not hear her grandmother send out the children to search for the star. "Sylvia," she heard her mother call. "Aren't you going to help find the star this year?"

Sylvia raced for the ballroom door, but Claudia and the cousins had made a good head start. She could only watch from a distance as they sped off in all directions, intent upon reaching the manor's best hiding places first. She ran for the front parlor, where Claudia had found the star the previous year, only to discover that a cousin had already claimed that room. She ran upstairs to the library, but two other cousins were already searching there. In every room it was the same: Claudia and the cousins raced about, laughing and shrieking and tearing the house apart in their quest for the star, leaving Sylvia with no choice but to dart out of the way.

Miserable, Sylvia went to the bedroom she and Claudia shared, knowing it was the one place no one would bother her. All of the fun had gone out of the game, but she would be disgraced if she returned to the ballroom before the star was found. Squeezing her eyes shut to hold back tears, she flung herself upon the bed—and gasped when her head struck something hard beneath the pillow. In a moment she was sitting upright on the bed, the star in her lap, its eight red-and-gold points glistening faintly in the dim light.

The star, beneath her own pillow. Elizabeth had left it where no one else would think to look. She had left it especially for Sylvia, her favorite.

Bursting with pride and gratitude, Sylvia climbed down from the bed and hurried downstairs, clutching the precious glass star to her chest. "I found it," she called out as she ran. "I found it!" She burst into the ballroom, breathless. "I found the star!"

The adults crowded around her, offering her hugs and congratulations. Someone called out to the other children that the game was over. In the distance, Sylvia heard their answering cries of dismay.

"Where did you find it?" one of the uncles asked.

Sylvia could not bring herself to tell him. "Upstairs," she said, and her eyes met Elizabeth's. Her cousin smiled at her, bright-eyed and mischievous, and raised a single finger to her lips. Sylvia, suddenly warmed by happiness, smiled until she laughed out loud.

The prize her grandmother awarded her was a small tin filled with red-and-white striped peppermint candy. At her mother's prompting, Sylvia offered each of the other children a piece, and her joy in the secret she and Elizabeth shared made it hardly matter at all that the tin was returned to her half empty.

All the while, Sylvia clung to the Christmas star. Suddenly, strong arms swept her up. "It's time, little miss," her father said, lifting her high above his head beside the tree. "Reach for the highest branch. You can do it."

Sylvia stretched out her arms and fit the star upon a strong bough that pointed straight up to the ceiling. Everyone applauded as her father lowered her to the ground. As the aunts lit the candles upon the tree, Sylvia stepped back so she could take in the whole of it, from the quilted skirt draped around the trunk to the star she had placed so perfectly upon the very top.

"It's beautiful," said Elizabeth. Her friend smiled and placed an arm around her shoulders, and she leaned into him with a sigh of perfect contentment. Sylvia glared at him, but neither he nor her cousin noticed.

At dinnertime, he earned another glare by stealing Sylvia's seat again, just as she had known he would. She had raced for the dining room as soon as they were called to supper, and she would have beaten him, too, except that her mother had taken her aside to wash her face and hands, sticky with peppermint candy. Sylvia was stuck at the far end of the table between Uncle William and Claudia.

After dinner was served, Uncle George rose and cleared his throat. "I know it's customary for Father to make the first toast on Christmas Eve," he said, with a nod to Grandpa, "but tonight I have a very special announcement, and I think Millie might burst if we don't share our secret with you at once."

Sylvia looked at her aunt and saw to her surprise that her face shone with happiness, though her eyes brimmed with tears. Aunt Millie reached for Elizabeth's hand and held it tightly. An expectant murmur went up from the table, but Sylvia's eyes were fixed on Elizabeth as she leaned over to speak encouragingly in her mother's ear, then, with a quick smile for her friend, turned her attention to her father.

"Many of you have known Henry longer than I have since he grew up around here, and I'm sure you're all aware of what a fine young man he is." He cleared his throat. Sylvia stared. Was he going to cry? "What you may not know is that he has become like a son to me. He tells me he loves my daughter, and my daughter assures me the feeling is mutual. It must be, because he asked her to marry him and she said she would. So please join me in wishing health and happiness to the beautiful bride-to-be and the luckiest man in the world."

The joyous clamor that followed was so deafening that Sylvia stuffed her fingers in her ears. She felt ill. If Henry came to live at Elm Creek Manor, Sylvia would never have her cousin to herself. Everyone else seemed so happy, even Aunt Millie, who was crying, but Sylvia could not imagine anything worse than allowing Henry to join the family.

A few days after Christmas—a hollow, anxious day in which the joy of the season was unbearable and even the presents Santa had left beneath the tree could not lighten her heart—Sylvia discovered that there was more to Elizabeth's wedding than she could have imagined.

She was playing with her toy horses and stable, a gift from Santa, when Elizabeth came to the nursery. "Hello, Sylvia," she said, tucking her skirt beneath her as she sat on the floor beside her. "Why have you been hiding up here all alone?"

"I'm not hiding, just playing," said Sylvia. "Where's Henry?"

"He's in the stable with your father and Uncle George, looking after the horses."

Sylvia knew what that meant. If her father and uncles were willing to share the secrets of Bergstrom Thoroughbreds with Henry, they already considered him part of the family. "I don't think the horses like strangers in their stables. He should go home."

Elizabeth laughed. "Oh, Sylvia. You don't like Henry very much, do you?"

Sylvia shook her head.

"Well, I do. He's my very best friend in the world, and it would make me very happy if you could learn to like him, too. Do you think you could try?"

"I don't think so."

Elizabeth sighed and drew Sylvia onto her lap. "Please? As a special wedding present to me?"

Sylvia thought about it. "If he promises to let me sit by you sometimes at dinner. And even after he comes to live here he should go away for a little while sometimes and let us play alone the way we always do."

Elizabeth went still. "Henry isn't coming to live here," she said. "Didn't you know?"

Sylvia shook her head, suddenly hopeful. If Henry wasn't moving in, then maybe things wouldn't be so bad after all. Sylvia could pretend he and Elizabeth weren't even married.

"But the day after Christmas we explained—" Elizabeth inhaled deeply. "But maybe you were too angry to listen. Darling, Henry and I won't be living at Elm Creek Manor after the wedding."

Sylvia twisted her head to peer into her cousin's face. She knew at once that Elizabeth was not teasing her. "Where are you going to live? Close?" If Elizabeth told her they were going to live with Uncle George and Aunt Millie, Sylvia thought she might burst into tears. They lived in Pennsylvania, too, but many miles away, in Erie.

Elizabeth held her tightly. "Henry bought a ranch out in California. We'll be leaving the day after the wedding, in the spring."

Sylvia's throat closed up around her grief. She scrambled out of Elizabeth's lap and fled the room, ignoring her cousin's pleas.

Sylvia didn't want to believe that Elizabeth was telling the truth, but the other grown-ups soon confirmed it. Worse yet, the wedding was not going to take place next spring, but this coming spring, barely three months away. After discovering this, Sylvia ran to her mother and begged her to make Elizabeth change her mind.

"I couldn't even if I wished to," Sylvia's mother told her gently. "Henry and Elizabeth want to make a life for themselves out in California. We will all miss them very much, but they've made their decision."

"Can't we make them wait?" cried Sylvia. "Why do they have to get married so soon? Can't they wait until next year?"

"Why should they wait?" interrupted Claudia. "They love each other, and weddings are so beautiful. Didn't you hear, Sylvia? Elizabeth said we could be flower girls."

"I don't want to be a flower girl!"

"Well, I do, and I won't let you spoil it." Claudia tossed her head. "You're just jealous because Elizabeth likes Henry more than you."

"She does not," shouted Sylvia. "I'm her favorite. She hid the Christmas star especially for me! She put it under my pillow where no one else would find it."

Claudia's eyes narrowed. "I knew you were too little to find that star all by yourself so fast. You cheated!"

"I did not!"

"You did so. Tell her, Mama. Tell her she and Elizabeth both cheated."

"We didn't cheat. It was just helping."

"Now, girls," their mother said. "Claudia, you can see your sister is upset. Let's not make things worse."

"But it's not fair."

"We can discuss that another time."

Sylvia tugged at her mother's hand. "Will you tell Elizabeth to wait? Please?"

In reply, Sylvia's mother shook her head sadly and reached out to console her, but Sylvia broke free of her embrace and ran off to find Great-Aunt Lucinda. Everyone listened to her. If she asked Elizabeth to wait another year, Elizabeth would do it, no matter how Henry complained.

She found Lucinda in the front parlor lost in thought as she worked on her Christmas Quilt. Reluctant to annoy the only member of the family likely to help her, Sylvia crept up to her softly and sat on the floor at her feet, resting her head against the ottoman. Lucinda offered her a brief smile but kept her eyes on her work. Sylvia watched as Lucinda joined one row of star points to others she had already assembled, her needle darting through the bright fabric, in and out, joining the pieces together. Before long she tied a knot at the end of the seam and laid the finished block on her lap, pressing it flat with her palms. Sylvia was struck suddenly by the similarity between the Feathered Star blocks her great-aunt had made and the star on top of their Christmas tree, the star Elizabeth had left beneath her pillow.

Silently she counted the blocks in the pile next to her great-aunt's sewing basket, remembering to add the one on her lap. "That makes six."

"Yes, that's right. Six down, fourteen to go." With a sigh, Lucinda gathered her sewing tools and returned them to her basket. "But they will have to wait for another day."

Sylvia's heart sank, and she had not thought it could go any lower. "Why? Why are you putting it away?"

"I don't have time to work on my Christmas Quilt now that your cousin is getting married," said Lucinda. "We have so much to do, and far less than the usual time to do it. I must help your Aunt Millie make the wedding gown, and of course we must have a wedding quilt, as well as a few good, sturdy quilts for every day and all the other things your cousin will need to take with her to California."

Sylvia chose her words carefully. "Maybe if you told Elizabeth you won't have enough time to finish all the sewing, she'll wait until next year to get married."

Lucinda laughed. "Oh, I see. That's a very clever plan, but I'm afraid it won't work. Henry has his heart set on leaving as soon as fair weather arrives. We'll have a wedding at the end of March whether we like it or not, so you and I will have to make the best of it."

Sylvia felt a small stirring of hope. Great-Aunt Lucinda wasn't completely happy about the wedding, either. Perhaps Sylvia had found an ally.

But then Lucinda dashed her hopes. "Don't worry, Sylvia. We'll get to your quilting lessons soon enough."

Sylvia could not speak for her despair. Great-Aunt Lucinda thought that Sylvia cared only for her quilting lessons, and worse yet, she intended to join in on the work that would hasten cousin Elizabeth's departure.

Sylvia was on her own.

New Year's Day came. Most of the relatives returned

to their own homes at the close of the Christmas season, but Elizabeth remained at Elm Creek Manor. This would have pleased Sylvia had she not known that she had stayed on for Henry, not for her favorite little cousin. Sylvia kept close to Elizabeth when her fiancé was not around, but as soon as he showed up, Sylvia ran off to the nursery or to the west sitting room, where her mother often sat reading or simply enjoying the afternoon sun and the view of Elm Creek. Her mother had a weak heart, the lingering consequence of a childhood bout with rheumatic fever. She often had to rest, but she was never too tired to offer Sylvia a hug or tell her a story.

But as the winter snows melted and buds began to form on the elm trees surrounding the manor, even her mother became so caught up in the preparations for the wedding that she had little time to comfort a sulky daughter.

On one rare occasion when Sylvia and Elizabeth were alone, Sylvia asked her, "Why do you want to go away from home?"

"You'll understand someday, little Sylvia." Elizabeth smiled and hugged her, but there were tears in her eyes. "Someday you'll fall in love, and you'll know that home is wherever he is."

"Home is here," Sylvia insisted. "It will always be here."

Elizabeth gave a little laugh and held her close. "Yes, Sylvia, you're right."

Happily, Sylvia realized that finally her cousin had come to her senses and had decided to stay. But when Elizabeth rose and ran off to the sitting room when Aunt Millie called her to a dress fitting, Sylvia's joy fled. Elizabeth intended to marry Henry, even though it was obvious she did not really wish to leave home. It was all his fault; Elizabeth wouldn't be going anywhere if not for him.

Sylvia realized that the only way to keep Elizabeth close was to drive Henry away.

From that moment on, Sylvia did all she could to prevent the wedding. She hid Aunt Millie's scissors so that she could not work on the wedding gown, but Aunt Millie simply borrowed Lucinda's. She stole the keys to Elizabeth's red steamer trunk and flung them into Elm Creek so that she could not pack her belongings. She refused to try on her flower girl dress no matter how the aunts wheedled and coaxed, until they were forced to make a pattern from the frock she had worn on Christmas. In one last, desperate effort, she told Henry that she hated him, that he was not allowed to sit in her chair at the dinner table ever again, and that everyone in the family including Elizabeth wished he would just go away, but they were too polite to say it.

Her efforts were entirely unsuccessful, of course. In late March, Elizabeth and Henry married and moved to California. Sylvia treasured every letter her beloved cousin sent her, even as they appeared less and less frequently over the years, until they finally stopped coming.

Sylvia never saw Elizabeth again. She often wondered what had become of her, why she had stopped writing. If Claudia had kept in touch with Elizabeth or her descendants, Sylvia had found no record of their correspondence in her sister's papers.

Sarah interrupted her reverie. "What do you think?" she asked, admiring her arrangement of the various pieces of the Christmas Quilt and looking to Sylvia for approval.

Sylvia dared not look at the quilt blocks for fear of what other memories they would call forth. "I think it's time to finish decorating." She rose from her chair and left the room without waiting to see if Sarah followed.

Chapter Two

A FEW MINUTES LATER, Sarah joined Sylvia in the foyer, where Sylvia had busied herself sorting the dining room linens from decorations that belonged elsewhere in the manor. "I couldn't reach Matt on the cell phone to remind him to bring home a tree," said Sarah. "We might have to cut down our own after all."

"Suit yourself."

"I'd prefer to suit all of us."

"Since I don't care one way or the other, whatever suits you will be fine with me." Sylvia stooped over to pick up a napkin ring shaped like a sprig of ivy. Once it had belonged to a set of twenty-four, but Sylvia would be satisfied if she could find three, one for each of the current residents of Elm Creek Manor. It was a pity they had decided not to run their quilters' retreat all year instead of only March through October. A dozen or so quilt campers certainly would liven up the place, and with their help, she and Sarah would make quick work of all the decorating Sarah apparently still had her heart set on, despite the new distraction of the quilt.

"Decorating the entire manor seems too ambitious considering our late start," said Sylvia. "Why don't we concentrate on only those rooms we use the most?"

Sarah mulled over the suggestion as if uncertain whether it was a practical idea or a plot to keep her from decorating as lavishly as she wished. "I guess that's a good idea," she said, clearly reluctant to abandon her original vision. "What rooms do you suggest?"

"The foyer, of course, since we have already begun, and to make a good impression on any visitors."

"Were you expecting visitors?"

"No, but one never knows at this time of the year." And one could always hope. Perhaps some of the Elm Creek Quilters might drop by if they found a lull in their family activities. "We could invite your mother."

"No way. Not a good idea."

On the contrary, it was a wonderful idea, such a perfect solution that Sylvia could have kicked herself for not thinking of it sooner. "Why on earth not?"

"For one reason, among many, I'm sure she's made other plans by now."

Sylvia doubted it. Sarah was Carol Mallory's only child, and she had sent at least one letter asking Sarah to come home. She had also phoned twice that Sylvia knew of. "If she has made other plans, she's free to decline our invitation, but at the very least we ought to give her that opportunity."

"It's too late," Sarah insisted. "Even if she could drop everything the moment we call, she would still have to pack and make that long drive. She wouldn't arrive until late tonight. We'd have Christmas morning together, but she'd have to leave by midafternoon so she can be home at a reasonable hour. She has to get up early for work the next day."

"How do you know she has to work?"

"She always works the day after Christmas," said Sarah flatly. "She always takes the early shift at the hospital to give another nurse the chance to take the day off. My mother would rather take the overtime than sleep in. It's our own family Christmas tradition."

Thinking of how long Sarah's widowed mother had

been the sole provider for their small family, Sylvia said, "Perhaps it was a matter of needing rather than merely wanting the overtime."

"I don't know. Maybe. She could have taken it any other day, though. Why take it the day after Christmas, when I was on school break and all my friends were busy with their families?"

Despite the sympathy evoked by images of a young Sarah left alone at home on the day after Christmas, Sylvia shook her head in disapproval. Sarah seemed incapable of seeing anything from her mother's point of view. She claimed it was too late to invite Carol to come for Christmas, but anyone with any sense could see she was just making excuses.

Sarah had turned away and had busied herself with sorting through a box of Christmas stocking hangers the Bergstroms had once lined up on the fireplace mantel each St. Nicholas Day. "After the foyer, where else should we decorate?"

Sylvia muffled a sigh, recognizing Sarah's attempt to change the subject but unwilling to pursue the matter. "The west sitting room. Perhaps we can move the armchair and set up the tree in the corner."

"Is that where your family usually put it up?"

"No, we used the ballroom, but in those days we needed the extra space to accommodate family and guests. The west sitting room would be much cozier for the three of us." The ballroom had been subdivided into classrooms for the quilt camp, too, and Sylvia didn't relish moving all of the partitions.

Sarah nodded and gestured toward the red-and-green tartan table linens. "What about the dining room?"

"Oh, let's decorate the kitchen and eat there as we

always do. The tablecloth will look just as festive on our usual table."

Sarah agreed, and as she gathered up the linens, Sylvia collected three of the holly napkin rings and picked up the Santa Claus cookie jar. They carried everything to the kitchen, one of the few rooms in the older wing of the house that Claudia had kept up with the times, more or less. The spacious room was painted a maple sugar hue that made the most of the afternoon sunlight, with the help of a copper light fixture that reminded Sylvia of an old-fashioned carriage lantern. It was suspended over the long wooden table and benches that filled the space between the doorway and the kitchen proper. Cupboards and appliances lined the walls except for the window over the sink, the door to the pantry in the southwest corner, and the open doorway that led to the west sitting room. A small microwave sat on the countertop beside the old gas oven Sylvia had cooked upon even before her abrupt departure so many years ago; it was a marvel of pre–World War II technology that it still worked at all. The refrigerator on the opposite wall appeared fairly new, perhaps less than ten years old, but the printed curtains had last been in style in the 1970s. The dishwasher Sarah had insisted they install stood out proudly, its gleaming stainless-steel finish intimidating every other appliance in the room. The kitchen was such a mishmash of old and new that Sylvia couldn't bear to change any of it, even though she knew it was not up to the standards of a professional kitchen and would prove hopelessly inadequate if their quilt camp grew at the pace Sarah predicted.

Sarah wiped off the long wooden table and draped the red-and-green tartan tablecloth over it. She placed two candlesticks in the center as Sylvia took clean cloth napkins from a drawer and tucked them into the holly wreath rings. Then Sylvia put the Santa Claus cookie jar between the candlesticks and declared that it made a fine centerpiece.

"Too bad it isn't full," remarked Sarah, lifting the lid to be sure.

"Even your sweet tooth couldn't handle fifty-year-old cookies," teased Sylvia, easing herself onto one of the benches. Images filled her mind, she and Claudia and her cousins swinging their feet as they sat on the bench dunking cookies into milk and leaving scuffmarks on the wooden floor with their shoes. A quick glance told her that time had worn away most of those marks, but some remained. She resisted the impulse to trace them with her fingertips.

"Maybe we should drive out to the bakery and fill it up with Christmas cookies," suggested Sarah.

"If you could find a bakery open on Christmas Eve, and if I thought you could do it without sending my great-aunt Lucinda spinning in her grave. Store-bought cookies in her favorite cookie jar? My dear, that's close to sacrilege in this house."

Sarah sat down on the opposite bench, amused. "I suppose you Bergstroms insisted upon homemade cookies."

"When you had a baker like Great-Aunt Lucinda in the family, you couldn't tolerate anything less. She made all the good German Christmas cookies precisely the way her mother had taught her. Lebkuchen—that's gingerbread; she made hers with grated almonds and candied orange peel. Aniseed cookies called anisplätzchen, and zimtsterne, cinnamon stars. She tried to keep that cookie jar filled from St. Nicholas Day through the Feast of the Three Kings, but we children ate them as fast as she could bake. It's no wonder she left the apple strudel to the other bakers in the family."

"I made apple strudel once," remarked Sarah. "You take the phyllo dough out of the box and place it on a cookie sheet, open up a can of apple pie filling, spread it all around, roll it up and bake it."

Sylvia cast her gaze to heaven. "Your generation will be forever remembered for its culinary ignorance."

"It was delicious," protested Sarah. "Especially with a little vanilla frosting on top."

"That is not strudel," said Sylvia. "Not real strudel, at any rate. If you had ever tasted my mother's, even your damaged taste buds would perceive the difference."

"I'm willing to learn. Teach me how to make the real thing."

Sylvia waved a hand, dismissing the notion. "I haven't made it since the war—the Second World War, before you get the idea that it was more recent. I would need at least a day to try to re-create the recipe from memory."

"You mean it isn't written down?"

"Of course not, dear. In those days, an accomplished cook didn't measure cups and teaspoonfuls; it was a heaping handful of flour here, a dash of salt there, bake in a hot oven until done. The instructions were never as specific as cooks require today."

And yet somehow food had always tasted better then, when recipes were handed down from mother to daughter and stored in one's memory rather than in a card file or on a computer.

From down the hall, she heard the back door slam; a moment later, Sarah's husband appeared in the doorway carrying two paper grocery sacks. "Looks nice," he remarked, admiring the festive table. "Does this mean Christmas isn't canceled after all?"

"Not even Sylvia can cancel Christmas," said Sarah. "No one can."

"Oliver Cromwell did," remarked Sylvia, rising and taking one of the bags from Matt. "In the 1640s, when he came to power in England. He thought it was too decadent. But I'm no Oliver Cromwell, and Christmas at Elm Creek Manor was never canceled. You shouldn't make assumptions based upon the lack of paper snowflakes and strings of colored lights. One doesn't need decorations to have Christmas."

"But it helps." To Matt, Sarah added, "Let's go out soon and get a tree. To me, it doesn't feel like Christmas unless it looks like Christmas."

"And sounds like Christmas," replied Matt. "We need to put on some carols."

"I left my CD player in the foyer," Sarah told him. He left the second bag of groceries on the counter and went to retrieve it, his curly blond head just clearing the doorframe. While they waited, Sylvia and Sarah put away the groceries Matt had purchased for their Christmas dinner, including sweet potatoes, cranberries, corn, apples, flour, onions, celery, and a contraband can of gravy Sylvia had deliberately crossed off the shopping list. Honestly. Canned gravy at Elm Creek Manor for Christmas dinner. When Sarah was not looking, Sylvia hid the gravy in a back corner of the pantry so that she would have no choice but to allow Sylvia to make theirs from scratch. Everything else they needed, they already had on hand. A turkey breast was defrosting on the bottom shelf of the refrigerator, and Sylvia had already torn a loaf of bread into cubes for the stuffing. She had made a pumpkin pie earlier that morning, before the young people came down for breakfast.

Sarah and Matt were quite right to attribute the holiday feeling to the sights and sounds of the season, but it was the smells and tastes of Christmas that flooded Sylvia with memories, transporting her to Christmases past as if she had lived those moments only yesterday and not decades ago. When Sylvia caught the scent of aniseed, no matter where she was or what the season, her thoughts immediately turned to Great-Aunt Lucinda, turning out batches of savory cookies for her eager nieces and nephews. The smell of baking apples and cinnamon and pastry called to mind her mother, and her grandmother, and even her great-grandfather's sister, Gerda Bergstrom, the first to make strudel in the kitchen of the farmhouse that would one day become Elm Creek Manor.

Gerda Bergstrom had brought the strudel recipe over from Germany when she emigrated in the 1850s; all of the family stories agreed upon that. Whether she had created it herself or learned it from her mother, no one knew. Either way, everyone who tasted Gerda's strudel affirmed that it was the most delicious they had ever tasted: the apples perfectly sliced and flavored with sugar and cinnamon, the pastry flaky and as light as air. Only a privileged few were ever treated to her strudel, and only at yuletide. All year she scrimped and saved her butter and egg money so that come December, she would have enough to purchase all the ingredients for the number of strudel she intended to make that year. She always made two for the family, which were devoured in a matter of minutes at breakfast Christmas morning. The others, sometimes as many as two dozen, she gave as gifts to her friends and to others whom she did not know as well, but who had earned her gratitude for a particular kindness they had shown her in the past year. Only one family other than her own received two strudels without fail every season: Dr. Jonathan Granger's, most likely because his services were so necessary and his friendship so valuable in a town with only one doctor. "I give you simply the joy and hope of the season," she would say as she offered a strudel to the lucky recipient, but neither the act nor the gift was as simple as she professed. Come Christmas Eve, when Gerda drove her brother's horse and wagon from farm to farm and through the streets of their small town distributing her gifts, everyone knew exactly where they stood with her. Some were pleasantly surprised; others ruefully resolved to be friendlier toward the outspoken spinster in the year to come.

As an unmarried woman living in her brother's household, Gerda would have been determined not to become a burden. By all accounts she was a hard worker, cooking for the family and tending her brother's children so her sister-in-law, a skilled seamstress, could earn extra money taking in sewing. Her strudel was already famous throughout the Elm Creek Valley by the time her nieces were old enough to learn her secrets. Later, when her nephews married, she taught their wives. Still, while every Bergstrom woman followed her instructions to the letter with results that would have been applauded in any other family, everyone agreed that Gerda's strudel remained unmatched in every regard.

After Gerda died, her cooking took on legendary attributes. More than one young bride marrying into the Bergstrom family fled to her room in tears after the strudel she had labored over for hours met with approving nods from her in-laws and fond reminiscences of the far superior crust or the more sublimely spiced apples Gerda had prepared long ago. Younger generations could only listen enviously as their elders recollected the Christmas feasts Gerda had created single-handedly in a kitchen that for most of her life boasted only a wood-burning stove and a root cellar. Once Sylvia was sent to her room for wondering aloud why Gerda could not have found any more productive use for her time than to haunt the kitchen peeling apples and stretching dough day and night, for that's what she must have done in order to produce as many pastries as family legend would have it.

But even though none could equal Gerda in the kitchen, every Bergstrom woman who learned her secret recipe had been armed with the power to win the admiration of young men, the respect of future mothers-in-law, and the envy of the other women whose family had been fortunate enough to receive a gift of the famous Bergstrom strudel.

Then a time came when so many women of the family knew how to make it that the next generation could not be bothered to learn. Why should they, when another aunt or cousin could be relied upon to make one for the family's Christmas breakfast and the several others necessary to fulfill Gerda's tradition of giving them away to the dearest friends of the family? It went unnoticed that, with each aged aunt who passed on or each young wife who moved away with her new husband, a little of Gerda's knowledge vanished into history.

Sylvia's mother was fortunate to learn from several of those who had been taught by Gerda herself: her mother-in-law and two of her husband's aunts, Lydia and Lucinda. Eleanor must have mastered the recipe quickly, for in Sylvia's earliest memories of watching the women of her family labor in the kitchen, her mother could handle the fragile dough as expertly as any Bergstrom-born.

Eleanor was also a talented quilter, but not only because of the Bergstroms' tutelage. She had learned to quilt as a child in New York City, and one of her most treasured possessions was the Crazy Quilt she had made with the help of her beloved nanny. When she first joined her husband's family at Elm Creek Manor, she had impressed the other women with her equal skill in patchwork and appliqué, whereas the Bergstrom women tended to favor one or the other. There were other differences; none of the Bergstroms had ever made a Crazy Quilt, a heavily embroidered, often delicate work created more for decoration than warmth, and they frequently knew the same patterns by different names. Over the years, they shared their knowledge and each woman considered her store richer for the collaboration.

Sylvia must have been seven or eight when Eleanor found Great-Aunt Lucinda's Feathered Star blocks tucked away in the family scrap bag with the leftover green and red fabrics. "These are too finely made to use for scraps," Eleanor protested when Lucinda explained that they had not found their way into the bag by mistake, for she had discarded them years ago. Her eyes were not as strong as they had once been, and she no longer felt capable of piecing together the tiny triangles as precisely as necessary. One of the aunts proposed stitching together the six blocks Lucinda had completed into a crib quilt, but after some discussion, all agreed that the eighteen-inch blocks were too large and overpowering to suit a baby's coverlet. Eventually Eleanor decided to continue making a full-size Christmas quilt, but rather than create additional Feathered Stars that would be compared to Lucinda's, she would appliqué holly wreaths and plumes to frame the older woman's work.

Eleanor worked on the quilt more consistently than Lucinda had, stitching the green holly leaves and deep red berries to ivory squares of fabric with tiny, meticulous stitches throughout the year. But although she did not put away the quilt at the end of the Christmas season, she progressed more slowly than Lucinda, for she could sew only for an hour or two at a time before headaches and fatigue forced her to set her handwork aside. Her health, which had never been robust, had begun a slow and steady decline after the birth of her youngest child and only son. Her condition had worsened markedly after the deaths of her mother and mother-in-law, less than a year apart. One by one she relinquished the activities she had once enjoyed: horseback riding, strolls along Elm Creek with Sylvia's father, picnics and games in the north gardens. The aunts took over her household duties without alluding to the necessity for Eleanor to rest. Her love for her family shone as strongly as ever, defying the weakness of her body, so that the children sometimes almost forgot her infirmity. She was their beloved Mama. It did not really matter whether she played with them, or if she merely held them on her lap and told them stories. They were happy in her company.

When December snows began to fall in Sylvia's ninth year, she offered to help her mother finish the Christmas Quilt in time for the holiday. She had recently finished a floral appliqué sampler and had improved her stitches so much that she was eager to take on a more important project. Her mother agreed, adding with a rueful laugh that without Sylvia's help, she might be obliged to give up as Lucinda had done.

Sylvia could not bear the thought of that, not after her mother had worked so hard to create such beautiful holly wreaths and sprays, so lifelike that Sylvia half-expected them to stir in the breeze. To spare her mother the effort, she traced her mother's leaf template onto stiff paper, cut out the shapes, paired them with pieces of green fabric, and basted the raw edges down until the fabric conformed to the paper. To make the berries, she placed a dime on the wrong side of a circle of fabric a quarter inch larger in diameter, then held the dime in place as she took small running stitches in the fabric circle all the way around the edge, leaving longer thread tails at the beginning and the end. She gently pulled the threads, drawing the fabric circle around the dime, and pressed with a hot iron. After loosening the threads to slip out the coin, she basted the edges of the fabric into a circle the size of a dime with perfectly smooth edges. All that remained for her mother to do was baste the leaves and berries in place on the background fabric and appliqué them securely.

Even with Sylvia's help, her mother tired easily and often rested with her sewing on her lap, watching two-year-old Richard play or supervising Claudia as she strung popcorn, berries, and nuts for the Christmas tree. Uncle William and his wife had needed four hours to choose a tree the previous year, which according to Sylvia's father was a new record. The delay forced the family to rush to finish decorating the tree before bedtime. Sylvia had overheard some speculation that

Uncle William and his bride had not spent all that time searching for a tree, but she could not imagine what else they might have been doing out there all alone in the snowy woods. Maybe they had gotten lost. In any event, Claudia was determined to be ready for an even longer search this year by preparing the decorations in advance.

Two days before Christmas, Great-Aunt Lydia announced her intention to make apple strudel that day, and anyone who wished to help would be welcome. Despite her weariness, Sylvia's mother took an interest. "How many do you plan to make?" she asked.

"Four," said Lydia. "One for us and three for the usual friends."

"Only four?" asked Eleanor. The family's interest in Gerda's tradition had diminished over the years as they had found other ways to express their affection and gratitude to their friends and neighbors. Quilted and knitted gifts were popular, but Sylvia had overheard Great-Aunt Lucinda tell Lydia that most families in the Elm Creek Valley would be grateful to find coal in their stockings this year. "Aunt Gerda always said the simple gifts were best," she had added, "but this year, simple is all most folks will be able to manage, and joy and hope may be in short supply."

They had been careful to speak of such things out of Eleanor's hearing, and now, confronted with her surprise, Lucinda and Lydia exchanged a look and Sylvia grew still. Her father and the other adults did their best to shield Eleanor and the children from distressing news, but Sylvia had perfected the art of eavesdropping on her elders. She knew what concerned her aunts, even if she did not entirely understand the cause.

In October, the First Bank of Waterford had lost all the family's money along with the savings of its other customers. For reasons that did not seem fair to Sylvia, a larger bank in a far-off city had called in a debt and had cleared out the Waterford bank vault in order to pay its own customers. Her father said that this was happening throughout the nation—banks failing, factories closing, everywhere men losing their means of earning a living. Rich men leaped to their deaths from skyscrapers rather than endure bankruptcy, and poor men sold apples on street corners.

Sylvia's mother knew what was happening around the country because the family could not hide the newspaper or turn off the radio without explaining why. What she did not know—what her husband had tried to conceal from her—was how seriously their own family had been affected. Eleanor did not know that their savings had been lost, or that the family business had not generated any income for months. The wealth of most of their former customers had been wiped out in the stock market crash. No one had the money to spend on luxuries like expensive horses. The Bergstroms would get by because they were moderately self-sufficient; they owned their own land and thus did not have to pay a mortgage, and they grew some of their own food. They had ample wood from their forest to heat the home if their supply of coal ran out before spring. The manor was full of desirable possessions they could use to pay off Eleanor's doctor bills and barter for whatever else they needed in town. But for the first time since Gerda Bergstrom's day, the family had to watch every penny. Lydia's expenditures on white flour, sugar, and cinnamon, a trifle any other Christmas, had already led to one argument with some of the men of the household.

"These are difficult times," Lydia tried to explain, reluctant to burden Eleanor with worries.

"And they will worsen before they improve," said Eleanor firmly, setting her quilting aside. "All the more reason for those of us who have been blessed to share our abundance with others."

The look of concern and dismay the other adults shared was so obvious Sylvia did not see how her mother could have misunderstood its meaning, but of course, Eleanor had no idea how much their abundance had dwindled. When she called for Sylvia to help her from her chair, Sylvia hurried to her mother's side and steadied her as she stood. On her feet, Eleanor looked around the circle of worried faces. "Will any of you help me?" When none of the aunts replied, Eleanor's mouth tightened almost imperceptibly. "Very well. Sylvia, would you?" Sylvia nodded. "That's a good girl. And you, Claudia?" More solemnly, Claudia nodded. "Good. It's time you girls tried your hand at Gerda's recipe anyway. You're old enough to do more than peel apples."

As Eleanor and her daughters left the parlor, Lydia opened her mouth to speak, but any protest she might have intended was abruptly silenced by a gesture from Lucinda. No one followed them down the hall to the kitchen, where Eleanor pulled out the bench and sat down at the table rather than standing at the counter as she used to do. She called for her mixing bowl, for flour, water, salt, and butter; Sylvia and Claudia scrambled to set everything before her. Their mother's mouth turned in a frown when she saw the limp flour sack, and Sylvia knew she was measuring with her eyes and calculating how far it would go.

"It will have to do," she murmured with a sigh. She ordered Claudia to fetch two eggs from the barn. She would make up the pastry dough two at a time and make as many as their larder would allow.

"Remember this, girls," their mother instructed when Claudia returned. She reached into the flour sack and put six large handfuls into her mixing bowl. She tossed in a pinch of salt, blended the two, and made a well in the center with a spoon. Into this she added an egg, a cup of water, and a dollop of fresh butter, which Sylvia brought to her. With both hands she mixed everything together, working in silence. Sylvia and Claudia exchanged a look, a silent warning not to speak, not to warn their mother that this was the last of the flour, that salt was scarce, that Great-Aunt Lucinda had been trading the eggs with neighboring farmers for sausage and ham. Sylvia was not sure it would have made a difference.

Eleanor turned the dough out onto a floured board and began kneading, the hard line of her mouth gradually relaxing as she worked. After a few minutes she called Claudia to take a turn squeezing, pressing, and folding the dough over and over again. Next Sylvia took a turn, kneading the dough until her hands and shoulders grew tired. Her mother took over for her, working the dough expertly with the heels of her hands.

"When I was a little girl," she said suddenly, "my parents employed a French chef who made *bûche de noël* for our Christmas dessert. Do you know what that is? It's a cake rolled and shaped to look like a yule log. He decorated it with chocolate frosting and meringue mushrooms. It was such a treat. My sister and I looked forward to it all year."

"Didn't your mother make strudel?" asked Sylvia.

Her mother laughed. "My mother? Oh, no, darling. My mother did not cook. I didn't taste strudel until I married your father and came to live here."

"Maybe we could make a yule log cake sometime," said Claudia.

"Perhaps someday. I prefer Bergstrom ways."

The dough had become a smooth, satiny ball beneath their mother's capable hands. She divided it into halves, separated them on the floured board, and covered them with a dishtowel. "Now we let the dough rest while we prepare the apples."

"We'll get them," said Sylvia quickly, motioning for Claudia to follow her down to the cellar. The apples, harvested from their own orchard and stored below where in winter it was as cold as the icebox, were heaped in bushel baskets along one wall, as red and crisp as the day they were picked. Choosing the nearest basket, each girl seized a handle and lugged the apples upstairs. Their mother sat up quickly and smiled when they returned, but it was obvious she had been resting her head on the table.

Sylvia fetched three paring knives from the drawer and sat down on the bench across from her mother and sister. Eleanor could peel three apples as swiftly as Sylvia peeled one, the red skin rolling off in a continuous, narrow ribbon as thin as paper. Sylvia tried to imitate her, but her strips usually broke as soon as they became long enough to touch her lap, and thick chunks of juicy white apple flesh sometimes came off with the peel. Eleanor wielded the paring knife so deftly that it was impossible to believe that she had not been preparing apples for strudel since she was Sylvia's age, or that she had ever spent Christmas anywhere but here.

"Mama?" asked Sylvia, forgetting her promise not to tire her mother with too many questions. "What was Christmas like when you were my age?"

"Very much like it is today," her mother said after a moment. "It was a day for celebrating the Lord's birth, for family, for special treats, beautiful carols, and if we had been very good girls, a visit from Santa Claus."

As piles of apple peelings collected on the table and their fingers grew sticky with juice, their mother told them stories of Christmases in New York—of fancy balls, concerts in the city, the annual trip to her father's department store on Fifth Avenue where she and her sister were allowed to choose any toy they wanted. She spoke more warmly of quieter celebrations in the nursery with her English nanny, who taught her about Christmas ghost stories and Christmas crackers and their obligation to help those in need, especially during the holidays but throughout the year. Sylvia wondered if the nanny's lessons accounted for her mother's determination to continue Gerda Bergstrom's tradition of giving.

When Eleanor decided they had peeled enough apples, her storytelling ceased. She demonstrated how to slice and cut the fruit into uniform pieces, once again finishing three apples to their every one. She sent Claudia to the linen closet for a freshly laundered sheet while she and Sylvia scooped the apple slices into a bowl and mixed them with two heaping handfuls of bread crumbs, a sprinkling of cinnamon, two handfuls of sugar, finely chopped walnuts, and a large spoonful of softened butter. The sweet smell of apples and cinnamon was too much for Sylvia, and she could not resist dipping her finger into the bowl to taste the sweet juice that had collected at the bottom.

"What do you think, girls?" their mother asked when Claudia returned from upstairs. "Has the dough rested sufficiently?" Sylvia did not know how to judge, but Claudia answered yes so confidently that Sylvia quickly chimed in her agreement rather than appear to know less than her sister. After the girls wiped the table clean, their mother covered the table with the sheet, pulled it smooth, and secured it in place with clothespins. She dusted the sheet with flour, but Sylvia noticed that she used far less than in previous years.

Eleanor instructed her daughters to wash their hands; when they returned from the sink, fingers freshly scrubbed and patted dry, they found her rolling out one of the dough balls into a rectangle in the center of the floured sheet. When she could roll the dough no thinner with the rolling pin, she set it aside. "Watch carefully," she instructed her daughters. "Someday you will need to know how to do this on your own."

She slipped her hands beneath the dough rectangle and gently stretched it, pulling carefully with the backs of her hands and her thumbs and allowing the dough to fall back upon the floured cloth. Stepping around to another side of the table, she repeated the motions until she had walked all the way around the table and stretched the dough on all four sides. "This will go faster if you two help me," she remarked, reaching beneath the pastry dough again. "And I won't have to walk around the table so many times."

Sylvia flushed with nervousness and pride as she took her place on the other side of the table from her mother. She had often watched her mother, aunts, and older cousins stretching the dough, but she and Claudia had never been permitted to join in. The fragile dough must be stretched to a uniform tissue-paper thinness everywhere, with no tears and no thicker patches to ruin the delicate texture. Sylvia's touch was at first tentative, but then as she saw how the dough responded as she gently drew it from the center out, she grew bolder.

"Mama," Claudia exclaimed just as Sylvia saw what she had done. "Sylvia tore a hole."

Mortified, Sylvia pulled her hands free of the dough and allowed it to fall to the table. A three-inch maw in the dough glared up at her.

"That's all right," said Eleanor, hurrying over. "It's easily mended." She gently pinched the tear closed and smiled reassuringly at Sylvia, but the seam was too visible and she knew she had ruined the strudel.

"I'm sorry, Mama," she said. What would the aunts say when they found out?

"Don't worry, darling," said Eleanor. "I imagine even Gerda Bergstrom tore the dough from time to time. When your grandmother first taught me to make it, I tore the dough so many times that it looked like a sweater the moths had found. We patched every hole and the strudel was still delicious, and I'm sure this one will be, too."

Sylvia felt better, but Claudia shook her head in silent disgust. Leave it to the careless little sister to ruin the Bergstrom reputation, her look seemed to say.

Eleanor urged her daughters back to the task. Sylvia obeyed, but more cautiously this time. Gradually the dough grew longer and wider until it was nearly translucent. Eventually the dough stretched to the edges of the table, impossibly thin. Their mother circled the table one last time, trimming off the thicker edges with a knife. She set the scraps aside—she would make soup noodles with them later—and beckoned for Sylvia to bring her the apple slices. While Sylvia held the bowl, Eleanor scooped out the apples and lined one long edge of the dough from one end of the table to the other, piling up the slices in the shape of a log.

When she had finished, Eleanor set the empty bowl on the counter, her face flushed. Worried, Sylvia watched her while she held on to the back of a chair to rest, but she paused only a moment. Then, starting at one end, she carefully folded the dough over the apples until they could not be seen. "This is where teamwork is essential, girls," she said, unclipping two of the clothespins. Her daughters had helped with this part before and knew what was to come. They took their places on either side of their mother and grasped the long edge of the sheet with both hands. Eleanor counted to three, and then they lifted the sheet so that the log of apples rolled away from them, wrapping itself up in dough as it went. Eleanor bent the strudel into a horseshoe, put it in a pan, and brushed it with butter left to melt on the stovetop. Claudia helped her slide the pan into the oven, and then, Sylvia thought with relief, they were finished.

"Well done, girls," their mother praised. "But the proof will be in the tasting."

Sylvia's mouth watered in anticipation, but she knew they would have to wait until breakfast Christmas morning to enjoy the fruit of their labors. Eleanor allowed them to savor their moment of pride for only a moment before reminding them of the second ball of dough waiting to be stretched. A few minutes before the second strudel was ready to shape for the pan, the first had finished cooking. The heavenly aroma of cinnamon apples poured into the kitchen as Eleanor opened the oven door and took out the baking pan. To Sylvia's joy, it looked exactly as it should, exactly like every strudel the Bergstrom women had made in that kitchen for generations.

With the second strudel in the oven, Sylvia was eager to begin another. "Shall we get more apples from the cellar, Mama?"

"Let's rest a while first," said Claudia, her eyes on their mother's face.

"Or you could allow us to help," remarked Great-Aunt Lucinda from the doorway. Great-Aunt Lydia peeked in over her shoulder, nodding.

"She asked you to help before and you refused," said Sylvia.

"Hush, darling," said her mother gently. She smiled at the aunts. "We'd be glad for your help. Many hands make light work."

As their more experienced aunts joined in, Sylvia and Claudia were reduced to their usual role of kitchen helpers. They fetched utensils and ingredients for their elders, provided an extra hand here or quick clean-up there, but mostly, they watched and they listened. Sylvia drank in their stories of Christmases from long ago, of the hardships and the joys the women of her family experienced within those walls. Her mother listened, too, peeling apples slowly and steadily in her chair, her face no longer flushed, but pale, her smile content but weary.

By late afternoon the flour sack was empty and the sugar bin nearly so, but fourteen flaky, golden brown strudel lay side by side on the wooden table. Lucinda and Lydia promptly turned their attention to their delayed dinner preparations while Sylvia and Claudia cleaned up the mess. Their mother rose to assist, but Lucinda encouraged her to go upstairs and lie down for a while. "I can't rest with so much yet to do before Christmas," she protested, but when the aunts insisted, she agreed to sit in the front parlor and work on the Christmas Quilt until they needed her.

Naturally, Lucinda and Lydia had no intention of calling her until the men came in and the meal was served. Even Sylvia knew that. She tried to listen in on the aunts' hushed conversation as she picked up apple peelings and washed dishes, catching words and phrases that convinced her they were discussing Eleanor's strange insistence upon baking so many strudel, more than the Bergstroms had made for gifts in years. But the elder women kept their voices deliberately low so that Sylvia learned nothing, not even what they planned to tell the men when they had no flour to bake bread the next day.

Due to their haste or, just as likely, the contents of the larder, dinner was a simple affair of biscuits left over from breakfast and sausages, apples, and onions fried up together in Grandmother's enormous cast-iron pan. Great-Aunt Lucinda told Claudia to set the dining room table while Sylvia went to the parlor to summon her mother. She found her asleep in the armchair, holly leaf appliqués scattered on her lap, thimble still on her finger.

If the men of the family were surprised to discover fourteen strudels displayed on the kitchen table, they said nothing of it at dinner. Maybe, Sylvia hoped, they had not gone into the kitchen at all. Maybe they would stay away until the pastries were wrapped in wax paper, tied with ribbon, and safely tucked away out of sight in baskets, ready for delivery. By an unspoken agreement, the women said nothing of how Sylvia's mother had spent her day. Throughout the meal, Sylvia found herself nervously waiting for her mother to divulge the truth, but Eleanor spoke little. As soon as dinner was finished, she excused herself and went upstairs to bed.

As soon as she was out of earshot, the men revealed that they were well aware of the secret. Uncle William criticized their wastefulness, while Sylvia's father wondered angrily why they had allowed Eleanor to work herself so hard.

"We couldn't have stopped her," said Lucinda. "Not without a good reason, not without divulging the truth about our finances. I don't even know if that would have convinced her."

"But you used up the last of the flour," said Uncle William.

"I have eggs to trade for more."

"We encouraged her to rest," added Lydia. "Most of the time she was simply sitting, peeling apples."

"Obviously that was enough to exhaust her." Sylvia's father rose and shoved in his chair, and only then did he seem to remember his three children still seated at the table, hanging on every word. Even two-year-old Richard looked solemn and anxious. "But she'll be fine after a good night's rest."

Sylvia knew her father had added the last for their benefit. She wanted to believe him.

The next morning, Sylvia came downstairs to breakfast to find her mother in the kitchen packing the strudel carefully into baskets. She was shaking her head in mild exasperation as her husband tried to coax her back to bed. "I am not tired, and I am not about to linger in bed on the morning of Christmas Eve," she told him. "I need to take these around to the neighbors now so that

I'll return before we send William and Nellie out to find a tree. I don't want to miss that."

"At least let me drive you," Sylvia's father persisted.

Eleanor stopped packing the baskets and looked him squarely in the eye. "Freddy, in all these years you have never treated me like an invalid and I forbid you to start now. You cannot protect me from what is coming, but you can make this time more bearable. Don't bury me before I've passed."

The anger in her mother's gentle voice shocked Sylvia. "Mama?"

Her father turned his head toward her with a jerk, but her mother looked up more slowly, as if she was not surprised to discover Sylvia in the doorway. "What is it, darling?"

"What's coming? You said something is coming. I heard you."

Her mother said nothing.

"Christmas," her father said abruptly. "Christmas is coming. Have you forgotten what day it is?"

Sylvia shook her head, both in response to his question and in rejection of his false reply. "Mama?" she said again, pleading. "Why are you angry at Daddy?"

Her mother hesitated. "Because I know he's right." She forced a smile, but Sylvia saw tears in her eyes. "I do work myself too hard sometimes, especially at this time of year. Freddy, I accept your offer to drive me. Thank you. Sylvia, would you come along, too, and help me give out the famous Bergstrom strudel to our friends? It's only fitting, since you helped make them."

"Of course, Mama," said Sylvia, forcing cheer into her voice. Silently she chastised herself for not heeding her father's wishes. How many times had he warned the children not to tire their mother? If Sylvia and Claudia had not agreed to help their mother make strudel, perhaps she would have stayed in her chair in the parlor, sewing on the Christmas Quilt and conserving her strength. Or perhaps she would have made the strudel alone, exhausting her last reserves of energy and rendering herself bedridden. Sylvia could not be sure if they had done right or wrong in helping their mother. It was all so confusing and strange. For years the adults of the family had cautioned the children that their mother was not well and that they should let her rest. Sometimes they forgot, but mostly they did as they were told. What good had it done? Quiet rest, visits from the doctor, concealing the truth about their finances—none of it made any difference as far as Sylvia could see. When was her mother going to be well and strong again?

Sylvia kept her worries hidden, a silent cry of fear and pain nestled close to her heart, as she and her parents dressed for the cold and carried the baskets outside to the car. Her father rarely drove anymore, conserving the expensive gasoline for emergencies. Sylvia's mother had been told that her husband preferred to exercise the horses rather than allow them to grow fat and lazy over the winter. As far as Sylvia knew, her mother had accepted this, even though it was not what the Bergstroms had always done. They did so many things differently now, and yet nothing had raised the suspicions of the woman who had always known the intimate details of the household, who had known things about her children she could not possibly have seen or heard. How could she be so unaware of what was going on around her? Suddenly Sylvia was seized by the longing to take her mother by the shoulders and shake her, shake the truth into her and out of her.

Sylvia climbed into the backseat with the baskets while her father helped her mother into the front. The car coughed out a puff of black smoke from the tailpipe when her father tried to start it, but after a moment, the motor rumbled steadily.

"The Craigmiles first," Eleanor said. Her father nodded and drove them to a farm less than a mile away. The Craigmiles had lived in the Elm Creek Valley for generations, and their family had been friends with the Bergstroms since Gerda's time.

Sylvia's father waited in the car while his wife and daughter went up to the house; Sylvia carried the strudel, and her mother rested a hand on her shoulder for support. When Mrs. Craigmile opened the door to Eleanor's knock, Sylvia could tell her mother was taken aback by how much she had changed. Though she was only ten years older than Eleanor, her dark brown hair had gone gray, and deep crevices of worry framed her eyes and mouth.

Eleanor swiftly composed herself. "Merry Christmas, Edith." She nodded to Sylvia, who placed a wrapped strudel in her neighbor's hands.

"Well, my goodness." Mrs. Craigmile stared at the gift. "Thank you. I'm grateful. We weren't expecting anything, not this year."

"Why not?" said Eleanor, clearly surprised. "You must know we'd never forget you."

"Yes, but this year . . ." Mrs. Craigmile shrugged. "Hard times have hit everyone. But you're looking well. It's good to see you're getting out of the house."

"I do shut myself indoors too much as soon as the weather turns colder. It must be my city constitution."

Mrs. Craigmile's lips curved in an unsteady smile. "You've lived among us so long you surely must be accustomed to our climate by now. I've never lived anywhere but here. I can't imagine what I'll do if we have to clear out."

"You want to give up your farm?"

"Want to? It's not even our farm, or so we're told. It's the bank's."

Eleanor gripped Sylvia's shoulder tighter. "But Craigmiles have worked this land for more than a hundred years. What does the bank have to do with it?"

"Remember when the Brennans put those fifteen acres along our north pasture up for sale?"

"Of course. You and Malcolm purchased them."

"Times were better then. We took out a loan from the Bank of Waterford to buy the land, and add that summer porch to the house, and get that new tiller." Mrs. Craigmile shrugged matter-of-factly, but her grief was palpable. "When the bank failed, they called in our debt. Now some bankers in Philadelphia say they own the land. I don't know whether we should pack up and leave with all we can carry before they take the clothes off our backs, or if we should do as Malcolm says and stay put until they force us off."

The shock on Eleanor's face made Sylvia sick to her stomach. Mrs. Craigmile must have sensed something amiss, for she hastily added, "But don't you worry about us. We'll be fine. What would a bunch of city bankers want with our farm? They're likely to leave us be, especially if we promise to send them a little something every month. We'll get by. You folks have a good Christmas, you hear?"

Eleanor nodded wordlessly. Sylvia breathed a quick Merry Christmas and accompanied her mother back to the waiting car.

"Did you know about the bank failure, Sylvia?" her mother asked.

"Yes, Mama," she replied in a small voice.

Her mother nodded, her eyes fixed on the car.

As they climbed into their seats, Sylvia held her breath, waiting for her mother to confront her father, to demand an accounting of their own circumstances. But she said nothing except to ask him to drive them on to the Shropshire farm, closer to town.

At every house they visited that morning it was the same. Friends and neighbors welcomed Eleanor and her gifts more gratefully than ever, inquired circumspectly after her health and the Bergstroms' prospects, and shared stories of misfortune that they clearly assumed Eleanor already knew. In town it was the same as on the farms. A schoolteacher said that half her pupils had dropped off the rolls. The wife of the editor of the *Waterford Register* confessed that she did not know how much longer her husband would be able to keep the paper going, and it would take all she had to scrape together a decent Christmas for the children. "But Santa won't forget them," she added, glancing at Sylvia as if noticing her for the first time. "Nor will he forget you."

She looked questioningly at Eleanor before adding the last. Whatever her silent question was, Sylvia's mother affirmed it with a quick nod and said, "I'm sure Santa will put in an appearance at our home tonight."

After the last strudel was delivered, Sylvia's father

turned the car toward home. Throughout the trip, Eleanor had remained mostly silent. Sylvia's father had glanced at her now and then to be sure she was all right, and no doubt he attributed her silence to fatigue. Sylvia wanted to warn him that her mother knew the secrets he had kept so well for so long, but she did not see how to do it without betraying her mother.

As they crossed the bridge over Elm Creek, Eleanor suddenly broke the silence. "Freddy," she said quietly, "our neighbors are suffering."

Sylvia's father said nothing for a long moment. "Of course they are. These are hard times for everyone."

"And I had no idea how hard until today. Oh, I knew our circumstances had to be worse than you were telling me, but I never conceived of anything so grim."

"Darling, I promise you we will manage. We won't lose the farm. The children won't starve."

"Perhaps, but what of our friends? What of the others? We must help them." Eleanor turned in her seat until she faced her husband. "The Craigmiles will lose their farm to the bank unless they pay off the loan. We must pay it for them."

"Darling—"

"Daniel Shropshire needs glasses. The Schultzes need food. No one has been able to pay Dr. Granger for months, so even his family is struggling. We must give more than simply the hope and joy of the season this year. We must give them what they need."

"Darling, we haven't the means."

Eleanor stared at him. "Then the bank failure—"

"Took our savings as well. Eleanor, as much as I long to help our friends, I'm doing all I can to keep our own heads above water."

Sylvia shrank back into her seat, sick at heart, wishing she were as deaf to their words as her parents seemed to believe. Her mother sat straight up in her seat, gloved hands clasped in her lap, as her father pulled the car into the old carriage house and shut it down. No one moved to leave the car, and at last Sylvia's mother said, "As Christians we are not called to give from our surplus but to give all we can. We must sell the horses."

"Eleanor." Her father's voice was full of compassion and pain. "I haven't been able to sell a horse in months. Believe me, I've tried."

"But our most loyal customers—"

"—are broke, or in the same shape we are. It's the same everywhere. We all have to weather this storm together."

"Yes. You're absolutely right." Eleanor opened the car door, climbed out, and slammed it shut. "Together. That is the only way we will endure. We can't think only of ourselves. And you mustn't hide the truth from me ever again."

Sylvia's father watched her stride briskly toward the house. Sylvia sat perfectly still, her heart pounding. She had never witnessed such a heated exchange between her parents, and it was a thing both terrible and exhilarating. *Look!* she wanted to shout to her father and the aunts, *Mama is not too sick for the truth. She is strong and angry and determined. She will prove all of you wrong and make everything better, including herself.*

"Come along, Sylvia," said her father tiredly. "Let's get inside before we freeze."

Inside, they found the rest of the family unpacking Christmas ornaments and teasing Uncle William and

Aunt Nellie as they dressed for a snowy walk through the woods in search of a Christmas tree. Sylvia's mother, Claudia reported, had briefly wished the couple well before heading upstairs to rest, or so everyone assumed. Sylvia joined in the decorating with a heavy heart. She wondered if anyone else noticed how often her father glanced to the doorway, how forced his smiles were.

The couple returned with a tree after little more than an hour had passed, earning them raised eyebrows and speculative looks instead of the thanks Sylvia thought they deserved for making up for the previous year by returning so promptly.

"Should we get Mama?" Claudia asked Sylvia as their father and uncle set the tree into its stand. "She wouldn't want to miss decorating the tree."

"I'll get her," said Sylvia. She slipped from the ballroom before her father could see her. He would not want her to disturb her mother.

Sylvia hurried upstairs to her mother's room, expecting to find her in bed, but instead discovering her seated on the floor taking clothes from a bureau drawer. Beside her was a pile of sweaters, neatly folded.

"Mama?" asked Sylvia. "What are you doing?"

"Sylvia, darling." Eleanor motioned for Sylvia to come to her. "I'm gathering clothes I no longer need. We'll take them to church tomorrow and ask Reverend Webster to distribute them to people in need."

Sylvia eyed the pile of sweaters. They were sturdy and warm, the kind her mother had worn when she helped exercise the horses. "Won't you need them?"

Eleanor shook her head. "They're too big for me now." And it was true; over the years her mother had grown thinner, a willow swaying in the wind. "I would like you to go to your closet and take out any dresses you've outgrown. Shoes, too. I'm sure the reverend can find a young lady who will be glad to have them."

"Now, Mama? Everyone is downstairs trimming the tree."

Eleanor started. "Oh, my goodness, of course they are. We mustn't keep them waiting. We can finish this tomorrow."

Spend Christmas Day sorting old clothes? Sylvia was about to protest, but the stories their neighbors had told of hard times and harder yet on the horizon tugged at her and she fell silent. She took her mother's hand and accompanied her downstairs. They passed Great-Aunt Lydia, sent out to hide the star. She seemed happily surprised to see Eleanor, and she teased Sylvia in passing about searching for the star before it was properly hidden. Ordinarily a remark like that would have left Sylvia feeling indignant and wrongfully accused, but too many other more upsetting things had been said that day for a harmless joke to trouble her.

When they entered the ballroom, Sylvia's father hurried over, took his wife's hands, and led her to a comfortable chair where she could observe the decorating and offer suggestions. Sylvia half expected her mother to argue that she did not need to sit, but Eleanor took the seat offered her and asked Sylvia to fetch her sewing. Sylvia ran to the parlor for the sewing basket and holly appliqués, and not long after she returned, her father sent the children out to find the red glass star. Sylvia remembered where Great-Aunt Lydia had hidden the star the last time she had taken a turn, three years before. Eager to return to her mother, Sylvia looked there first and discovered the star on a bookshelf in the library, though not the same bookshelf. Sylvia took Richard by the hand and guided him to it; he crowed with joy and raced back to show his parents what he had found.

And so Christmas Eve passed as all those in Sylvia's memory had passed, or nearly so. Great-Aunt Lucinda read aloud Christmas greetings from distant family, including cousin Elizabeth's letter from California. Sylvia's father read "A Visit from St. Nicholas" aloud to the children, and Great-Aunt Lydia followed with the story of the Nativity from St. Luke. Sylvia's mother sewed holly berry appliqués to her Christmas Quilt, and Great-Aunt Lucinda passed around a plate of her Christmas cookies. But there were fewer cookies than last year, and fewer presents beneath the tree. Sylvia hoped Santa would not forget that most of those were gifts the adults would exchange, and that there was room beneath the tree for more for the children.

The children were sent off to bed with hugs and kisses. Sylvia led toddler Richard by the hand and tucked him into bed, as she did every night. When she went to her own room, Claudia was already under the covers. "What happened when you and Mama and Daddy went out this morning?" Claudia asked as Sylvia climbed into bed.

"We took strudel to the neighbors, just like always."

"But you were gone so long."

"Mama made more strudel this year."

"She might think this will be the last year for it."

Sylvia felt a thundering in her skull as the nagging suspicion she had tried to ignore all day erupted to the surface. It was true. Each giving that day had been an expression of friendship, of sympathy during hard times, of the joy and hope of the season—but also of farewell.

Musing, Claudia added, "It's almost as if Mama thinks we'll always be this poor, that we'll never have enough flour to bake properly again."

Gratefully, desperately, Sylvia seized on to her sister's innocent explanation and held fast. Of course their mother's gifts were linked to the hard times in Waterford. Of course she would want to give out as many strudel as possible to make sure their friends had a special breakfast Christmas morning. From what Mrs. Craigmile and the others had said, even the most ordinary meals of the past had come to seem luxurious. Their mother's gifts would remind their friends that better times were sure to come again. She was offering them hope and encouragement with every bite of delicate pastry and cinnamon apples.

"We aren't poor." Sylvia pulled the quilt up to her chin. "We're a lot better off than most people, especially the families who live in town. We'll always get by as long as we have the farm."

"That's true. Daddy can always sell some of the land."

"That's not what I meant. We have the farm and the orchards and our home. We'll never starve and we'll always have a roof over our heads. That's all we need."

"Everyone needs money, even if they own a farm. We have to pay taxes and buy the things we can't make or grow." Claudia spread her glossy brown curls in a fan on her pillow to keep her hair free of snarls, as she did every night. She slept on her back and in the morning her hair would still be spread out obediently, without the smallest tangle. Sylvia could never figure out how Claudia managed to keep still all night, while Sylvia always woke tangled in the bed sheets.

"I don't mean sell all of the land," Claudia added. "We would never sell the manor and leave us without a home. But Daddy will sell the land if he has to. I know I would."

Anger stirred within Sylvia. "It's a good thing Elm Creek Manor will never be yours to sell."

She rolled over on her side and folded her pillow around her head, her back to her sister. Claudia was a fool, a silly little fool. The farm sustained their family. The land took care of the Bergstroms as much as they took care of the land. Their father knew this. Every Bergstrom with an ounce of sense understood that implicitly, just as they understood the necessity of air to breathe and food to eat. How Claudia could so blithely contemplate selling off Bergstrom land filled Sylvia with equal parts astonishment and anger.

Christmas morning dawned gray and cold. Snow had fallen overnight, and the dense clouds gave a twilight cast to the morning air, but the weather had not prevented Santa from coming. Sylvia forgot her frustration with her sister and her worries about their neighbors in the particular happiness that was Christmas morning. Santa had come. He had forgiven her the innumerable acts of naughtiness she had committed throughout the year and had placed her on his good list, a surer sign of his love and his faith in her potential than an accurate evaluation of her behavior. She could even be happy for Claudia, who had received the china doll she had longed for. Little Richard had found a wooden train beneath the tree and was happily pushing it around in circles on the floor. Sylvia received a sewing basket of her very own, exactly like her mother's except for the color—a cheerful pine instead of dark cherry wood.

"Santa must have seen you helping me with the Christmas Quilt," her mother remarked. "He must have decided you needed scissors and needles of your own."

Sylvia would have been content with that one gift, but just then her father peered curiously into the branches of the tree. "What's that?" he asked, gesturing.

"I don't see anything," said Claudia, "just a bit of paper. Maybe it fell from Sylvia's angel. The wings have always been loose. She didn't use enough paste."

Sylvia glared at Claudia before remembering that Santa might already be watching and taking notes for next year.

Her father shook his head, puzzled. "It's a bit of paper, all right, but look up to the higher branches. The wings of Sylvia's angel are right where they belong. Sylvia, will you see what it is?"

Sylvia closed her sewing basket and set it aside. She rose on tiptoe and reached into the tree where a small bit of white was visible through the branches and needles. It was a piece of heavy writing paper, folded over and sealed with a spot of red wax. Her own name was written in fancy script upon it.

"It's a letter, I think," she said. "To me."

"A letter?" Sylvia's mother glanced at her father, surprised. "Who is it from?"

"Santa?" joked Uncle William.

"Who else would have left a surprise in our Christmas tree?" said Sylvia's father. "Read it aloud, Sylvia. Tell us what old St. Nick has to say for himself."

Quickly Sylvia broke the seal and unfolded the paper. "'Dear Sylvia,'" she read. "'I hope you like the sewing basket I left for you. I trust you weren't too disappointed that I could not bring you all the toys you wanted. I'm sure you know that folks have fallen on hard times in your part of the world. This year I had to fill up my sleigh with food and clothes as well as toys for all those good little children who don't have warm homes and plenty to eat, like you and your sister and brother do. Unfortunately, my sleigh was too heavy for my reindeer to pull, so I had to leave a few bags of toys back at the North Pole. I will do my best to bring them next year, but you're such a generous, kind little girl that I know you'll understand.'"

"He can't be talking about Sylvia," interrupted Claudia. "I think he put her name on there by mistake."

"Claudia," admonished their mother.

Sylvia ignored her sister and read on. "'I know you won't miss those toys when you find out what a special present I've planned for you to receive soon. I couldn't bring it on my sleigh and it wouldn't fit under the tree. I know you'll take very good care of it because you're so helpful to your mother and your great-aunts, and because you take such loving care of your little brother.'"

"Now I know he got our names mixed up," declared Claudia.

"Claudia, hush," said their father.

"What present wouldn't fit under a tree?" asked Uncle William, scratching his head. "What's that jolly old elf talking about? Maybe he's been sipping too much eggnog."

Claudia giggled, but Sylvia kept reading. "'I'm sure you know Blossom is due to have her foal soon. You tell your father that I said you get to have that foal for your very own horse.'" Sylvia stopped reading and looked up at her father.

"Go on," her mother prompted. "This has suddenly become quite interesting."

"I'll say," said Uncle William.

Sylvia took a deep breath and plunged ahead. "'I know you'll take very good care of your horse and that you will make me very proud. Until next year, I remain very truly yours, Santa Claus. P.S.: Merry Christmas!'" She gulped and looked from her mother to her father. "Can he do that? Can he make you give me one of the horses for my very own?"

Her father shrugged. "Who am I to argue with Santa Claus? If he thinks you're ready to join the family business, I'm going to trust his judgment."

"Why is Sylvia the only one who gets a horse?" protested Claudia.

Their mother turned to her. "Why, Claudia, do you want a horse?"

Claudia's mouth worked in a scowl. "No," she grumbled.

"Santa probably knows you're scared of horses," reasoned Sylvia. "And you got the doll and all those clothes. And Richard's too little to take care of a horse. So it's just me. Daddy, can we go see Blossom right now?"

"After breakfast," her father promised.

Sylvia had almost forgotten that breakfast would include the strudel she and Claudia had helped her mother make. She knew it was the same one because she had pinched an edge of the pastry just so, wanting to be sure she would recognize it later. To her relief, it was as flavorful and flaky as those her grandmother had made. Everyone around the table said so.

After breakfast, Sylvia went with her father and uncle

to the stables. She greeted Blossom gently, fed her a special Christmas treat of oats and apples, and promised always to take very good care of her little foal.

The snow fell heavily throughout the day, keeping away visitors who had not arrived on Christmas Eve. It was a smaller, quieter Christmas than in years past, and the older members of the family spoke wistfully of loved ones who had passed on, how they would have admired the tree, enjoyed the girls' first strudel, and marveled at the letter from Santa Claus. Later that day, Sylvia's mother sent the girls off to collect clothing and toys in good repair to give to the less fortunate. This became another Bergstrom tradition, and when prosperity returned, their gifts became more generous—new clothes and toys instead of old, sacks of groceries for the food pantry, checks to the soup kitchen the students of Waterford College established near campus. In years to come, Sylvia was pleased to think that so much had come from her mother's compassionate insistence that they must give more than what they thought they could afford, and if they did, they would surprise themselves with the unsuspected depths of their good fortune.

A few months later, when Blossom's foal was born, Sylvia named her Dresden Rose after one of her mother's favorite quilt blocks. The gentle horse provided Sylvia with the comfort of a loyal friend as her mother's health waned. A day arrived when Eleanor no longer had the strength to come downstairs to the parlor to sit and quilt and fondly watch over her children. Then she no longer left her bedroom at all.

Once, in the night, Sylvia heard her mother weeping. She stole from bed and listened at her parents' door, and as she listened she learned that her mother wept not because she could not bear the physical pain, but because she did not believe she would live to see her children grow up. What grieved her most of all was that Richard was so young, he was not likely to remember her, to remember how dearly she had loved him.

For once, Sylvia regretted eavesdropping on her elders. She crept back to bed and cried into her pillow until she fell asleep.

Eleanor Bergstrom died before the end of summer. She was laid to rest in the Bergstrom plot of their church's small cemetery. Her father dug up a lilac bush from Eleanor's favorite place on the estate and replanted it near her grave, so that in springtime she would once again be near the fragrant blossoms that had brought her so much pleasure.

The first Christmas of what came to be known as the Great Depression was Eleanor's last. For Sylvia, no Christmas that followed was ever as joyful or as blessed as those that lived on in her memory, when her family was whole, when she was a child loved by a mother.

"If I could have just one more day with my mother," said Sylvia. "Just one more day to quilt with her, to taste the meals she prepared with such love, to tell her—oh, I would have so much to tell her. And your mother is just a few hours' drive away, and you cannot even pick up the phone and invite her to come for Christmas. I tell you, Sarah, someday you are going to regret not making that call."

Sarah gaped at her, her hand frozen in the act of shelving a box of dehydrated potatoes in the pantry. "I'll call her," she said when she found her voice. "If I had known how much it meant to you, I would have done it earlier."

"Don't do it for my sake but for your own," said Sylvia, an ache of longing catching in her throat.

Chapter Three

Sylvia left Sarah alone in the kitchen. On her way out, she passed Matt carrying the CD player back to the kitchen. "Tell Sarah not to disappoint me," she told him firmly. She would leave it up to Sarah whether to explain what she meant.

Sylvia crossed the marble foyer, still gaily strewn with Christmas decorations, and climbed the grand oak staircase to her bedroom on the second floor. If Carol accepted her daughter's invitation—and why would she not?—they would need to finish decking the manor's halls at record speed. Now Sylvia regretted her earlier strategic interference in Sarah's decorating, and she had half a mind to hurry back downstairs and send the young couple out for a tree that minute—but rather than risk interrupting Sarah's phone call, she would wait.

They would have a tree up soon enough, and it would be fitting to have a present for Carol beneath it. Sarah and Matt had likely mailed her gifts already. Carol would not be expecting anything else, and certainly, the hope and joy of the season manifest in her daughter's invitation would be gift enough. But even so, Sylvia would like to give Carol something herself. She had recently finished a blue-and-white Hunter's Star quilt that she had intended to sell on commission at Grandma's Attic, Waterford's only quilt shop; it would make a lovely gift. If Sarah kept to her promise to call her mother, with any luck, Carol would be there to unwrap it Christmas morning.

Sylvia found a box for the Hunter's Star quilt and wrapped it in cheerful red-and-white striped paper, and then attended to Sarah and Matt's gifts. For Matt she had purchased a set of gardener's tools he had admired in a catalog; for Sarah, she had chosen a wheeled art cart with three drawers full of notions and gadgets guaranteed to thrill the heart of any quilter. Matt had helped her assemble it, but Sylvia had packed the drawers herself, arranging the acrylic rulers and rotary cutters just so. It was no mean feat to wrap the contraption, and after some early thwarted attempts to conceal the entire cart, she decided to cover only the sides and the top and to leave the wheeled underside alone. Sarah would not mind.

Sylvia was nearly finished when she heard the phone ring down the hall in the library. *Carol,* she thought. She must have been away from the phone when Sarah called and was returning her message. Sylvia continued wrapping gifts, allowing Sarah the opportunity to answer. But the ringing continued uninterrupted until it was abruptly silenced when the answering machine picked up. "Oh, for heaven's sake," grumbled Sylvia, hurrying to the library while the outgoing message played. She snatched up the phone just before the beep. "Good morning. Elm Creek Quilts."

"Good morning, Sylvia." The caller's voice was difficult to make out over the background of children's shrieks and laughter. "It's Agnes."

"Why, hello, dear." Sylvia sat down behind the large oak desk. "It sounds like you have a houseful."

"That's an understatement. I don't know who's causing more commotion, the five grandchildren or the four parents trying to settle them down."

"At least with you there the children don't have the adults outnumbered." Sylvia winced at the sound of glass shattering. "What was that?"

"Nothing, just a bowl." Agnes's voice became muffled, as if she had covered the mouthpiece. "Sweetie, stay off the kitchen floor until Grandma cleans that up. You have bare feet."

"Is there anything I can do? Do you need some spare quilts or pillows? Or perhaps a rescue squad?"

"No, we're all fine here. A little cramped, but we'll manage. I'd rather be crowded than alone on Christmas, wouldn't you?"

"That depends," said Sylvia. She would be happier alone if it meant Sarah was en route to her mother's.

"Oh, Sylvia. I don't buy that for a minute. Even you want company at Christmas. Which brings me to the point. Are you going to be home later this afternoon? I wanted to stop by and wish you a Merry Christmas in person."

Sylvia smiled at her sister-in-law's poorly disguised hint that she wanted to drop off Sylvia's Christmas present. "I don't have any plans to go out. Stop by anytime. Bring the grandkids."

"Thanks, but we're trying to contain this hurricane. It will just be me and one of my girls."

They made plans for her visit, and Sylvia hung up the phone, disappointed. Her invitation to the children was sincere, as much for herself as for Agnes. She missed the sounds of children playing in Elm Creek Manor, running through the halls and thundering up and down the stairs the way she and her siblings and cousins had done.

Perhaps next year.

Sylvia returned to her room. After wrapping her gifts and fixing the bows and tags in place, Sylvia went downstairs to the foyer, where the decorating had apparently made little progress since the last time she had passed through. Perhaps, she thought hopefully, Sarah was finally on the phone with her mother, making arrangements for her visit, offering driving directions, assuring her she did not need to bring anything for Christmas dinner the next day. Smiling, Sylvia found herself humming carols as she unpacked a box of red velvet ribbons of varying widths. She and Claudia had used them to tie up boughs of greenery they gathered from the strand of pines beyond the orchard. Perhaps she could send Matthew out to cut some before he and Sarah went searching for a tree. The Bergstroms had loved to put evergreen branches throughout the manor—on fireplace mantels, above mirrors and picture frames, everywhere that a touch of green and the scent of pine would make a room more festive. Claudia had liked to set candles among them; the effect was lovely, especially on a snowy night.

Sylvia added a few last touches to the foyer and decided that fresh greenery was all she needed to make the room complete. She went to the front parlor and rapped softly on the door before entering, but Sarah was not on the phone. Sylvia headed for the kitchen, quickening her pace. It was not necessarily a bad sign that the phone call had ended so soon. Perhaps they had needed only a few minutes to make Carol's arrangements.

From the hallway outside the kitchen, Sylvia heard the familiar clatter of a sewing machine. Frowning, she strode into the west sitting room and discovered Sarah bent over Sylvia's Featherweight sewing machine, stitching Eleanor's holly sprays to a row of Lucinda's Feathered Stars. Matthew was nowhere to be seen.

"What do you think you're doing?" exclaimed Sylvia.

Sarah looked up, startled. "I'm working on the Christmas Quilt. What's wrong? Did you want me to sew by hand instead?"

"What I wanted was for you to call your mother."

"I did call her," said Sarah, indignant. "I told you I would, and I did."

"And?"

"And we talked. She received the gifts Matt and I sent. The sweater fits but she doesn't like the color, so she's going to exchange it."

Exasperated, Sylvia nearly shouted, "Is she coming to visit or isn't she?"

"No." Sarah busied herself with pinning a seam. "She thanked you for the invitation, but she had already made other plans. The neighbors across the street invited her to celebrate with their family. They always have a big crowd, and my mom's known them for years. She'll have a good time."

Sylvia raised a hand to her brow and sighed, defeated.

If only she had thought to ask Sarah to invite her mother weeks ago. Next year, she would remember. Or better yet, she would ask Carol and make all the arrangements herself. Sarah needn't know of it until her mother walked through the front door, suitcase in hand. Let Sarah try to wriggle out of talking to her mother then!

Sarah studied her, curious. "Just this morning you insisted you wanted a quiet Christmas all alone, and now you're the picture of despair because my mother turned down a last-minute invitation. I don't get it, Sylvia."

Wasn't it obvious? All Sylvia wanted for Christmas was a peaceful exchange between two stubborn women, a few cautious but determined steps toward reconciliation. Carol had reached out by inviting Sarah home, but Sarah had rebuffed her, and now she seemed relieved—cheerful, even—that her mother was not coming.

"At least you tried," said Sylvia, doubting her young friend had extended the invitation graciously. "Maybe next year."

"No, next year it's Matt's father's turn."

"But you skipped your mother's turn."

"No, *she* skipped it. She doesn't get a do-over."

"My goodness, Sarah, this is your relationship with your mother we're talking about, not a game of Parcheesi. No wonder your mother declined, if you invited her this grudgingly."

Sarah's cheeks flushed. "If you knew the whole story, you wouldn't side with my mother. If you could see for yourself how she treats Matt, you'd understand why I don't want to force him to endure her company."

"It can't be as bad as all that."

"You're right. It's worse. Matt is a wonderful man and he loves me, but my mother thinks I've married beneath myself because he's not some white collar professional. She refuses to believe he's anything more than a maintenance man. And even if he were, what's wrong with that? Having a blue collar job doesn't make you a bad husband any more than working in an office cubicle guarantees you'll be a good one."

Though her loyalties were to Sarah and Matt, Sylvia tried to look at the situation from Carol's point of view. Sarah and Matt had met as students at Penn State, where Sarah earned a bachelor's degree in accounting and Matt in landscape architecture. Upon graduating, Sarah found a position as a cost accountant for a local convenience store chain in State College, while Matt was promoted to a full-time position from his former part-time job working on the Penn State campus. Unfortunately, Matt lost his job when the state legislature slashed the university's budget, and when his search for another position in State College proved fruitless, he looked farther afield, to Waterford. In agreeing to the move for Matt's sake, Sarah had admittedly taken a risk in sacrificing her secure position and steady income, but it was a tedious and uninspiring job, and she had been glad to be free of it. Their gamble had paid off in a multitude of ways, but parents tended to be cautious where their children were concerned, and perhaps Sarah and Matt had taken too many risks with their careers for Carol's taste.

Sylvia tried to shed a positive light on Carol's concerns. "She probably only needs reassurance that he will be a good provider. Many parents believe that no one is good enough to marry their children."

"I'm not going to forward copies of his pay stubs just to appease her," Sarah declared. "It wouldn't help anyway. She's so convinced he'll never amount to anything that she twists his every achievement into a sign of his imminent failure. When he received his degree at Penn State, she started calling him 'that gardener.' When he accepted the job that brought us to Waterford, she carried on about how he was dragging me off to the middle of nowhere and ruining my career. When he switched jobs to work as your caretaker, she sent me a three-page letter warning me about the dangers of allowing our incomes to be dependent upon the whims of an old woman."

Sylvia sucked in a breath. "She said that?"

"And much more, from the day I first told her we were dating. Sylvia, I know you think I've stayed away out of petulance or spite, but that's not it. I can't forgive my mother for the cruel things she's said about the man I love, and I'm keeping them apart so she can't hurt him." Sarah frowned and fingered one of the Feathered Stars. "Until she can promise to treat my husband with respect, I don't want to share the same room with her."

Sylvia sat down heavily on her chair—then rose quickly and moved the forgotten book to the side table. "I had no idea it was as bad as all that. I thought you were—"

"Exaggerating?"

Sylvia nodded.

Sarah let out a short laugh, empty of humor. "I knew it. Believe me, the opposite is true. I could tell you stories— Okay. Here's one, just to give you a taste. Matt and I had been married for about two years when we spent Christmas with my mother for the first time. Do you know what she had under the tree? Season tickets to the Pittsburgh Steelers for her then-boyfriend, a gorgeous Italian leather briefcase for me, and do you know what she had for Matt?"

Sylvia muffled a sigh. "I dare not hazard a guess."

"A fruitcake."

"You can't expect me to believe that."

"It's true! A fruitcake in a tin shaped like Santa's workshop."

"Well—" Sylvia struggled for a positive interpretation. "Why not? It's a holiday favorite. I bet it was a very good fruitcake."

"That's a bet you would lose. It was the exact same fruitcake she had received as a gift from the hospital board of directors five years before. All of the nurses get something from the same mail order company each year. She probably thought I forgot, but I didn't."

"It seems odd that she would save a fruitcake so long," said Sylvia. "How can you be certain she didn't buy it for Matt that year because the one she had received from the hospital was so delicious?"

Sarah gave her a look that said, *because I'm not stupid.* "It came sealed in plastic with a very visible 'Use Before' date stamped on it."

"Oh, dear."

"I was so proud of Matt. He thanked my mom and actually looked pleased that she had given him something. I think maybe he really was."

"Well," said Sylvia weakly, "it is the thought that counts."

"Exactly! What was she thinking, giving him stale fruitcake? It wasn't even edible. Compare that to the expensive gifts she bought for me and her then-boyfriend. It would have been better if she had given us nothing."

"Well—" Sylvia did not know how to defend Carol, and she was no longer sure she wanted to. "I imagine you confronted your mother."

"Not really. I merely trapped her in her own deceit. On Christmas Day, with all the relatives present, I suggested that we serve the fruitcake with coffee for dessert. I took it into the kitchen and sawed off a few slices and set them on a nice serving plate. My mother hovered over me the entire time making a fuss about how she had already made a pecan pie and she didn't want it to go to waste and how I really should have let Matt take the fruitcake home. Later, when her then-boyfriend took a piece from the buffet, she swooped in and snatched his plate before he could break a tooth. Fortunately, no one else took a piece or she would have been grabbing plates left and right for the rest of the day. I don't know what happened to the tin. Before we left the next morning, I asked my mother for it, saying that I wanted to use it to store Christmas cards. She said it was in the dishwasher but she couldn't open the door in the middle of the cycle, so she would mail it to us. Of course she never did."

"Perhaps it was lost in the mail."

"Oh, sure. That's fair. When in doubt, blame it on the hardworking postal service instead of my malicious mother."

Sylvia was at a loss. "How does Matt feel about all this?"

"You know him, the eternal optimist. He still believes that once my mother has a chance to get to know him, she'll accept him. I'm a realist. I know it would take a miracle for that to happen."

"Christmas is a time for miracles."

"This would take a miracle on the order of the parting of the Red Sea, and I'm not holding my breath." Sarah shook her head and slid fabric beneath the presser foot of the sewing machine. "See, Sylvia, your family has its Christmas traditions: German cookies and decorating a tree in the ballroom. My family has ours: using Christmas gifts to express our spite and taking extra early-morning shifts so we can avoid our family. Maybe now you can understand why I'd rather stay here."

The bitterness in her young friend's voice pained Sylvia. Her mother had acted with appalling rudeness, but even so, Sylvia could not help marveling at the pettiness of it all. To harbor such anger and resentment over a Christmas gift! Sylvia regretted that Carol Mallory had been so unkind to steadfast, good-natured Matt, but she could not condone Sarah's decision to keep the two apart because of it. She rather agreed with Matt. Surely if Carol had more opportunity to discover what a fine young man he was, her disapproval would lessen until it eventually ceased.

Sylvia sat pondering while Sarah worked on the Christmas Quilt, ruefully aware that her plan to bring together Sarah and her mother had been doomed from the beginning. Their relationship was clearly in worse shape than Sylvia had realized, and no thrown-together Christmas reunion would rectify things. Christmas was the season of peace, but somehow people often forgot to include the harmony of their own family in their prayers for peace on earth and goodwill toward all. The stress and excitement of the holidays often laid bare the hairline cracks in the facade of ostensibly functional families. No wonder Sarah preferred to work on another family's abandoned quilt than on her own family's unresolved disagreements.

Sarah did seem to be making remarkable progress on the quilt, although Sylvia was not quite certain how she intended for those very dissimilar blocks to come together harmoniously. She had attached border sashing to some of Lucinda's Feathered Stars and joined four together in pairs. With a few added seams, Eleanor's holly sprays had been transformed into open plumes, which Sarah was in the midst of attaching to Claudia's Variable Stars.

"That's a sure way to ruin it," muttered Sylvia. Louder, over the cheerful clatter of the sewing machine, she added, "Sarah, dear, I thought I told you not to bother including Claudia's blocks in the quilt."

Amused, Sarah said, "You suggested that I could leave them out if I thought they would ruin the quilt, and I told you that I wouldn't dream of leaving her out of a family quilt. I measured, and you're right; her blocks vary in size almost a half-inch, but my layout will account for that."

"But they're so plain and simple," protested Sylvia. "They aren't as intricate as the blocks my mother and great-aunt made."

"That's precisely why they work so well." Sarah continued sewing, completely indifferent to Sylvia's consternation. "Sometimes a simple block is needed to set off more elaborate designs. You taught me that."

Sylvia had always suspected that someday her preaching would come back to haunt her. "This is a very special quilt. You shouldn't include a block of inferior quality for sentimental reasons."

"A quilt, like a family, doesn't have to be perfect, but it does have to be inclusive."

"That's a remarkable philosophy from someone who refuses to give her mother a second chance to truly get to know her son-in-law."

"Said the woman who held a grudge against her sister for fifty years."

Sylvia had no reply.

"I'm sorry," said Sarah quickly. "I know what happened between you two was much more than a grudge. I didn't mean to make light of it."

But Sylvia knew Sarah was not entirely wrong. "Think nothing of it. We've exchanged strong words before and survived."

Sarah searched her face for a moment to be sure Sylvia was not angry, frowned briefly in uncertainty, and returned to her work with an almost imperceptible shake of the head.

Sylvia watched as the hapless Variable Star blocks were joined with her mother's exquisite appliqué and knew that somewhere, Claudia was laughing.

Sylvia had once overheard her father say that she had come into the world looking for a fight, and as the Bergstrom closest to her in age, Claudia had quickly become her unwitting rival. Sylvia, naturally, saw the situation differently. It was Claudia who was constantly competing with her, Claudia who sparked the arguments and stirred up animosity and yet somehow always managed to appear blameless to the adults of the family.

Even as a child Sylvia understood why adults preferred Claudia. She was such an obvious favorite that Sylvia almost did not blame them for it. Claudia was two years older, but since Sylvia was bright for her age and tall, everyone treated them as if they were the same age, and comparisons were unavoidable. Claudia was the beauty; she had been blessed with their mother's grace and the best features of the Bergstroms. The oldest members of the family declared that she was the very image of Great-Grandmother Anneke, a famous beauty of her day, but they respected their ancestors too much to hold any of them responsible for Sylvia's appearance, even though her remarkable height, strong chin, and assertive posture were unmistakably Bergstrom. Claudia's hair, the rich brown hue of maple sugar, hung down her back nearly to her waist in glossy waves, while Sylvia's, the color of the burnt bits scraped off toast, tended to be snarled and windblown from the time she spent outdoors hanging around the stables, pestering her father with pleas to be allowed to ride. Sylvia was the better student, mastering her lessons easily and impatient for more, but Claudia won the teachers' hearts with her obedience and charming manners. She never failed to be sweet and cheerful, even as she misspelled half the words in her themes. For her part, Sylvia was moody and sensitive, and she could not hide her resentment at being compared unfavorably to the lovely creature who had passed through that teacher's classroom two years before. For as long as Sylvia could remember, she had been convinced that she was a terrible disappointment to their mother, an inferior second effort after the overwhelming success that was her firstborn.

From an early age, each of the sisters had struggled to prove herself better than the other in every conceivable quality or activity. Sylvia won in academics, quilting, and innate ability with horses; Claudia, in everything else. Still, although Sylvia was best in what she considered the most important categories, her success was unsatisfying because Claudia seemed unaware of it. While Sylvia's report cards gave Claudia no alternative but to concede she was the better student, Claudia feared horses and did not care how well Sylvia rode or how docilely the strongest stallions responded to her attentions. She also would never admit, even when Sylvia confronted her with side-by-side comparisons of their stitches, that Sylvia was the more adept quilter. No matter how often Sylvia proved herself to be her sister's equal or better, Claudia refused to treat her as anything but a tag-along little sister, a nuisance, an afterthought.

Quilting—which for so many women and girls was an

enjoyable, harmonious activity that encouraged friendship, sharing, and community—only sharpened their competitive natures. Their first quilting lesson with their mother turned into a race to see which girl could complete the most Nine-Patch blocks and win the right to sleep beneath the finished quilt first. When Sylvia gained an insurmountable lead, Claudia burst into tears, declared that she hated Sylvia, and ran from the room, scattering her meager pile of Nine-Patch blocks as she went. When Eleanor found out the reason for her outburst, she told Sylvia to apologize to her sister—which Sylvia did. "I'm sorry I sewed faster than you," she told Claudia, which outraged her sister and displeased all the grown-ups.

Sylvia ended up finishing that quilt alone. She gave it to a cousin, Uncle William and Aunt Nellie's four-year-old daughter, since Claudia would not allow it into their room.

A more sensible pair of girls would have avoided working together on a quilt again, but their second attempt came a year later, when their mother announced that she was expecting another child. Originally each girl had planned to sew her own quilt for the baby, but when they began to argue over which quilt their new brother or sister would use first, Eleanor decreed they would work together: Sylvia would choose the colors, Claudia the pattern, and each would sew precisely half of the blocks necessary for the top. It seemed like a reasonable plan, until Claudia did the unthinkable and chose the Turkey Tracks pattern. Not only was this a challenging block Sylvia doubted her sister could make well, but according to their grandmother, it also had a history of foreboding consequences. Once better known as the Wandering Foot, its name had been changed to divert the bad luck associated with it. Legend told that a boy given a Wandering Foot quilt would never be content to stay in one place, but would forever be restless, roaming the world, never settling down. A girl receiving such a quilt would be doomed to an even worse fate, so bleak that Grandmother refused to describe it. Eleanor and Claudia had heard Grandmother's warnings as often as Sylvia, but they laughed off Sylvia's concerns and told her not to be upset by silly superstitions. Defeated, all Sylvia could do was to select her lucky colors, blue and yellow, and hope that would be enough to offset the pattern's influence.

After their mother died, the fire went out of the girls' competitiveness around the quilting frame. Without their mother to impress, without a chance that she would finally admit a preference for the handiwork of one daughter over the other, there seemed no point to it.

Less than three years after losing their mother, Sylvia and Claudia decided to collaborate on a quilt once again, out of necessity rather than any anticipation of enjoyment. In January 1933, while browsing through a catalog from which their father often purchased farm tools, they learned about a marvelous quilt competition sponsored by Sears, Roebuck, and Company. If their quilt passed elimination rounds at their local store and at the regional level, it would be displayed in a special pavilion at the World's Fair in Chicago and be eligible for a $2,500 First Prize. Neither Sylvia nor Claudia had ever possessed such an enormous sum of money, and they were determined to enter.

In order to complete an entire masterpiece quilt by the May 15 deadline, they had no alternative but to work together. Claudia interpreted the rules to mean that each quilt must be the work of a single quilter, so she signed their entry form under the name "Claudia Sylvia Bergstrom," provoking Sylvia's ire when she discovered her billing had been reduced to her sister's middle name, or so everyone would believe. A more significant point of contention was the design of the quilt. Sylvia wanted to create an original pictorial quilt inspired by the World's Fair theme of "A Century of Progress," but Claudia thought the judges would be more impressed by a traditional pattern presented in flawless, intricate needlework. After wasting several weeks debating their design, they agreed to a compromise between tradition and novelty. Sylvia designed a central appliqué medallion depicting various scenes from Colonial times until the present day, which Claudia framed in a border of pieced blocks. To Sylvia's exasperation, Claudia selected the Odd Fellow's Chain pattern, squandering an opportunity to select a pattern with a more appropriately symbolic name. Sylvia did not complain, however, since it was a visually striking block her sister could handle more or less successfully, and it did inspire an intriguing title for their work: "Chain of Progress."

Despite their unpromising start, the sisters agreed on one point: "Chain of Progress" was the best quilt either had ever made. They took first place at the local competition in Harrisburg, but lost at the regional level in Philadelphia. Later that year, when their father took his three children by train to see the World's Fair, the sisters agreed on a second point: Their quilt was easily as lovely as any of the twenty-nine finalists displayed. Claudia was so disappointed by the loss of the admiration and status that would have accompanied a victory that Sylvia hadn't the heart to suggest that her uneven quilting stitches had probably cost them a place among the finalists.

Sylvia did not mind the loss as much as her sister. Though times were still hard and the Bergstroms had to watch every penny, their father had splurged on the trip to the World's Fair, reward enough for Sylvia. She also knew that, at age thirteen, she had many quilt competitions and blue ribbons in her future.

Time passed and other concerns left little room in her thoughts for mulling over her disappointment—namely, her younger brother Richard's progress in school. He was an apt pupil when it came to learning about horses—which pleased their father—but although he was bright, he had little patience for the classroom. Headstrong and mischievous, he dodged Sylvia's efforts to tutor him, and if she left him alone with a lesson to study, she would return later to find that he had run off to the barn, or the orchard, or more likely than not, the stables.

Sylvia blamed that Wandering Foot quilt.

In spite of his reluctance to study, he was clever enough to do well on his school work even when he only gave it half his attention. That, his kind heart, and his charm were his saving graces at school. He had light brown, wavy hair that brightened to gold in the summer, long-lashed, green-brown eyes that his sisters envied, and a dimple that appeared in his right cheek when he grinned, which was often. The teachers adored him and smiled when they called him a rascal, and he was popular among his classmates—not because he followed the crowd, but because he could usually persuade the crowd that his way of doing things was more fun.

In the autumn of the year after the Bergstroms' trip to

the Chicago World's Fair, a new family moved into a ramshackle house on the outskirts of town. The parents and a young daughter were rarely seen, but their oldest child, a boy, attended the elementary school in Waterford. He was enrolled in Richard's class, and Sylvia often spotted him sitting alone by the fence when she and Claudia dropped off their brother on their way to their own school, a block away. She was appalled that any mother or father could send a child to school in such filthy clothes. His face was always peaked, weariness hung in his eyes, and his sleeves were often not long enough to cover the bruises on his arms.

Most of the schoolchildren shunned the newcomer, whose presence hinted at a darker world than the one they inhabited, one they might have sensed they themselves had escaped only by an accident of birth. Some of the bolder children teased him, but Richard put a stop to that. Sylvia observed the whole incident through the fence on the day Richard suddenly walked off the pitcher's mound and approached the boy as he watched from his usual spot by the fence. Richard asked the boy's name and invited him to join in the game. When the other boys protested, Richard said, "Okay, if you don't want Andrew on our team, him and me'll play catch instead."

"But you have the only ball," a boy in the batter's box shouted. "We can't play without you."

Richard grinned and shrugged as if that had not occurred to him. "Then I guess you can't play without Andrew, either."

The loss of Richard's favor was worse than the loss of the ball, so the other boys quickly agreed to allow Andrew to play. Although their father expected them home, Sylvia stood on the other side of the fence watching the game, her heart swelling with pride.

As autumn waned, Sylvia watched as Richard and Andrew became fast friends. Andrew was as skinny and filthy as ever, but he smiled more, and although he was still quiet around the other children, sometimes he would whisper a joke that would leave Richard howling with laughter. When she spotted Andrew on the schoolyard wearing a jacket Richard had outgrown, she did not need to ask how he had come by it. At home Richard spoke about his friend so often that their father encouraged him to invite Andrew over to play. One day Andrew was waiting with Richard at the gate when his sisters came to escort him home.

"Andrew's coming over to play," Richard informed them. "And he's staying for dinner."

"Oh, really?" said Claudia. "Does Father know?"

"It'll be fine," Sylvia interjected. She smiled at the wary little boy. "Father has asked Richard to invite him many times."

"Do his parents know?" Claudia asked dubiously.

"They won't mind," Andrew piped up. Sylvia was sure they would not. She doubted anyone would even notice whether he returned home.

After that, Andrew came home with Richard nearly every day. Sometimes Sylvia gently probed him with questions about his home and his family, but Andrew said little. Still, his guarded replies were enough for Sylvia to deduce that he was unhappy and worried about his little sister. Sylvia did not know what to do. Extracting details from Andrew was so difficult that she was unsure just how bad things were, and she did not want to do anything to compel him to run away, as so many other children had when their fathers lost their jobs and their mothers could not feed them. An unhappy home was safer than the life on the rails so many other men and boys had chosen. So Sylvia found reasons to give Andrew the sturdy clothes Richard had outgrown but not worn out, and she filled her brother's lunch box each morning with food enough for two boys. Andrew began to fill out, and he must have begun brushing his hair and washing his hands and face at school. Sylvia suspected that a kindhearted teacher had taken an interest in his welfare, but Claudia teased that the young boy had taken it upon himself to improve his appearance because he had a crush on Sylvia.

When winter snows began to fall, Sylvia's thoughts turned to Christmas. That winter would bring their fifth Christmas without Mama. Every year since she had left them, the Bergstroms had celebrated in a subdued fashion, in part because of their reduced circumstances, but also because Sylvia's father was the head of the household and his heart simply wasn't in it. He found no joy in the old Bergstrom traditions without his beloved wife by his side, and his daughters found it difficult to keep them on their own. When Sylvia thought of Andrew, though, she decided that even a quiet Bergstrom holiday would likely surpass any warmth and happiness he might find at home. They must invite him to spend Christmas Eve and Christmas Day with their family because if anyone needed the joy and hope of the season, Andrew did.

It was Claudia, however, who came to Sylvia with the notion that they must bring back the old Bergstrom traditions in all their splendor. Sylvia was dubious. How could they afford to rival lavish Christmases past? How could they proceed without their mother's guiding hand? She hesitated to voice aloud her sense that it was wrong, somehow, to enjoy the holiday without their mother.

As the days passed, Claudia wore her down with her persistence, and finally reminded her that if they did not restore their traditions, no one would, and all the Bergstrom stories would be lost. Richard's memories of their mother had grown dim. He had been so young when she died, and their brokenhearted father could rarely bring himself to speak of her. The sisters owed it to Richard and their mother to fill in the spaces of their younger brother's memory with their own.

Sylvia, who would do anything for her darling little brother, needed no further inducement to join Claudia in reviving their family's traditions. Their father was surprisingly willing to go along with the plan. "It's been too long since we've had a truly Merry Christmas around here," he said, smiling wistfully at his daughters. He opened his billfold and paid them a special "Christmas allowance" to spend on their celebration—modest, but still more than they had hoped for. The sisters decided to spend it upon gifts for their father, Richard, Andrew, Andrew's little sister, and ingredients for their favorite Christmas treats—Great-Aunt Lucinda's German cookies and the famous Bergstrom strudel. As they made their preparations, the holiday spirit returned to the home, so gradually and quietly that it came as an unexpected delight when Sylvia discovered Lucinda whistling a Christmas carol as she folded the laundry, or caught Uncle William and Aunt Nellie kissing beneath a sprig of mistletoe. Great-Aunt Lydia took them shopping for gifts and groceries, and in the week before Christmas, Elm Creek Manor was once again filled with the aromas of gingerbread, anise, and cinnamon. Sylvia and Claudia wrapped store-bought presents for the boys and their father, and made gifts for the rest of the family.

It felt like Christmas again. Until the joy and hope of the season had been restored to her, Sylvia had not realized how much her heart had longed for them.

If only Mama were there.

On the day before Christmas Eve, Sylvia and Richard were upstairs in the nursery playing baseball with a broom handle and a bundle of knotted socks when Claudia entered. "I need you in the kitchen," she told her sister. "It's time to start the strudel."

"I'll be down in a minute." Sylvia caught a grounder and tagged out Richard before he reached first. "The inning's almost over."

Richard trotted back to home plate and picked up the fallen broom handle. "No, it's not. I still have two more outs."

Sylvia grinned and wound up to pitch. "Like I said, I'll be down in a minute."

"We need to start now, while the kitchen's free." Claudia's nose wrinkled in disapproval as she observed the game. "You shouldn't play baseball in the house anyway."

"It's not a real baseball." Sylvia tossed the knot of socks toward her brother, who swung the broom handle, connected, and sent the makeshift ball careening toward left field.

"It's a sockball," said Richard helpfully as he ran for first base.

"Whatever it is, it could still break something." Claudia turned for the door. "If you can't be bothered to help, I'll do it myself."

Sylvia could imagine the disaster that would ensue if she allowed that to happen. "No, wait. I'm coming." She scooped up the sockball and lofted it to Richard, who caught it easily. "Sorry. I'll have to finish you off later."

"Says you." Richard grinned and went off to play with his model airplanes.

"We couldn't have waited ten minutes?" Sylvia asked as she followed her sister downstairs.

"Great-Aunt Lucinda just finished her last batch of cookies but she'll need us out of the way when it's time to make supper. She said we may make strudel now or not at all."

Sylvia knew that was a valid reason for haste, but couldn't admit it. "You could have said so before."

"You didn't give me a chance. You were too busy arguing for your right to play 'sockball.'"

Sylvia clamped her mouth around a retort. She wouldn't be the one to start a fight, not so close to Christmas, not with the family seeming more content than they had been in years.

She hoped allowing Claudia the last word would put her in a sweeter temper, but in the kitchen, Claudia became even more imperious. She sent Sylvia down into the cellar to fetch a basket of apples, a task they had always handled together. When Sylvia returned, huffing from exertion, she found Claudia taking flour, sugar, nuts, and spices from the pantry—and wearing their mother's best apron.

"What's that you're wearing?" she demanded, setting down the basket with a thud.

Claudia glanced down at her clothes. "It's an apron, of course. You should put yours on, too, or your dress will get covered in flour."

"That's Mama's apron."

Claudia regarded Sylvia with exasperation. "You know my old one is worn out. Aunt Lucinda said I should wear this one. If it bothers you so much, you can wear it and I'll wear yours."

"Never mind," muttered Sylvia, taking two paring knives from the drawer.

Claudia sighed and shook her head. "When you're done being ridiculous, would you please bring a sheet from the linen closet?"

"Why don't you do it?"

"Because I'm doing this." Claudia indicated the pastry ingredients in her arms. "Why are you being so disagreeable?"

"Why are you being so bossy?"

It was a charge Claudia hated, perhaps because she knew how often her behavior merited it. "I'm not being bossy. I just want to make sure this is done right. Don't you see? It's up to us to make this a happy Christmas for everyone. If we can't do it this year, they might not give us another chance."

"They can't cancel Christmas."

Claudia nudged the basket of apples closer to the kitchen table with her foot and set her burdens on the counter. "No, but they can tell us not to try, and then we can go back to the same gloomy Christmases we've had for the past four years. Is that what you want? More importantly, do you think that's what Mama would want?"

Claudia began flinging handfuls of flour into a mixing bowl, her mouth in a defiant line. Sylvia watched her for a moment, then, without another word of complaint, she hurried upstairs, retrieved a clean sheet from the linen closet, and draped it over the long wooden table as their mother had always done, and other women of the family had done before her. She pulled the thin fabric smooth and fastened the corners to the legs of the table with clothespins. As she dusted the sheet with flour, Claudia cautioned, "Not so much." Sylvia said not a word in reply.

They took turns kneading the dough—pressing it into the floured board with the heels of their hands, folding it over, turning it, pressing again. Sylvia was surprised how quickly her arms tired from the effort. It had not seemed so difficult in years past—but she and her sister had never kneaded the dough for more than a minute or two at a time, as one of the elder Bergstrom women had always shouldered the burden of the chore. After ten minutes had elapsed, Sylvia suggested they set the dough aside to rest, but Claudia insisted they continue for another two minutes apiece. Sylvia was tempted to tell her to do all four of the minutes herself if she felt that strongly about them, but she bit her tongue and did her share.

Finally Claudia divided the smooth ball of dough into two halves, separated them on the floured board, and covered them with a flick of the dishtowel that reminded Sylvia, painfully, of a similar gesture their mother used to make. How pleased she would be to see her two daughters working together to make the famous Bergstrom strudel, Sylvia thought, and she resolved to finish the task in a manner that would make their mother proud.

Yet no matter how agreeably Sylvia followed the directions her sister unnecessarily provided, the more Claudia chided her. Sylvia took off too much apple flesh with the peel. She was not peeling fast enough, and the apples would turn brown before they could be baked.

She sliced the apples too thin. She did not chop the nuts finely enough. With every word of criticism, Sylvia's temper flared, but she would not allow Claudia to provoke her into an outburst, ruining what should have been a significant moment in the history of their family. The two Bergstrom sisters were renewing a beloved tradition they had last shared with their mother, a tradition that reached back into the past to the first Bergstroms to come to America and possibly even earlier.

On behalf of all the Bergstrom women who had preceded them, it was essential that they work together. Especially when the apples were prepared and it was time to stretch the dough. Especially since they would be spending many hours together to make the ten strudel Claudia had decided they needed that Christmas, one for the family and nine to give away.

"It's rested enough," remarked Claudia as she pulled back the dishtowel covering the two flattened balls of dough. Sylvia, who had observed the making of strudel nearly as many times as her elder sister and knew as well as she did how long the dough needed to rest, merely murmured her assent. She was reminded of how graciously their mother had always asked the opinion of the other women and girls present, even her novice daughters, achieving consensus before deciding it was time to stretch the dough.

Claudia rolled out the ball of dough into a rectangle, then beckoned Sylvia forward to help stretch. Sylvia obliged, and in unison, they reached beneath the dough and pulled it toward themselves with the back of their hands. When Claudia stepped to her right, Sylvia mirrored her, so they always faced each other on opposite sides of the table. At first, Sylvia was amazed by how quickly the familiar motions came back to her, and as the sisters fell into a rhythm of reaching and stretching, she once again marveled at the dough's transformation from a smooth ball into a thin, translucent sheet.

She was so involved in the methodical process that it was Claudia who first noticed the trouble. "This isn't right," she muttered.

"What? There aren't any tears."

"No, but we haven't made it any wider or thinner for quite a while."

Sylvia had paid little attention to the time. She could not honestly say how much progress they had made in the last two minutes, or the last five. "It seems fine to me."

"The dough should have reached the edges of the table by now." Claudia paused, wiped a smear of flour from her face with the back of her hand, and studied the dough. "Something's wrong."

"Did you count how many handfuls of flour you used?"

"Yes."

"Did you use the usual cup for measuring the water?"

"Yes, of course," snapped Claudia impatiently. "I did all that."

"We could give it another few minutes," suggested Sylvia. "Or we could ask Aunt Lucinda—"

"No. We need to do this on our own, remember?" Claudia slid her hands beneath the dough and indicated with a sharp nod that Sylvia was to do the same. Sylvia complied, and this time when she released the dough and allowed it to fall back to the table, she noticed that instead of draping gracefully across the floured sheet, it sprang back slightly, like a rubber band.

Claudia was watching her face. "That time you saw it, too."

Sylvia nodded as they reached beneath the dough again. Lift, stretch, fall—and again, that almost imperceptible motion of the dough as it sprang back into its former shape. Their mother's dough had never done that. Neither had their grandmother's. "It's . . . rubbery," said Sylvia, searching for the least offensive term.

"I made it exactly the same as always," said Claudia. "You saw me."

That Sylvia had been out of the kitchen for most of the time Claudia mixed the dough was hardly worth mentioning given the mounting problems at hand. Sylvia could now see that while the dough was suitably thin in the center, the outer edge of the rectangle was as thick as a fist, as if it were a heavy frame around a delicate canvas.

"I think somehow we have to stretch the edges more without stretching the center," Sylvia finally said.

"And how are we supposed to do that?"

"I don't know *how*; I just know *what*."

"That's not very helpful," grumbled Claudia, but after a moment, she took up the rolling pin and tried to flatten the edges. It helped somewhat, and after Claudia had made two trips around the perimeter with the rolling pin, she told Sylvia to resume stretching. "Harder this time."

"Are you sure?" asked Sylvia. "The center is already so thin."

"Yes, I'm sure." To demonstrate, Claudia thrust her hands beneath the dough and pulled firmly toward the edges—and gasped in horror as a long tear running the length of the rectangle appeared on Sylvia's side of the table.

"We can patch it," said Sylvia, already setting to it.

"If you had pulled equally from your side—"

"You didn't give me a chance! The tear still would have happened, just in a different place."

"Never mind." Claudia came around the table to the other end of the tear and began pinching it closed. "Let's just fix it. There's no need to place blame."

Apparently there wasn't, Sylvia thought, unless she was at fault. But she said nothing as the sisters worked from the ends toward the middle until the tear was mended with a seam of pinched dough. Afterward, Claudia circled the rectangle one last time, trimming off the thick frame with a knife.

"What are you doing?" asked Sylvia. On every side, the dough rectangle fell several inches short of the edge of the table.

"It wasn't going to stretch any farther."

"It's not big enough."

"But it is almost thin enough, and it will taste the same."

Sylvia wasn't so sure. What if whatever alchemy had made the dough more difficult to stretch had also affected its flavor? "I'll get the apples," she said instead, careful to allow no trace of annoyance or worry into her voice. At least they would have extra noodles for soup.

The dough rolled around the apples as easily as ever, to their unspoken relief, and soon their first strudel was baking in the oven. They did not have nearly as much difficulty stretching the second ball of dough—in part because they had learned from their mistakes and took care not to leave a thick rope of dough around a thin center rectangle—but when they could stretch the dough no more, it still was thicker than their mother's, and it did not come within two inches of the table's edges.

Still, the first strudel came out of the oven a beautiful

golden brown, and the aroma of baked apples and cinnamon drew other members of the family into the kitchen. Most of them praised the sisters and declared that they couldn't wait to taste the strudel on Christmas morning, but Uncle William took one look at their first attempt cooling on the table and said, "Looks like the runt of the litter."

"We won't bother saving any for you, then," Sylvia teased right back, but Claudia busied herself at the sink full of dishes until he left the kitchen so he would not see her scarlet face.

"Eight more to go," Sylvia remarked on her way to the cellar for more apples.

"Maybe two are enough," said Claudia wearily.

Sylvia stopped short on the stairs. "You don't mean that. Uncle William was just teasing."

"No, it's not that. I suppose I had no idea how difficult this would be without—" Claudia composed herself. "Even when Mama was ill, she managed everything with such ease. Next year—maybe next year we can try to do more."

Sylvia was surprised by her sister's admission of weakness, or at least the closest thing to an admission of weakness Claudia was likely to let slip. As for herself, she hated to abandon any task until she had no choice but to admit defeat—but she also did not relish the thought of spending the rest of the day in the kitchen. The temptation to leave the kitchen overruled her perseverance, and so Sylvia agreed that the two strudel they had already made would be sufficient, as it meant one for the Bergstroms and one for Andrew to take home to his family. Their friends and neighbors had not received the famous Bergstrom strudel since Eleanor's last Christmas and would not expect it this season. Next year, Sylvia and Claudia promised each other, they would be pleasantly surprised.

The next morning, Christmas Eve morning, Andrew arrived at the back door while the Bergstroms were finishing breakfast. Sylvia's father, who had planned to pick him up later that afternoon in the car, joked that the boy's haste would do nothing to speed Santa's visit, but as the boy cast a longing gaze toward the remains of the meal, there could be no mistaking what had sped him to their door. Lucinda welcomed him to the table and signaled for Claudia to bring an extra plate, and soon the scrawny boy was bolting down everything they set before him.

After breakfast the boys ran off to play. The women tidied the kitchen then sent Uncle William and Aunt Nellie out to find a tree. "Isn't anyone else in this family ever going to get married?" Uncle William grumbled as he shrugged into his coat.

"Don't look at me," said Lucinda.

He peered hopefully at Claudia. "How old are you again?"

"Sixteen," she said, straightening proudly.

"Forget it, Will," said her father. "The job is yours for at least ten more years."

"Daddy," protested Claudia.

"We don't mind," Aunt Nellie assured the girls' father. She linked her arm through her husband's and smiled up at him. "In fact, this year, we're going to pick out the best tree Elm Creek Manor has ever had."

The couple left through the back door, following a trail broken through the soft layer of snow on their way toward the bridge over Elm Creek. Watching through the kitchen window, Lucinda remarked to Sylvia's father, "Looks like it's going to be another four-hour search this year."

"I'm sure William hopes so," he replied, grinning.

"Well, the ornaments are ready in the ballroom," said Claudia, missing the implications. "Whenever they do get back, we can begin decorating."

"In the meantime, I'll fix lunch," said Lucinda.

Claudia nodded. "And I have some sewing to do."

Sylvia had small gifts to wrap, knitted socks and scarves she had completed the night before. She left her festive packages in the ballroom, not surprised to find that her aunt and uncle had not returned, then went looking for Claudia. Her sister sat in the front parlor, in their mother's favorite chair, threading a needle. At her feet lay piles of fabric she had sorted by color.

"What are you working on?" Sylvia drew closer to the familiar-looking scraps. "Is that the Christmas Quilt?"

Claudia nodded, holding the needle between pursed lips while she tied a knot at the end of the thread.

Sylvia looked from the triangles on her sister's lap to the stack of Feathered Star blocks on the table at her right hand. "Those pieces are too big for a Feathered Star. They should be less than half that size."

"I'm not making Feathered Stars." Claudia took the needle from her mouth and speared its tip into a white triangle and a green one. She nodded to their mother's old sewing basket, which she had long ago adopted. Upon its open lid Sylvia spied a few red-and-green Variable Star blocks.

Sylvia picked up one and immediately spotted the mistakes. The tip of one star point had been lopped off by an adjoining seam. A pair of green star points did not meet at the tip of the central red square. On the back of the block, instead of pressing her seams flat and smooth, Claudia had folded them over carelessly, creating a thick lump of fabric layers that would be difficult to quilt through later. Sylvia compared the block to a second.

"Did you do this on purpose?" asked Sylvia, matching the top corners of the blocks and holding them together to estimate the difference in size. "Did you mean for this one to be a half-inch smaller than the other?"

Claudia snatched the blocks from her grasp. "Don't be ridiculous. I used the same templates for all of them."

She must have varied her seam allowances, then. "You'll have to block them with the iron. You'll need a lot of steam—"

"I know how to block a quilt."

"You could have avoided that step if you had sewed more accurately. Why are you making Variable Stars instead of—" Sylvia broke off, remembering just in time that the last thing she wanted to do was encourage her sister to attempt a far more difficult pattern when she could barely manage one of the simplest star blocks in her repertoire. "If you try to sew these blocks together, you'll be able to match up either the star points or the corners, but not both. Does Aunt Lucinda know what you're up to? She won't appreciate it if you ruin her quilt."

"I will not ruin her quilt, and yes, I already asked her if I might finish it."

"And she said yes?"

"Of course she said yes, or I wouldn't be sitting here working on it. Honestly, Sylvia."

Sylvia thought of the time and talent their mother and Great-Aunt Lucinda had sewn into their Feathered

Stars and holly plumes. All of their work would go to waste if Claudia distorted their handiwork with her poorly constructed Variable Stars. "Maybe you should let me help."

"Maybe you should find something of your own to work on."

Why should she? The Christmas Quilt was as much hers as it was Claudia's. "If I make some of the blocks, we'll finish more quickly. That way you'll also have an example to follow when you're steaming or trimming your blocks to the right size. I think your trouble is your seam allowances—"

"My trouble is that I have an annoying little sister who doesn't have anything better to do on Christmas Eve than criticize me. Great-Aunt Lucinda said I could finish the quilt and that's what I'm going to do. You're just angry because you didn't think of it first. If you had, you wouldn't have let me help you, and you know it."

Every word struck home, and Sylvia's temper flared. In the distance she heard the double doors to the foyer slam, followed by the happy clamor of voices. Uncle William and Aunt Nellie had returned with a tree and the sisters were needed in the ballroom, but Sylvia couldn't resist one parting shot: "The word 'variable' in your 'Variable Stars' shouldn't refer to their size."

She hurried from the parlor before Claudia could have the last word.

Richard and Andrew must have flown down from the nursery. She tried to keep them out of the way as Uncle William and her father hauled the tree into the ballroom and set it up in its familiar place on the dais. Great-Aunt Lucinda brought in trays of food so they could lunch while they trimmed the tree, and someone switched on the radio. Suddenly the room was filled with music and laughter, and Sylvia felt a pang of longing for her mother. Her eyes met her father's, and she knew he shared her thoughts. In his arms he carried the paper angels she and Claudia had made years before in Sunday school. He put Claudia's on a high branch and placed Sylvia's exactly even on the opposite side of the tree—not one branch higher, not one lower. His great deliberation signaled to Sylvia that he had seen Claudia's stormy expression and had identified Sylvia as its source.

She flushed guiltily and looked away, pretending to be absorbed in the boys' antics as they wrapped garlands of popcorn and cranberries around the lower branches of the tree. *Wait until she finishes piecing the top of the Christmas Quilt and wants help layering and basting it,* Sylvia thought bitterly. Sylvia would not lift a finger or a needle to help her. And she was through with letting Claudia carry on as if she were the lady of the house. If anyone held that role with Mama gone, it was Great-Aunt Lucinda, not a silly sixteen-year-old girl.

The tree was all but finished when Great-Aunt Lucinda noted that someone ought to hide the star. "I'll do it," said Claudia, smiling as she removed the eight-pointed ruby-and-gold star from its box.

"No, I will," said Sylvia, snatching it from her hand.

"You could do it together," their father and Lucinda said in unison.

Sylvia smothered a groan. "I'll be right back," she said, and she raced from the room before Claudia or anyone else could object.

But where to hide the star? She would have been tempted to choose an especially difficult hiding place for the pleasure of tormenting her sister, but she suddenly doubted Claudia would take up the search. Richard was younger, but that did not mean Sylvia should choose a more obvious location for his sake. He knew all the manor's secret places and would be disappointed if he found the star too soon. Then Sylvia remembered Andrew, and she decided that she wanted him to win. Even the competitive Richard would be pleased if his friend won the game and could add a prize to the gifts Santa would leave for him beneath the Bergstroms' tree.

Perhaps Sylvia could help him in the search the way cousin Elizabeth had once helped her. Andrew had no pillow of his own in the Bergstroms' home to look beneath, and he was not likely to run crying to Richard's room as Sylvia had fled to hers so many years before. Andrew spent most of his time at Elm Creek Manor in the nursery. Perhaps, if that was where he felt most comfortable, he would begin his search there.

Taking the steps two at a time, Sylvia raced upstairs to the third floor and burst into the nursery. Andrew loved Richard's model trains. Sylvia hurried across the room and hid the star in the wooden crate that held the engine and its cars, leaving only one golden tip visible.

She returned to the ballroom, pleased with herself, but her satisfaction fled with one look from her father. She glanced at Great-Aunt Lucinda, who shook her head even though a faint smile quirked at her lips.

"I hid the star," she announced, managing a weak grin. Her father sent the younger children out to search for it, and Sylvia busied herself with rearranging a few of the ornaments upon the tree, more to conceal her blush than any aesthetic purpose. She resolved to avoid provoking Claudia or anyone else until Christmas was over. With any luck, the sight of her snatching the star from her sister's hand would fade from the adults' memories. She knew Claudia would never forget.

They finished trimming the tree, all but the very highest bough, and then they were left with nothing to do but listen to the radio, admire the tree, and chat, as no triumphant child had returned with the glass star held tightly in a small fist. "You did hide it in the manor, right, Sylvia?" asked Uncle William after an hour had passed. "You didn't throw it out a window into a snowbank?"

"It's in the manor," said Sylvia, glancing toward the door worriedly. At first she had hoped only Andrew would find the star; now she would be glad if anyone did.

"Did you hide it where a child would think to look?" asked Claudia. Her tone, her stance, her look of disappointed resignation pointedly telegraphed that she was not at all surprised her younger sister had found a way to ruin a beloved holiday tradition. If Claudia had been allowed to hide the star, it would be shining on the top of the tree by now.

"Of course." The crate of model trains was right there on the floor of the nursery, not on a high shelf or tucked away in a closet. Surely she had not hidden it too well.

Just then the ballroom door burst open. "We can't find it," said Richard, panting from his sprint through the manor.

"It's a big house," said Uncle William. "Keep looking."

Richard shrugged and ran off again. "Maybe I should give them a hint," Sylvia appealed to her father. At his assent, she dashed after Richard and told him to look on the third floor—and to make sure he passed the message along to the other children. He promised, grinning because his sister knew him so well, and soon the ballroom echoed with the thunder of many feet racing up the stairs.

A half hour later, Richard returned to the ballroom, Andrew at his heels. "When you said third floor, did you mean the attic? Because I thought we weren't allowed up there."

Claudia whirled on her sister. "You didn't put it in the attic, did you? Someone could get hurt on those stairs."

"No! Richard, the attic would be the fourth floor. Did you try the nursery?"

"Yes. Everyone's been in the nursery for at least an hour."

Sylvia knew he was exaggerating, since it had been only a half hour ago that she had given him the hint. Even so, with so many children in the nursery, someone should have stumbled upon the star within minutes.

With Richard and Andrew leading the way, Sylvia, Claudia, their father, and Great-Aunt Lucinda climbed the stairs to the third floor. The nursery lay directly above the library—an unfortunate oversight in planning that Sylvia's grandfather had not noticed until the first time his reading was disturbed by noisy play overhead. Like the library, the nursery stretched the entire width of the south wing and welcomed in sunlight through east, west, and south facing windows. In the twilight, large flakes of snow blew against the glass, but the children were too busy playing to notice. Uncle William's daughter served tea to Sylvia's old dolls, two boys were engaged in a battle with Richard's toy soldiers, and other cousins read or built block towers or played games of their own invention. After an hour and a half of fruitless searching, perseverance had finally succumbed to the allure of toys. The quest for the star had been abandoned.

But no child was playing with the model trains.

"You haven't given up already, have you?" asked Sylvia. The little girl cousin to whom she had given the Nine-Patch quilt looked up and smiled, but the other children were too engrossed in their play to hear.

"Perhaps another hint is in order," suggested Lucinda. "Animal, vegetable, or mineral?"

Richard and Andrew looked up at Sylvia, hopeful.

"Mineral," she said. "A form of transportation." The two boys began to wander the room, moving aside scattered toys, heading in the opposite direction from the crate of model trains. "Think of something used to transport passengers or cargo over long distances. Oh, for heaven's sake." Desperate to salvage the game, she made train noises, mimed the movement of wheels, and tugged on the cord of an imaginary steam whistle.

Richard brightened and ran across the room to his model trains, Andrew right behind. They dug through the crate, emptying it of engines and boxcars with amazing speed, until the last one lay on the floor. The boys looked across the room at Sylvia, expectant and puzzled.

"Great hint," Claudia scoffed. "You sent them to the wrong place."

But she hadn't. Quickly Sylvia joined the boys and peered into the crate to see for herself. It was empty.

Lucinda saw trouble in her expression. "This is where you hid the star?"

Sylvia nodded, puzzled. She scanned the clutter of train cars to see if the star had accidentally been set aside in the boys' haste, but it was not there. "I don't understand. I put it right here."

"Among the trains," said Claudia, skeptical. "Then where is it?"

"I don't know."

"Are you sure you hid it here?" asked her father. "Perhaps you had second thoughts and returned later to move it to a more difficult hiding place. Think hard."

"I'm certain." The question stung. She wouldn't have forgotten where she had hidden the star.

"Perhaps someone else moved it." Aunt Lucinda raised her eyebrows at Richard. "As a little Christmas joke?"

Richard's eyes went wide and innocent. "Not me."

Andrew shook his head vigorously, his expression terrified.

Sylvia knew that, like her, her father and Great-Aunt Lucinda had instantly conjured up images of what punishments a prankster might face in Andrew's house. She forced a smile. "It's a very funny joke," she said, and made herself laugh. Her father let out a chuckle, and the fear in Andrew's eyes relaxed.

"I don't think it's funny at all," declared Claudia.

"Okay, young man." Great-Aunt Lucinda smiled and held out her palm to Richard. "You had us fooled, but now the joke's over."

Richard frowned. "I told you I didn't touch it." Suddenly he looked excited. "Hey, what if a ghost did it? A spirit like in that Christmas story Sylvia read me last night."

Andrew's frightened expression returned. "He's just teasing," Sylvia hastened to reassure him. She believed that Richard had not taken the star, but then, who had? She searched the other children's faces for a clue, but they played on, barely paying attention to the drama unfolding by the model trains. Not a trace of guilt or glee colored their expressions.

"Richard, why don't you put away your trains now,"

advised Sylvia's father. As Andrew joined in to help, Sylvia's father beckoned the women out of their hearing. "Perhaps the star was found—and broken before the finder could return to the ballroom. It's surprising it hasn't happened sooner."

"I always did think it was a bad idea to send children running through the house with a glass star," mused Lucinda. "It's possible, perhaps even likely. But the question remains, who?"

"Not Richard," said Sylvia, eager to exonerate her brother. She knew instinctively that he had spoken the truth. "Could it be Andrew?"

"What makes you think so?" asked her father.

"Because he was the most likely to find the star," Sylvia explained, reluctant to direct blame toward a boy who, as far as she knew, had never broken a single rule in his many visits to the Bergstrom home. "I hid the star among the trains because the nursery is his favorite place in the manor and the trains are his favorite toys. I wanted to help him find the star as cousin Elizabeth helped me."

"You mean as cousin Elizabeth helped you cheat," said Claudia. "Anyway, the nursery isn't Andrew's favorite place in the manor. The kitchen is."

Sylvia wished she had considered that because, of course, Claudia was right.

Great-Aunt Lucinda shook her head. "If the star was broken, I doubt Andrew did it. Remember when he broke that glass on the veranda after I warned the boys not to put them down in the line of fire of their marbles? He picked up every shard, brought them to me, and apologized. He would have done the same thing here."

"This isn't a drinking glass, one of many," said Claudia. "This is a family heirloom."

Sylvia's father nodded, thoughtful, and called the children over. When they had gathered around him, he tried to tease the truth out of them, but no one admitted to finding the star. In a voice too low for anyone but Sylvia and Lucinda to hear, Claudia muttered that he ought to threaten them with a spanking, but Sylvia thought his disarming humor was the right approach. Even Andrew was smiling. But even Sylvia had to admit that her father's questions yielded little useful information. The timeline of the children's whereabouts that he managed to piece together told them nothing more than that all of the children had been in most of the rooms of the manor at some point during the search, sometimes alone, but most often in the company of at least one other child.

Eventually Sylvia's father must have decided that the perpetrator needed a stronger motivation to confess. "If no one has found the star," he warned, "no one can collect the prize."

"There's a prize?" said Andrew.

Richard nodded. "It's usually a toy or candy."

Andrew nudged him. "Come on. Let's keep looking."

Sylvia's heart went out to him. He of all the children wanted a prize so badly that he would continue searching despite the obvious futility of the task. As badly as the game had turned out, she did not regret her attempt to help him. "Can't we let them share the prize?" she asked her father.

"That's against the rules," said Claudia.

Their father held up his hands, somber. "Claudia's right. We won't be able to put the star on top of the tree tonight, so we can't award the prize. I'm disappointed no one wants to come forward and tell the truth, and I'm sure Santa Claus isn't very happy, either."

The children exchanged looks of surprise and dismay, but no one looked any more guilty or worried than the others.

"I'll tell you what we can do," her father continued. "If the star is on the kitchen table tomorrow morning in time for breakfast, I won't ask who left it there, and everyone can share the prize equally."

"Is it candy?" piped up one of the youngest cousins.

"It is," said Sylvia's father. "Now, let's go downstairs and enjoy the rest of our Christmas Eve. It's almost bedtime."

When they returned to the ballroom without the star for the top of the tree, Sylvia's father treated the astonished adults to a lighthearted account of the missing star and repeated his promise to the children. Then he read aloud "A Visit from St. Nicholas" as he had done every Christmas for as long as Sylvia could remember. Afterward, he gave up his chair to Aunt Nellie, who read St. Luke's account of the Nativity.

When she finished, the children rose from their places around the tree to collect hugs and kisses before going off to bed. Gazing at their sweet, beloved faces, Sylvia could not believe any of them capable of hiding a guilty secret. "I wish Father would have let them have the prize anyway," she said with a sigh.

She had only been thinking aloud, but Claudia heard her. "If you wanted them to have the prize so badly, you should have let them find the star."

"I tried. I hid it, and obviously someone found it."

"So you say."

Sylvia stared at her. "Do you think I still have it?"

"I think you know where it is."

"I don't," Sylvia retorted. "I haven't the faintest idea where it could be. One of the children probably broke it and is too upset to confess, just as Father said."

Claudia searched her face, frowning. "If that's so, then where are the pieces? I intend to search every dustbin and look beneath every carpet. None of the children has left the manor since before the search began. If the star is broken, the pieces must be here. And if they aren't—"

Claudia left the words unspoken as she volunteered to help the aunts put the children to bed. At first Sylvia was too stunned to follow, but then she steeled herself with a deep breath and offered to see to Richard and Andrew. After she had supervised their teeth-brushing, heard their prayers, and tucked them into the twin beds in Richard's room, she crept upstairs to the nursery. She discovered Claudia rummaging through the dustbin.

"Any luck?" asked Sylvia quietly.

Claudia shook her head.

Together they searched every place a frantic child might have hidden the ruby-and-gold shards of broken glass. Claudia seemed glad to have her sister there—not because she wanted the company, but to assure herself that Sylvia could not dispose of the star, whole or in pieces, while unobserved. It was late when they gave up, and Claudia was even angrier than when they had begun. Sylvia began to wish that she had kept the star. She would have confessed to it then and there just to make peace with her sister on Christmas Eve.

"We should go to bed," she said tiredly. "Everyone

else has, and it's possible whoever took it is waiting until everyone is asleep to leave it on the kitchen table."

Claudia folded her arms. "So that's how you're going to end this charade."

Sylvia was too exhausted to argue. "Oh, stop it, Claudia."

She left her sister standing there and went off to bed.

Christmas morning dawned silvery white. Sylvia woke to the sound of hushed voices and quick footsteps passing in the hall outside her door. Smiling, she rose and dressed for church in a green velvet dress Claudia had outgrown. It had been Claudia's best dress, worn only on special occasions, and Great-Aunt Lucinda had helped Sylvia make it over so that it fit her properly and looked almost like new. She brushed her hair and tied it back with a matching ribbon. Sometimes, if she looked in the mirror at precisely the right angle, she thought she looked almost as pretty as her sister. Standing far away from the mirror helped.

She greeted Aunt Nellie in passing as she hurried downstairs, eager to reach the kitchen, certain that the Christmas star would be on the table. From the foot of the stairs, she spied a cluster of cousins still clad in their pajamas gathered around the door to the ballroom. Every Christmas Eve, Great-Aunt Lucinda locked the door before retiring for the night so no one would disturb Santa if he came by, but the children always checked in case she had forgotten. Richard had his eye to the keyhole. "I can't see anything," Sylvia heard him say. "The lights are out. Quit shoving! Wait a minute—I think—yes! There's something under the tree!"

The other children pressed closer. "What?" Andrew cried. "What do you see?"

"Just shadows. It's too dark to see anything more. Keep your voices down. We're not supposed to peek."

"That's right," said Sylvia. The children jumped guiltily and stepped away from the door, all save Richard, who barely glanced up from the keyhole. "You should be getting dressed for church. I bet that's where your parents think you are."

"Can't we open the door and look to make sure Santa came?" asked one of the younger cousins. "We won't step even one little baby toe into the room."

The other children joined in, begging for just one look, just to be sure. Sylvia held up her hands, laughing, glad that it wasn't her decision. She would be tempted to let the children tear into their gifts right away, even if it made them late for church. "Do you really all have such guilty consciences?" she teased. "You really aren't sure whether Santa put you on his 'Good' list?"

She scooted them toward the stairs and waited at the bottom until the last reluctant straggler had reached the landing. Then, with one last entreaty to hurry, she continued toward the kitchen.

She met her father in the hallway. His expression told her what she needed to know, but still she asked, "Was it there?"

Her father shook his head. "They still have time. I said in time for breakfast, and we won't have breakfast until after church."

Sylvia nodded, but she could sense that his concern ran deep. Bergstrom children were raised to respect their elders and to do as they were told. Such blatant defiance of her father's wishes was unthinkable. Like children everywhere, the Bergstroms broke rules and made mistakes—Sylvia was proof enough of that—but they never failed to accept the consequences of their actions, even if, deep down, they wouldn't admit that they had done anything wrong. The taking of the star and the refusal to return it, even broken, was something new and disturbing in their household.

The adults stayed away from the kitchen as they helped the children dress in their finest for church services, offering the guilty child every opportunity to return the star unobserved. The children were so excited they could hardly stand still long enough to have their hair combed, and more than once, Sylvia had caught an older cousin sneaking off to test the doorknob to the ballroom.

As members of the choir, Sylvia and Claudia were expected to arrive at church a half hour before services to don their robes and warm up their voices. Richard and Andrew rode with Sylvia in the backseat when Father drove her and Claudia to the same church in Waterford their family had attended for generations. By the time the sisters filed out of the music room and climbed the stairs to the loft with the rest of the choir, the pews were nearly full. Sylvia spotted the rest of the family among the throng, but she was disappointed not to find Andrew's parents and little sister.

She soon forgot their absence in the glory of the day. Her heart filled with joy and gratitude as she sang the traditional carols she loved so dearly. How the Lord must have loved the people of the world to send them His only Son! And how He must love them still, despite their sin, despite their weakness, despite the shadow of the Cross that fell upon the Manger even on this most joyous of days. At that moment Sylvia felt touched by the light of grace, and she knew that if she could remember that feeling after she left that gathering, even in her darkest hours, she would never be alone.

The feeling of joyful gratitude lasted throughout the service and soared when the entire congregation rose after the final blessing and sang "Joy to the World" as the church bells pealed an accompaniment. The service ended, but still the congregants lingered, wishing one another a Merry Christmas. Every embrace, every greeting was a prayer for good health and peace in the coming year. Sylvia spotted Claudia putting away her choir robe with the other sopranos. She scrambled down the risers and flung her arms around her sister.

"Merry Christmas, Claudia," she said, her voice muffled by her billowing robe.

"What's the matter with you?" Claudia exclaimed. "You scared me half to death." Beside her, her friends smirked. They had known Claudia too long to be surprised by the antics of her difficult little sister.

Sylvia ignored them. "I just want you to know that I love you."

"Well, I love you, too, of course, but I don't have to tackle you in the choir loft to prove it."

"Maybe you should just send her a Christmas card next time, Sylvia," suggested one friend.

Another chimed in, "Or give back the Christmas star."

Sylvia looked sharply at Claudia. She was not sure what astonished her more: that Claudia had blabbed to her friends about a family matter, or that she still blamed Sylvia for the disappearance of the star. "I don't have it," she said, the warmth and fellowship inspired by the Christmas worship slowly ebbing.

"I don't want to talk about that here." Claudia yanked Sylvia free of her choir robe, bundled it up, and dumped it into her sister's arms. "Give this back to Miss Rosemary. The other altos are already gone."

Biting back a retort, Sylvia did as Claudia commanded, shutting her ears to the older girls' laughter.

Great-Aunt Lucinda waited until every member of the family had returned home from church before unlocking the ballroom. Children rushed past her through the open door like water through a floodgate, and their shouts and squeals of delight upon discovering presents beneath the tree were deafening. Santa had come. Sylvia watched the children race from one gift to another searching for their names, seeing in their faces the utter happiness and delight that only a visit from Santa could bring. She missed feeling so captivated by wonder, swept up in the magic of Christmas, a magic that had once seemed as real as every other Bergstrom tradition. She smiled wistfully as she watched the younger children, wishing that just for Christmas morning she could be their age again—believing, trusting, not knowing everything she knew now. Still, it was such a joy to witness her brother and cousins enjoying a moment of complete happiness that she felt a surge of love for each of them, and a joy that in its own way was as magical and as full of wonder as what the children felt.

In the midst of all the clamor and excitement, Andrew sat on the floor, an island of stillness. He was so close to the tree that he was almost concealed within the branches, his eyes full of astonishment as he clutched two gifts, each with his name written in elegant script upon it.

"Don't open them yet," warned Richard, although Andrew clung to the boxes so tightly Sylvia doubted he could be compelled to set one down so he could open the other. "We have to eat breakfast first."

"That's right, children," called Great-Aunt Lucinda, clapping her hands for their attention. "Breakfast, then gifts. You know the rules."

A great moan of despair went up from the children, but then they remembered their hunger and raced off to the dining room. They gobbled their breakfast—eggs and sausage and apple strudel—and dashed back to the Christmas tree, unable to stay away from Santa's bounty for one moment longer than necessary. The older Bergstroms ate more leisurely, knowing that the older children would remind the younger that they were not allowed to open their gifts until everyone had finished breakfast.

"We should take our plates in there instead of taking our time and torturing them like this," remarked Uncle William, as he did every year. Everyone murmured assent and continued eating at their same, leisurely pace.

"The strudel is delicious, girls," said Aunt Nellie, who had watched her mother-in-law make strudel once and had vowed never to learn the recipe.

"It is," agreed Sylvia's father, smiling warmly at his daughters. "I'm proud to see that you're carrying on the Bergstrom tradition. Your mother would have been proud of you two."

Sylvia smiled and was about to thank him for the compliment when Uncle William added, "With a few more years' practice, folks might not be able to tell the difference between your strudel and those of the more experienced bakers in the family."

"And even we are no match for Gerda," remarked Great-Aunt Lucinda. "She could make the lightest, flakiest pastry so effortlessly it could make you cry. I think that's why I always preferred to bake Christmas cookies.

I couldn't help feeling like a failure when I compared my strudel to hers, so I gave up trying. Don't follow my poor example, girls. Stick with it and you might find that one of you has inherited Gerda's gift for pastry."

Sylvia caught her sister's eye and they shared a long look of commiseration. No Bergstrom girl escaped comparison to Gerda, and they were overdue for their turn. Sylvia cheered up when she thought of how much their second attempt to stretch the dough had improved upon their first. Next year, they would do even better. Judging by the few crumbs left on the plate where their strudel had been, their first attempt had been a success despite its flaws. The pastry was chewy where it should have been light and flaky, but the apple filling was as delicious as any Sylvia had tasted.

She would have taken more pleasure in the famous Bergstrom strudel had the Christmas star awaited them on the kitchen table. Though none of the adults mentioned the star at breakfast and Sylvia suspected most of the children had forgotten that it was still missing, she knew the prankster's disregard for her father's offer of amnesty troubled all of them.

Any hope that the prankster might have had a last-minute change of heart vanished as Sylvia helped Lucinda carry dirty dishes from the dining room to the kitchen. Only the jolly Santa Claus cookie jar and six red-and-green tartan placemats sat on the long wooden table.

"What will we put on the top of the tree?" Sylvia asked her great-aunt as they washed and dried the dishes, side by side.

"I don't know. We've used that star as long as I can remember." Great-Aunt Lucinda shrugged. "Perhaps we'll just leave it bare and let the emptiness prick the conscience."

"You don't think I still have the star, do you?"

"No, Sylvia. I saw your face when you searched the empty crate and I know you were as bewildered as the rest of us."

"Then who?"

Lucinda was silent for a moment. "I have my suspicions, but I'll keep my own counsel."

Sylvia did not pester her, for she was suddenly taken by suspicions of her own. Who had been most eager to lay blame? Who had the most reason to want Sylvia's first attempt to hide the star fail?

Claudia.

"Aren't you coming?" called Richard, racing into the kitchen. "Everyone's waiting."

"I suppose the dishes won't get any dirtier if we save them for later." Smiling, Great-Aunt Lucinda shook soapsuds from her fingers and dried her hands on Sylvia's dishtowel. Richard whooped in delight and ran off to the ballroom where the other children were waiting eagerly with their gifts. Sylvia wished everyone could tear into their gifts all at once, as some of her friends' families did, but the Bergstroms took turns opening one gift at a time, proceeding in order from youngest to eldest. Sylvia received a beautiful cardigan Great-Aunt Lucinda had knit from the softest wool, a coordinating skirt from Claudia, W. B. Yeats's *Collected Poems* from her father, and from her brother, an illustrated story of a stagecoach robbery in the Wild West starring thinly fictionalized versions of the Bergstrom children.

The story Richard had written for Andrew was a slightly different version featuring the two boys. Andrew seemed pleased by his friend's gift, but he could hardly take his eyes off what Santa had brought him: a steel train set with an engine, two boxcars, a passenger car, and a bright red caboose. His expression, utter delight mixed with disbelief, touched and amused Sylvia. She suspected it was the nicest gift he had ever received. Suddenly she thought of his little sister and wondered what, if anything, she had found upon waking that Christmas morning. She had a horrible thought: How would that little girl feel when Andrew came home with beautiful new toys from Santa when she had received nothing?

She would think Santa had forgotten her.

How old was Andrew's sister—four? Five? Four, Sylvia decided. She looked younger, but Andrew, too, was small for his age. She was just about the age to enjoy—Sylvia looked around the room and her gaze fell upon Uncle William's youngest daughter, who was cradling the rag doll Santa had brought her. A doll. Of course. But Claudia's old dolls were too worn and faded from so many years of hard love, though they remained in the nursery for the cousins' visits. Sylvia had never cared for dolls, so she had none to give away.

Except—

Then she remembered a gift from her grandmother Lockwood, her mother's mother. The children had never met her until the day she came to live at Elm Creek Manor a few months before her death. When she first arrived, she had given Claudia an heirloom silver locket containing a picture of their great-grandparents that her own mother had given to her long ago. To Sylvia she gave a fine porcelain doll with ringlets of golden hair, dressed in a gown of blue velvet. It was a beautiful doll, but Sylvia had always preferred to play with toy horses and hardly knew what to do with it. But she had sense enough, even at eight years old, to hug the doll and pretend she liked the gift to show respect to the grandmother she barely knew.

Her grandmother had explained that the doll once belonged to Eleanor. "They were inseparable until she decided she was too old for dolls," said Grandmother Lockwood in a voice as dry and as crisp as a cracker. "Then she sat on a shelf in the nursery gathering dust, the poor, neglected thing."

"I didn't neglect it," Sylvia's mother had said, her voice carrying a hint of sharpness. "You're thinking of Abigail. That was her doll, not mine."

"That's not so," said Grandmother Lockwood. "I recall very clearly giving it to you for Christmas when you were four."

"That was Abigail. She said Santa brought it. When Abigail no longer wanted her, she gave her to me, but by then I was no longer interested in dolls, either."

"You would have liked them still if Abigail had." Grandmother Lockwood turned a sharp eye upon Sylvia. "Well, my dear, it seems I've given you the doll no one wanted. I suppose you, too, will abandon her."

Sylvia did not like the dismissive tone her grandmother used to address her mother, but she nodded gravely and promised she would never abandon the beautiful doll. She had kept her promise, although she had not showered the toy with the affection Grandmother had likely hoped to inspire.

The beautiful doll had once been a Christmas gift, and it had already been handed down twice. It would not be parting with a family heirloom to pass it on to a deserving little girl.

Sylvia slipped away from the party and dashed upstairs to her bedroom, where she stood on a chair on tiptoe to reach to the back of the top shelf where the box had sat untouched for years. She pulled down the heavy white cardboard box, blew off the dust, and removed the lid. The doll was as lovely as the day Sylvia had put her away, her blue velvet frock and white pinafore spotless, her golden curls perfectly arranged. When Sylvia picked her up, the blue eyes opened above the button nose and rosebud mouth. For a moment she considered giving it to her favorite little cousin, who still enjoyed dolls and would adore this one. But she had so many dolls—she had received a new one just hours ago—and so many other toys as well. Resolved, Sylvia tucked the doll carefully into the box and replaced the lid, then wrapped it and tied it with ribbon.

The children were distracted with their toys when she returned, and the other women were off in the kitchen seeing to Christmas dinner. When her father and the other men were not watching, Sylvia slipped the box unnoticed beneath the tree, then strolled away and waited for someone to notice the new gift. After a while, when no one did, Sylvia pointed to it and exclaimed, "Isn't that another present? How did we miss it?"

Her father gave her a speculative look as the children hurried to the tree and discovered the unexpected gift. "That wasn't there before," said Richard.

"Are you sure?" asked Sylvia. "Santa couldn't have returned while we were here. We would have seen him."

Richard threw her a brief, quizzical frown, but

Andrew quickly drew his attention. "Sally Jane," he read. "That's my sister's name."

"We don't have a Sally Jane in the Bergstrom family," said Sylvia's father. "It must be for your sister. I wonder why Santa left it here."

"Maybe he made a mistake," piped up one of the cousins.

"Maybe he wants me to take it to her," said Andrew slowly. "I don't think he knows where we live now."

A shadow of concern passed over Sylvia's father's face. "I'm sure that's what Santa intended," he said. "He knows you're a responsible boy and that he can trust you to get this to your sister safely."

"I will," said Andrew solemnly. Then he smiled, and for a moment, Sylvia glimpsed a boy as happy and as certain that he was loved as her own dear Richard.

The rest of the day passed happily but all too soon. The children played with one another's new toys while the adults spoke of Christmases past and read aloud from the letters of absent loved ones. Cousin Elizabeth and her husband, Henry, had sent a whole box of oranges from their ranch in California. Great-Aunt Lucinda read Elizabeth's letter aloud so they could all enjoy her amusing stories about going to the beach in November and thinking of the folks back in Pennsylvania shivering by the fire, glimpsing a genuine movie star in a theater—in the audience, not on the screen—and of her exasperation when, just after she had wiped away a blanket of dust that had settled throughout the house after a minor earthquake, an aftershock came along and threw another layer down. Sylvia shivered with excitement imagining her brave cousin pacing impatiently and waiting for an earthquake to stop, worried only about the mess she would have to clean up and completely indifferent to the danger.

Then Elizabeth's tone grew wistful. "I do miss Elm Creek Manor and all who reside therein, especially at this time of year," Great-Aunt Lucinda read. "I wish I could spend just one more Christmas surrounded by family. I make the famous Bergstrom strudel here, but it just isn't the same without the aunts and uncles there to tell me mine doesn't taste as good as Grandma Gerda's. On Christmas Eve, know that I will be thinking of you all and wondering which lucky child placed the star upon the tree that night." Great-Aunt Lucinda cleared her throat. "Good-bye for now and God Bless. Merry Christmas from your loving Elizabeth."

Sylvia ached to see her cousin again. She would even be glad to see Henry if only he would bring her beloved cousin home.

Christmas dinner was delicious. They had scrimped and saved for months so that they might have a feast that day, just as the first Bergstroms who had settled in that country had done. They savored the tender jagerschnitzel—grilled pork loin with mushroom gravy—sweet potatoes, creamed peas, and all the dishes without which Christmas would not seem complete. After the children were excused, the older members of the family lingered at the table, sharing Christmas memories and hopes for the year to come. The Depression couldn't last forever, Uncle William said, as he had the previous year. Better times were sure to come. The horses were thriving, and the Bergstroms would be ready when their old customers returned. In the meantime, the Bergstroms would weather the storm as they always had.

"What was in the box you gave to Andrew's sister?" Sylvia's father asked her.

"A doll," she replied. "She's like new. I rarely played with her."

"I can't remember ever seeing you with a doll," remarked Aunt Nellie. "It must have been very long ago."

Claudia leveled her gaze at her sister. "You don't mean Grandmother Lockwood's doll, do you?"

"Yes, that's the one."

"But she was Mama's!"

"No, she wasn't. She was Aunt Abigail's."

"But after that she was Mama's."

"Mama never played with her, and neither did I." Sylvia looked from her sister to her father, worried. "I thought Andrew's little sister would like to have her."

"It's a generous gift," said Great-Aunt Lucinda. "I'm sure little Sally Jane will adore her."

Claudia looked shocked. "You don't mean to let her go through with it?"

Great-Aunt Lucinda shrugged. "We can hardly take it back now."

Sylvia's father regarded Claudia, concerned. "Did you want the doll for yourself? Aren't you a little old for dolls?"

"I don't want it to play with. It's a family heirloom."

"You never showed any interest in it before."

Sylvia detected the trace of irritation in her father's voice and wondered if her sister did, too.

Indignant, Claudia replied, "I never dreamed Sylvia would give it away or I would have."

"What's done is done," said their father firmly. "It's a fine doll—for all that I know about dolls—but it was never a cherished family heirloom. Aunt Abigail played with it as a child but your mother never did, and even if she had, she would have been the first to offer it up to a little girl who hasn't had a tiny fraction of the blessings you children have received every day of your lives, Depression or no Depression. Your mother was generous that way, and it seems that Sylvia has learned from her. And for that, I am grateful."

Shocked, Sylvia could only stare at her plate, her face hot. She had never heard anyone speak so sternly to Claudia. In a strangled voice, her sister asked if she could be excused. Their father dismissed her with a nod, and she hurried from the dining room as quickly as she could without running.

"Nephew," chided Great-Aunt Lucinda after she had gone.

"I'm sorry, Aunt, but I just couldn't bear any selfishness today. Not on Christmas. Eleanor would have been so disappointed. And as for you, young lady—"

Sylvia quickly looked up. "Yes, Father?"

"You could have asked your sister first before giving away the doll." He held up a hand to stave off her protest. "I realize she never played with it, but you know how she loves the stories your mother used to tell about her life in New York. This doll is a link to the world she knows only through your mother's stories. Even so, I think she would have gladly given it to Andrew's sister if you had allowed her to have a say in the decision."

Ashamed, Sylvia lowered her eyes again. "I—I should have thought of that."

"Well, give her back the Christmas star and I'm sure she'll forgive you." Great-Aunt Lucinda laughed at Sylvia's expression. "I'm teasing, dear."

Sylvia's father glanced out the window. Although they

had dined early, already it was dusk. "I suppose I'd better take Andrew home," he said, pushing back his chair.

The rest of the family saw them off, except for Claudia, who had not been seen since she left the supper table. Andrew seemed reluctant to go until Sylvia's father made a joke about how the car was so full of gifts that it reminded him of Santa's sleigh. The boy brightened at the idea and willingly climbed into the front seat beside Sylvia's father.

After they departed, Sylvia helped Aunt Nellie and Great-Aunt Lucinda tidy up the kitchen and dining room. They had almost finished when they heard her father return, opening the back door and stomping his feet on the steps to knock the snow from his boots before coming inside. Sylvia was putting away the dry dishes, but she heard her father talking to Lucinda at the back entry.

"We should have invited the whole family," he said, removing his coat. "I don't think they had much of a celebration."

"No Christmas dinner?" said Great-Aunt Lucinda.

"I'm not sure they had any dinner at all. Aunt, if you could see the squalor they live in—" He sighed, frustrated. "No man should have to raise his children that way. What is wrong with our country that we allow this to happen?"

"I don't know that our country is to blame."

"We *are* the country, Aunt. People like us. We all have to do what we can to help one another, just as my Eleanor said. But so many men out of work for so many years—That's not a problem that will resolve itself. Something must be done."

Fondly, Great-Aunt Lucinda teased, "Why, Frederick, are you asking for a Christmas miracle?"

"If there were any chance of getting one, you'd better believe I'd ask." He fell silent for a moment. "Do you know what the boy said to me as I drove him home? He said that this was the best Christmas he had ever known. You and I, William and Nellie—and perhaps even the older children—we've compared these past few Christmases to those of the twenties and note how we've come down in the world, and yet this little boy was overwhelmed by our abundance."

"That's a lesson for us all."

"Aunt Lucinda—" He hesitated. "I can't help thinking how much more we could do for Andrew and his little sister if—"

"No, Frederick. I know your heart's in the right place, but you can't take children from their parents."

"If you could see their home, you'd feel differently."

"Perhaps, but that doesn't change the fact that there is much more to a home than material comforts."

"I'm not so sure that Andrew's home has all those intangibles."

"And I can't say for certain whether you're condemning them simply because they're poor. Nephew, dear, there are so many families like the Coopers. Are you going to take in all their children?"

"No," he said. "No, I suppose that would be impossible. But I can help this child and his sister."

"We will continue to share what we have with Andrew, just as we always have." Great-Aunt Lucinda sighed. "We should have thought of the little girl. Thank goodness for Sylvia's generous heart. We can and we should do more for Sally Jane, but at least today, she learned that Santa has not forgotten her."

Sylvia's father and great-aunt walked off down the

hall, their conversation fading until Sylvia could no longer hear them. Was it true, as Great-Aunt Lucinda had said, that she had a generous heart? No one had ever said such a thing before, and she had never thought of herself that way. She just couldn't bear the thought of a little sister believing she was less loved than an older sibling. Santa couldn't remember Andrew and not Sally Jane. It simply would not be fair.

Christmas of 1934 was drawing to a close. Sylvia helped see the children off to bed, then curled up in a chair in the ballroom with the book of poems her father had given her, reading and enjoying the beauty of the lights on the Christmas tree, which seemed unfinished without the ruby-and-gold star on the highest bough.

She remembered then that she had not seen Claudia in hours. Marking her place in the book with a scrap of ribbon from a Christmas gift, she set it aside and went looking for her sister. She eventually found her kneeling on the floor of the front parlor, packing the Feathered Stars, appliquéd holly plumes, and haphazard Variable Stars into a box. Inside, Sylvia spotted the larger cuts of fabric from which Lucinda, Eleanor, and Claudia had taken the pieces for their blocks.

"Christmas is over, so you're putting the Christmas Quilt away?" asked Sylvia, amused in spite of herself. "I see you're following in Great-Aunt Lucinda's footsteps."

"Exactly," said Claudia shortly. "To the letter."

"What do you mean?"

"I mean I'm quitting, too. I suppose that pleases you."

Strangely, it did not please Sylvia at all. "Why quit when you've already made five blocks?"

"Because I've already wasted too much time on this wretched thing." Claudia closed the box and rose, then stood there with the box at her feet, regarding her sister challengingly, as if daring her to continue the conversation.

"Maybe you'll feel differently next Christmas," said Sylvia. "Maybe that's how you'll follow Great-Aunt Lucinda's example, by working on it only during the Christmas season."

"I will never sew another stitch of this quilt," Claudia vowed. "I don't want anything to remind me of this miserable Christmas."

Sylvia stared at her, bewildered. "What are you talking about?"

"Oh, for heaven's sake, Sylvia, don't pretend you don't know. It isn't like you to sympathize with me and I'm not fooled. This Christmas has been a disaster from start to finish, from the moment the strudel dough turned rubbery until ten minutes ago when I tried to sew two of my Variable Stars together and couldn't get the points to match. I used the exact same templates and measured each before I cut, and yet it still would not come together properly."

The trouble was her seam allowances, not her templates, Sylvia thought, but she decided to wait for a better moment to mention it. "The strudel was fine, and the proof is that only crumbs were left. And one bad quilt block isn't a disaster."

"It's not just that. It's everything."

Sylvia knew she was thinking of the missing Christmas tree star, Aunt Abigail's doll, Sylvia's embarrassing show of affection in the choir loft—everything. Or nearly so. Apparently she had forgotten the beautiful Christmas tree alight with candles, Great-Aunt Lucinda's delicious Christmas dinner, the sublime joy of the church service, the unbridled happiness of the children, and the loving company of their aunts and uncles and father. How could any of that be branded a disaster?

"When Father took Andrew home," said Sylvia, "the little boy told him that this was the most wonderful Christmas he had ever known."

Claudia looked away. "Well, of course it would be, for him."

Sylvia wanted to argue that it had been so, not only for Andrew, but for all of them, but she ached with longing for her mother and could not honestly say that any Christmas was as full of joy and hope as those Eleanor had shared with them. Of course that could not be so. But this Christmas had been full of blessings, and she could not understand why her sister could not see them.

Great-Aunt Lucinda was certain the ruby-and-gold glass star would be discovered when the family put away the trappings of the holiday after Twelfth Night, but it was not. Sylvia never saw the star again, and she doubted Claudia ever stopped suspecting she played a role in its disappearance.

In the year that was to come, Sylvia's father discovered that his instinct to remove Andrew and Sally Jane from their unhappy home was justified. Richard and Andrew were eight years old when Andrew ran away from home and hid out for days in the wooden playhouse Sylvia's father had built for Richard near the stables and exercise rings. Richard smuggled blankets and food to his friend, but he inadvertently led Sylvia right to him one early autumn night when she woke to the sound of her brother creeping past her bedroom door. When Sylvia's father contacted the authorities, whatever they discovered about the Cooper home compelled them to take Andrew and Sally Jane from their parents the first day of their investigation. Sylvia's father immediately offered to take them in, but an aunt was found in Philadelphia, and while the local authorities respected Frederick Bergstrom, the law said that the children belonged with family.

Andrew and his sister were sent away to the city. For months after his sudden departure, Richard missed his friend and wrote him letters, but the Bergstroms did not know where to send them. For years thereafter, the Bergstroms counted Andrew and his little sister among those absent loved ones with whom they longed to spend Christmas once more.

And on every one of those Christmases, Sylvia hoped her sister would reflect upon that year and realize that it had truly been a joyous time despite the mishaps and misunderstandings, and that she would finish the Christmas Quilt, even with her well-intended but imperfect stitches. If Claudia ever did see the Christmas of 1934 in a different light, she never shared that epiphany with her sister, nor did she ever add another stitch to the Christmas Quilt.

Chapter Four

SYLVIA KEPT SARAH company in the sitting room as she finished attaching Claudia's Variable Stars to the Feathered Stars and holly plumes. As the disparate sections of the Christmas Quilt came together, Sylvia began to see a pattern emerging, but whether Sarah would succeed in creating something harmonious and beautiful, Sylvia could not yet determine.

The sight of Claudia's handiwork intermingled with their mother's and great-aunt's gave her mixed feelings. While Claudia's piecing skills were inferior to those of her predecessors, her pattern choice simpler, Sarah had arranged the Variable Stars so that they set off the complexity of the other blocks without competing for the observer's attention. They seemed to fit with an ease that made Sylvia question her reaction to her sister's pattern choice so many years before. Perhaps Sarah had not chanced upon a flattering arrangement. Perhaps this layout was what Claudia had intended all along.

It remained to be seen how Sarah would accommodate the blocks Sylvia had made, or whether a Bergstrom sister would be excluded from the quilt after all—just not the sister Sylvia would have predicted.

In a moment when the clattering of the sewing machine had paused, Sylvia asked, "Would you care to help me finish putting up the Christmas decorations?"

"When I finish this section," Sarah promised, winding a new bobbin. "I'll meet you in the foyer, okay?"

Sylvia shrugged and left her to it. She returned to the

boxes of Christmas decorations scattered across the marble foyer, and she cast a critical eye upon the work they had already completed. She made a few changes, made a mental note to have Matt collect some greenery, and, in armfuls she could manage, brought the rest of the decorations to the kitchen. On one of her trips, she discovered that the sewing machine had fallen silent, and that Sarah and Matt were discussing something in hushed voices within the sitting room.

She considered eavesdropping, but reminded herself that she rarely learned anything pleasant that way. So she went to the doorway and regarded the pair, who were speaking earnestly, their heads bent close together. She caught a few words—"mother," "impossible," and "never"—just enough for her to identify the topic of conversation.

"I hate to interrupt," she said, hiding a smile when they sat up too quickly. "But if we're going to finish decorating, I'll need your help."

"You're not interrupting anything," said Matt.

"We were just debating . . . which Christmas carol is the most depressing," said Sarah. "Matt says 'I'll Be Home for Christmas' because it's about longing for home rather than actually being there, but I think 'Have Yourself a Merry Little Christmas' is more melancholy. What do you think?"

"What an odd way to pass the time." Sylvia didn't believe her for a moment, but she decided to play along. "My vote goes to the 'Coventry Carol.'"

"Which one is that?"

"It's a traditional piece." Sylvia hummed a few measures. "It's about King Herod's slaughter of the innocents in his attempt to kill the Christ Child."

"You win," said Matt.

"Naturally. I have experience and wisdom on my side." Not to mention years of practice debating Claudia on every conceivable topic. "Now then. If Sarah is willing to take a break from her sewing, I believe it's time you two went out and found us a tree."

Sarah and Matt agreed, so Sylvia reminded them of the borders of the Bergstrom estate, which had contracted significantly since her youth due to Claudia's sale of parcels of land in Sylvia's absence. She described a particular region of the woods that had yielded many fine Christmas trees in the past, advised them to take the old toboggan along, and sent them on their way.

Sylvia watched from the back stairs as they trudged off across the parking lot—empty of cars in the off-season, although Matt kept it cleared of snow in case of unexpected visitors—and crossed the bridge over Elm Creek. So many other couples had made that trek before them. It was a tradition that had begun with Hans and Anneke Bergstrom, as they went off to find a tree while Gerda, the superior cook, remained at home to attend to their Christmas Eve supper. Their simple, practical decision became ritual as younger generations married and the family grew. Once Sylvia's parents had been the newlyweds sent off to find the Christmas tree, their love steadfast and hopes for the future bright despite the doctors' grim prediction that Eleanor's health would not allow her to bear children. Years later, their daughter Sylvia set off for the snowy wood with her beloved husband, James.

Dear, wonderful James.

They met at the state fair when Sylvia was sixteen. Every year she and Claudia entered their quilts in the show in hopes of winning a ribbon, and Great-Aunt Lucinda entered her best preserves. Their father showed his prize horses and spent hours debating the merits of various breeding and training practices with other men in the business, some of whom were his rivals. Nine-year-old Richard shadowed his father, absorbing every word the men exchanged. Like Sylvia, he had always known that one day he would take his place beside his father and uncle with Bergstrom Thoroughbreds.

Although Sylvia cared as much about the business as her brother, at the fair, she was too absorbed in her riding competitions to pay much attention to business trends and competitors' rivalries. She took first place in nearly every competition she entered, which she attributed as much to her father's fine horses as to her own skill. When she saw her father beaming at her proudly as the judges awarded her ribbons and draped a wreath of flowers around her mount's neck, she knew she was doing her part to strengthen the reputation of Bergstrom Thoroughbreds. After years of struggling, the family business was steadily regaining its former prominence. Recent outstanding showings in the Preakness had brought them new customers, and just as Uncle William had always predicted, many of their former clients had returned when they could afford to once again.

That year at the fair, a young man she did not recognize came often to the practice ring and leaned against the fence to watch while Sylvia rode Dresden Rose. Once, when he caught her eye and called out a greeting, she replied with a nod and pretended to ignore him. She had come to find his presence disconcerting and wondered if a rival had sent him to ruin her concentration and leave her vulnerable to mistakes in the ring. With dismay she realized that the plan, if it was a plan, had a good chance of succeeding. The young man was undeniably handsome, tall and strong with dark eyes and dark, curly hair, impossible to ignore.

Later, as she tended to Dresden Rose, the young man from the practice ring joined her in the stable. He complimented the mare, which he immediately recognized as a Bergstrom Thoroughbred, and inquired if Sylvia often rode their horses.

"Of course," said Sylvia.

"They're supposed to be the finest horses around."

"A lot of people think so."

He smiled. "I know I shouldn't admit this, but the best of my family's stable can't match the worst of Old Bergstrom's."

"Oh, really?" Sylvia was so astonished she nearly laughed. "I suppose 'Old Bergstrom' would be delighted to hear that."

"I bet he already knows." The young man went on to confide that his father intended to catch up to Old Bergstrom in a generation, but that he did not believe his father would succeed. One day, however, he himself would breed horses even finer than the best Old Bergstrom had to offer.

After that admission, when he asked for her name, Sylvia thought it prudent to offer only her first. When he introduced himself, she was startled to learn he was James Compson, the youngest son of her father's strongest rival.

James did not discover who Sylvia's father was until her next riding competition later that day. From atop Dresden Rose, she spotted her family cheering in the spectators' seats and waved to them, her confidence bolstered.

Then, as she looked away into another part of the stands, her eyes met James's. His gaze was so steady and intense that the encouraging grin he offered completely unsettled her. She looked away and fought to compose herself as the announcer called out the names of the riders.

When it was her turn, the announcer's voice rang out so that all could hear. "Our fifth competitor—Sylvia Bergstrom!"

As Dresden Rose trotted into the ring, Sylvia risked a glance at James Compson and was pleased to see him staring at her with an expression of shock, bewilderment, and chagrin. Later, when he did not reappear at the practice ring, she regretted having fun at his expense. She should have told him who she was the moment he identified Dresden Rose as coming from her father's stables. Surely he did not believe she had run to her father with his idle talk about his father's plans—although part of her felt disloyal for not divulging what she knew.

James must have forgiven her, for the next time they met a few years later, he was as warm and friendly as ever. They struck up a correspondence that lasted several years as their friendship blossomed into love. When Sylvia was twenty and James twenty-two, they married, and James joined the Bergstrom family and the family business at Elm Creek Manor.

Their first Christmas as husband and wife marked a time of renewed hope and happiness in the Bergstrom household, which had grown smaller since the year Claudia had attempted to finish the Christmas Quilt. Great-Aunt Lucinda, the last child of Hans and Anneke Bergstrom, had passed away after a brief illness. Uncle William died after being thrown from a horse, and when Aunt Nellie remarried, she moved away with her children. Other cousins left the Elm Creek Valley, too, pursuing the promise of better jobs elsewhere when the family business faltered. Elm Creek Manor, which had once seemed so full and bustling with life, suddenly became unbearably large and empty to its few remaining residents. Though the threat of a war in Europe loomed on the horizon, James's arrival in the household promised that they had reached a turning point, that he would help the business to thrive, and that one day the manor would be restored to its former glory.

On their first Christmas Eve as husband and wife, Claudia hid her jealousy poorly as Sylvia and James pulled on their coats and boots in preparation for their snowy trek into the woods, but Sylvia gave her credit for trying. Claudia had known her beau, Harold, since high school and in all fairness should have been the first sister to marry, but Harold had yet to ask her. No one doubted that he would get around to it eventually, but it chafed Claudia that once again her younger sister had preceded her. "It's true you get to be first to bring in the tree," she had remarked as they made the famous Bergstrom strudel earlier that day. "But I will get to be the newlywed until Richard marries, which means I will have more turns than you."

Sylvia was in such good spirits that she had conceded Claudia's point and pretended to be annoyed that her term as the most recent bride might soon end. She did not mention that Harold did not seem to be in much of a hurry, and that if he didn't propose soon, Richard might very well be old enough to marry before Claudia did.

With the rest of the family wishing them good luck from the back door, Sylvia and James headed out, stopping first at the barn for the ax, a coil of rope, and the toboggan. "Give you a ride?" James offered, inclining his head to the toboggan, his face lighting up with his smile.

"This is for the tree," Sylvia reminded him, placing a mittened hand close to his around the towrope.

A thick blanket of snow as soft as powder had fallen overnight, and though the sky was concealed behind thick clouds, the air was clear and still. They walked in a companionable silence until James stopped short at the base of a thin white pine. "How's this?"

"It's tall enough, but the branches are too sparse," replied Sylvia. "I like a fuller tree, don't you? The ballroom is so large, if we don't have a full tree, it disappears in the space."

"Then let's keep looking." James gave the rope a tug and they continued on. "In my parents' house, my father always wanted a floor-to-ceiling tree, but my mother preferred a small one to stand on a tabletop. She said that was the way her family had always done it, and to please her, my father went along with it. Over the years they collected too many ornaments to fit on one small tree, but instead of getting a larger one, they chose two small trees and kept them in different rooms. By the time I was in school, we had small trees on tabletops in almost every room of the house. When visitors came, my next-oldest sister and I would lead tours to make sure they didn't miss any of them."

Sylvia smiled at the image of her beloved husband as a boy on Christmas morning. "We could do that instead if you like, choose several little trees instead of one large."

"No, this is the Bergstrom home and we'll do it the Bergstrom way."

"This is the Compson home now, too." Sylvia linked her arm through his. "Compson children will be born here and live here. We must give Compson traditions their pride of place."

"Some Compson traditions," James conceded. "I will miss Christmas Eve church services and staying home Christmas morning, opening presents in my pajamas."

Sylvia laughed. "Maybe we could try that next year." She paused and gestured to a tree several paces to the left. "What about that one?"

James left the toboggan behind and broke a trail through the snow. "It looks great, all right," he said, reaching out to touch the middle limbs. "It's full enough, but the branches are too slender. They won't hold much weight."

He demonstrated how easily they bent, and Sylvia could picture the whole tree slumping under the load of ornaments and garlands. "We need something sturdier," agreed Sylvia. "That's more important than its appearance, unless we want to be sweeping broken glass off the ballroom floor for the whole twelve days of Christmas."

They returned to the toboggan and ventured deeper into the stand of conifers. As they walked along, side by side, passing the stumps of past Christmas trees, Sylvia thought of all the Bergstrom women who had made this journey before her. Once they had been as young and hopeful and as full of love for their husbands as she.

"James," she said suddenly. "Promise me you'll never leave me."

"I promised you that when I married you."

"Promise me again."

He stopped and took both her hands in his, amused. "I, James Compson, promise you, Sylvia Bergstrom Compson, my lawfully wedded wife, that nothing on earth could compel me to leave you."

"Not even a war?"

He hesitated. "If we do get pulled into the war in Europe, I might not have a choice. You know that."

"Promise me you won't enlist. Wait until you're drafted. Promise me you'll go only if you have no other choice."

"You're asking me to make promises about something that might not happen." No trace of amusement remained in his face. "What if I have no choice but to enlist? What if it's my duty?"

"Make your duty be to me," Sylvia implored. "To this family. I lost two uncles to the Great War, and I know how my father's service haunts him. I don't want that for you. For us."

"Sylvia—"

"Please, James."

He fell silent, gathering up the rope to the toboggan. "All right," he said quietly. "I won't enlist unless it's what I have to do to protect you, to protect this family. What I ask in return is that you allow me to decide when that time has arrived."

She longed for him to correct his speech, to say that he had meant to say "if" instead of "when," but he did not. "Very well," she said. "Let us pray that time never comes."

He handed her part of the toboggan rope and they continued on.

Soon James halted and indicated a tree a few yards ahead. "How about that one?"

In amazement, Sylvia took in the blue spruce from trunk to highest bow. It was the most magnificent tree she had ever beheld. Their journey had taken them off the usual footpaths into a section of the Bergstrom woods she rarely visited, but still she wondered how she could have missed this tree before. Somehow, she thought, she should have known it was here.

"It's beautiful," she breathed. And it was—strong and full and tall. Perhaps too tall. "It looks about forty feet high."

"I would have guessed forty-five."

Sylvia smiled. "We'd never get that back to the house. We'd have to bend it in half to fit it in the ballroom, and even then it might still brush the ceiling."

James grinned, agreeing. "Pity, though. It's a beautiful tree."

"It's unfortunate we can't just lop off the top."

James studied the tree. "Who says we can't?"

"Common sense. You'd have to climb all that way carrying the ax, and then—"

James picked up the coil of rope, shouldered the ax, and headed for the base of the tree.

"James, no." Sylvia caught him by the sleeve of his coat. "Have you lost your mind? You could fall and break your neck."

"I've climbed a few trees in my day."

"But you're no lumberjack. Don't be foolish. There are other trees."

He placed a hand on a lower branch. "Not like this one."

Sylvia imagined the top of the tree crashing to the ground, her husband close behind. She pictured it falling the wrong way, pinning her beneath its weight. "We could both get very badly hurt; you do realize that, don't you?"

He brushed her cheek and grinned. "Sweetheart, have a little faith."

Sylvia threw up her hands and backed away. Even

burdened by the rope and ax, James scaled the blue spruce with remarkable speed. Sylvia could not tear her eyes from him as he climbed, as if her line of sight held him aloft, and if she looked away for the barest instant, he would tumble to the ground. Soon only bits of his clothing were visible through the thick branches—the heel of his brown boot, the red wool scarf she had knit him.

Then she heard the chopping sound of metal biting wood and, minutes later, a shout of warning.

Instinctively she flung up an arm to shield her face as the top of the tree seemed to hang suspended in the air for a moment, before it tipped, deceptively slowly, and plummeted to the ground. A smaller shape followed.

Snowdrifts muffled the sound of two impacts.

Sylvia found that she was holding her breath, and that she had looked away. Frantically she searched the tree until she spotted James climbing down, the coil of rope upon his shoulder. The ax. He had tossed down the ax rather than carry it. The height, her worry—all had deceived her into misjudging the size of the second object to fall.

Sylvia ran to him and flung her arms around him just as his feet touched solid ground. "Never do that again, understand? You scared me half to death."

James regarded her, surprised. "I got you the perfect tree, didn't I?"

"You're more important to me than any tree."

"I'm glad to hear it."

Sylvia was still trembling, but she followed James to the fallen treetop and helped him raise it. It was undamaged, as full and perfectly shaped as it had seemed from far below. They loaded it on the toboggan and tied it down with the rope.

"We'll take this part back for everyone else to see," said James as they pulled the toboggan toward home. "We'll know what it really is—just a small part of something greater than anyone else can imagine."

"And the tree will keep growing," Sylvia added. They were not leaving only a stump behind. Their tree would continue to grow and if all went well, it would one day regain its former height. In twenty years, perhaps, they could return to the same tree—but surely they would no longer be the most recently married couple by then. If someone chose that tree again, it would have to be another pair of newlyweds passing on the Bergstrom traditions.

Together they pulled on the towrope and brought back their first Christmas tree to the family awaiting them inside in the warmth and light.

Sylvia and James chose the Bergstrom Christmas tree for three more seasons.

By their fourth Christmas as husband and wife, the anticipated additions to the family—a baby, Claudia's beau Harold—had not come, but otherwise the family's fortunes had prospered since their wedding day. Through the years, Richard's wanderlust had grown, and when he was sixteen, he finally persuaded their father to allow him to attend a young men's academy in Philadelphia. A few days after the term began, he wired home with the astonishing news that he had found Andrew and that they had resumed their close friendship. Sylvia was delighted that her brother had a friend at school, especially one who knew the city well, but she missed Richard terribly. Still, she usually kept her lonely worries to herself. It was the autumn of 1943, and with so many families losing brothers and sons every day, she had no right to complain when her brother was merely away at school.

That year she looked forward to Christmas with greater anticipation than ever before. On the day Richard was expected home for the school holidays, the manor buzzed with expectation and excitement. All day Sylvia paced around, taking care of last-minute preparations but rarely far from a window, looking out through the falling snow for her brother. Suddenly one of the cousins ran downstairs from the nursery shouting that a car was coming up the drive. Sylvia ran to the foyer, threw open the front door—and discovered that Richard had not come alone. She would not have minded if Andrew had accompanied him, but instead she found herself gaping at a small figure standing so shyly behind Richard that she might have been attempting to hide. The biggest blue eyes Sylvia had ever seen peered up at her from beneath a white fur hood, but nearly all of the rest of a small, pale face was hidden behind a thick woolen muffler.

Richard laughed, kissed his sister on the cheek, and guided his companion indoors.

That was how Sylvia met the love of her little brother's life.

Agnes Chevalier easily surpassed Claudia in beauty, her skin so fair and features so delicately perfect that she reminded Sylvia of a dark-haired version of the porcelain doll she had given to Andrew's sister years before. Aside from her loveliness, though, Sylvia concluded within hours of her arrival that it was impossible to understand what her brother saw in the girl. He must have lost his mind, because why else would he have brought her, without a chaperone, all the way from Philadelphia to disrupt the Bergstroms' Christmas? Didn't her own family want her?

Soon Sylvia discovered why they indeed might not,

for as surely as she was the prettiest girl Sylvia had ever seen, she was also the silliest and most spoiled creature ever to set foot in Elm Creek Manor. Worst of all, Richard was obviously besotted with her and indulged her every whim. When she asked for coffee after supper just as Sylvia appeared with the tea service, Richard raced into the kitchen to put on the coffeepot. Even after Richard showed her the estate and explained to her about the business he would run someday, she still referred to the stable as a "barn" and a young horse as a "calf." At eleven o'clock on Christmas Eve, she came downstairs dressed for Midnight Mass—and without missing a beat, Richard escorted her to church even though all his life he had attended Christmas morning services like every other Bergstrom. At breakfast Christmas morning, she insisted that the legendary Gerda Bergstrom's strudel could not possibly taste as delicious as the one Sylvia and Claudia made, which was an entirely ridiculous assertion given that she had absolutely no proof one way or the other.

It irked Sylvia that her father seemed to find the fifteen-year-old child charming, and that James and Claudia seemed unaware of the flaws that were so obvious to Sylvia. James even warned Sylvia that she had better get used to Agnes because she might become a permanent addition to the family. Sylvia shuddered at the very thought, but she resolved to conceal her feelings for Richard's sake. Surely time would prove Richard's interest to be nothing more than a passing fancy, and next Christmas, they would celebrate with just the Bergstrom clan again—and Harold, who always joined them. But that was fine with Sylvia, as he had been Claudia's beau so long he might as well be family.

Sylvia's prediction could not have been more wrong.

In the following spring, Richard responded to the increasing anti-German sentiment in the country by deciding to lie about his age and enlist to prove his patriotism and loyalty. His best friend, Andrew, planned to join up with him. Alerted to their intentions, James and Harold raced to Philadelphia; but arrived too late to stop them—too late as well to prevent Richard and Agnes from marrying. They were no different from so many other young couples faced with separation who married in haste, but Agnes's parents must have consented only reluctantly because she was no longer welcome in their home.

Richard and Andrew were given two weeks before they were due to report for basic training, so Richard accompanied his bride when James and Harold brought her back to Elm Creek Manor. It was only then that Sylvia learned that James and Harold had enlisted, too, because if they did so immediately they were promised that they could remain together.

"It was the only way, Sylvia," James insisted as she reeled from shock. "It was the only way. I'll look after him. I promise you that. I promise we'll all come home safe to you."

There was nothing she could do. He had enlisted; he could not take it back. Nor could she rage at him for breaking the promise he had made to her that Christmas Eve. He had enlisted in order to look after her beloved younger brother. He believed he was doing what was necessary to protect her, to protect their family.

The men's last days at Elm Creek Manor flew swiftly by. Harold asked Claudia to marry him, and she accepted. Sylvia half expected them to wed at the county courthouse before Harold departed, but Claudia said they would marry after he came home. Harold did not seem pleased by the delay, but he could hardly complain considering that it was his fault they had not married years earlier.

Before Sylvia could come to terms with the men's imminent departure, they left for eight weeks of basic training. Sylvia saw her husband one last time before he shipped out, spending more than she could reasonably afford on train fare and a boarding house because she could not bear to stay away. Though James was the only one of them granted overnight leave, she managed to see the other three men at the base before they shipped out. Richard and Andrew were proud and excited about their deployment, while Harold was reticent and wary and wore his fatigues uncomfortably. Only James seemed unchanged, the same beloved man but for the uniform.

She was not the only wife or sweetheart who had come to bid a lover farewell. When it was time to part, she stood behind a chain-link fence with other women as the men marched back to their barracks, some shouting encouragement to the soldiers, others waving and promising to write, many weeping. Sylvia held the men in her sight as long as she could, wanting James and Richard's last glimpse of her to be a comfort to them while they were away. They needed to know she would be strong, that she would hold the family and the business together in their absence. She wanted their last memory of her to be a source of courage and pride.

But Harold ruined it. At the last moment, he sprinted back and linked his fingers with hers through the chain link fence. "Will you give Claudia a message?"

Sylvia nodded. "Of course. Anything."

"Will you ask her to wait for me?"

At first Sylvia was confused. "I thought she accepted your proposal."

"Yes, but—" He hesitated. "I may be gone a long time, and she's a beautiful girl . . ."

Sylvia's heart hardened. "My sister has loved you since she was seventeen years old," she snapped. "It's outrageous that you would doubt her loyalty now. You've had every opportunity to marry her. It's not her fault you squandered your time."

She turned from his startled, wounded face and strode away as quickly as she could. She did not turn around to see if James had witnessed the exchange, if his last memory of her would be of anger and spite.

Within weeks of the men's deployment, Sylvia discovered she was pregnant.

Months passed. Letters from the men were infrequent and cherished, though sometimes they were censored so thoroughly Sylvia could hardly make sense of them. Sylvia threw herself into sustaining her household, volunteering for the war effort however she could, organizing scrap metal drives, and buying war bonds—anything. She would have joined the WACs or moved to Pittsburgh and taken a job in one of the factories that had been turned over to war production if she had not been needed at home to manage Bergstrom Thoroughbreds. And if she had not thought it might endanger the baby.

She thanked God for the baby, for a piece of James she carried with her always. His child gave her hope, a future to look forward to. By late autumn, her morning sickness had eased, but no one looking at her would have guessed she was expecting. Claudia told her to count her blessings, but Sylvia longed for a round belly, proof that the child was real and alive and growing. Once, when the last brown leaves had fallen from the trees in the winds of early winter, Sylvia confided to her sister that she would be devastated if James did not return home in time to hold his newborn child. Claudia told her not to worry. She had heard on the radio that the Allies had made so many gains in Europe that the war would be over by Christmas. Sylvia prayed she was right.

December came, with no sign that the war would end soon. Sylvia devoted herself to managing the business and the household—and her young sister-in-law, who tested Sylvia's patience with her tearfulness and need for consolation. Sylvia feared for her husband and brother too, but she did not pace frantically on the veranda if the postman was late, or dissolve into sobs if a wistful romantic song played on the radio. She knew they had to be strong, to accept without complaint their hardships and loneliness. Nothing they faced at Elm Creek Manor could compare to what their men endured.

Sylvia would have thought a girl as anxious as Agnes would have avoided stories from the front lines, but she dragged Sylvia and Claudia to the theater in Waterford at least once a week to watch the newsreels. The tension in the audience mirrored Sylvia's own as scenes of battles flashed upon the screen; she scanned every soldier's face for James and Richard and Andrew—even Harold. She worried about his safety, too, for Claudia's sake. She had not passed on his last message to her sister. What good would it have done them? What he had meant as a profession of love seemed to question her fidelity. Sylvia thought it a kindness to forget he had ever spoken.

Watching the newsreels provided the Bergstrom women with an odd sort of comfort, allowing them a glimpse into their men's lives and, in knowing what they endured, helping to share their burden. Newsreels of other women's husbands and sweethearts sufficed when they had no word from their own. Letters were their lifeline, but weeks often passed between letters from the Pacific, then several would arrive at once, their dates often spanning several weeks.

If Claudia were in an especially pensive mood, she would skip the news and arrive only in time for the feature, but Agnes studied the newsreels as unflinchingly as Sylvia. Over time, Sylvia developed a grudging respect for the girl. She had stolen a peek at several of Agnes's letters to Richard, and was surprised to find not one word of complaint, only loving encouragement and amusing descriptions of how she spent her days. Agnes joined Sylvia in all of her volunteer activities, and although she couldn't sew to save her life, she could knit with impressive speed and never dropped a stitch. Although her clothes, her speech, and her general unfamiliarity with all things practical indicated that she had led a life of privilege before marrying Richard, she had somehow learned frugality along the way, for she darned socks and mended torn sweaters so well that her repairs were nearly invisible. If she came upon a garment that had been outgrown or could not be mended, she unraveled the stitches, wound the yarn into balls, and knit socks and washcloths for the Red Cross to give to soldiers.

Perhaps this was the side of Agnes that had won Richard's heart.

Two days before Christmas, Sylvia's longing for her husband became almost too much to endure. She sat in the front parlor with Claudia and Agnes, stroking her swelling abdomen and dreaming of James holding their baby. Claudia cut templates for her wedding quilt and mused about her gown, while Agnes's knitting needles provided accompaniment to "I'll Be Home for Christmas" on the radio.

Sylvia couldn't bear it. "Turn that off," she ordered. Claudia paused in the middle of a description of possible bodice designs and stared at her. Sylvia hauled herself from her chair and snapped off the radio. "I can't listen to that anymore. They aren't coming home for Christmas, so what's the use of dreaming about it?"

"Sometimes dreams are all we have," said Agnes softly.

It was exactly the sort of thing Sylvia might have expected her to say. Sylvia needed more than dreams. She needed James beside her. She needed Richard home and safe.

"What we need is a Christmas miracle," said Claudia. "For the war to end. If ever we ought to pray for peace on earth, this is the time."

"The war will end when we win," said Sylvia tiredly. "However long it takes, however many lives it takes."

They fell silent. Embarrassed by her outburst, Sylvia was about to turn the radio back on when Claudia spoke. "We haven't done anything to prepare for Christmas."

"We sent the boys their packages," said Agnes.

"Yes, but we've done nothing around here." Claudia gathered up her quilt pieces and set them aside. "We should make cookies from some of Great-Aunt Lucinda's old recipes."

"We don't have enough sugar rations," Sylvia pointed out.

"Then at least we should decorate." Claudia rose and reached for Agnes's hand. "Come on. We need something to remind us of the joy and hope of the season. Let's get those boxes out of the attic. Not you, Sylvia. You shouldn't carry anything heavy in your condition. Sit and rest."

"I've been sitting and resting all day," Sylvia grumbled, but her interest had been kindled. When Claudia and Agnes did not immediately return with the decorations, she went to the kitchen and checked the pantry for flour, sugar, and spices. She already knew they had plenty of apples down in the cellar. The ample harvest that year had been a mixed blessing, for with the men away, their abundant crop had been too much for the four remaining Bergstroms to harvest on their own. Rather than allow the apples to rot on the ground, they took enough for themselves and sent word throughout the town that anyone willing to pick the apples was welcome to take away whatever he could carry. Friends and neighbors as well as townsfolk they scarcely knew accepted the offer, and some left gifts of surplus produce from their own gardens in trade. One sunny afternoon, an entire Boy Scout troop arrived and harvested bushel after bushel of the ripe fruit. Each boy took some home to his family, but most were delivered to hospitals and soup kitchens throughout the state. Many more were sent to VA hospitals or USO outfits, nourishing wounded soldiers as well as those who had not yet seen battle.

Apples the Bergstroms had in abundance, and they had enough of the remaining ingredients to spare for one strudel. Tomorrow, Sylvia resolved, she and Claudia would make one. Perhaps Agnes would like to learn.

She returned to the foyer just as Claudia and Agnes began unpacking the decorations. She joined them, stopping by the parlor first to open the door and turn on the radio so they could listen as they worked. A quiet happiness filled her as she unwrapped the familiar trappings of the holiday—Richard's soldier nutcracker, the paper angels she and Claudia had made in Sunday school, Great-Aunt Lucinda's Santa Claus cookie jar. They had never found the ruby-and-gold glass star for the top of the tree; the highest bough had remained bare every year since it went missing. Sylvia had been sorry to see the traditional search for the star go, but this year, there were no children in the house to hunt for it anyway—unless, she thought saucily, they counted Agnes.

"Look what I found," said Agnes, peering into a white cotton pillowcase, plumped full as if a lumpy pillow were inside. For a moment, Sylvia thought she had discovered the star, but the colorful pieces she took from the pillowcase were fabric, not glass. "Is this a quilt?"

A lump formed in Sylvia's throat and she looked to Claudia, who stood frozen in place. "Pieces of one, anyway," said Sylvia, when her sister did not reply.

Agnes laid the Feathered Star blocks on the marble floor. "These are lovely."

"Our great-aunt made them," said Claudia quietly. She resumed setting candles into brass holders on the windowsills.

Agnes reached into the pillowcase again. "This appliqué is lovely," she said, admiring the holly plumes. "If I thought I could make something so beautiful, I might be tempted to learn to quilt."

"It's not as easy as it looks," said Sylvia.

Agnes regarded her mildly. "I didn't say it looked easy."

"I could teach you to quilt," offered Claudia.

"No, thank you." Agnes gave the quilt blocks one last admiring look before returning them to the pillowcase.

Sylvia was disappointed that Agnes had not emptied the makeshift bag. Claudia might not offer quilting lessons so freely after Agnes gave her opinion of those Variable Star blocks. "Why didn't your great-aunt finish?"

"She wasn't the only one to work on it," said Sylvia. "My mother did the appliqué, and Claudia pieced five other stars. They're probably still in the case if you want to look."

"Didn't you make anything for the quilt?"

"Why, no." Sylvia glanced at Claudia, who was feigning disinterest as she unpacked ornaments from the green trunk. "Claudia said she wanted to finish it herself, so I—"

"You may complete it if you like," said Claudia. "I have too much sewing for my wedding to spend time on another project. It was never that important to me anyway. I haven't touched it in ten years."

Sylvia knew she had not; Sylvia had not seen one thread of the quilt since Claudia put the fragments away on that Christmas Day so long ago. How the pieces had ended up in a pillowcase in the trunk with the Christmas decorations, she had no idea.

Uncertain, Sylvia studied her sister. "You honestly wouldn't mind? You said you never wanted to see any part of this quilt again. You said you couldn't bear to be reminded of the worst Christmas ever."

Claudia laughed shortly. "I think we would all agree that *that* Christmas hardly deserves that title anymore."

"Don't say such things." Agnes rose, holding the pillowcase carefully, as if it contained something precious and fragile. "This may be a lonely Christmas, but it is still Christmas. Sylvia, I agree that you should finish the quilt. It will help put us all in the holiday spirit."

Agnes held out the pillowcase, and when it seemed that she would stand there with her arm outstretched forever unless Sylvia took it, she did so. "I couldn't possibly finish it by Christmas Day."

"I might not know how to quilt, but I do know that much." Agnes smiled and returned to the blue trunk. "Why not set yourself a goal of finishing it before next Christmas so that you and James can play with the baby upon it beneath the Christmas tree?"

Sylvia's heart warmed at the image that played in her mind's eye. The Christmas tree, blooming with light and color. James, home and safe, beaming proudly at their child. Their precious son or daughter, with bright eyes, a rosebud mouth, sitting up or crawling—goodness, what would the baby be doing at this time next year? The Christmas Quilt, a soft comfort beneath them all.

Sylvia ached to begin, but she hesitated. "The decorations—"

"We can finish without you," Agnes assured her.

"You should be sitting with your feet up anyway," remarked Claudia, without looking up from her work.

Sylvia was about to retort that she wasn't an invalid, but she reconsidered. It was, after all, the perfect excuse. "I'll be in the sitting room," she said, and went off with the pillowcase in hand to find her sewing basket.

In her favorite room just off the kitchen, Sylvia spread out the blocks on the floor and studied them. The fabrics remarkably had not faded through the years; the colors were as bright and merry as the day Great-Aunt Lucinda chose them so long ago. The Feathered Star blocks and holly plumes were as lovely as she remembered, and since Claudia's Variable Stars used many of the same fabrics, it might be possible to scatter them among the finer handiwork so that their flaws would not be apparent. But what should Sylvia's contribution be? What could she add to help bring the disparate pieces together harmoniously?

Sylvia thought back to the Christmas when Lucinda had set aside the quilt for the last time in order to help with the sewing for cousin Elizabeth's wedding. The Bergstrom women had made Elizabeth a beautiful gown and a Double Wedding Ring bridal quilt embellished with floral appliqués. A few weeks before the wedding, little Sylvia found Great-Aunt Lucinda working on a new quilt, a pattern of concentric rectangles and squares, one half of the block light colors, the other dark. It resembled the Log Cabin block so closely that at first Sylvia mistakenly believed them to be practice blocks for her quilting lessons.

But Great-Aunt Lucinda told her that this was another quilt for cousin Elizabeth, a sturdy scrap quilt for everyday use, something to remember her great-aunt by. "This pattern is called Chimneys and Cornerstones," she explained. "Whenever Elizabeth sees it, she'll remember our home and all the people in it. We Bergstroms have been blessed to have a home filled with love from the chimneys to the cornerstone. This quilt will help Elizabeth take some of that love with her."

Sylvia nodded to show she understood. It did not matter that these were not Log Cabin blocks. The upcoming wedding had left her so morose that the further postponement of her quilting lessons had lost the power to disappoint her.

Great-Aunt Lucinda traced a diagonal row of red squares, from one corner of the block to the opposite. "Do you see these red squares? Each is a fire burning in the fireplace to warm Elizabeth after a weary journey home."

"You made too many," said Sylvia, counting. "We don't have so many fireplaces."

She laughed. "I know. It's just a fancy. Elizabeth will understand. But there's more to the story. Do you see how one half of the block is dark fabric, and the other is light? The dark half represents the sorrows in a life, and the light colors represent the joys."

"Then why don't you give her a quilt with all light fabric?"

"I suppose I could, but then she wouldn't be able to see the pattern. The design appears only if you have both dark and light fabric."

"But I don't want Elizabeth to have any sorrows."

"I don't either, love, but sorrows come to us all. But don't worry. Remember these?" Great-Aunt Lucinda touched several red squares in a row. "As long as these home fires keep burning, Elizabeth will always have more joys than sorrows."

The meaning of the quilt had comforted Sylvia as a child, and now, the memory of Great-Aunt Lucinda's love warmed her heart once again. Cousin Elizabeth had journeyed so far that none of the Bergstroms expected to see her again. God willing, Sylvia would see her husband and brother, and Andrew and Harold. Until then, the Bergstrom women would keep the home fires burning. They would keep a candle in the window to welcome their loved ones home.

And while they waited, Sylvia would stitch her joys and sorrows into the Christmas Quilt, using the fabrics of the women who had gone before her to make the Log Cabin blocks she had never had the chance to make with her great-aunt.

She chose red scraps for the center of the Log Cabin

blocks and sewed rectangles of evergreen and snowy white around them, alternating the colors so that one half of the block was light and the other dark, divided along the diagonal. Sometimes the greens were so dark they appeared almost black, and often an ivory or muslin scrap slipped in among the white. The variations added depth and dimension to her work, subtle nuances that enhanced the beauty of the clearer hues.

Lost in reminiscences of Christmases past and the Christmas future she yearned for, Sylvia passed the day in sewing and reflection. Later, when hunger beckoned her from the sitting room, she discovered her home transformed by the loving attention of her sister and sister-in-law. All the old familiar decorations adorned the foyer, the ballroom, the other nooks and corners where so many memories lingered. Candles glowed softly in the windows; wreaths of holly and ivy graced the doors.

"We need a tree," said Agnes as they prepared a simple dinner for themselves and Sylvia's father, who was in bed recovering from a bout of the flu and needed his meal brought up to him on a tray.

Claudia glanced out the window. The sun touched the horizon, and the elm trees along the creek cast long shadows that stretched across the snowy ground and brushed the manor as if longing to come inside into the warmth. "We can't look for a tree tonight," she said. "It's too late. It will be dark by the time we finish dinner."

"Tomorrow, then," said Agnes cheerfully. "That's the proper day, isn't it? Richard told me your family always chooses the tree on Christmas Eve."

Sylvia wondered what else Richard had told her.

After dinner, she returned to the sitting room to work on the quilt. Claudia and Agnes joined her, each tending to her own work, but not so absorbed that they did not pause from time to time to admire Sylvia's progress.

The next morning, Sylvia returned to the Log Cabin blocks after breakfast and sewed until Claudia suggested they make strudel. The sisters set Agnes to peeling apples while they mixed and kneaded the dough, then took up their paring knives to assist her while the dough rested.

"In Philadelphia, my parents employed a chef who had trained in Paris," Agnes said as they sliced the peeled apples into uniform pieces. "Every year he made the same dessert, a rolled cake decorated to resemble a yule log."

"Bûche de noël," said Sylvia, her mother's words suddenly rising to the forefront of her memory.

"Yes, that's what he called it." Agnes gave her a curious look. "Have you ever made one?"

"Never, but my mother's family served it every year when she was a child."

Agnes nodded thoughtfully, and Sylvia suddenly wondered what her mother would have thought of the young woman. They might have more in common than Sylvia had ever suspected.

When the apple filling was prepared and the dough had rested, Sylvia and Claudia demonstrated how to stretch it. Agnes was impressed, but too worried about ruining the dough to try her hand at it. Sylvia was willing to let her be, but Claudia would not tolerate such reluctance. "You're a Bergstrom woman, and Bergstrom women need to learn this recipe," she insisted. "Besides, Sylvia really ought to get off her feet and I can't finish on my own."

Sylvia knew her sister could manage perfectly well, but she said nothing because the fib finally convinced

Agnes to roll up her sleeves and try. Standing opposite Claudia, she reached beneath the dough and pulled it toward her with the backs of her hands, mirroring her sister-in-law. At first her efforts were so timid that she made no difference at all, but with encouragement from Claudia and teasing from Sylvia, she grew bolder. The dough had nearly doubled in area when Agnes's wedding ring snagged on the dough, tearing it.

"You should have removed your jewelry first," said Sylvia, leaving her stool to help Claudia seal the gap.

"Never," said Agnes. She closed her right hand around her left fingers so fiercely that Sylvia and Claudia laughed. Agnes worked more carefully after that, but she still tore the dough twice more before it reached the edges of the table.

Before long the strudel was in the oven baking, filling the kitchen with the enticing aroma of apples and cinnamon. "It smells divine," said Agnes, inhaling deeply as she swept up apple peelings from the floor.

"It does," Claudia agreed, "but it doesn't smell half as wonderful as Gerda Bergstrom's did."

"How would you know?" demanded Sylvia.

Claudia looked at her, surprised. "I suppose I don't," she said. "I've heard it repeated so often I assumed it was true."

Sylvia laughed.

"Now that we've finished the strudel, should we set out to find a tree?" asked Agnes.

Sylvia's mirth vanished. "We can't leave the house while the strudel's baking. It might burn."

"We don't all have to go," said Claudia. "One of us could stay behind."

"It would take all our combined strength to bring in

a tree," countered Sylvia. "You've never done it, so you don't know. It's a heavy load to haul on the toboggan, even with a strong man at your side."

Agnes shrugged. "So we'll pick a smaller tree. We can't have Christmas without a tree."

Sylvia thought back to the four Christmases of her marriage, to the four times she and James had ventured out into the woods to search for the perfect Christmas tree. None of the later searches had been as dramatic as the first, but each had been memorable in its own right. Each blessed them with a revelation about their marriage—how they worked together, made decisions, showed respect, disagreed—some facet of their relationship that had been present all along, brought to the surface for them to accept with joy, or to resolve to change. After sharing so much with James every Christmas Eve of her married life, she could not bear to have anyone else take his place at her side, not even a sister.

"It is a Bergstrom family tradition that the most recently married couple chooses the tree," said Sylvia. "James is not here, I can't bring in a tree alone, and I don't want to go with anyone else. Rather than break family tradition, I've decided against having a tree this year."

Claudia peered at her. "So you believe that the most recently married couple, or bride, in this case, should decide whether we have a tree."

"Exactly."

"That sounds reasonable to me."

"Good," said Sylvia, surprised that her sister had conceded so easily.

With a triumphant grin, Claudia turned to Agnes. "It's up to you, then. Should we have a tree this year or not?"

Startled, Sylvia spun to face Agnes. She had forgotten. It was too cruel to admit, but it was sometimes difficult for her to remember that Richard was married, that Agnes was more than a visitor.

"If it's up to me . . ." Agnes avoided Sylvia's eyes. "I would like to have a tree."

Claudia's smile broadened in satisfaction, sparking Sylvia's anger. "You'll have to bring it in yourselves," Sylvia said, and strode off to the sitting room to work on the Christmas Quilt.

She heard them at the back door dressing to go out into the snow, but she did not move from her chair. She worked on the Christmas Quilt, pausing only to take the strudel from the oven—baked to a perfect golden brown—and fix lunch for her father. She placed a bowl of soup, some crackers, and a mug of hot tea with lemon and honey on a tray and carried it up to the library, where her father was reading a book in an armchair in front of the fireplace, wrapped in a blue-and-white Ocean Waves quilt her mother had made long ago.

"Lunchtime," she announced. "Chicken noodle soup and tea with honey."

"Better than any medicine." Carrying his book and holding the quilt around himself, her father joined her at the large oak desk and seated himself in the leather chair as she placed the tray before him. "What are you girls up to down there? I thought I heard the back door open."

"Claudia and Agnes went out for a Christmas tree." Sylvia nudged a stack of business papers out of the way and moved the bowl of soup closer.

"Oh?" Her father brightened. "That's a fine idea. I was beginning to think you girls didn't want a tree this year."

"Agnes had her heart set on it."

"Do you need me to help place it in the stand?"

"We'll manage, Father. Thank you."

"Nonsense." A fit of hoarse coughing interrupted him. "I'm feeling fine."

"Oh, yes, I can see that you are. You should be in bed." At his warning look, she held up her palms. "Fine. You're on the mend. I'm not going to argue with you."

"You're the one who should be in bed," he pointed out, indicating her abdomen with a nod.

"Now *that* is nonsense," said Sylvia, dismissing his advice with a smile. "I'll let you know when the tree is in place so you can help decorate."

Not long after she returned to her quilt, she heard the back door open. A moment later, Claudia stood in the sitting room doorway, still in her coat and boots. "Sylvia," she said, fighting to catch her breath, "I need your help."

Alarmed, Sylvia hauled herself awkwardly to her feet. "What's wrong? Is Agnes hurt?"

"No, but she's— I can't explain. Just come with me."

Quickly Sylvia threw on some old winter clothes of James's, having outgrown her own coat, and followed her sister outside. They trudged through the snow toward the largest stand of evergreens, following the narrow trail Claudia and Agnes had broken earlier.

They had not ventured far. They were still within sight of the manor when Sylvia spotted Agnes's coat and hood through the bare-limbed elms on the other side of the creek. The young woman stood fixed in place, gazing up into the branches of a Frazier fir. It was full, tall, and straight, and as they drew closer, Sylvia could see why Agnes had chosen it.

"What's the matter?" Sylvia asked, lowering her voice. "Is she afraid she'll hurt herself with the ax? Do you need me to do it?"

"You're welcome to try, if she'll let you."

As they reached Agnes, Sylvia realized that the emotion in her sister's manner was exasperation, not worry. "Agnes?" she asked carefully. "Is something wrong with the tree?"

"No." Agnes stared up at it, her expression unreadable. "It's perfect."

Sylvia looked around for the ax and spotted it on the toboggan. "Then let's cut it down and take it inside."

"No!" Agnes caught Sylvia by the coat sleeve before she could lift the ax. "Don't you see? There's a bird's nest up there."

She pointed, and Sylvia followed the line of her finger to a spot just above the midsection of the tree. After a moment's scrutiny, she was able to discern a nest of twigs, brown leaves, and straw hidden within the spruce branches.

"I told her it's abandoned," said Claudia. "All the birds have flown south for the winter."

"Not all of them," countered Agnes. "Some chickadees don't. Neither do owls and woodpeckers."

"What sort of bird made that nest?" asked Sylvia.

Agnes hesitated. "I don't know."

"Then it most likely belonged to a robin who left for sunnier skies months ago." Claudia shook her head. "It's almost certain that's an uninhabited nest."

"*Almost* certain," said Agnes. "I don't want to destroy the home of a living creature if we can't do any better than 'almost.' Even if the bird did migrate, what will it think when it returns home in the spring and discovers its home is gone?"

Sylvia had never given much thought to what birds thought, or even if they did. "Perhaps the bird would be glad to have the excuse to build a nice, new nest in a tree deeper in the woods."

Incredulous, Agnes looked at her. "Is that how you would feel? Is that how you think the boys would feel if they came home from the war and found that we had torn down Elm Creek Manor and moved into the old Nelson farmhouse because it was closer to town?"

Claudia threw up her hands. "This is so far beyond reasonable that I don't think the word has been invented yet to properly describe it."

Agnes, hurt and close to tears, turned her gaze back to the tree. Sylvia saw that she was biting the inside of her cheek to keep from crying.

"I have a solution," she said carefully. "Why don't you pick another tree, one without a nest in it?"

"No." The set of Agnes's jaw showed that she was resolute. "It has to be this one. I knew the moment I saw it."

"But—" Sylvia threw Claudia a helpless glance, but Claudia just shook her head. "We have so many trees, and you haven't spent much time looking. I'm sure you'll find another tree just as lovely."

"No, I won't. I didn't set out to find an adequate tree or the most convenient tree. I set out to find the right one, and I did. This is the one I choose. Haven't you ever found something and known in your heart that it was meant to be yours?"

Sylvia had, once. She sighed. "Well, you found it all right, but you can't keep it."

"I know that," said Agnes.

Sylvia thought for a moment. "We could move the nest to another tree."

"You are not climbing a tree in your condition," said Claudia. "Let Agnes do it."

"I don't know how to climb trees," said Agnes defensively. "One doesn't get much practice in a city."

"You know a lot about the migratory habits of the birds of Pennsylvania for a girl who's never climbed a tree."

"Stop bickering," ordered Sylvia. "I'm trying to think." Claudia was right to say Agnes was not being reasonable, but Sylvia had never seen the younger girl dig in her heels before, and she had to admit it was a change she approved of. She also sensed that something else lay beneath the surface of Agnes's insistence. Somehow the fate of the absent bird, their men overseas, and Agnes's own exile from her family home had become intertwined in the young woman's mind, and although Sylvia didn't quite understand it, she longed for a solution that would bring peace to Agnes's troubled heart and restore contentment to the family.

A light gust of wind stirred the trees, sending a light dusting of snow upon Agnes's fir. The tiny crystals glittered like diamonds in the midday sun.

Suddenly it came to her. "Let's decorate the tree out here."

The others stared at her, Claudia bewildered, Agnes hopeful. "Out here?" echoed Claudia.

"Yes, why not? It's within sight of the house. We can enjoy it from the ballroom windows."

Claudia was aghast. "Hang ornaments that have been in the family for generations on a tree outside in the dead of winter?"

"We don't have to," exclaimed Agnes. "We've already strung popcorn and cranberries and nuts. We can trim the trees with those—"

"And apples, for a bit of color," added Sylvia.

"And candles for the light—"

"Oh, yes, by all means," interrupted Claudia. "What's Christmas without a forest fire?"

"Very well, forget the candles." Agnes beamed at Sylvia. "Will you help me?"

Sylvia smiled. "Of course."

Once Claudia saw they had made up their minds, she resigned herself to Agnes's peculiar choice and would not be left out of the decorating. They went back to the house for the apples, popcorn garlands, and strings of cranberries and nuts, which they wrapped around the Frazier fir by tossing one end of the strings into the highest branches they could reach and unwinding as they walked around the tree. With bits of twine, they tied apples by their stems to the ends of branches, which dipped slightly beneath the weight. Inspired, Sylvia sent Agnes back to the house for cookie cutters, which they used to carve stars and circles from packed snow, frosted shapes they arranged on the boughs like ornaments. Claudia turned out to be quite good at it. Soon she was enjoying herself as much as the others, and she led them in Christmas carols, including a few of her own invention.

"Don't sit under the Christmas tree, with anyone else but me," Claudia sang, and the others burst into laughter. She pretended to be insulted. "Don't laugh. I'm composing a holiday classic."

"I'm sure Glenn Miller can't wait to record it," said Sylvia.

Afterward, they stood back to admire their work. Agnes glowed with happiness, and Claudia admitted that their tree was pretty in its own way. "It's certainly unique," Sylvia agreed, and the women linked arms as they trudged through the snow back to the manor, pulling the toboggan behind them.

The next morning, Sylvia's father felt well enough to accompany the women to church. The mood of the congregation was more subdued than celebratory, more longing than joyful. Sylvia knew that nearly every person gathered there yearned for a brother, father, husband, or son overseas, or was grieving for someone lost to the war. Even the pastor had a brother serving in France, and in his sermon he referred to the men they all missed and their longing for peace.

"We must not give in to despair," the pastor said. "We must have faith that the Lord who loves us will not abandon us. Though far too many of us have sewn gold stars on the service banners displayed in our front windows, though so many of us mourn, we must not believe that God has ceased loving us. He has not forgotten us. In our moments of weakness, we may fear that we walk alone, but we must never forget that God has sent us the light of his love and mercy. The light shines in the darkness, and the darkness shall not overcome it.

"The miracle of Christmas is that in sending to us His only Son, whose birth we celebrate this morning, God kindled a light in the darkness that shrouded the earth, a light that continues to shine brightly and will never be extinguished. Today, my dear brothers and sisters, we are confronted by darkness—the darkness of war, of tyranny, of oppression, of loneliness, of evil manifest in the world. Today, with the entire world at war, this darkness seems very deep indeed, but we must not forget that Jesus Christ brought the light of peace, and hope, and reconciliation into the world, and no darkness shall ever quench it. Each of us must bring light into the world, so that the darkness will not prevail."

Transfixed by his compassionate words, heart aching for her husband, Sylvia found herself fighting back tears of grief and anguish. If James and Richard did not return to her, she did not know how she could endure it. She knew that she could not. She was desperate for the light the pastor had spoken of to shine through the darkness of her life, but she was so afraid, and so lonely. The darkness surrounding her was so opaque she feared no illumination could penetrate it. In silence, she cried out for God's mercy, for the comfort only He could provide.

A hand clasped hers—Claudia's—and she reached out her other hand to Agnes, and then Sylvia understood. They were all lonely and afraid. They had to be light for one another.

The three Bergstrom sisters held fast to one another for the rest of the service. They held hands still as they rose to sing the final hymn. As the last notes of the song faded away, Sylvia felt peace settling into her heart, and she whispered a prayer of thanks for her two sisters. They would sustain one another, whatever came, whatever darkness threatened them.

Back at home, the family breakfasted on the famous Bergstrom apple strudel and coffee, and then gathered in the ballroom to exchange gifts. Sylvia's eyes filled with tears when she unwrapped Agnes's gift—a beautifully knitted cap, receiving blanket, and booties done in a seed stitch in the softest, finest of blue-and-pink stripes.

"Where did you ever find the yarn for this?" asked Sylvia, fingering the precious garments.

"I found a worn layette in the attic," confessed Agnes.

"Moths had eaten through the blanket, but I washed it thoroughly and most of the yarn was still useable. I wish I could say it was new."

"Nonsense," declared Sylvia. "It's as good as new. Better. It has family history."

Agnes was so pleased she blushed.

Later, after the presents were opened and admired, the women read aloud from their men's letters, saved for this occasion so that they would feel as if the family had reunited on Christmas Day. It had taken all of Sylvia's willpower not to tear open James's letter as soon as it had arrived a week before, but now she was grateful she had agreed to Claudia's proposal. The men had been promised a hot Christmas dinner instead of the usual rations, James had written. Turkey with dressing, cranberry sauce, mashed potatoes, green beans, and apple pie for dessert. It wouldn't compare to anything Gerda Bergstrom might have prepared, but to the men hungry for a taste of home, it would seem like a feast for a king.

Harold reported a mild case of dysentery; Richard was learning how to drive a tank. Andrew had sent one letter to them all, thanking them for the pictures of the girls on the back steps of the manor. "I don't have a sweetheart to write home to," he confessed, "so I especially welcome your letters." He promised to look after Richard and thanked Sylvia's father for the memories of the best Christmas he had ever spent, which, he said, would be a comfort to him this season spent in the heat of the South Pacific, far from the snowy forests and fields of home.

Sylvia's father cleared his throat several times as the last letter was read, and when Agnes finished reading, he went alone to the window and gazed outside to the gray sky that spoke of snow to come. Sylvia wished there had been more letters. Cousin Elizabeth had not written for the third or possibly fourth Christmas in a row; Sylvia had lost track. But she knew that what her father longed for most he could not have: for his son to walk in the door that moment, his wife to be standing at his side holding his hand, his brother to be making jokes and teasing the children, his aunt Lucinda and his mother to be holding court in their chairs by the hearth.

"Sylvia," he said suddenly, beckoning to her. "Come take a look at this."

She went to him and looked out the window. Just beyond the elms on the other side of the creek, she saw Agnes's Christmas tree, simply but beautifully adorned. As she watched, she detected movement, and suddenly a doe and fawn emerged from the woods and carefully picked their way through the crust that had formed on top of the snow. They approached the Christmas tree, and the doe stretched out her head to nibble a popcorn garland. Her fawn cautiously bit into an apple.

Sylvia's smile broadened as a flurry of motion heralded the arrival of a flock of chickadees. Soon other birds joined in the feast, and squirrels as well, busily harvesting the popcorn, fruits, and nuts from the Christmas tree.

Claudia and Agnes came to see what engrossed them. "Our tree," Claudia lamented when she understood what was happening, but Agnes laughed out loud.

"I knew that nest wasn't abandoned," she cried. "I knew that tree was still a home to someone."

"If it wasn't before, it is now," remarked Sylvia, and her father chuckled.

"We should make this a new tradition," said Agnes as

they watched the feast. "Every year we should bring in one tree for ourselves and decorate that one for the animals."

Amused, Sylvia asked, "What if next Christmas Richard wants to cut down that tree and bring it indoors?"

"I'll talk him out of it," said Agnes, without a moment's hesitation.

"Next year we will all be together again," said Claudia, with such resolve that for a moment they all shared her certainty that it would be so. "Next Christmas, the war will be over and the boys will be home."

And Claudia and Harold might be the newlyweds, Sylvia thought. It would be their turn to bring in the tree. Their nephew or niece would be enjoying his or her first Christmas, and God willing, in the years to come many cousins would join her, filling the house with love and laughter again.

Let this be our Christmas miracle, Sylvia prayed, watching from the window as the wildlife of Elm Creek Manor enjoyed an unexpected Christmas feast while snow began to fall.

Chapter Five

THE BLESSINGS OF Christmas lingered in Sylvia's heart into the New Year, sustaining her through the difficult last months of the war.

But the Christmas future with her husband and child that she had prayed for did not come to pass. Of the four men they were longing to see that day, only Andrew and Harold returned.

A few months after Christmas, James died attempting to save Richard's life, determined to the end to protect him as he had promised.

The shock of the news sent Sylvia into premature labor. Her daughter, born too soon, fought for life for three days, but eventually slipped away.

Devastated, maddened by grief, Sylvia remembered little of the aftermath. As if looking through a fog of sorrow, she saw herself lying in a hospital bed, holding her baby's small, still body and weeping. She recalled begging the doctors to release her so she might attend the funeral of her father, who had collapsed from stroke, unable to bear the shock of so much loss.

Eventually Sylvia was released from the hospital and sent home. For weeks afterward, she felt as if the world were shrouded in thick woolen batting. Sounds were less distinct. Colors were duller. Everything seemed to move more slowly.

Gradually the numbness that pervaded her began to recede, replaced by the most unbearable pain. Her beloved James was gone, and she still did not know how he had died. Her daughter was gone. She would never hold her again. Her darling little brother was gone. Her father was gone. The litany repeated itself relentlessly in her mind until she believed she would go mad.

A few hesitant visitors from the Waterford Quilting Guild came by to express their sympathies and see what, if anything, they might do to help, but Sylvia refused to see them. Eventually they stopped coming.

The war ended. Harold returned to Elm Creek Manor thinner, more anxious—a pale shadow of the man who had left. Perhaps seeking a distraction or a return to normalcy, Claudia threw herself into planning her wedding. As her matron of honor, Sylvia was expected to help, but though she tried, she could not summon up any interest and had difficulty remembering the details of the tasks Claudia assigned to her.

One day a few weeks before the wedding, Andrew paid an unexpected visit on his way from Philadelphia to a new job in Detroit. Sylvia was glad to see him. He walked with a new limp and sat stiffly in his chair as if still in the service, and although he was pleasant to everyone else, he had barely a cold word for Harold, who seemed to go out of his way to avoid Andrew. Sylvia found this odd, since she had always heard that veterans shared a bond almost like that of brothers. Perhaps seeing each other dredged up memories of the war that were still too painful to bear.

That evening after dinner, Andrew found Sylvia alone in the library. He took her hand and pulled her over to the sofa, shaking from the effort to suppress his anger and grief. He had seen everything from a bluff overlooking the beach where they had been killed. He had been a witness to it all and powerless to help. He offered to tell her how her brother and husband died, but warned her she would find no comfort in the truth.

Without thinking of the consequences, Sylvia told him to tell her what he had seen. Haltingly, every word paining him, he described how Richard had come under friendly fire, how James had raced to his rescue, how he would have succeeded with the help of one more man. How Harold had hidden himself rather than risk his own life. How Andrew had run straight down the bluff to the beach where his friends lay dying, knowing that he would never make it in time.

"I'm so sorry, Sylvia," said Andrew, his voice breaking. "He saved me when we were kids, but I couldn't save him. I'm so sorry."

Sylvia held him as he wept, but she had no words to comfort him.

Andrew left Elm Creek Manor the next morning. Sylvia brooded in silent rage as the days passed and the plans for the wedding continued. Finally, she could keep silent no longer. Her sister had to know the truth about the man she intended to marry.

But to Sylvia's shock and outrage, Claudia denied the truth, blaming Sylvia's accusations on jealousy that Harold had come back and James had not. Torn apart by this unexpected betrayal, Sylvia left Elm Creek Manor that day, unable to bear the sight of the man who had allowed her husband and brother to die, unable to live with a sister who preferred a disloyal lie to the truth. Into two suitcases she packed all she could carry—photographs, letters from Richard and James, the sewing basket she had received for Christmas the year before her mother died. Everything else she left behind—beloved childhood treasures, favorite books, unfinished projects, the Christmas Quilt. Everything except memories and grief.

She intended never to return.

Fifty years later, when she received word of Claudia's death, she tried to find someone else to inherit the manor—a distant relation she had never met, anyone. She even hired a private detective, but his search promptly turned up nothing—so promptly that she sometimes suspected he had not searched as thoroughly as his fees merited. But with no one to pass on the burden to, she returned to Elm Creek Manor as the sole heir to the Bergstrom estate.

And here she would live out her days, no longer consumed by regrets, thanks to the intercession of Sarah and Matt McClure. She would always long for what might have been, but she would also accept with gratitude the blessings that had come to her late in life.

If only Claudia were there to share them with her.

She heard the back door open and Sarah and Matt came in, laughing. "We found a tree," Matt called.

Sylvia rose to join them.

In the back entry, a six-foot blue spruce lay on the floor. "What do you think?" Sarah asked, as she and Matt removed their coats and boots.

"It doesn't look like much, lying down," Sylvia remarked. She glanced at her watch. Bringing in the tree had taken them a respectable hour and a half. That spoke well for the couple—better, in fact, than she had expected. They had clearly not wasted time in argument, nor in indecisiveness, with neither willing to hold to a position for fear of offending the other. Nor had they returned too quickly, indicating that only one of them had chosen the tree and the other had been unwilling to suggest an alternative, or had spoken up only to be ignored. If a husband and wife could not work together in a simple task like choosing a Christmas tree, it did not bode well for the more important decisions they would face in their life together.

Sylvia thought Sarah and Matt would do just fine.

"Shall we set it up in the west sitting room?" asked Sarah.

"All in good time," said Sylvia. "First I need to pay a call on someone I've too long neglected, and I would appreciate a lift."

Sylvia sat on the passenger side of Sarah and Matt's red pickup truck, the pinecone wreath she and her mother had made on her lap. They passed the old red barn Hans Bergstrom had built into the hillside, rounded a curve, and drove downhill along the edge of the orchard. The gravel road narrowed as they entered the woods, bouncing and jolting over the potholes, until they emerged a quarter of a mile later and turned left onto the paved county highway that led to the town of Waterford proper.

"Do you mind telling me where we're going?" asked Sarah. "Or is it a surprise?"

Sylvia gestured toward the road ahead. "Just keep heading into town."

Sarah shrugged and did as she was told.

As they drove north, the rural landscape gave way to planned neighborhoods that had sprung up on the farmland during Sylvia's absence, and a couple of strip malls that looked like every other strip mall one might find in the more urban regions of Pennsylvania. As they approached the heart of town, the buildings showed more age, and more character, though most of the shops Sylvia had frequented as a young woman had been replaced by quirky boutiques, restaurants, and bars catering to the students and faculty of Waterford College.

"Turn here," Sylvia said as they approached Church Street.

A block from the town square, Sylvia asked Sarah to park in the church's lot. As Sylvia gazed through the windshield at the small churchyard enclosed within a low iron fence, Sarah asked, "Do you want me to come with you?"

Sylvia roused herself and unbuckled her seatbelt. "No, dear," she said. "I need a word in private."

Carrying the wreath, she made her way carefully across the parking lot and passed through the gate into the cemetery. Like the parking lot, the walking paths had been cleared of the previous night's snowfall, but a light dusting of snow had blown across the paths since then, and in the footprints left behind Sylvia read the longings of the other mourners who had come to pay respects that day. Few had been buried in that churchyard since the 1950s after the larger cemetery was established east of town, but the Bergstroms owned a family plot, and many generations had been laid to rest in the shadow of the old church steeple.

The lilac bush her father had planted remained, dormant now in the depths of winter but thriving, larger than she remembered. In the spring, the winds would shower her parents' graves with fragrant blossoms. Sylvia gazed down upon the headstone engraved with both of their names, the dates they had died fifteen years apart. They had made the most of the time granted to them, and Sylvia wished she had followed their example. She understood too late how wise they had been.

She said a silent prayer and looked about for the headstone she had seen only once, a few days after her return to Waterford. It was smaller than her parents', low to the ground and engraved only with Claudia's married name, date of birth, and the day she had died. It was simple and modest, chosen by two women from the church, who apologized when they showed it to Sylvia. Claudia had set aside a little money for her burial, they said, but it did not stretch far. If they had known she had surviving family, they would have waited, but as it was they followed Claudia's instructions the best they could. If Sylvia liked, she could replace the headstone with something more suitable.

"No," Sylvia had told them. "This is what she requested, and it will do. Thank you for seeing to it for me."

As she had on that first visit two years before, Sylvia studied the headstone and wondered why Claudia had selected this plot for herself and had buried Harold in the newer, larger cemetery. Why had she not wanted to be interred beside her husband, as their parents had done? Why was Harold's headstone as stark as Claudia's, with no fond epitaph to show the world that he had once been loved?

Sylvia suspected she knew. If Claudia had come to believe the truth about Harold's role in Richard's and James's deaths, Sylvia could not imagine how she had endured living so many years as his wife. Elm Creek Manor was not so large that they could have avoided each other indefinitely. Sylvia knew so little of Claudia's life after her abrupt departure. Agnes had remained at Elm Creek Manor for several years until she left to marry a history professor from Waterford College, but she had told Sylvia very little of those days, probably wishing to spare her pain. Sylvia had so few clues to tell her of the woman her sister had become—a few unfinished quilts, the overgrown gardens, the dilapidated state of the manor—but none of her own words, not one single photograph. Forever Claudia would remain fixed in Sylvia's memory precisely as she was the day their final argument compelled Sylvia from their home.

If only Sylvia had remembered how they had been each other's light in the darkness on the last Christmas of the war. If only she had remembered that, and come home.

"I'm sorry," Sylvia said aloud. "I'm sorry I was too proud to come home. I'm sorry I never had the chance to apologize to you. All these years I've blamed you for driving me away, but that's not why I left, not really. It's not because you married Harold. It's not even because I couldn't bear the sight of him, although it did take me a long time to stop hating him."

Sylvia inhaled deeply, her nostrils stinging from the cold, her breath emerging as a stream of ghostly mist. "I ran away because I was afraid. I didn't think I could endure the daily reminders of the happiness I once had and had lost. Now I know I should have stayed. Together you and I and Agnes could have helped one another bear our burdens. Instead I ran away, but I took my grief with me, and I've regretted it ever since."

She bent down to lay the wreath on Claudia's grave, arranging the red velvet ribbon with care. Then she straightened. "I wish—" She hesitated. "I wish I knew that wherever you are, you've forgiven me."

She murmured a quiet prayer, then turned and made her way back to the waiting truck. Sarah offered her a sympathetic smile as she took her seat, but thankfully did not trouble her with questions.

Back at the manor, Sylvia and Sarah found the Christmas tree still lying on the floor just inside the back entrance. Matt was in the west sitting room, putting the last screws into a metal tree stand he must have purchased earlier that day because Sylvia had never seen it before. He had moved furniture aside to clear a corner of the room for the tree, setting the sewing machine against the wall and stacking the pieces of the Christmas Quilt neatly on the sofa. Boxes of ornaments lay scattered on the floor between the coffee table and the two armchairs by the window.

Matt looked up and smiled as they entered. "Just in time," he said. "Sarah, could you give me a hand with the tree?"

Sylvia scooted out of the way while the young people hefted the tree and carried it from the hallway into the sitting room. She offered directions as they wrestled it into the tree stand, pushing it this way and that until it stood straight and tall. Then they set it back into the corner, rotating the stand so that its best side faced out.

It was a beautiful tree, full and tall and fragrant.

Sylvia nodded her approval as Sarah and Matt stepped back for a better look. "You chose well," she praised them. "I believe you must have found the finest tree in the forest."

"There was another one we liked better, closer to the manor between the creek and the barn," said Sarah. "We decided not to cut it down because there was a bird's nest in it."

Sylvia gave her a long look. "Indeed?"

"The nest looked abandoned to me," said Matt, "but we decided not to disturb it just in case."

"I understand completely," said Sylvia, inspecting the

tree. "I see you had to trim off a bit here," she said, indicating the top of the tree, where the severed trunk was hidden among the boughs. "Was it crooked, or did you think the tree would be too tall?"

"We didn't cut off the top," said Matt. "See how the wood has weathered? The top of this tree was cut off long ago. We just took off the next six feet down."

Sylvia stared at him, then at Sarah. "What you mean is that when you had that arborist out here last spring, he pruned this tree."

Matt shook his head. "No, that's not what I meant. When I say long ago, I mean decades. Maybe between forty and sixty years, but I'm just guessing."

"Fifty-five," murmured Sylvia. It was an unlikely coincidence. Out of all the trees in the forest, Sarah and Matt had just happened to pick the same blue spruce that she and James had chosen? She was too skeptical a soul to believe that.

But how could they have known?

She shook off a quickening of excitement. Coincidence, she told herself firmly. Nothing more.

They strung tiny white lights upon the tree, the candles of Sylvia's childhood gone the way of other hazards they had once accepted with blissful ignorance. As Sarah's CD player serenaded them with carols, they adorned the tree with the beloved, familiar ornaments from Sylvia's youth—the ceramic figurines from Germany, the sparkling crystal teardrops from New York City, carved wooden angels with woolen hair from Italy. Beneath the tree, Sarah arranged the nativity scene Sylvia's grandfather had carved, while Matt placed Richard's soldier nutcracker and Grandmother's green sleigh music box on the table. Sylvia found the paper angels she and Claudia had made in Sunday school, yellowed and curled with age, but so dear to her that she would not dream of leaving them out. She placed them in prominent places high upon the tree, Claudia's on one branch and her own on the opposite side of the tree exactly even with her sister's—not one branch higher, not one lower.

"What should we put on the top of the tree?" asked Sarah, digging through the boxes. "I haven't found an obvious tree topper, like a star or an angel or something."

"For many years, we left the highest bough bare," said Sylvia.

"Why? Is that symbolic of something?"

Loss, Sylvia almost said. "No. For many years we used a red-and-gold glass star, but it went missing one year and we never replaced it."

"I think I know why," said Matt, nodding toward the paper angels with a grin. "You and your sister fought over whose angel should be above the other's. Neither of you would give in, so you didn't use anything."

"You know us too well," said Sylvia lightly, although until that moment, it had never occurred to her to wonder why no one had ever suggested using their angels in that fashion. Perhaps the bare top of the tree was meant to prick the prankster's conscience, an annual reminder that the loss of the star had not been forgotten. More likely, their father had not wanted to suggest anything that might stir up an argument between the sisters.

Just then, Sylvia heard a knock on the back door and a slight pause before it swung open. "Hello," a voice called out. "Is anyone home? Don't bother denying it because we saw the truck in the lot."

Sylvia smiled, recognizing the voice. "We're in here, Agnes."

A moment later, Agnes appeared in the doorway, petite and white-haired, her blue eyes beaming behind pink-tinted glasses. Behind her stood her eldest daughter, Cassandra, a head taller than her mother but with the same blue eyes and raven black hair of her youth, bearing only the first traces of gray. They had both removed their coats, and Cassandra carried a white bakery box.

"Merry Christmas," Agnes greeted them. She embraced Sylvia first, then Sarah and Matt. "What a beautiful tree."

"Sarah and Matt chose it," Sylvia said.

"Naturally. They are the newlyweds." Agnes's merriment turned to surprise as she spotted the Christmas Quilt on the sofa behind Sylvia. "My goodness. You've brought out the Christmas Quilt. You're putting it together at last."

"Yes, well—Sarah is," said Sylvia.

Agnes hurried over and picked up a section of the quilt where Sarah had joined Feathered Stars and holly plumes together. "It's just as lovely as I remembered. Your mother's appliqué was my inspiration, you know. I never forgot her beautiful handiwork. When Joe asked me to marry him, I was determined to learn to appliqué so I could make us a beautiful heirloom wedding quilt."

"I never knew that," said Sylvia.

"You should see it," said Cassandra, smiling at her mother. "It's exquisite. All those beautiful rosebuds."

"I wouldn't say exquisite," said Agnes, but they could all tell she was pleased. "Not with so many mistakes. I was just a beginner, in over my head."

"We all have to start somewhere," said Sarah.

"I couldn't agree more." Agnes gave the holly plumes a fond caress and returned them gently to the sofa. "I'm so pleased to see someone working on this quilt after so many years."

"I'm surprised Claudia didn't throw it out after I left," said Sylvia. "She already associated it with so many unpleasant memories even before I took it up, and I'm sure my departure didn't help. I suppose she was all too willing to pack it away where she would never have to lay eyes on it again."

Agnes peered at her curiously, her pink lenses giving her a rosy, girlish air. "Why, no, that's not the case at all. Claudia worked on it every Christmas that I lived here. She brought it out on St. Nicholas Day and put it away with the rest of the Christmas things on the Feast of the Three Kings. For the few years that I lived here, Claudia fully intended to finish that quilt. Even when times grew difficult between her and Harold, she had her heart set on it."

"But—" Sylvia glanced at the sofa and swiftly counted five Variable Star blocks. "I know she finished those Variable Stars long before I left home."

"I didn't say she made more Variable Stars," said Agnes. "You really didn't notice? How many Log Cabin blocks did you make, Sylvia? Fifteen or twenty?"

"That sounds about right," said Sylvia.

"There are far more than that here," said Sarah. "I counted at least fifty."

"That can't be." Sylvia counted for herself, examining the quality of the needlework as she did. Each of fifty-two blocks was as finely sewn and precise as any block Sylvia had ever made. She could not distinguish between her work and her sister's. "But why would she make more of the pattern I selected rather than her own?"

"Maybe she understood why you chose as you did," said Sarah. "Apparently she trusted your judgment more than you thought. Maybe this was her way of telling you so."

Perhaps it was true. Could it be that all those Christmases Sylvia had spent alone, longing for home, Claudia had been missing her, too?

For Sylvia it was all too overwhelming. She sat down on her favorite chair by the window and stared at the quilt, still in pieces, but coming together thanks to Sarah's loving attention.

"I was afraid, since the Christmas decorations had been stored away so long," she said softly, "that Claudia stopped celebrating Christmas after I left."

"You forgot about the aluminum tree," said Sarah. "Remember? Maybe she couldn't have a traditional Bergstrom holiday on her own, but she did celebrate Christmas."

"And of course there was also the— Oh, my goodness. You're not the only forgetful one." Agnes beckoned her daughter forward. "Cassie, would you give Sylvia her present, please?"

Cassandra placed the white cardboard bakery box on Sylvia's lap. "You should open it now," she said, smiling. "Don't wait for Christmas morning."

Sylvia lifted the lid, and on any other day she would have been astonished to find an exact replica of the famous Bergstrom strudel, but not that day.

"Where on earth did you buy this?" she exclaimed. "I thought the German bakery on College Avenue closed years ago."

"She didn't buy it," said Cassandra proudly. "She made it. And what a production it was!"

"Claudia taught you," said Sylvia in wonder. "She did keep the old traditions."

"Not this one, I'm afraid," said Agnes. "We made strudel the Christmas after you left, but it was such a bleak and empty season without you, without Richard and James, that we couldn't even bear to eat it. We made two and gave them both away. As far as I know, that was the last time anyone made strudel in the Bergstrom kitchen."

"And you remembered the recipe yourself after all those years." When Agnes shook her head, Sylvia said, "Then Claudia wrote it down for you."

"No, in fact, many years after I married, I came by and asked Claudia for it, but she said it had never been written down, and that she had forgotten it. Then, years later, she sent me a Christmas card with the recipe enclosed. She remembered how I had asked for it, and so she got it from a distant relation out west. A second cousin, I believe."

Sylvia could scarcely breathe. "Do you remember her name? When was it she wrote to Claudia?"

Agnes shook her head. "I'm afraid I don't recall."

Sylvia's heart sank. It was, she knew, too much to hope for.

"But I have the letter at home."

In the twenty minutes it took Cassandra to return to her mother's home for the letter, Sylvia's thoughts raced with possibilities. The only relative she knew of who had gone to live "out west" was Elizabeth, and although Sylvia had always called her cousin, as the daughter of Sylvia's great-uncle George, it would have been more accurate to call her a second cousin.

"Oh, what could be keeping Cassandra?" exclaimed Sylvia, pacing in the sitting room.

"It's ten minutes there and ten minutes back," said Agnes soothingly. "She'll be here soon."

"But what if she can't find it?"

Agnes assured her this was unlikely. "Just bring the whole box," she had instructed her daughter, referring to a small cedar chest in which she kept some of Richard's belongings. She had described its location, inside a larger steamer trunk in the back of Agnes's bedroom closet. It ought to be easy to find.

After what seemed to Sylvia an interminable wait, Cassandra returned, the small wooden box in her hands. "I would have been back sooner," she said breathlessly as she gave the box to her mother and pulled off her coat and gloves, "but I had trouble staying on the road in your woods."

"We must do something about that road," said Sylvia. "Well, Agnes? Is it there?"

"It was there this morning when I used the recipe," she said, with a hint of amusement. "Would you please sit down? You're rattling the Christmas ornaments with all of that pacing."

Sylvia dropped into her favorite chair and clasped her hands anxiously while Agnes took a seat in the nearest armchair. Sylvia held her breath as Agnes lifted the lid and removed a folded sheet of yellowed, unlined paper. With a fond smile, she passed it to Sylvia.

Sylvia slipped on her glasses, unfolded the page, and read:

December 6, 1964

Dear Claudia,

How wonderful it was to hear from you after so many years! Your letter was truly the best Christmas gift I am likely to receive. I apologize for not writing to you for so long. I suppose I fell out of habit. (Isn't that a dreadful thing to say about keeping in touch with one's family? That it should be a habit, like getting your daily exercise and remembering to take your vitamins.)

All excuses aside, I promise to send you a longer letter soon, full of news of me and the family. For now, I assure you that we're doing all right out here in sunny Southern California. It's more crowded than it used to be, but the weather is fine and we like it. I'll add you to my Christmas letter list, so check your mailbox in a week or two for more news than you probably can stand about us.

While we're on the subject, would it have hurt you to send some news about yourself and the rest of the family at Elm Creek Manor? How are you? How's Harold? How is my dear little Sylvia and baby brother Richard? I suppose they aren't so little anymore. Please tell Sylvia to write to me and tell her I'm sorry her old cousin hasn't written in so long. It would serve me right if she's forgotten me entirely.

Well, on to the purpose of this letter. I still make the famous Bergstrom strudel every Christmas, winning praise from all who are privileged enough to taste it. I still bake it in the old way, measuring by touch and sight and taste rather than cups and teaspoons. But since you are my sweet little cousin (and perhaps because I have a guilty conscience for neglecting you so long), I made strudel this morning, first measuring my ingredients the old way, and then scooping each one into measuring cups so I could give you the standard measurements you asked for. You'll find the recipe on the back of this page. If my measurements are off a pinch of this or that, please accept my apologies. It probably won't matter. Once you start making the strudel again, I'm sure it will all come back to you.

An early Merry Christmas to you and the family. Please send me a letter packed full of news next time. I know you are capable of it! And make it soon, please. I miss you throughout the year, but especially at Christmas.

With Much Love from Your Cousin,
Elizabeth

Sylvia turned over the letter and found a recipe printed in Elizabeth's neat hand on the back, just as she had promised.

She read the date again. Elizabeth was still in Southern California in 1964, and—Sylvia checked the letter to be sure—she had a family. Elizabeth would be ninety-three if she were still alive, but even if she were not, perhaps her descendants were, regardless of what that private detective had concluded.

"Do you have a return address?" she asked, her voice choked with emotion.

"I'm sorry." Agnes shook her head, sympathetic. "Claudia sent me only that page. I don't know what became of the envelope."

"I understand." Still, it was something to go on, and perhaps that Christmas letter Elizabeth had promised Claudia was somewhere in the manor. Sylvia had not gone through all of Claudia's papers; there were so many. She had every reason to hope an address could be found among them.

"Why don't you show her the rest, Mom?" prompted Cassandra. "The letters and things?"

Agnes went pink. "Oh, not the letters. Not even after all this time. Forgive me, Sylvia, but Richard was a romantic and I couldn't bear for anyone to see them. I don't even know if Joe suspected I had kept this box of things hidden away from him. He wasn't the jealous sort, but even so . . ."

"I won't pry into your romance with my baby brother," said Sylvia, amused. She tried to peer into the box, but the lid blocked her view. "If you have anything in that box of a less private nature, I would be grateful if you would share it with me."

"Certainly." Agnes looked much relieved. "Some of these things you've seen before, but it was so long ago . . ."

She handed over a stack of photographs: Richard and Andrew at school, Richard and Agnes on the front steps of Independence Hall, the three friends laughing on a sunny day along the Delaware River with the Philadelphia skyline behind them. There were other snapshots of Richard alone, including a formal portrait in uniform and other snapshots taken during the war. Sylvia lingered over a photograph of Richard and James in fatigues, arms slung over each other's shoulders, grinning.

"You should keep that one," said Agnes.

Sylvia thanked her softly.

"I suppose you should keep this, too," Agnes remarked, taking from the box a ruby-and-gold glass star, with eight serrated points resembling the Feathered Star blocks

Great-Aunt Lucinda had made so long ago. Only a small chip in one of the golden tips and a hairline seam where a ruby star point had been broken off and reattached with glue distinguished it from the one in Sylvia's memory.

Sylvia stared, shocked into silence. "Where on earth did you find *that*?" she finally managed.

"It was Richard's." Agnes turned the star over in her hands, shook her head in bemusement, and handed it to Sylvia. "I'm not quite sure what the story behind it is. It was December, right before the semester holiday, when I first saw it. We were all out together one day when Andrew suddenly pulled this from his overcoat pocket, repaired exactly as you see it here, gave it to Richard, and said, 'Merry Christmas. I guess you'll win the prize this year.' Richard laughed like it was the funniest joke he had ever heard and said, 'I knew it was you! I knew it all along. I'm never playing poker with you again.' And then they both had a good laugh, and Richard said, 'I can't wait to see their faces when they wake up Christmas morning and find this on the tree.' But he must have forgotten about it in all the commotion because he didn't put it on the tree after all."

"What commotion?" asked Sarah.

Agnes threw Sylvia an embarrassed glance. "Well, in a manner of speaking, I invited myself along when Richard went home from school for the holidays. I met him at the train station with my suitcase and asked if I could join him. He said yes without a moment's hesitation, although I'm sure he knew my parents didn't know of my plans."

"I suspected as much," declared Sylvia. "I knew there must have been a very good reason Richard had not warned me you were coming."

"Warned?" echoed Cassandra.

"Told," Sylvia hastily amended.

"The star was among Richard's belongings from school," Agnes explained. "He packed up so quickly after enlisting that I never took the time to sort through his trunk. After he died—well, it was simply too painful. I opened the trunk to put this box and his uniform and a few other things inside, but I couldn't bear to sort through everything. When I left to marry Joe, I took the trunk with me. A few years later I wanted to see these old photos again, and that's when I stumbled across the star."

"But why didn't you tell us you had found it?" asked Sylvia.

Agnes shrugged. "I didn't know it was missing."

"It isn't missing anymore," said Sarah. "Sylvia, why don't you do the honors?"

Holding the star tenderly, Sylvia rose, went to the Christmas tree, and reached up to the highest bough, where she carefully fixed the ruby-and-gold glass star to the cut tree trunk. It caught the sunlight streaming in through the west windows and sent reflections of red and gold dancing on the walls and ceiling and floor just as it had on the long ago Christmas when Elizabeth had hidden the star beneath her pillow and her father had lifted her up in his strong arms to adorn the tree Uncle William and Aunt Nellie had chosen. From a distance the repair and the chip were hardly noticeable.

She would not go so far as to call any one of the unusual incidents of that day a Christmas miracle. The standard for miracle, she thought, stood a bit higher. But taken as a whole—that business with the tree, hearing from Elizabeth, even in an old letter—well, she would be a fool to ignore the signs. She didn't need a burning bush or Jacob Marley rattling chains in the halls to know when she ought to pay attention.

Very well, Claudia, she thought, smiling. *I can take a hint.*

Sylvia was forgiven. She knew that now. Despite their differences, despite Sylvia's mistakes, her sister loved her, and always had. But the realization was bittersweet because Claudia was not there to enjoy the wonder of that Christmas Eve, the Christmas that joy and hope returned to Elm Creek Manor.

But she could still make a difference in the life of a friend.

Sylvia turned to Sarah. "I've tried reasoning with you. I've hinted and suggested and resorted to subterfuge, but nothing has worked. But you must do it, and I won't take no for an answer."

Sarah stared at her. "No for an answer to what?"

"Visiting your mother for Christmas."

Sarah rolled her eyes. "We've been over this. I thought you understood—"

"I understand, all right. I understand that you and your mother need to make peace before you end up like me—realizing too late where I went wrong and reconciling with memories instead of living, breathing people." She tapped Sarah on the chest, and the young woman was too startled to step back out of the way. "You, young lady, are not going to make that mistake. I'm going to see to it."

Warily, Sarah asked, "What exactly did you have in mind?"

"I'm throwing you out."

"What?"

"Just for the holiday. You're welcome back any time after Christmas."

Sarah shook her head. "This is crazy."

"It's been a crazy sort of day. I suppose it's infectious." Sylvia held up her hands to forestall an argument. "Now, I've made up my mind, so don't argue. I realize I can't force you to visit your mother. I suppose you could sleep outside in the truck or take a hotel room somewhere, but I can only hope you won't be that stubborn."

"Sylvia . . ." Sarah studied her, shaking her head in bewilderment. "Why is this so important to you?"

Sylvia grasped her gently by the shoulders. "Because you are important to me. I don't want you to look back on your life someday and wonder if you did everything you could to make the best possible use of your time on this earth. We all are responsible for bringing the peace of Christmas into the world, Sarah. Starting with our own families."

"I can't make peace with my mother if she doesn't meet me halfway," Sarah retorted, but then she hesitated. "If it means that much to you, I'll try. I'll go see her. But I can't promise that she'll welcome us with open arms."

"As long as you greet her with an open mind, that's all I ask."

"What about you?" asked Sarah. "You can't spend Christmas here alone."

Sylvia shrugged. "We'll have our celebration tonight. You and Matthew can leave for your mother's place first thing in the morning."

"Sounds good to me," offered Matt.

Sarah was not satisfied. "That still leaves you alone on Christmas Day."

"Sylvia can spend Christmas at my home," said Agnes. "With me and the girls and the grandkids. There's always room for one more."

"No, there isn't," said Sylvia, remembering their phone conversation earlier that day. "So you and your family should spend Christmas with me."

Agnes brightened. "Here at Elm Creek Manor?"

"We could spend it in the barn if you prefer but the manor will be warmer." Sylvia smiled. "Why not here? We have a tree, all the fixings for a Christmas dinner, and plenty of room for the children to run around."

Agnes looked inquiringly at her daughter, who said, "It's fine with me, Mom, and I know Louisa will agree. She was worried about the kids trashing your house, so this will be a load off her mind."

"The children are more than welcome to trash my house instead," declared Sylvia.

Agnes beamed, and for a moment, Sylvia glimpsed in her lined face the girl her brother had loved. "In that case, we'd be delighted to accept your invitation."

On Christmas morning, Sylvia, Sarah, and Matt rose early for church and returned home to a breakfast of Agnes's apple strudel. The famous Bergstrom recipe was as delicious as Sylvia remembered. The cinnamon spiced apples and flaky crust immediately took Sylvia back to those Christmas mornings of childhood, when the people she loved gathered around the table and reminisced about Christmases past and absent loved ones. Gerda Bergstrom could not have done any better.

They exchanged gifts, and after Sylvia reassured them that she would be perfectly content, Sarah and Matt loaded their suitcases into the red pickup and drove off to Uniontown to spend a few days with Sarah's mother. Sarah called later that afternoon to tell Sylvia that her mother had loved the Hunter's Star quilt. Carol had given

Sarah and Matt jeans, identical blue-and-white striped sweaters, and knit Penn State hats. "Can you believe it?" said Sarah in a low voice so she would not be overheard. "Matching outfits, like we were five-year-old twins or something." But she sounded pleased.

Not long after Sarah and Matt departed, Agnes and her brood showed up, and the children promptly filled the manor with enough noise and play and laughter for twice their number. Santa had apparently gone on a Christmas Eve shopping spree, too—in a red pickup rather than a sleigh—because there were toys for each child beneath the tree. After some consideration, Sylvia decided against reviving the tradition of hiding the ruby-and-gold glass star.

It was a wonderful, blessed day.

When her guests departed, Sylvia tidied the kitchen and settled down in the sitting room with a cup of tea, her heart content. She put on her glasses and read Elizabeth's letter once more, then sighed, folded it, and tucked it away for safekeeping. Somewhere out in California, Elizabeth's children and grandchildren might be gathered around their own Christmas tree, thinking of Elizabeth fondly just as Sylvia was. Or perhaps Elizabeth was present among them, watching over her family from a favorite spot near the fireplace, the Chimneys and Cornerstones quilt on her lap. Wherever she was, she was also with Sylvia in Elm Creek Manor, for as the Christmas Quilt had shown Sylvia that day, those she loved lived on in their handiwork and in the hearts of those who remembered them.

Tomorrow, Sylvia decided, she would string popcorn and cranberries into garlands and decorate a tree near the creek. The wildlife of Elm Creek Manor had gone too long without a Christmas feast of their own. She would search through Claudia's old papers and see if she could find the letter Elizabeth had promised to send, and perhaps with it, an address, a promising lead to the descendants she might have left behind.

But that was for tomorrow. Tonight, in the last few hours of Christmas Day, Sylvia intended to work on the Christmas Quilt, to complete a task too long neglected. In her home full of memories, she felt the presence of all those whom she loved, blessing her and wishing her well. At last she understood the true lesson of the Christmas Quilt, that a family was an act of creation, the piecing together of disparate fragments into one cloth—often harmonious, occasionally clashing and discordant, but sometimes unexpectedly beautiful and strong. Without contrast there was no pattern, as Great-Aunt Lucinda had taught her long ago, and each piece, whether finest silk or faded cotton, would endure if sewn fast to the others with strong seams—bonds of love and loyalty, tradition and faith.

The New Year's Quilt

To Marlene and Leonard Chiaverini,
who know how to ring in the New Year in style

Acknowledgments

A bottle of fine champagne for Denise Roy, Maria Massie, Rebecca Davis, Annie Orr, Aileen Boyle, Honi Werner, Melanie Parks, David Rosenthal, and everyone at Simon & Schuster for supporting the Elm Creek Quilts series.

Party hats and noisemakers to Tara Shaughnessy, the world's most wonderful nanny, who plays with my boys and allows me time to write.

A chorus of "Auld Lang Syne" to the friends and family who have encouraged me through the years, especially Geraldine Neidenbach, Heather Neidenbach, Nic Neidenbach, Virginia Riechman, and Leonard and Marlene Chiaverini.

A sky full of fireworks for my husband, Marty, and my sons, Nicholas and Michael, for making every New Year the happiest yet.

Chapter One

SYLVIA SPUN THE RADIO DIAL through pop songs and talk shows until she came upon a station playing big band versions of holiday favorites. "We should break the news to her gently," Sylvia said. "We should sit her down, give her a stiff drink, and tell her in calm, soothing voices what we've done."

"You're likely to find that drink thrown in your face," Andrew retorted. "No, we should just tell her straight out, like tearing off a bandage. The sooner we tell her, the sooner she can start getting used to the idea."

Andrew knew his daughter better than Sylvia, but she doubted the direct approach would work. "How about this?" she suggested. "We'll say, 'Amy, dear, we have some bad news and some good news. The bad news is that we've gotten married. The good news is that since we got married on Christmas Eve, you won't have to buy us a separate wedding present.' "

"I don't like calling our marriage 'bad news.' "

"I don't either, but I'm sure that's how Amy will look at it."

"If she had any idea how happy I am that you finally consented to be my bride, I can't believe she'd refuse to be happy for us."

"Perhaps you should tell her how happy you are," said Sylvia. "Perhaps it will be as simple as that."

They considered that for a moment, and then in unison said, "I doubt it." Andrew chuckled, and Sylvia caressed his cheek before returning her gaze to the passing scenery, to snow-covered hills alight with the thin sunshine of a late December morning. She could not remember the last time she had been so content. Her husband of nearly two days was by her side, the pleasures of a winter honeymoon awaited them, and dear friends—a second family—would welcome them home to Elm Creek Manor after the New Year.

If only Andrew's daughter had not objected to the marriage, Sylvia's happiness would be complete.

She muffled a sigh, reluctant to allow Amy's perplexing disapproval to ruin her good spirits. If only she could rid her thoughts of Amy's last visit to Elm Creek Manor, of her disappointed frown and the determined set to her shoulders when she reminded her father of Sylvia's stroke two years earlier, of how deeply Andrew had grieved when Amy's mother died of cancer. Sylvia and Andrew tried their best to put Amy's concerns to rest, but she had made up her mind, and nothing they said could persuade her that their marriage would not inevitably end in sorrow. "We all would love for you to have many, many years together," Amy had said, "but the end is going to be the same."

Eventually Andrew had heard enough. "If being by your mother's side throughout her illness taught me anything, it showed me that nothing matters but sharing your life with the people you love. Your mother had a great love of life. I'm ashamed that in her memory, you want me to curl up in a corner and wait to die."

Amy went scarlet as her father stormed off. Sylvia tried to reassure Amy that she had fully recovered from her stroke, she was in excellent health for her age, and she had sufficient resources to ensure that she would not become a burden to anyone, but Amy could not be appeased. Having failed to persuade her father, Amy appealed to Sylvia instead, but although Sylvia offered a sympathetic smile to soften her words, she resented the younger woman's ridiculous implications that she was on her deathbed and spoke more bluntly than she should have. "I'm sure you mean well," she said, "but we've made our decision, and I'm afraid you're just going to have to live with it."

Amy's startled expression told Sylvia that Amy had never expected her concerns to be dismissed so quickly. How could she have expected anything else? She should have known that Andrew had too much honor to withdraw a marriage proposal merely to please stubborn children, especially when it went against his own wishes and all common sense.

Sylvia sighed as the winter scenery rushed past her window, dreading their arrival in Hartford and the unpleasant scene that was sure to unfold when Andrew broke the news that they had married on Christmas Eve. She was grateful for the reprieve their two-day honeymoon in New York City would provide, but she knew they were only delaying the inevitable. In her more optimistic moments, Sylvia hoped that Amy would set aside her foolish objections when she realized the deed was done, her father was married, and nothing would change that. More often, however, she feared that learning about the wedding after the fact would only inflame Amy's anger, and the recent months of estrangement between father and daughter would become a permanent condition.

The wedding had been lovely, for all that it had been pulled together in a matter of weeks. Sylvia and Andrew had hoped Amy would attend with her husband and three children, and naturally, they had invited Andrew's son, his wife, and their two daughters as well. Months earlier, Bob and Kathy had expressed misgivings when Andrew announced the engagement, but after the shock wore off, they seemed to accept his unexpected decision to remarry. Even Amy's husband had privately told the couple that he wished his own widowed father had been fortunate enough to find a second love as they had.

Sylvia and Andrew had invited everyone to Elm Creek Manor for Christmas without mentioning the wedding, a secret they had divulged only to the young couple that would act as witnesses and the judge who would officiate at the ceremony. They had intended to tell Andrew's children about the upcoming nuptials once they arrived at Elm Creek Manor, a few hours before Sylvia and Andrew would exchange their vows—enough time for them to get used to the idea but not enough for them to arrange flights home before the ceremony. Perhaps, Sylvia reluctantly admitted to herself, their plan had been misguided, even underhanded, and far more likely to backfire than to win the children over. Not that it mattered. Amy had turned down the invitation with a weak excuse about wanting to spend a quiet Christmas at home, and Bob, unwilling to risk angering his sister by appearing to take sides, had stayed away, too.

They had missed a beautiful wedding. Sarah McClure, Sylvia's quilting apprentice and business partner, and her husband, Matt, had staged a holiday wonderland. The candlelit ballroom of Elm Creek Manor glimmered with poinsettias, ribbon, and evergreen boughs. Andrew had built a fire in the large fireplace, then added the nostalgic decoration of the nativity scene Sylvia's grandfather had carved and that her father had brought back from a visit to the Bergstroms' ancestral home in Baden-Baden,

Germany. The youngest Elm Creek Quilter, Summer Sullivan, had taken charge of the musical entertainment, setting Christmas carols wafting on air fragrant with the scents of pine and cinnamon and roasted apples. Just across the dance floor, the cook and two assistants—his daughter and her best friend, or so Sylvia had overheard—placed silver trays of hors d'oeuvres and cookies on a long table and prepared the buffet for hot dishes still simmering in the kitchen. Someone had opened the curtains covering the floor to ceiling windows on the south wall, and snowflakes fell gently against the windowpanes.

Sylvia could not have imagined a more festive place to spend a Christmas Eve.

Soon guests began to fill the ballroom—the Elm Creek Quilters and their families, other friends from the nearby town of Waterford, college students Sylvia had befriended while participating in various research projects, and Katherine Quigley, the mayor, who was one of the few people in on Sylvia and Andrew's secret. Cocktails were served, followed by a delicious meal of roasted Cornish game hen with cranberry walnut dressing that reminded Sylvia all over again why some quilters claimed they came to Elm Creek Quilt Camp for the food alone. Summer put some big band tunes on the CD player and led her boyfriend to the dance floor. Other couples joined them, and soon the room was alive with laughter, music, and the warmth of friendship.

"I don't think I've ever had a happier Christmas Eve," said Sylvia as she danced with Andrew. "I hate to see it end."

"Is that so?" He regarded her, eyebrows raised. "Does that mean you've changed your mind?"

"Of course not," she said, lowering her voice as the

song ended. "In fact, I was just about to suggest we get started."

He brought her hands to his lips. "I was hoping you'd say that."

Sylvia signaled to Sarah, who found Mayor Quigley in the crowd and told her that the time had come. Andrew smiled as Sylvia fidgeted with her bouquet. "Nervous?"

"Not at all," she said. "I just hope our friends will forgive us."

"They'll have to, once we remind them that you and I never said anything about waiting until June."

"May I have everyone's attention, please?" called Sarah over the noise of the crowd. Someone turned down the volume on the stereo. "On behalf of Sylvia and Andrew and everyone who considers Elm Creek Manor a home away from home, thank you for joining us on this very special Christmas Eve."

Everyone applauded, except Andrew, who straightened his tie, and Sylvia, who took the arm of her groom.

"It is also my honor and great pleasure," said Sarah, "to inform you that you are here not only to celebrate Christmas, but also the wedding of our two dear friends, Sylvia Compson and Andrew Cooper."

Gasps of surprise and excitement quickly gave way to cheers. Sylvia felt her cheeks growing hot as their many friends turned to them, applauding and calling their names.

"You said June," one of the Elm Creek Quilters protested.

"No, *you* said June," retorted Sylvia.

"But I already bought my dress and picked out your gown!"

All present burst into laughter, and, joining in as

loudly as anyone, Sarah held up her hands for quiet. "If you would all gather around, Andrew would like to escort his beautiful bride down the aisle."

The crowd parted to make way for the couple, and Summer slipped away to the CD player. As the first strains of Bach's "Jesu, Joy of Man's Desiring" filled the air, Sylvia and Andrew walked among their guests to where the mayor waited.

To Sylvia, every moment of the simple ceremony rang as true as a crystal chime. They pledged to be true, faithful, respectful, and loving to each other until the end of their days. They listened, hand in hand, as the mayor reminded them of the significance and irrevocability of their promises. They exchanged rings, and when they kissed, the room erupted in cheers and applause. As Sarah and Matt came forward to sign the marriage license, Sylvia looked out upon the assembled friends wiping their eyes and smiling, and she knew that she and Andrew had wed surrounded by love, exactly as they knew they should.

If only Andrew's children and grandchildren had come to share this moment. If only they could be as happy for Sylvia and Andrew as their friends were. Sylvia looked up at her new husband and saw in his eyes that he shared her wistful thoughts.

She reached up to touch his cheek. He put his hand over hers, and smiled.

It had truly been a marvelous wedding, exactly the celebration she and Andrew had wanted. Even the Elm Creek Quilters had enjoyed themselves too much to complain that they would have to abandon their own plans for a June wedding.

The only shadow cast upon their happiness was the absence of Andrew's family.

Sylvia, who considered herself something of an expert on the subject of familial estrangement and its consequences, knew that Amy was the key. If they could win her over, the others would follow, relieved to see family harmony restored. Amy had clearly inherited her father's stubbornness, but with any luck, she had also inherited his kind heart.

As Bing Crosby crooned "I'll Be Home for Christmas," Sylvia forced her worries aside and reached into the back seat for her tote bag. Mindful of Andrew's travel mug in the cup holder between them, still half-full of coffee from the Bear's Paw Inn, she took out her current work-in-progress, a patchwork quilt in blues, golds, and whites with touches of black scattered here and there wherever the whim had struck her. The quilt had a wintry feel to it, or so she had always thought, and it had suited her to work on it when the days were short and the nights long and cold. In recent months, she had decided to finish the quilt once and for all, and not only for the satisfaction of crossing another item off her Unfinished Fabric Object list. The one task that remained was to sew on the binding, the outermost strip of fabric that concealed the raw edges of the quilt top, batting, and lining. Usually Sylvia found such simple handwork tedious, the least creative and enjoyable task of the quilting art, but today she welcomed the distraction.

Andrew glanced over as she threaded her needle. "Is that our wedding quilt?"

"I'm sorry, dear, but it isn't." Deftly Sylvia drew her needle through the raw edge of the quilt, hid the knot within the batting, and began sewing the binding to the back of the quilt with small, barely visible ladder stitches. "It's only a lap quilt, not big enough for our bed. You'll have to wait a few months if you want a wedding quilt from me."

"Maybe the Elm Creek Quilters will make us one."

They were her dearest, closest friends, so perhaps they would. On the other hand . . . "After they've had a chance to recover from their surprise, they might."

Andrew grinned. "And if they forgive us for denying them the wedding of their dreams?"

"Precisely." In sharp contrast to Andrew's children, the Elm Creek Quilters had been so delighted by the announcement of their engagement that they had been carried away with wedding-planning enthusiasm. Sylvia felt a twinge of guilt for spoiling their plans after her friends had gone to the trouble of choosing the wedding cake, finding the perfect wedding gown in a bridal magazine, and setting the date for the ceremony after a comparison of their schedules ruled out half the Saturdays in June, but it had to be done. Sylvia and Andrew couldn't bear the thought of putting on an enormous production knowing that his children would refuse to attend. This way, they could make themselves believe that Amy and Bob and their families would have come for Christmas if they had known that a wedding would take place. This way, in the years to come, Andrew's children would not be haunted by guilt for refusing to attend their father's wedding.

Sylvia hoped to spare Amy and Bob regrets they were too young to know lay ahead of them.

"Though it's not our wedding quilt," Andrew said, "it still must be important or you wouldn't have brought it along on our honeymoon."

"It is, indeed." Sylvia spread it open on her lap so he

could glimpse more of the colorful patchwork, although he would not truly be able to appreciate the quilt's loveliness in such cramped quarters. "It's a quilt for the season. I call it New Year's Reflections."

"Reflections, not resolutions?"

"Reflections should precede resolutions, or so I've always thought."

Andrew shook his head. "I don't believe in making New Year's resolutions. If someone needs to change, they should change, and not wait for the New Year to do it."

"Some people don't have your self-discipline," said Sylvia, smiling. "Some people need an important occasion to herald a time for change."

"Some people, meaning yourself?"

"Perhaps. I'm very much in favor of New Year's resolutions, and I support anyone who chooses to make one. They are a sign of optimism and hope in an increasingly cynical world. Someone who makes a New Year's resolution is declaring that they have hope, that they believe they can improve their lives, that we can change our world for the better."

"You don't need to change. I wouldn't change a thing about you."

"Spoken like a true newlywed," teased Sylvia. "It's very good that you don't want to change me, because you can't, you know. And it's not because women of a certain age are set in their ways or any such nonsense. No one can make another person change. One has to change oneself."

But that did not mean a caring friend couldn't point out a new direction to someone headed down the wrong road, and hope they took heed. The New Year's Reflections quilt never failed to remind her of that, or that a new path chosen without careful reflection would lead even the most resolute traveler in a broad circle, back to where she had begun, and no better off than when she had set out on her journey.

Andrew fell silent while Sylvia methodically sewed down the binding, each stitch bringing her closer to the completion of an on-again, off-again quilt nearly six years in the making. Out of the corner of one eye, she observed Andrew frowning slightly as he pondered the mystery of her quilt's presence on their honeymoon. "Did you bring the quilt because last year you resolved to finish it before midnight on New Year's Eve, and you're running out of time?"

"No," said Sylvia with a little laugh. "I brought it along because it's a gift for Amy."

"But we sent the kids their Christmas presents weeks ago."

"It's not a Christmas gift. It's a New Year's gift." Sylvia hesitated before deciding to tell him the whole truth. He was, after all, her husband now. "It's a gift to thank her for accepting my marriage to her father."

Andrew shot her a look of utter bewilderment. "But she didn't," he said, quickly returning his gaze to the road ahead. "She doesn't. She made that perfectly clear when I told her I was going to marry you whether she liked it or not. Sylvia, I think you should prepare yourself. This peace offering of yours—it's a pretty quilt and a nice gesture, but it might not be enough. This whole trip might be a waste of time."

"I refuse to believe that," said Sylvia. This attempt at reconciliation was for the newlyweds as much as it was for Amy. It would do them some small good to know they had tried, even if Amy rebuffed them.

And while it was true that Amy had not accepted her father's engagement and almost certainly would not welcome news of his marriage, perhaps by the time the New Year dawned, she would have a change of heart. Sylvia would put her trust in the power of the season to inspire new beginnings, even if Andrew did not.

As they drove through eastern Pennsylvania on their way to New York, Sylvia chatted with Andrew and worked on the New Year's Reflections quilt, every stitch a silent prayer that Andrew and his daughter would reconcile. She could not bear to be the cause of their estrangement. She knew all too well the ache of loneliness that filled a heart that learned forgiveness too late.

For more than fifty years, bitterness and grief had separated Sylvia from the home she loved—and the sister whom she blamed unfairly as the cause of all her sorrow. Every New Year had offered her an opportunity to start over, but she had stubbornly awaited an apology that never came, an apology she perhaps did not deserve. Only after Claudia's death did Sylvia return to Elm Creek Manor and discover that her sister had missed her and had longed for her return. If only Sylvia had not cut off her ties so completely, Claudia might have been able to find her, to send word to her, to offer the apology Sylvia had resolutely awaited. If only Sylvia had not allowed obstinate pride to prevent her from reaching out to Claudia first.

Sylvia would not allow Andrew and Amy to repeat her mistakes. Some good had to come of her hard-earned lessons. Their disagreement was not longstanding; surely the wound would heal if they tended it quickly and did not allow the infection of anger to take deeper root.

Sylvia tucked the needle into the edge of the binding and held up the quilt to inspect her work. The double-fold bias strip of dark blue cotton lay smooth and straight, without a single pucker, a perfect frame for the twelve blue-and-gold patchwork blocks of her own invention, twelve variations of the traditional Mother's Favorite block.

Claudia probably would have had something to say about Sylvia's choice. Each daughter had longed to be their mother's favorite, and as a child, Sylvia had wavered between fear and certainty that she wasn't it. Claudia probably would not have believed that Sylvia had chosen the pattern despite its name, not because of it. It was visually striking, with a four-inch central square set on point by white triangles and framed by narrow strips of blue. Triangles pieced from lighter blue trapezoids and white triangles made up the corners of the block, creating a distant resemblance to the better-known Pineapple block. But Sylvia had complicated an already difficult pattern by substituting miniature patchwork blocks for the solid, four-inch squares in the centers. These blocks she had indeed chosen for their names, for their symbolism, for the memories of long-ago New Year's celebrations that came to mind whenever she worked upon the quilt.

Sylvia ran a hand over the patchwork surface, wishing the pieces of her life fit together with such precision. It was difficult to look to the year ahead with anticipation and hope when she could not help glancing over her shoulder with regret at the mistakes of the past. Throughout her long, lonely exile from Elm Creek Manor, picking out the threads of her past mistakes had become a New Year's Eve tradition for her, as much a part of the holiday as the countdown to midnight and "Auld Lang Syne."

It had not always been that way. She had not learned that melancholy habit at her mother's knee, or from any of the other Bergstrom women who passed down family traditions through the generations. When Sylvia was a girl, the Bergstrom family ushered in the New Year with joy and merriment whether the world beyond the gray stone walls of the family home was at peace or at war, enjoying prosperity or enduring hardship.

A lifetime ago, as 1925 approached, the Bergstrom family had had much to be thankful for: the comfortable manor large enough to accommodate their extended family, the sustenance their farm provided, the company of those they loved, and unprecedented success and prosperity mirroring the nation's rise in fortune. During the few years before, newly wealthy businessmen from as far away as Chicago and New York City had flocked to Elm Creek Manor, eager to add prized Bergstrom Thoroughbreds to their growing lists of possessions. Even little Sylvia understood that they wanted to impress friends and rivals and to prove themselves the equals of the "old money" families who had kept Bergstrom Thoroughbreds in their stables almost from the time Sylvia's great-grandfather had founded the business before the Civil War. Although Sylvia mourned the departure of each elegant mare or proud stallion, she did not complain. She knew the family owed their livelihood to these stout businessmen in fine suits who spoke in brash accents as they puffed their cigars and watched her father and uncles put the horses through their paces. She was old enough to understand that each horse the men bought meant food on their table, new dresses and shoes to wear to school, and money to pay her mother's doctor bills.

Sylvia's favorite cousin, Elizabeth, had more reason

than any Bergstrom for happiness that season, as she had recently become engaged to her longtime sweetheart, Henry Nelson, a young man from a neighboring farm. The wedding plans had already begun in earnest despite the holiday because, much to Sylvia's dismay, Henry and Elizabeth planned to marry at the end of March and move to California, where Henry had purchased a cattle ranch.

Sylvia had never liked Henry. Whenever he came around, Elizabeth forgot her favorite little cousin and went off riding or walking or picking apples with Henry instead. When he stayed for supper, he took Sylvia's chair at the table without even asking permission, as if he had more right to sit at Elizabeth's side than Sylvia. No matter how often Sylvia scowled at him or spoke impertinently or squeezed herself between Henry and Elizabeth when they sat by the fire turning pages of a book, Henry seemed stupidly unaware of how unwelcome he was. Whenever Elizabeth visited from Harrisburg, Henry included himself in every holiday gathering at Elm Creek Manor, and he wasn't even family.

But he would be, soon. Sylvia felt sick at heart as she realized that when Henry and Elizabeth married, she would lose her favorite playmate and confidante forever.

Even Elizabeth's promise that Sylvia and Claudia could be flower girls at the wedding did nothing to console her. Instead, Sylvia strengthened her resolve to persuade Henry to go away and never come back. If he went to California without Elizabeth, that would be best of all, but Sylvia would be satisfied if he stayed on the other side of the fence separating the Nelson farm from the Bergstroms'.

Sylvia tried her best, but she was not naturally devious and she had to be careful not to raise the ire of her parents, aunts, and uncles, who did not seem to realize that Henry had to be stopped. One day, inspiration struck as she came upon Henry waiting in the parlor while Elizabeth finished a wedding gown fitting upstairs with Sylvia's mother and aunts. "Is Elizabeth still crying?" she asked him, strolling into the room and plopping down on her grandma's favorite upholstered chair.

Henry regarded her warily. "What do you mean?"

Sylvia fingered a loose thread on the ottoman and did her best to look nonchalant. "Oh, you know. She's always crying these days. Grandpa says she's 'turning on the waterworks.' "

"Is that so?" Henry's brow furrowed. "Do you know what she's crying about?"

"I'm not sure. She never cries when she's with me." Sylvia felt a thrill of delight when Henry's frown deepened. "But I heard her tell my mama . . ."

"What?" Henry prompted.

"I'm not supposed to listen at doors."

"I won't tell anyone."

"Promise?"

Henry nodded, barely containing his impatience. "Of course. Go on. What did Elizabeth say?"

"She told my mama that it would break her heart to go to California and never see her family again."

Henry sat back in his chair. "She said that?"

Sylvia nodded. What Elizabeth had really said was that she would miss Elm Creek Manor terribly and she dreaded the moment of her departure, but she loved Henry and it would break her heart to stay behind and let him go to California without her. That was what Elizabeth had said, but Sylvia knew Elizabeth and she understood the real meaning hidden behind her words. Henry was wrong to take her away, and since Elizabeth was too afraid to hurt his feelings, it was up to Sylvia to tell him the truth.

Henry rose and strode from the room. Sylvia jumped up and peered through the doorway after him, but her heart sank in dismay when she spied him crossing the black marble floor of the front foyer on his way to the grand oak staircase instead of slinking off down the west wing hallway to the back door. Jolted by guilty alarm, she hurried off the way Henry should have chosen, barely pausing to pull on her boots and coat before racing outside into the snow.

She hid out in the barn, keeping warm in the hayloft while the cows scuffed their hooves and lowed complaints below. She had missed lunch, and her stomach growled. When her mittened fingers grew numb, she had no choice but to return indoors. Henry's boots no longer stood in a puddle of melted snow just inside the back door. She tried to find encouragement in his absence, but her stomach was a knot of worry.

She tiptoed upstairs to the nursery to find her mother and Claudia sitting on the window seat reading a book. Claudia glared, accusatory and triumphant. Sylvia could not bear to meet her mother's gaze.

"Claudia, darling, would you please wait for me downstairs?" Sylvia's mother asked.

"Now you're going to get it," Claudia whispered, brushing past Sylvia on the way out the door.

"Sylvia, come here." Her mother patted the window seat.

Sylvia obeyed, dragging her feet across the nursery floor. She sat beside her mother, eyes downcast, and did not resist when her mother took her hands. "Goodness, Sylvia," she exclaimed, chafing her daughter's hands with her own. "You're half frozen. Where have you been hiding?"

"In the barn."

"I would have guessed the stable—you love the horses so much."

The stable would have been Sylvia's first choice, but she would have risked discovery there. Her father and uncles were in and out of the stable all day, tending the horses.

Mama was silent for a moment, but then she sighed. "Darling, I know how much you love Elizabeth. I know you're going to miss her when she goes to California. But Elizabeth loves Henry, and she is going to marry him. Being mean to him won't change that."

Tears sprang into Sylvia's eyes. Henry had told on her. She had always known he couldn't be trusted.

"I suppose I've been too lenient. I've excused your little pranks because of the holidays, because I know how much you admire your cousin, how important it is for you to be her favorite . . ." The distant look in her mother's eyes suddenly disappeared, and she fixed Sylvia with a firm but loving gaze. "I'm sure you want what's best for Elizabeth. She loves Henry, and Henry loves her. Our family has known him since long before you were born. If I thought he wouldn't make her happy, if I suspected for one moment that he wasn't a good man, don't you think I'd be with her right this moment trying to talk her out of it?"

"I . . ." Sylvia had not thought about it. "I guess so."

"Once, long ago, I almost married the wrong man for the wrong reasons, so trust me when I say I've learned to recognize a bad match—" Mama caught herself. "But that's a story for another day. The problem, Sylvia, isn't Elizabeth's choice or your feelings about it. The real problem is that you lied."

Surprised, Sylvia blurted, "No, I didn't."

"Yes, you did. It was very naughty of you to tell Henry that Elizabeth doesn't want to go to California with him. It was wrong for you to make him think he was making her unhappy."

But he was making her unhappy. He made Elizabeth cry. Elizabeth didn't want to leave Elm Creek Manor; Sylvia had heard her tell Mama so. "But I didn't lie. What I said was true, I know it was."

"Sylvia." The single word, gently spoken, was reproach enough for Sylvia. She knew she hadn't lied, but Mama believed she had and could not hide her disappointment. Sylvia wished she had never come in from the barn. The one rule her father and the other grown-ups of the household upheld before all others was that no one should upset Mama. She had suffered a terrible illness that had injured her heart when she was a little girl no bigger than Sylvia. Although Father could not stop Mama from romping with the children in the nursery or riding her favorite horse, his worried admonitions alarmed the girls and made them cautious. Whenever Mama was forced to take to her bed, Sylvia hid from Dr. Granger as he raced up the steps, black bag in hand, certain he would scold her for whatever she had done to make his visit necessary.

What if, by trying to keep Elizabeth close, Sylvia had harmed Mama?

Sylvia flung her arms around her mother. "I'm sorry," she said, her voice muffled by her mother's sweater.

Mama stroked Sylvia's long, tangled curls. "It's all right, darling. I know you won't do it again. I can't ask you to like Henry, but for all our sakes, please try to be kinder to him. Perhaps for the New Year you can make a fresh start. Elizabeth loves him. Perhaps you can resolve to try to love him a little, too."

Sylvia couldn't imagine ever feeling anything but anger and resentment for Henry, especially now that he had turned out to be a big tattletale, but she nodded to please her mother. She wished the grown-ups understood that she was only doing what was best for everyone. She could not imagine how Elizabeth would ever be happy, so far away in California with only dreary Henry for company.

Concealing her dislike wouldn't be easy, but Sylvia would have to try because the alternative was to hide in her room until the holidays passed, and she couldn't bear to miss out on all the fun. This year, Great-Aunt Lucinda had decided to revive an old tradition her parents and aunt had brought to America from Germany, a Sylvester Ball on New Year's Eve. The last time the Bergstrom family had celebrated the night of Holy St. Sylvester was before Sylvia was born, so Sylvia had no memory of those happy occasions. Great-Aunt Lucinda said there would be dancing, singing, and lots of delicious treats to eat and drink. She also promised Sylvia that she and Claudia could stay up until midnight to welcome the New Year. Sylvia knew that any more naughtiness could cost her that privilege, so she vowed to behave herself, at least until January 2.

Snow fell on the morning of December 31. Sylvia and Claudia spent most of the day outside, sledding and building snowmen, until their mother called them inside for a nap. Claudia went inside without complaint, but Sylvia balked at going to bed in the middle of the day. Only when her mother warned her that she would never be able to stay up until midnight if she did not rest first did she reluctantly come inside.

Cousin Elizabeth passed her on the landing, breathless, her golden curls bouncing, her eyes alight with pleasure and mischief. How could Sylvia not adore her? "Hello, little Sylvia," Elizabeth sang, sweeping her up in a hug. "Where are you off to on this last day of the year?"

When Sylvia reported that she had been sent to bed, Elizabeth gave her a quizzical frown. "You don't look sleepy to me."

"I'm not," said Sylvia, glum. "Naps are for babies."

"I couldn't agree more. Come on." Elizabeth took her by the hand and quickly led her up another flight of stairs to the nursery. "This is your first big dance, and we don't have a lot of time to get ready."

Sylvia threw a quick, anxious glance over her shoulder, but no one was around to report to her mother. "Claudia will tell on me when I don't come to bed."

"Oh, don't worry about her. When I passed your room she was already snoring away. She'll never know what time you came in."

Sylvia hated to disobey her mother so soon after resolving to be good, but a chance to spend time alone with Elizabeth might not come again for a very long while, if ever. She tightened her grasp on her cousin's hand until they shut the nursery door behind them. Elizabeth slid a chair in place beneath the doorknob. "That'll give you time to hide should anyone come snooping," said Elizabeth. "We'll have to keep our voices down. Take off your shoes and show me what you know."

Sylvia took off her Mary Janes and bravely demonstrated the few ballet steps her mother had taught her and Claudia, half-afraid that Elizabeth would laugh and send her off to take a nap after all. Then she stood in first position, awaiting her cousin's verdict. "Well, you're not a lost cause," said Elizabeth. "In fact, that's a very good beginning. I started out in ballet myself. Your aunt Millie insisted. But that's not the kind of dancing we're going to be doing tonight. You have a lot to learn and not a lot of time."

Elizabeth took her hands and, over the next two hours, introduced Sylvia to grown-up dances she called the fox-trot, the quickstep, and one Sylvia had seen her parents do—the waltz. When Sylvia proved to be an apt pupil, Elizabeth praised her and taught her the tango and the Charleston. Dancing hand in hand with her cousin, gliding over the wood floor in her stocking feet, smothering laughter and asking questions in stage whispers, Sylvia realized she had not been so happy since before Elizabeth announced her engagement. Henry Nelson seemed very far away, as if he had already gone off to California, alone.

Sylvia gladly would have danced on until the guests arrived, but suddenly Elizabeth glanced at the clock and exclaimed that they had better return downstairs quickly and get dressed if they didn't want the neighbors to catch them in their underthings. Giggling, Sylvia crept downstairs to her bedroom, where she rumpled her quilt, opened the blinds, and woke Claudia, who never suspected her sister had not just risen from a nap herself.

Soon Mama bustled in, slim and elegant in her black velveteen gown, to make sure the girls had scrubbed their hands and faces and put on their best winter dresses. Sylvia's was only a hand-me-down, Claudia reminded her, while her own was new; Grandma had sewn it for her especially.

"Now, girls, don't bicker," said Mama, brushing the tangles from Sylvia's hair and tying it back with a ribbon that matched the dark green trim of Claudia's outgrown dress. Sylvia wanted to protest that she wasn't bickering, that Claudia was the only one who had spoken, but she had already upset Mama once that day and didn't want to push her luck, even if it meant letting Claudia get the last word.

Soon the guests arrived, friends and neighbors from nearby farms and the town of Waterford, two miles away. Sylvia stuck close to Elizabeth until Henry Nelson arrived with his family and Elizabeth dashed off to welcome them. Sylvia scowled at them from across the foyer as Elizabeth kissed his cheek and helped his mother out of her coat. It didn't matter. When the dance began, Elizabeth would come back. Hadn't she said that Sylvia was a swell partner? Hadn't they spent two hours practicing? Hadn't she declared that together they would show everyone what Bergstrom girls could do?

The Sylvester Ball began with a supper of lentil soup, followed by pork and sauerkraut. Pork roasted with apples was one of Sylvia's favorite dishes, and she loved Great-Aunt Lucinda's sauerkraut, chopped much finer than Great-Aunt Lydia's, mildly flavored, and thickened with barley. Since the Bergstroms enjoyed pork and sauerkraut every New Year—although they usually ate the meal on New Year's Day rather than the night before—Sylvia was surprised to see some of their neighbors wrinkling their noses at the aromatic, fermented cabbage. "Try it," she urged Rosemary, Henry's younger sister, but Rosemary shook her head and gingerly pushed the shredded cabbage around her plate with her fork. A few of the more reluctant guests took tentative bites only after Great-Aunt Lucinda insisted that the meal would bring them good luck in the year to come. Germans considered pigs to be good luck, she explained, because back in the old days, a farm family who had a pig to feed them through the long, cold winter was fortunate indeed. "Why do you think children save their pennies in piggy banks," she asked, "when any animal could have done as well?" And since cabbage leaves were symbolic of money, a meal of pork and sauerkraut would help secure good fortune throughout the New Year.

"Dig in, son," Uncle George advised his future son-in-law, and Henry gamely took an impressive portion of sauerkraut. Sylvia wished he had refused. That would have convinced everyone that he didn't belong in the family.

Afterward, the party resumed in the ballroom, where the musicians Uncle George had hired from Harrisburg struck up a lively tune that beckoned couples to the dance floor. Sylvia looked around for Elizabeth, but Claudia grabbed Sylvia's hand and dragged her over to a corner where they could play ring-around-the-rosie in time to the music. Sylvia had no interest whatsoever in playing a baby game to what was obviously a quickstep, but when she saw Elizabeth on Henry's arm, she gloomily played along to appease Claudia. When the song ended, she slipped away and wove through the crowd to Elizabeth, but now her beautiful cousin was waltzing with Uncle George, and Sylvia knew she would be scolded if she interrupted.

Her turn would come, she told herself, but dance after dance went by, and always Elizabeth was with Henry, or her father, or Henry's father, or one of her uncles. Mostly she was with Henry. When she finally sat out a dance, Sylvia raced to her side. "There you are," Elizabeth exclaimed, and as far as Sylvia could tell, her cousin was delighted to see her. "Are you having a good time?"

Sylvia was miserable, but Elizabeth could easily fix that. "Can I have a turn to dance with you?"

Elizabeth fanned herself with her hand. "Absolutely, right after I rest with some of your father's punch." She looked around for Henry, but Sylvia quickly volunteered to get Elizabeth a cup, and she hurried off through the crowd of dancers and onlookers to the fireplace at the opposite end of the room.

Her father sat by the fireside, joking with his brothers and Henry's father, who waited impatiently to sample her father's renowned *Feuerzangenbowle*. Into a large black kettle he had emptied two bottles of red wine, some of the last of his wine cellar. Sylvia caught the aroma of rich wine and spices—cinnamon, allspice, cardamom—and the sweet fruity fragrances of lemon and orange. Her father stirred the steaming brew, careful to keep the fire just high enough to heat the punch without boiling.

"At this rate it'll be midnight before we can wet our whistles, Fred," one of the neighbors teased.

"If you're too thirsty to wait, have some coffee and save the punch for more patient men," Sylvia's father retorted with a grin. "Sylvia can show you to the kitchen."

Sylvia froze while the men laughed, relaxing only when she realized none of the men intended to take her father up on his offer. Although many of their neighbors of German descent had brewed their own beer long before Prohibition, few could obtain fine European wines like those Father's customers offered him to sweeten their deals. They wouldn't leave the fireside without a glass of Father's famous punch, and neither would Sylvia. She was determined to serve Elizabeth before Henry did, to prove just how unnecessary he was.

Father traded the long-handled spoon for a sturdy pair of tongs, grasped a sugar cone, and held it over the kettle. With his left hand, he slowly poured rum over the sugar cone, or *Zuckerhut* as the older Bergstroms called it, and let the liquor soak in to the fine, compressed sugar. At Father's signal, Uncle William came forward, withdrew a wooden skewer from the fire, and set the sugar cone on fire. Sylvia watched, entranced, as the bluish flame danced across the sugar cone and carmelized the sugar, which dripped into the steaming punch below. When the flame threatened to flicker out, her father poured more rum over the *Zuckerhut* until the bottle was empty and the sugar melted away. With a sigh of anticipated pleasure, the uncles and neighbors pressed forward with their cups as Father picked up the ladle and began to serve. Sylvia found herself pushed to the back of the crowd, and not until the last of the eager grownups had taken their mugs from the fireside was she able to approach her father.

He eyed her with amusement. "This isn't a drink for little girls."

"It's not for me." Sylvia glanced over her shoulder and spied Elizabeth still seated where Sylvia had left her, laughing with Rosemary, Henry's sister. "It's for Elizabeth."

"I don't know if Elizabeth should be drinking this, either."

"If she's not old enough for punch, maybe she's not old enough to get married."

Her father was so astonished that he rocked back on his heels and laughed. Sylvia flushed and turned away, but her father caught her by the arm. "Very well, little miss, you may take your cousin some punch. Mind you don't sample it along the way."

Sylvia nodded and held very still as her father ladled steaming punch into her teacup. With small, careful steps, she skirted the dance floor and made her way back to Elizabeth. She scowled to find that Henry had replaced Rosemary at Elizabeth's side.

"Here you go," Sylvia said, presenting the cup to her cousin. Elizabeth thanked her and took it with both hands. Pleased with herself and relieved that she had accomplished the task without spilling a single drop, she sat down on the floor at her cousin's feet, ready to block her path should Henry take her hand and attempt to lead her to the dance floor.

"Your father won't be happy to see you drinking," Henry warned in a low voice that Sylvia barely overheard.

"My father is the last person who should complain about anyone's drinking."

"He's not drinking tonight."

"Yes, and don't you find it interesting that he can exercise some self-control while all the family is watching, and yet he can't muster up any fortitude at home?"

Sylvia heard Henry shift in his chair to take Elizabeth's cup. "Maybe you've had too much already. You're not used to this stuff."

"Henry, that's truly not necessary. I only had a sip—"

Infuriated, Sylvia spun around to glare at him. "My daddy made that punch and it's very good. You're just mad because I brought it to her instead of you. You have to spoil everything!"

Henry regarded her for a moment, expressionless, his hands frozen around Elizabeth's as she clutched the cup. A thin wisp of steam rose between them. "Never mind," said Henry, dropping his hands to his lap. "If you want to drink it, drink it."

"No, no, that's fine." Elizabeth passed him the cup so quickly he almost spilled it. "I'm not thirsty after all."

Henry clearly didn't believe her, but he set the cup aside. "Do you want to go for a walk?"

"I promised Sylvia I would dance with her."

Sylvia was too overcome with relief that Elizabeth had not forgotten her promise to pay any attention to Henry's reply. When he rose and walked away, she promptly scooted his chair closer to Elizabeth's and sat down upon it. Absently, Elizabeth took her hand and watched the dancers in silence. Sylvia pretended not to notice that her cousin was troubled. Elizabeth was here, she was going to give Sylvia her turn, and Sylvia was not going to probe her with questions that might make her too unhappy or distracted to dance.

At last the song ended, and after a momentary pause another lively tune began. Elizabeth smiled at her and said, "Are you ready to cut a rug?"

Sylvia nodded and took her hand. Elizabeth led her to the dance floor and counted out the first few beats, then threw herself into a jaunty Charleston. Sylvia struggled to keep up at first, distracted by the music that drowned out Elizabeth's counting and the many eyes upon them, but she stoked her courage and persevered. She felt a thrill of delight when she spotted Claudia watching them, mouth open in astonishment. Henry's disgruntled frown filled her with satisfaction, and she kicked higher and smiled broader just to spite him. Most of the guests had put aside their own dancing to gather in a circle around the two cousins as they danced side by side. Sylvia mirrored her graceful cousin's spirited steps as closely as she could, praying her family and the guests wouldn't notice her mistakes.

All too soon the song ended. Breathless and laughing, Elizabeth took Sylvia's hand and led her in a playful, sweeping bow. She blew kisses to the crowd as she guided Sylvia from the dance floor while the musicians struck up a slow foxtrot and the couples resumed dancing. To Sylvia's chagrin, Elizabeth made her way directly to the far side of the room, where Henry waited beside one of the tall windows overlooking the elm grove and the creek, invisible in the darkness. He had eyes only for Elizabeth as they approached.

"You've been practicing," he remarked, smiling at her with fond amusement.

"I have to do something to keep myself busy when I'm bored and lonely back home in Harrisburg and you're tending the farm up here. Did you think I sat home every night pining for you?"

"I had hoped so." He slid his arm around Elizabeth's waist and pulled her close. Sylvia tried to keep hold of Elizabeth's hand, but her cousin's slender fingers slipped from her grasp. Elizabeth laughed and kissed Henry's cheek. He murmured something in her ear, and Sylvia was struck by the certainty that she had been entirely forgotten.

Unnoticed, she slipped away from the couple and searched out her mother. Mama's face lit up at the sight of her. "I had no idea you were such a fine dancer," she said, pulling Sylvia into a hug.

"Elizabeth taught me." And now that they had shown

everyone what Bergstrom girls could do, Elizabeth had returned to Henry. Sylvia had done her best, but anyone could see that Henry was her cousin's favorite dance partner, no matter what she had declared as they practiced in the nursery.

Sylvia climbed onto her mother's lap and watched the dancing for a while, her eyelids drooping. When her mother offered to take her upstairs to bed, Sylvia roused herself and insisted that she meant to stay up until midnight, like everyone else. She went off to find Claudia, who demanded that Sylvia teach her the Charleston. Sylvia showed her the few steps she knew, but dancing with Claudia was not as much fun as performing with Elizabeth, and she soon lost interest. When she spotted Great-Aunt Lucinda carrying a tray of her delicious *Pfannkuchen* to the dessert table, she hurried over and took two of the delicious jelly-filled doughnuts. Licking sugar from her fingertips, she considered taking a plate to Elizabeth, but her lovely cousin was once again circling the dance floor in Henry's arms. He was not much of a dancer, Sylvia observed spitefully. He knew the steps well enough but he seemed to be going through the motions without a scrap of enjoyment. But Elizabeth was having a wonderful time, and Sylvia could not pretend otherwise.

She finished her dessert and went off to find a dance partner. She would show Elizabeth that she, too, could have just as much fun with someone else.

Her father was pleased by her invitation to dance, as was her grandpa after him. Claudia found her and they made up their own dance, holding hands and spinning around in a circle until they became so dizzy they fell down. When they had come too close to crashing into dancing aunts and uncles too many times, their mother begged them to find some other way to amuse themselves. At that moment the musicians took a break, and Great-Aunt Lucinda called everyone to the fireside for *Bleigiessen*. "See what the New Year will bring you," she joked. "Unless you'd rather not know."

Only Grandma, who found fortune-telling unsettling, declined. "I'd rather have another jelly doughnut than a prediction of bad news," she said, settling into a chair near the dessert table, waving off the others' teasing protests that she should not assume that the news would be bad.

Sylvia, who had seen lead pouring on other New Year's Eves, knew that the game would almost certainly promise good fortune to everyone, since the funny shapes were rarely so obvious that the observers could reach only one conclusion. She darted through the crowd and found a seat on the floor close to the fireside. Great-Aunt Lucinda went first, melting a small piece of lead in an old spoon held above the flames. When it had turned to liquid, she poured it into a bowl of water, and everyone bent closer to see what shape the lead would take.

"It looks like a pretzel," Great-Aunt Lydia declared. "You're going to become a baker."

Everyone laughed. "I'm already a baker," said Great-Aunt Lucinda, passing the spoon to a neighbor. Everyone who had ever tried her delicious cookies or apple strudel chimed in their agreement.

One by one family and friends held the spoon over the fire, poured the melted lead into the water, and interpreted the shapes the metal took as it rapidly cooled. Those gathered around broke into cheers and applause when stars or fish promised good luck, when triangles promised financial improvement, or bells heralded good news. They burst into laughter when one elderly widow's lead formed an unmistakable egg shape, announcing the imminent birth of a child. "It must mean a grandchild," she speculated, but that did not stop her friends from teasing her, claiming that if she had tried *Bleigiessen* the previous New Year's Eve, the lead surely would have taken the shape of a mouse, symbolic of a secret love.

When Sylvia's father took a turn, an anchor shape showed that he would find assistance in an emergency. The crowd mulled this over while Aunt Millie took the spoon, for while it was good to know that he would have help in a time of need, it would be better to avoid the emergency altogether. "This *Bleigiessen* isn't very helpful after all," said Aunt Millie as the lead shavings turned to liquid over the fire. "It tells you just enough to worry you, and not enough to steer you clear of trouble." With that, she poured the lead into the bowl of water and exclaimed with delight when the lead sank and hardened into a lopsided cylinder she insisted was a cake.

"That doesn't look like any cake I'd want to taste," said Great-Aunt Lucinda.

"We can't all be bakers, like you," Aunt Millie retorted. "We all know that a cake means a celebration is coming, and of course that must refer to the wedding." With that, she handed the spoon to her future son-in-law.

Sylvia inched forward, holding her breath as Henry melted the lead then shrugged noncommittally as he poured it upon the water. The liquid metal thinned and elongated as it sank to the bottom of the bowl, and a gasp went up from the onlookers as two interlocking rings appeared. Sylvia waited, willing the rings to break, for that meant separation—and perhaps, perhaps, an end to the engagement. She waited, but the rings remained stubbornly joined.

"I've never seen rings form like that," Great-Aunt Lydia breathed. "A single ring alone signifies a wedding. Rings joined in this fashion surely indicate that you two will have a happy, enduring marriage. Congratulations, young man."

Henry's skepticism promptly vanished, and he flashed a grin to his future bride, who beamed and reached for his hand. Sylvia muffled a groan of disgust and snatched up the spoon from the hearth. She hoped for a ball to announce that good luck would roll her way, but instead the figure in the bowl resembled Grandma's eyeglasses. Sylvia scowled as her family debated which of the two possible interpretations to choose, whether she would one day be very wise or very old, and decided that old age was the more likely of the two. "It could be both," she protested, handing the spoon to her sister. "Why not both?" And why did her family—with the exception of her mother and Great-Aunt Lucinda—find it so difficult to believe that Sylvia could one day be wise?

Claudia went next, biting her lip hopefully as she peered into the bowl of water. "What is it?" she asked. "A tree? An arrow? What does it mean?"

"Looks like an ax to me," offered a neighbor.

When Claudia turned to Great-Aunt Lucinda for confirmation, the older woman reluctantly nodded. "It does resemble a hatchet."

"You saw one of those yourself, when we were girls," cried Great-Aunt Lydia. "Oh, but that can't be right. For you, perhaps, but not for pretty little Claudia."

"Thank you, sister dear," said Great-Aunt Lucinda dryly, and when the guests pressed her for an explanation, she held up her hands to quiet them. "Now, now, it's supposed to mean that you'll find disappointment in love, but take heart, Claudia. The fortune is only meant to tell you what the year ahead may bring, not what might happen when you're a grown woman. I don't think you need to worry about being unlucky in love at your age."

Claudia held back tears. "But what if it's not just for the year ahead? What if it's for my whole life?" A few well-meaning women reached out to comfort her, but she shook off their reassurances. "Sylvia won't reach old age in a single year, but that's what her fortune says."

"Many of these symbols have more than one meaning," Aunt Millie reminded her. "Your hatchet must mean something else."

"Maybe you're going to become a lumberjack," Sylvia suggested.

Claudia glared at her as the adults rocked with laughter. "Make jokes if you want. I don't think this game is fun anymore." She flounced off to join Grandma by the dessert table.

"After that, I'm almost afraid to take a turn," said Elizabeth, reaching for the spoon Claudia had flung down on the hearth. With a quick smile for Henry, she melted a few of the remaining lead shavings and let them fall from the spoon into the water. At first the lead gathered itself up into a ball—"Good luck will roll your way," an onlooker said—but then a dimple appeared along one side, and the opposite edge seemed to flatten.

"A heart," Henry's mother announced, beaming at her future daughter-in-law. "Elizabeth has found true love."

As Elizabeth's face glowed from happiness in the firelight, Sylvia boiled over with impatience. "That's not a heart," she declared. "A heart has a pointed tip. That looks like . . . like a piece of fruit, that's all."

Elizabeth gazed into the bowl, her smile slowly fading. Then she looked up and gave Sylvia a wistful smile. "I suppose you're right." She turned away to gaze into the bowl. "The question is, what sort of fruit, and what does it mean?"

"It looks like an apricot to me," said Great-Aunt Lucinda. "See the slightly elongated shape, and the indentation along the edge? That part could be the stem—"

"It's a heart," said Henry's mother, but less convincingly.

"Maybe it's an orange," said Henry, making his way to the fireside. He offered Elizabeth his hand and helped her to her feet. "An orange ripening on a tree in a grove on a ranch in sunny southern California."

"It's an apple," Sylvia shot back. "It looks exactly like one of the apples we picked from our own trees last autumn."

"Whatever variety of fruit it may be," Sylvia's mother broke in gently, "I think we can all agree on the meaning. For Elizabeth, the year ahead is certain to be sweet and good and flavorful."

All of the adults chimed in their agreement, but Sylvia scowled, pretending not to notice her mother's warning look. The shape was an apple and it meant that Elizabeth ought to stay close to Elm Creek Manor, where she could enjoy the harvest year after year.

Only a few lead shavings remained when Sylvia's mother came forward to try her hand. A few guests who had wandered away from the game returned to the fireside to see what the future held for their beloved hostess. Sylvia saw neighbors exchange glances and overheard their whispers, and her heart swelled with pride. Everyone loved Mama, and everyone wanted her to receive the best fortune of the evening. Sylvia hoped that the lead would take the shape of a cow, which represented healing, and she resolved to call the lump of lead a cow if it even remotely resembled any four-legged animal. If Elizabeth and Henry's mother could interpret the figures liberally to suit themselves, so could she.

Sylvia's mother hesitated before dribbling the melted lead into the bowl of water. A hush fell over the room. Sylvia's mother bent over the bowl, then sat back on her heels and took a deep, shuddering breath. Sylvia inched closer to see, and her stomach suddenly knotted in cold, sickening dread.

The metal had hardened in the shape of a cross. There could be no mistaking it. And crosses signified death.

Someone broke the silence with a low moan, but was quickly hushed. Sylvia's mother looked around at the faces of her friends and family and forced a smile. "Perhaps I should have followed Grandma's example after all," she said, her voice trembling.

"It's just a foolish game," said Great-Aunt Lucinda. "It's not real."

"What's wrong?" said Henry. "That looks like a sign of good fortune to me."

Sylvia balled her hands into fists and glared at him. "Don't you know what crosses mean?" He was so stupid, so stupid!

"That's not a cross." Henry bent over the bowl to scrutinize the figure within, and then straightened, shaking his head. "That second line's too thin and not straight enough. Anyone can see that's a threaded needle. That has to be a good sign for a family full of quilters."

"Of course. I see it now," said Great-Aunt Lucinda

quickly. "Perhaps it means you're going to make many quilts this year, Eleanor."

"Or perhaps the meaning is more symbolic," said Elizabeth. "Needles are useful and necessary, just as you are to all of us. Needles can make a home warmer and more beautiful. Needles are used for . . . for mending."

Henry put his arm around Elizabeth's shoulders, but his eyes were on Sylvia's mother. "Looks like you'll be doing some mending in the year ahead, Mrs. Bergstrom."

An inflection he gave the word suggested healing rather than darning socks or repairing little girls' torn hems. Sylvia's mother trembled with another deep breath, but then she offered Henry a warm, grateful smile. "Of course. I see it now." She reached out a hand, and Henry and Elizabeth helped her to her feet. "I do hope this doesn't mean I have to rush off to my sewing basket until after the party."

A ripple of laughter went through the crowd, but Sylvia caught the undercurrent of sadness. Her mother must have heard it, too, for she turned a brilliant smile on her loved ones and gestured to the musicians to strike up another tune. As the first merry notes sounded, Sylvia's father was at Mama's side, inviting her to dance.

Sylvia no longer felt like dancing. She wished that she had come up with the new interpretation of the symbol her mother had seen in the water, wished that she had been the one to protect her mother from the bleak foretelling, the one to bask in the warmth of her mother's grateful smile. And yet she felt oddly grateful to Henry for speaking up when she and everyone else had been paralyzed with foreboding. As much as she disliked him, she was glad he had been there.

Now, if only he would go home.

Sylvia curled up in an armchair and watched the couples circle the dance floor like snowflakes in a storm—her mother resting her cheek on her father's chest, Elizabeth gazing lovingly up at Henry. They danced on, not knowing what the year ahead held in store, but determined to face the best of times and the worst of times together.

Sylvia's mother did not die in the year to come, but her weak heart did not mend itself as they all prayed it miraculously would. She had always been the peacemaker of the family, so perhaps the mending the symbol foretold was the gentling of arguments and the soothing of hurt feelings within the family circle. Or perhaps the lead shape had carried a simpler, more literal meaning, for Sylvia's mother, like all the women of the family, sewed furiously that winter, making quilts, a trousseau, and a beautiful wedding gown for Elizabeth.

For Sylvia's beloved cousin did not come to her senses as Sylvia hoped, but married Henry and left Elm Creek Manor for a ranch in southern California. Whether Elizabeth had indeed found her true love, or only oranges and apricots, Sylvia never knew, for as the years passed, letters from Triumph Ranch appeared in their mailbox less frequently until they finally stopped coming.

Sylvia's mother saw four more New Years come and go, until she finally succumbed to death quietly at home, with her loved ones around her. Doctors had been predicting her death since childhood, but no amount of time would have been enough to prepare themselves for life without her. On that dark day, they thought only of their loss, and no one remembered the lead cross she had seen in the water.

If Claudia remembered the dire prediction she had

received that New Year's Eve, she never spoke of it. As a pretty and popular young woman, she enjoyed the admiration of all the young men of the Elm Creek Valley and seemed, for a time, to have escaped the unhappy fate the lead figure in the water had foretold. Her disappointment in love came many years later, after the war, after her marriage to the man whose cowardice led to the deaths of Sylvia's husband and their younger brother. This was the great betrayal that had compelled Sylvia to abandon the family home, the breach no apology could heal.

As for the eyeglasses Sylvia had seen in the bowl of water, she did indeed achieve a ripe old age. Whether she had attained wisdom as well—that was another thing altogether. She certainly had not attained it in time to reconcile with Claudia before her death. Whenever Sylvia reflected upon that New Year's Eve, she could not help but wonder whether the hatchet had warned not only of Claudia's unhappy marriage but also of the severing of ties between two sisters.

If ever Sylvia needed wisdom, she needed it now. She sighed and ran a hand over the quilt top, pausing to study the changes she had made to three of the Mother's Favorite blocks. For one, she had substituted a Hatchet block to remind her of the fortune Claudia had cast that long-ago winter night. A True Lover's Knot in the center of another block called to mind her parents, who had loved each other like no other man and woman Sylvia had ever known. Another block boasted an Orange Peel pattern, which Sylvia had sewn as a tribute to Elizabeth and Henry. She hoped they had been blessed with true love and all the sweetness life had to offer. How she wished she had not been so selfish, so jealous of their blossoming affection. If only she had understood that in loving Henry, Elizabeth had not depleted her heart's store of love. There had always been enough left over for her favorite little cousin. Had Sylvia not tried to keep Elizabeth's love all for herself, perhaps Elizabeth would have stayed in touch with the family. Perhaps Sylvia would know what had become of her, and why her letters from Triumph Ranch had stopped coming.

Sylvia and Andrew drove on, leaving the rolling, forested hills of Pennsylvania behind them. Sylvia had always considered herself a reasonable person, sensible and not given to superstitious flights of fancy, and yet she could not help wondering if Henry had a hand in her current predicament. She could not miss the similarities between his situation and that which she now faced, and she suspected he would be amused, if he were still alive, to witness her current predicament. Now, at long last, she understood how he had felt, how Elizabeth had felt, when confronted with Sylvia's foolish objections to their wedding. Now, too late for it to do any good, she understood how it must have pained Elizabeth that Sylvia had withheld her blessing.

On that New Year's Eve so long ago, a more reasonable child might have chosen to mend her ways and make a new start with Henry, as befitting the New Year. Not Sylvia. A few days into the New Year, she resumed her silly pranks with renewed determination to prevent the wedding. She hid Aunt Millie's scissors so that she could not work on the wedding gown, but Aunt Millie simply borrowed Great-Aunt Lucinda's. She stole the keys to Elizabeth's red steamer trunk and flung them into Elm Creek so that her cousin could not pack her belongings. She refused to try on her flower girl dress no matter how the aunts wheedled and coaxed, until they were forced to make a pattern from the frock she had worn on Christmas. She even came right out and told Henry that she and everyone else in the family hated him, but Henry did not believe her, and he did not go away until he took Elizabeth with him to California.

Just as Andrew's children misjudged Sylvia, so had she misjudged Henry. She had seen him through the filter of a young girl's jealousy and had never considered that he might cherish Elizabeth and bring her joy. On that New Year's Eve, when he had turned foreboding into hope by imagining another future for her mother, Sylvia had been offered a glimpse of the man he truly was, a man of kindness, reassurance, and generosity of spirit. If only she'd had the sense to be grateful that her beloved cousin had found such a partner.

Could she hope for more from Andrew's children than she had been willing to give? If Andrew's children never accepted their marriage, wasn't it precisely what she deserved, a just punishment for her own selfishness so long ago?

Perhaps. She could not deny it. But Andrew had done nothing wrong. He deserved better even if Sylvia did not.

Two days in New York awaited them, two days to savor the Christmas season in the city, alight with anticipation of the New Year. Sylvia intended to enjoy their honeymoon, but she would also make time to complete her quilt before they continued east to Amy's home in Hartford, Connecticut.

She would find out soon if Amy possessed the insight that had eluded Sylvia as a child.

Chapter Two

Sylvia continued to sew down the binding as she and Andrew drove across New Jersey, but she put the quilt away as they approached the Lincoln Tunnel. Soon they had arrived in Manhattan, where a light flurry of snow whirled down upon the minivan from a clear blue sky. Sylvia clasped her hands in her lap in girlish delight as they drove through Midtown, passed Central Park, and turned onto East 62nd Street on the Upper East Side. She had not been to the city in many years, and it seemed new and familiar all at the same time. She considered it a stroke of good fortune that they found a parking spot not far from their bed and breakfast inn, a five-story brownstone called the 1863 House. One of the proprietors was a regular guest at Elm Creek Quilt Camp, and every year she urged Sylvia and Andrew to come stay with them anytime they were in New York. "It's the least I can do to repay your hospitality," she said. "Your classes inspire me, and Elm Creek Manor restores my soul. Where would I be without you?"

Adele, who had retired from a successful career on Wall Street in her mid-forties to pursue quilting and other artistic interests, was given to such dramatic statements, so Sylvia was at first not convinced that she was meant to take the offer seriously. But when Adele repeated the invitation in a Christmas card Sylvia received just after she and Andrew had decided to move up their wedding date, she finally accepted.

Since the newlyweds had set their Christmas Eve

wedding date only a week ahead of time, they did not expect Adele and her husband, Julius, to have a room available on such short notice. Andrew even suggested they stay in a large chain hotel rather than impose on their generosity, but Sylvia had faith in Adele and suggested they at least inquire. A bed and breakfast in one of the finest neighborhoods in the city would be much more charming than an impersonal hotel room, and Sylvia couldn't bear to pass up the opportunity to see firsthand the historic inn she had caught glimpses of in the amusing stories Adele had shared at quilt camp.

In a stroke of good fortune, although the 1863 House was usually fully booked through the Christmas season, a last-minute cancellation had freed up what Adele promised was one of their most charming rooms. "Don't overbook yourself during your stay," Adele warned. "I promised the staff of the City Quilter I'd bring you by if you ever came to town." Sylvia rarely turned down an invitation to browse through fabric bolts and admire ingenious new quilting gadgets, so she happily agreed to leave plenty of time to visit Manhattan's best quilt shop.

Adele was off at the market when they arrived, but Julius welcomed them and showed them to the Garden Room on the first floor. The former drawing room boasted a twelve-foot ceiling and a large, south-facing bow window with lace curtains that made the most of the winter sunlight. French doors led to a private terrace garden, dusted with late December snow, and a mahogany wardrobe stood beside a marble fireplace with an elegantly carved wooden mantel. Along the near wall, a striking, multicolored scrap quilt adorned a grand four-poster bed. Sylvia quickly set her suitcase down and went to examine it. "This isn't one of Adele's creations," she remarked, noting the antique fabric prints and colors. The block design resembled the Thousand Pyramids pattern, with four corner triangles composed of thirty-six smaller triangles separated by rectangular sashing arranged around a small, cheddar-yellow Sawtooth Star.

"It's one of Adele's favorite discoveries," Julius confirmed. "She insisted we bring it out for you to use in honor of your wedding. Adele said she could think of no one who would appreciate it more."

Delighted, Sylvia ran her hand over the bright, scrappy top. Adele had indeed discovered a treasure. The fabrics indicated that it dated from the mid- to late-nineteenth century, but its excellent condition belied its age. Someone must have cherished this quilt, for it had been given the gentlest of care.

"I imagine this quilt has quite a story to tell," she murmured, thinking of the unknown quiltmaker who had spent months, perhaps years, sewing the tiny triangles together by hand.

"I'll bet this house does, too," said Andrew admiringly, resting his hand on the carved mantelpiece.

"The quilt's provenance is somewhat uncertain, as it is for so many antiques," said Julius. "But Adele and I would be glad to tell you what we know about the house over dinner tonight, unless you have other plans?"

They had tickets for a popular Broadway musical that one of Andrew's old buddies from his army days had managed to get for them. ("His daughter has connections," Andrew had explained when Sylvia marveled at their good fortune. "She's going with a fellow who works in the ticket office.") An early dinner with their proprietors would suit them perfectly. They arranged to meet later that afternoon, and Julius returned to his work while Sylvia and Andrew unpacked.

With a few hours to spare before dinner, Sylvia and Andrew decided to stroll along the Museum Mile to stretch their legs after the long drive, enjoy the sights and sounds of the city, and make plans for the rest of their visit. The air was brisk, but not unbearably so, and the wind was light enough that Sylvia's wool coat, scarf, and mittens warded off the cold. "Should we take advantage of the after Christmas sales?" she teased, tucking her arm through Andrew's as shoppers hurried past with bags from Bergdorf Goodman and FAO Schwarz. She laughed at her husband's disconcerted expression as he struggled to find a good excuse to refuse. She knew that the afternoon of shopping he had promised her was not his favorite item on the honeymoon itinerary.

At four o'clock, they circled back and met Adele and Julius at Mon Petit Café, a charming bistro only steps away from the 1863 House. Adele greeted Sylvia with a warm embrace. "Such a lovely bride," she exclaimed, and told Andrew that he was a lucky man. Andrew proudly agreed, but a wry twist to his smile told Sylvia that he did not expect to receive such a resounding endorsement at the next stop on their honeymoon tour.

Inside the bistro, a low murmur of voices and the aromas of roasting meats and spices warmed the air. Their table near the window offered a sunny view of Lexington Avenue, but Adele's irrepressible joy diverted Sylvia's attention from the sights outside. She seemed about to burst with a happy secret, and Sylvia hid a smile, knowing that her expressive, demonstrative friend would not be able to keep them in suspense for long.

Andrew, a quintessential steak-and-potatoes man,

at first looked askance at the menu when he saw the French names for each dish. Just as the waiter appeared, he brightened and ordered Steak Frites—which as far as Sylvia could discern, was French for steak and fries. Since one of them ought to be daring, she chose Magret de Canard, roast duck breast in raspberry coulis with wild rice, even though she had only tried duck once and had no idea what a coulis was. "Don't tell me," she said when Julius began to explain. "I want to be surprised. Perhaps that should be my New Year's resolution: to take more chances and seek out more surprises."

"That's my resolution every year," said Adele, raising her wine glass in a toast to herself.

"It's worked well for you so far," remarked Julius. "Think of all you've accomplished because you're willing to take chances. We should all have your courage."

"You make me sound much braver than I am," Adele protested, but her smile thanked him.

When Sylvia and Andrew urged them to explain, Adele reminded Sylvia of how she had once had a lucrative career as a stockbroker. "I was successful by most people's standards. I had a corner office, great salary, all the perks—but I was working eighty-hour weeks. I had no time for my friends. I gobbled all my meals on the run. I read stock reports on the treadmill at the gym and answered cell phone calls in the bathroom. You laugh, but I'm serious. I was always working. It never stopped."

"Just imagining it wears me out," said Andrew.

"It wore me out, too," Adele confessed. "But whenever thoughts of slowing down or taking a vacation crossed my mind, I drove them away. I had always pushed myself beyond other peoples' expectations, and to stop doing so would be a sign of weakness, or worse yet, some kind of moral failing. I couldn't let myself down."

"I don't know who she was doing it all for," Julius confided to the older couple. "She makes it sound like she was under constant scrutiny and judgment, but I've always believed that people are far too wrapped up in their own concerns to pay much attention to others' struggles."

"For better or for worse, that does seem to be the case," admitted Sylvia, although she could have shared many personal anecdotes of small-town life to the contrary.

"I don't blame anyone but myself for the pressure I felt in those days," Adele said. "All around me were colleagues with the same responsibilities, long hours, and stresses I had, but they were thriving. They enjoyed waging the daily wars. It took me a long time to admit to myself that I wasn't happy. But I didn't know what to do. I didn't know how to stop without giving up, without admitting defeat."

Sylvia nodded, although she did not see how leaving a miserable job could be construed as admitting defeat. There was far more virtue to be found in diverting from a course that clearly wasn't working than in plodding down a road one knew led to a bad end.

"So I went through the motions." Adele sighed and toyed with her fork. "And then came September eleventh."

When she fell silent, Andrew gently asked, "Did you lose loved ones?"

"I don't know anyone who didn't. I lost several friends that day, acquaintances I knew through work, clients—" Adele took a deep breath. "There are no words. There just aren't any words for it."

Her listeners nodded.

"Adele also lost her home when the Towers collapsed," said Julius.

"Oh, dear," said Sylvia. "I had no idea. You never mentioned it."

"My apartment building was covered with soot and debris," Adele explained. "None of the residents could go home. I stayed with a friend—slept on her sofa, tried to figure out what to do next. Weeks passed before we were allowed to return for some belongings. Everything I owned was covered in a thick, white shroud of dust. I threw a few salvageable things into a bag and never looked back. It was hard to care about *things* when so many innocent people had lost their lives."

Sylvia reached out and patted her hand. "I understand, dear."

"I had long since returned to work. After all that had happened, it seemed trivial to brood over my dissatisfaction with my career. My feelings hadn't changed; I just stopped thinking of them as important enough to act upon. Then one December afternoon, I was out apartment hunting when I passed the 1863 House."

"She went inside, took a tour, and made an offer within a week, even though she had never run a bed and breakfast in her life," her husband broke in, shaking his head in proud incredulity.

"It didn't happen quite that quickly," Adele said, laughing. "I did my due diligence. I made a business plan. But if I hadn't seen that quilt in the window, I might still be toiling away on Wall Street."

Sylvia was eager to hear how a quilt had played a role in Adele's story, and she urged her friend to continue. Adele explained that not long before she bought the 1863 House, her therapist had encouraged her to take up a creative hobby—something for pure enjoyment completely unrelated to her job. Since her grandmother had quilted and because at that low point in her life she felt drawn to items of warmth and comfort, she signed up for a beginner's quilting class at the City Quilter.

"I was a newly minted quilter, with all the zeal of a recent convert," said Adele. "When I walked past the brownstone that day, I glimpsed a quilt through the window, a Crazy Quilt draped over the davenport. I wanted a closer look, but rather than risk arrest by peering through the window, I knocked on the door and asked the proprietor if I could come inside for a closer look."

The proprietor was a quilter herself, and so pleased by Adele's interest that she offered to show her all the antique quilts in the inn. One very special quilt she saved for last, withdrawing it from a custom-made, muslin-lined wardrobe in the family's private quarters on the fifth floor.

"It was the quilt I placed on the bed in your suite," Adele said, confirming Sylvia's guess. "Can you imagine sewing together all those tiny triangles by hand? And those fabrics—it's a veritable catalog of mid- to late-nineteenth-century prints. The proprietor unfolded the quilt with such reverence that I had to know why. She told me that the quilt had come with the brownstone when she and her husband bought it forty years before. The previous owners had told her that the quilt was there when they purchased it, too. Intrigued, she traced its ownership as far back as she could and finally concluded that the quilt had probably belonged to the original owners of the house.

"As she returned the quilt to the wardrobe for safekeeping, she remarked that the quilt and the house had been together so long that it would be a shame to part them. She only hoped that whoever bought the house would cherish both quilt and residence as much as she had." Adele smiled. "That's when I knew I had to make an offer."

"Was it the quilt you wanted, or the house?" asked Andrew.

"I couldn't have one without the other," Adele pointed out with a laugh. "I wanted the quilt, sure, but I wanted the house and the life at least as much. Talk about hubris. I didn't think there would be anything to running an inn. Change the sheets every once in a while, take reservations, serve bagels and coffee—" Adele rolled her eyes. "I thought if I could handle Wall Street, I could handle a little B&B. Let's just say I had a very sharp learning curve. But I never regretted it. I closed on the property on the afternoon of New Year's Eve. As I signed the papers, I told myself that 2002 would be my new beginning. No more would I stay in a safe, predictable routine that made me miserable. Predictability is a trap and safety is an illusion. Love and happiness, on the other hand, are real, but you don't find them without taking chances." She smiled at Julius. "Love for my work eventually led to love of another kind."

After she took over the inn, she explained, she wanted to discover all she could about its history. The previous owners shared what they knew, but Adele suspected the former single-family residence had a richer and more intriguing story to tell. Since Hunter College was nearby, she contacted its history department for advice. That phone call led to a meeting with Julius, a professor who had written several books on New York history. They fell in love, and a year later, they married.

By that time Adele had settled into her new career.

She loved everything about her new life—meeting people from around the world, sending off her guests each morning with a delicious breakfast, introducing them to intriguing places off the usual tourist track, making them feel like true New Yorkers no matter how brief their stay in the city. When she found the time, she continued to research the history of the lovely old brownstone. With Julius's help, she learned enough about research methods and historical scholarship to qualify for a Master's degree, if only she had been officially enrolled.

Sylvia, who had heard some of Adele's stories at Elm Creek Quilt Camp, said, "I do hope you'll share some of that history with us."

Adele promised she would, and as soon as their delicious meal was finished, they returned to the inn. "The name 1863 House comes from the year the brownstone was built, as I'm sure you've already guessed," she told them as they climbed the front stairs. Inside, she showed them down a long hallway that had been converted to a gallery, displaying framed enlargements of black-and-white illustrations that appeared to be political cartoons. Sylvia recognized caricatures of Jefferson Davis and Robert E. Lee in various states of distress, and others of a somber but noble Abraham Lincoln in metaphorical narratives—sewing a divided nation together, visiting his Southern rivals in their nightmares. Other drawings parodied long-forgotten political figures and controversies, while another seemed to mock the simultaneous efforts of both the North and the South to recruit freed slaves for their armies.

"The man who built this residence was an artist and political activist named John Colcraft," Adele said. "You wouldn't know it from his political cartoons, but he was a South Carolinian by birth."

"I wouldn't have guessed that," Andrew remarked, peering closely at an illustration of a particularly tough-looking Union general wiping his shoes on a map of the Confederate states.

"His family had made its fortune in cotton, and as the second son, John often traveled North on business for his father. On one of those journeys he met a Quaker woman named Harriet Beals, who was born in Chester County, Pennsylvania, to a family of staunch abolitionists. By 1858, John had embraced her faith, renounced slavery, and married her, although not necessarily in that order."

"I've always wondered how a man who owed his livelihood to the exploitation of slave labor managed to win the heart of a dedicated abolitionist," Julius remarked.

"He must have been a fine talker," said Adele, with a glance that suggested she knew another man who fit that description. "Don't forget, he did renounce slavery. He also begged his father to free his slaves, but his father refused and disowned his son. Or the son disowned the father, it isn't entirely clear. John Colcraft later wrote that on that day he had lost his birthright but regained his soul."

"Fine words, indeed," said Sylvia, though her own experiences had made it impossible to consider any familial estrangement without regret, without wondering what might have been.

"The couple settled in Philadelphia for a time, which is where John began his artistic career." Adele led them down the hall at a pace that allowed them to examine the framed cartoons more carefully. "As a Quaker and a pacifist, he battled the evils he saw in the world around him with a pen rather than a sword. He began with innocuous illustrations for a city neighborhood, but as the Civil War approached, his drawings took on a more editorial slant. As his fame—or in certain circles, notoriety—grew, he moved to New York and became a regular artist for *Harper's*."

"Which brought them here," Sylvia guessed, admiring the front room of the house as Adele and Julius led them inside and invited them to sit.

Adele nodded. "At the end of 1862, John received a considerable inheritance from his mother's side of the family—'untainted by the stain of slavery,' as he put it—and he used it to build this home for Harriet and their two children. They moved into it in the spring of 1863, at a time of rising tensions in the city."

The Emancipation Proclamation had been in force for several months by then, Adele reminded them. Proslavery organizations responded to the increasing political power of abolitionists by warning working-class New Yorkers of the increased competition for laborers' jobs that would inevitably follow should slavery be abolished and the freed slaves move North. A new, stricter draft law only fanned the flames of unrest: Every male citizen between the ages of twenty and thirty-five, as well as all unmarried male citizens between thirty-five and forty-five, were considered eligible for military service and could be chosen for duty by lottery. Certain exceptions could be made, however. If a man could hire a substitute to take his place or if he could pay the federal government a three-hundred-dollar exemption fee, he would not have to serve. African-Americans were not subject to the draft because they were not considered citizens.

Working-class men, who would bear the brunt of the new law, were outraged. "Then, as it would now, the conflict played out in the press," said Adele. "John Colcraft was right in the thick of it, skewering his political opponents and satirizing racism and hypocrisy on both sides." She gestured to the four walls. "His most significant work was created in this very room. That desk is a reproduction of the one he used, based upon his own sketches of the original."

Fear, anger, and racial tensions rose throughout the city as spring turned into summer and the first lottery approached, Adele told them. On July 11, the first names were drawn, and for nearly two days the city remained quiet, holding its breath, waiting to see if the danger had passed. But early in the morning of July 13, the tensions erupted in violence and bloodshed. At first the rioters targeted only military and government buildings, which to them represented all that was unfair about the new conscription process. People were safe from attack as long as they did not attempt to interfere with the mob's destruction. Before long, however, the rioting took an uglier, more sinister turn as the long-simmering racial tensions finally boiled over. Mobs began attacking African-American residents, their businesses, and any other symbol of black community, culture, or political power.

"Even children were not safe," said Adele. "A mob armed with clubs and bats descended upon the Colored Orphan Asylum at Fifth and Forty-Second, where more than two hundred children lived. They looted the place of anything of value—food, clothing, bedding—and then they burned down the building."

"They attacked an orphanage?" gasped Sylvia. "Had they no shame?"

"What happened to the children?" asked Andrew.

"The building was a total loss," said Adele. "Somehow

the matron, superintendent, and a handful of volunteers managed to get all the children outside unharmed—but the mob was still there, destroying property, attacking and even killing African-Americans unlucky enough to fall into their hands. The superintendent split the children into two groups to try to lead them through the rioting to safety. Two hundred and thirty-three children followed the matron and superintendent to the police station at Thirty-Fifth Street. The remaining twenty-nine made their way here under Harriet Beals Colcraft's protection."

"For five days this house was their sanctuary," Julius added. "For five days the children were sheltered in these rooms while the worst atrocities you can imagine were carried out in the streets."

"I'd prefer to only imagine them, if you please," said Sylvia, when Julius seemed prepared to describe those horrors with a historian's eye for detail.

"While Harriet cared for the children, she must have been out of her mind with worry," said Adele. "She had led the orphans to an empty house. John had gone out, perhaps to the newspaper office to check on the safety of friends, perhaps to witness the events unfold so he could draw about them later. Only after the rioting subsided did Harriet receive word that her husband was in the hospital. He had been discovered unconscious and badly beaten on the waterfront, where white longshoremen were attacking black dockworkers and sailors. He must have come between the two sides."

"Or a political enemy recognized him and took advantage of the uproar and confusion to exact some personal revenge," said Julius. "That's my pet theory, anyway."

"I think it's more likely he rushed to a victim's aid

only to fall prey to the attackers himself," said Adele. "He never fully recovered from his injuries, but suffered pain and difficulty walking for the rest of his life. He considered it a blessing that his attackers had struck him on the back and legs and left his arms unscathed so he could still draw, and therefore could still support his family."

"Some blessing," said Andrew. "If they had tried to hit him but missed, well, *that* I'd call a blessing."

"Adele has been entertaining her guests with stories of the Colcraft family ever since," said Julius. "Almost every time, at the end of the tale, one of her listeners will say, 'You should write a book.' "

"I was going to make that suggestion myself," remarked Sylvia. "The Colcrafts certainly experienced an interesting chapter of New York history, and you have a gift for words."

"I thought about it," said Adele. "Julius has written two books for university presses, and I've lost count of how many articles he's written for academic journals, so I knew something of the publication process. I wanted to tell the Colcrafts' story, but the thought of writing a book was so daunting. I couldn't imagine tackling such an enormous project. And what if I couldn't finish? Or what if I did finish and no one cared? What if every publisher in the world rejected it? What if the writing turned out to be one big waste of time?"

"She found every logical reason not to try," said Julius. "I tried to encourage her, but—" He shook his head ruefully. "Why listen to me? I'm just her husband."

"Then last Christmas my mother gave me a book on New York history," said Adele. "It seems like the perfect gift for a history buff, doesn't it?"

"It made her miserable," said Julius.

"But don't ever tell my mother," Adele warned them. "She doesn't know. Anyway, for a few days after Christmas I alternated between reading chapters of the book and moping around the inn in a brood. Whenever our guests couldn't overhear, I complained to Julius about relevant historical details omitted from the book, other sources that the author should have consulted, and conclusions that didn't fit the historical record. Again and again I asked, 'How can this guy get his book published and I can't?'

"Finally, Julius must have heard enough, because he retorted, 'How? By having the courage to actually sit down and write his book, and send it out into the world so that people like you could stew in jealousy and gripe about how you could have done better.' "

"You said that?" Andrew asked Julius. "How many nights did you have to sleep on the sofa afterward?"

"Not long," said Julius. "Less than a week."

"Oh, don't believe him," said Adele, laughing. "I knew he was right. And yes, I had been duly chastened. But the task of sitting down and writing an entire book was still too overwhelming to contemplate. Then I had a revelation: I didn't have to write the entire book in one sitting."

Everyone laughed.

"That might seem obvious to you," said Adele, "and anyone else with common sense, but it wasn't something I had consciously considered before. Finally I realized that the only way I would ever be a published writer was if I sat down and wrote something."

"That *is* an important part of the process," said Julius, his mouth quirking in a grin.

"I had to push thoughts of failure out of my mind," said Adele. "I told myself that even if I never published my book, it was important to record all I had learned about the Colcrafts and the history of this wonderful brownstone. I was sure our guests would enjoy learning what my research had uncovered, even if no publisher thought the story was worth putting on bookstore shelves. So I made a New Year's resolution: Every day I had to sit down and write a few sentences. I stopped thinking about writing an entire book and instead just focused on those few sentences each day."

"Did you keep your resolution?" asked Sylvia.

"Even on weekends and holidays," said Julius proudly, with an affectionate smile for his wife.

"Running the B&B was still my first love, and I have high standards, so it wasn't easy to find writing time," said Adele. "But I managed. As the weeks passed, I accumulated more and more pages, I wrote for longer stretches of time, and my confidence increased. I was doing it. I was actually writing my book, something I feared I could never do."

"She printed out one copy for each guest room in the inn and had them spiral bound," said Julius. "Our guests read the book, and loved it, and some even asked for autographed copies to take home."

"I had Julius read through the manuscript before I made the guests' copies," Adele hastened to add. "I wanted some editorial oversight, at least. I do have my pride."

"One day, one of our guests asked Adele if she minded if he showed her book to a friend who worked for a publisher," said Julius. "By that time Adele had been sending the manuscript around to literary agents, and had even submitted it to a few contests, but received only rejection letters in reply."

"That was a fun time," said Adele dryly. "Our guest's

offer was the first real glimmer of hope I'd seen. Did I mind if he showed it to his friend? Was he crazy? I would have driven him to his friend's office and watched him personally deliver the manuscript if I hadn't thought that would seem too desperate. If I had known that his friend was a senior editor at New York University Press, I might have been too terrified to let him do it, so it's a good thing he didn't mention that until he was on his way out the door with the manuscript in his briefcase."

"Please do tell me that this story has a happy ending," said Sylvia, remembering how upon meeting her friend at the restaurant, she had strongly suspected that Adele was concealing a secret. Now Sylvia was certain she knew why.

A smile lit up Adele's face. "My book is coming out next fall."

Sylvia and Andrew cheered and embraced her, offering their congratulations and promising to buy copies for all of their friends. "It's not going to be a best-seller," warned Adele. "I'm just hoping it will do well locally and in academic bookstores and libraries."

"Don't downplay your success," Sylvia admonished her. "What a wonderful achievement. I'm sure the Colcrafts would be proud."

"All this came about because of a New Year's resolution," Andrew marveled.

"A New Year's resolution that I kept," Adele emphasized. "Anyone can make promises. The challenge is in following through."

They peppered Adele with questions about her forthcoming book until Julius glanced at the clock and reminded them of the time. With a start, Sylvia remembered their theater tickets. She and Andrew hurried off to the Garden Room to dress, and before long, they were on their way.

Sylvia gazed out of the cab window, drinking in the beauty of the city at night and reflecting upon all that Adele had shared with them. Sylvia admired her resolve and her determination to put aside her fears and find a more fulfilling path. Sylvia had made a similar choice not long ago, when she accepted a challenge from a young friend, Sarah McClure, and transformed her family estate into a quilters' retreat. Embarking upon that journey had been a risk, the most significant chance she had taken in decades, but at that point in her life, she'd had very little to lose. She wondered how her life might have been different if, like Adele, she had taken measures to change her life years earlier, and not waited for her sister's death to return home to Elm Creek Manor. If only on one lonely New Year's Eve she had made a resolution as Adele had done, and had come home to ask forgiveness instead of waiting for Claudia to apologize first.

Resolving to start a New Year with a vow to mend broken ties with her sister never occurred to her, Sylvia thought ruefully as their cab pulled on to Broadway. Even if it had, Claudia would not have responded well to the gesture. The sisters had a fractious history when it came to New Year's resolutions, and as much as Sylvia wanted to blame Claudia for that particular conflict, at her ruthlessly honest core, she knew she was at fault.

Sylvia was six years old when her mother and father announced that a new baby brother or sister would be joining the family in the coming winter. Sylvia was torn between delight over the exciting news and worry for her mother's health. On more than one occasion, she had heard her father gently admonish her mother for overexerting herself. He was always encouraging her to rest, to sit down with some quilting or a book instead of chasing around after her daughters. Her mother tried to accept his suggestions graciously, but Sylvia saw her mouth tighten even as she allowed her husband to help her into an overstuffed chair. Sylvia knew that a baby meant sleepless nights and busy days, and she resolved to help her mother care for the baby so that she could get the rest Sylvia's father and old Dr. Granger insisted she needed.

Sylvia would even willingly change diapers, something Claudia had already confided that she would never do. "Babies are stinky and noisy and they cry all the time," Claudia warned. "Mama and Father will spend all their time with the baby and we'll only get what's left over. You wait and see."

Her sister's warnings filled Sylvia with apprehension, but she brushed them aside when she realized that no one else in the family said such things and that Claudia delivered her dire pronouncements only when she and Sylvia were alone. When the adults of the family were around, Claudia was all smiles and cheerfulness and eagerness to help care for the precious little newborn. The aunts and uncles praised her and called her a good girl whenever she went on in that way, but Sylvia, who secretly hoped for a brother, knew what her sister was up to. Claudia wanted to be the best big sister the Bergstrom family had ever seen only because she had to be the best at everything, not because she really wanted to help, and definitely not because she liked babies. As far as Sylvia could tell, Claudia couldn't stand them.

That was one reason why Sylvia was especially annoyed when Claudia suggested they make a quilt for the baby. Sylvia agreed, wishing she had thought of it first. Sylvia was the better quilter, but Claudia was two years older, so she declared herself in charge of the project. When Sylvia balked, Claudia threw up her hands in frustration. “Fine,” she snapped. “I’ll make my own quilt for the baby.”

Not about to be outdone, Sylvia announced that she would make her own quilt for the baby, too. The argument escalated as they fought over whose quilt the baby would use first, until their voices became so loud that Mama came to investigate. “It’s lovely that you want to make a quilt to welcome the baby,” she said, short of breath, settling herself carefully into a chair. “But you don’t have much time. You’ll have to work together if you hope to finish before the baby comes.”

She smiled to conceal her weariness, but a stab of guilt reminded Sylvia that their mother needed peace and quiet. Only for her sake did Sylvia agree to work with her sister on a single quilt. At their mother’s prompting, they agreed that Sylvia could select the block pattern and Claudia the colors. Sylvia chose the Bear’s Paw, a pretty block that even Claudia could not mess up too badly, since it had no curves or set-in pieces. She imagined cuddling Mama’s new baby within its soft folds, but Claudia’s next words spoiled her contentment: “For colors, I want pink and white, with a little bit of green.”

Sylvia protested that those colors would do fine for a baby sister but not for a little boy. “It’s a baby. It won’t care,” said Claudia, rolling her eyes at her sister’s ignorance.

“If he’s a boy he’ll care. Let’s pick something else.”

“You picked the pattern. I get to pick the colors. You can’t pick everything.”

Mama broke in before the argument could become heated. "Compromise, girls."

One glance at her mother's beloved face, tired and disappointed, compelled Sylvia to swallow her pride. "Okay," she told her sister. "You pick the pattern and I'll pick the colors."

Claudia considered only a moment. "Then I pick Turkey Tracks."

Sylvia couldn't believe what she was hearing. Could there be any worse choice for a baby quilt? Not only was it unlikely that Claudia could manage the difficult pattern, but every Bergstrom quilter had heard Grandma's foreboding stories about the pattern once better known as Wandering Foot. A boy given a Wandering Foot quilt would never be content to stay in one place, but would forever be restless, roaming the world, never settling down; a girl would be doomed to an even worse fate, so bleak that Grandma refused to elaborate. "Some people think that by changing a block's name, you get rid of the bad luck," Grandma had once said, watching over Sylvia as she practiced quilting a Nine-Patch. "I know that bad luck isn't so easily fooled."

Sylvia knew it would be far better to give a boy a pink quilt than to give any baby a quilt full of bad luck, but her mother and sister dismissed her concerns and told her not to be upset by foolish superstitions. Against the two of them, united, there was nothing Sylvia could do but select her lucky colors, blue and yellow, and hope for the best.

If anything proved that Claudia was not a responsible, loving elder sister, her insistence upon that quilt pattern should have done so. Why had Claudia insisted upon that bad-luck block instead of choosing from among her favorites? Was she only trying to annoy Sylvia, as she so often did, or was she deliberately wishing her new sibling misfortune?

Despite Sylvia's reluctance, they finished the quilt in two months. Her mother's proud smile as she draped the blue-and-yellow quilt over the cradle filled Sylvia with warmth and happiness, easing her worries. If Mama said everything was all right, if Mama thought the quilt was not to be feared, then surely it must be so.

The weeks passed and their mother's slight figure grew rounder, but only around her tummy. Her limbs were thin and pale, her face shadowed. Sylvia woke one morning to find that Dr. Granger had been summoned in the night. Mama was all right, Great-Aunt Lucinda assured her, but the doctor had ordered her to remain in bed until the baby was born. Great-Aunt Lucinda made the girls promise not to play loudly in the house, and not to trouble their mother with any unpleasantness. "If ever we needed you two girls to get along, this would be the time," she said with a sigh. "Try not to argue, but if you must, please do it in whispers. Outside."

"What if it's snowing?" asked Claudia. "What if it's dark?"

"I don't care if it's a blizzard at midnight. If you're so angry at your sister that you must express it or burst, take it outside to the barn."

After Great-Aunt Lucinda hurried away to their mother's bedroom, Claudia whirled upon Sylvia. "Did you hear that? You'd better behave yourself." She trotted off after Great-Aunt Lucinda without waiting for a reply.

Sylvia gritted her teeth, balled her hands into fists, and stalked upstairs to the nursery, sick with anger and worry. The baby was not supposed to come until the middle of January, which meant that Mama had to stay in bed a whole month. She would miss Christmas and New Year's Eve. Sylvia did not know what might happen if Mama disobeyed the doctor's orders—she dared not ask—but she could imagine the worst. This time Mama must listen to Father and rest.

No matter how Claudia provoked her, Sylvia would not shout and argue. She would let Claudia have her way and the last word in every discussion if she had to hold her own mouth shut with her hands. Until the baby was born and Mama was allowed out of bed, Sylvia would be the perfect daughter her mother deserved.

For the first few days, Sylvia stuck to her vow so diligently that her father asked her if she felt all right and Great-Aunt Lydia often frowned and felt her forehead as if she believed only illness could subdue Sylvia's naughtiness. Claudia glared at her, suspicious, but was apparently unwilling to be the one to break the tentative truce. Sylvia tried to make her newfound obedience less obvious, but she couldn't help feeling annoyed by the attention her good behavior drew. Did everyone really believe she was ordinarily so naughty that a few quiet days made such a difference?

At first Sylvia's mother submitted to the doctor's orders without complaint, but after a week, she grew restless and bored. One morning, Sylvia passed by her parents' bedroom door and overheard her mother telling her father that she felt strong enough to leave bed. She longed to sit on the front porch, watch the snow fall, and breathe deeply of cold, fresh winter air. "As long as I rest, it shouldn't matter if I'm in bed or in a chair," she said. "Dr. Granger didn't mean for us to take his suggestion so literally."

"It was an order, not a suggestion, and you can ask him to be more specific on his next visit." Sylvia's father tucked the bedcovers around his wife, but she impatiently flung them off again. "Until then, we're going to assume that 'bed rest' means 'rest in bed.' "

"I'll come back straight away if I feel so much as a twinge of pain."

"By then it might be too late. Think of all those stairs. Darling, think of the baby."

Sylvia recognized that tone in her father's voice and knew her mother had lost the argument before it began. Sylvia's mother must have sensed that, too, but she persisted until she had persuaded her husband to allow her more visits with the children. Delighted, the sisters agreed to all of their great-aunts' conditions: no arguing, no loud voices, no bad news, and no complaints. They could read to their mother, or sew, or tell amusing stories, or take her meals on trays. They could not stay too long, only one of them could visit at a time so they did not overtire her, and under no circumstances were they to ask her to get out of bed and play.

Every morning the girls raced downstairs to the kitchen so they could be the first to offer to take Mama her breakfast, knowing she would let them linger until it was time to go to school. Sylvia usually reached the kitchen a few steps ahead of her sister, but Claudia would remind everyone that she was the eldest and more responsible, Sylvia more prone to knocking over her milk at the table and running in the halls. Sylvia protested, but most mornings she sat down glumly to her own breakfast at the kitchen table while her sister glided off bearing the tray without so much as rattling a single dish. Sylvia longed for her to trip on a loose floorboard and send teacup and oatmeal flying through the air, but old Great-Grandfather Hans had built the house too well for that.

Sometimes after school, Sylvia was allowed to take the mail up to her mother and stay to read aloud from one of her schoolbooks or talk about her day. On the last day before school holidays began, Sylvia raced upstairs with an envelope bearing a New York postmark. It could only be from Grandmother Lockwood, her mother's mother. Grandfather Lockwood had died before Sylvia was born, but he had been a very successful businessman and had founded the most prestigious department store on Fifth Avenue. None of the Lockwoods had ever visited Elm Creek Manor and the Bergstroms never went to New York, except when Father or one of the uncles traveled on business, so the Bergstrom girls had never met anyone from their mother's side of the family. It was probably too far to travel, Sylvia speculated, or Mama was too tired or Grandmother Lockwood too old.

Sylvia was certain the letter would lift her mother's spirits, but instead of tearing open the envelope, her mother turned it over in her hands, felt its thickness, and traced the postmark with a fingertip.

"Aren't you going to read it?" Sylvia asked.

"Not now." Mama smiled briefly and set the letter on the nightstand. "Later. I'd rather hear about your day. How was school? Did you learn anything interesting? Did anyone do anything that made you laugh?"

Sylvia sat down on the edge of the bed and happily told her nearly every detail of all that she had done and seen since leaving the house that morning. A few days later, when she saw the envelope tucked into a book at her mother's bedside, she wondered what news Grandmother Lockwood had sent from New York. Probably nothing terribly interesting, she decided, or her mother would have mentioned it. Grandmother Lockwood didn't work or quilt, and although she used to go to lots of parties when Grandfather Lockwood was alive, as far as Sylvia could discern from the few details Mama had shared through the years, all that concerned her these days was the weather and her health. She no longer lived in the house where Sylvia's mother had grown up, so she wouldn't have any gossip about neighbors and old friends to pass along, either. Still, it was a letter from family, so it must have been a welcome distraction from boring bed rest. Sylvia couldn't wait until the baby came and everything could return to normal.

Christmas approached. Great-Aunt Lydia and Grandma made the famous Bergstrom apple strudel as gifts for the neighbors, and Great-Aunt Lucinda kept the Santa Claus cookie jar filled with her delicious German cookies—*Lebkuchen, Anisplätzchen,* and *Zimtsterne.* Sylvia ached to see her mother among the other women of the family in the warm, fragrant kitchen, kneading strudel dough, peeling apples, laughing, gossiping, and reminiscing about holidays past. The conversations were more subdued that year, the laughter less frequent, as if no one felt like celebrating without Mama in the room. She was the gentle, loving center of every family gathering, and even though she was only upstairs, her absence was sorely felt.

On Christmas morning, Sylvia left Claudia in the ballroom marveling at the presents Santa had left beneath the tree and stole away to the kitchen. Great-Aunt Lucinda glanced through the doorway as if expecting Claudia to follow close behind, and when she didn't,

Great-Aunt Lucinda asked Sylvia in a conspiratorial whisper if she wanted to carry Mama's breakfast up to her. Sylvia agreed with a quick nod, afraid that Claudia would overhear and come running to snatch the tray from her hands.

Cautiously she made her way upstairs to her mother's bedroom, torn between determination not to drop a single crumb and worry that if she did not move quickly enough, the tea would cool before she reached the top of the stairs. To her relief, the teacup was still hot to the touch when she reached her mother's bedroom. She took a deep breath and nudged the door open with her foot.

"Breakfast time, Mama," said Sylvia as cheerfully as she could, taken aback by the sight of her mother lying still and pale against the pillows. Was this how she looked every morning upon waking? Had she slept at all?

As her mother smiled and sat up awkwardly, Sylvia set the tray on the nightstand and hurried to assist her. "It's apple strudel and tea," she said, although her mother could surely see that for herself. To cover her embarrassment, Sylvia smiled, tucked the quilt around her mother, and placed the tray on her lap.

"It wouldn't feel like Christmas morning without the famous Bergstrom apple strudel." Mama took a small bite and closed her eyes, savoring the spicy sweetness and the delicate pastry. "Delicious."

"I helped peel the apples."

"I thought so. They seem especially well peeled this year." Mama smiled and patted the bed beside her. "Would you mind keeping me company for a while?"

Sylvia wasn't sure that Father would approve, but she nodded and climbed into bed, careful not to jostle the tray. She snuggled close and rested her hand on her mama's tummy, waiting for the baby to respond. When an especially strong kick pushed Sylvia's hand away, Mama laughed. "I think he knows his big sister is waiting for him to come out and play."

"Do you really think it's a boy?" asked Sylvia. "Claudia wants another sister." A better sister, Claudia had implied.

"I think so, but we won't know until the day comes." Her mother grimaced and rubbed her lower back. "Which I hope will be soon."

"Not too soon," said Sylvia, thinking of how often she saw her father bent over his calendar in the library, counting and recounting the weeks as if his diligence could keep the baby from coming.

"No, not too soon," her mother agreed. She finished her breakfast and asked Sylvia to take the tray away so she could lie down again. Sylvia returned the tray to the nightstand and climbed back into bed beside her mother.

Her mother stroked her hair gently. "I've missed you, darling. I'm sorry I haven't been able to play with you."

"That's all right," said Sylvia. "I understand."

"After the baby comes, I'll be as right as rain again. You'll see."

Sylvia nodded and hugged her. She wanted to believe it, but the house was so full of apprehension that some days she thought the windows might shatter and the darkness stream from the house like billowing black smoke.

"Everything will be fine, darling," her mother said. "Don't worry."

"I can't help it," Sylvia blurted. "Everyone says not to upset you and I'm trying, I'm really trying, but what if it's already too late? What if the bad luck is already hurting the baby? You touched the quilt, and maybe that's all it takes."

She regretted the words the moment they passed her lips, but to her surprise, her mother let out a gentle laugh. "Oh, Sylvia, is that what's troubling you? That silly superstition?"

That wasn't it. At least, that wasn't everything, but she couldn't bring herself to query her mother about the doctor's visits and Father's constant anxious frowns and the adults' hushed conversations when they did not know children were listening. Sylvia could not give voice to those other fears, so she nodded. Everything would be so much better if only the quilt worried her.

"I promise you that the quilt is not bad luck," her mother said firmly. "How could anything made with so much love bring the baby anything but comfort and happiness?"

"Grandma says the pattern—"

"I know what Grandma says. I've heard the old wives' tales. Have you? Have you really listened to what the folklore says about that pattern?"

"It says—" Sylvia hesitated, trying to remember Grandma's exact words, certain it was a trick question. "If you give a boy a Wandering Foot quilt, he'll be too restless to stay in one place. He'll roam the world, never settling down."

"That's what it says," her mother confirmed. "And although I don't believe the superstition, not for a moment, if that's our little baby's fate, I don't think that's so terrible."

Sylvia propped herself up on her elbows. "You don't?"

"Not at all. What's wrong with a little wanderlust? I like to think that your little brother or sister might have adventures, see the world, and visit all the places I've only read about in books." Her mother reached up and stroked her cheek. "You see, darling, I was always too ill to travel when I was a little girl. My parents took my older sister with them when they went abroad, but I stayed at home in New York with my nanny. Until I married your father and came to Elm Creek Manor, the most exotic place I had ever visited was our summer house."

"That's not fair. If you couldn't go, they all should have stayed home."

"I admit there were times when I was jealous of my sister, but as I grew older, I resolved to be happy for her. I decided it wouldn't be fair to deny her travel and fun just because I was too fragile to do anything—or so everyone thought." A brief frown clouded her features. "Everyone but my nanny. Now that my sister is gone, I'm grateful that she had so many wonderful experiences when she was young."

Sylvia had to admit that it didn't sound so bad to wander the world and have adventures, not the way her mother put it, but one nagging worry remained. "But what about that part that says he'll never be happy to stay in one place?" she asked. "Doesn't that mean that he won't want to stay here at Elm Creek Manor with the rest of the family? What if he goes far away and we'll never see him again, just like Elizabeth?"

"We don't know that we'll never see Elizabeth again," her mother corrected. "It's a long way to travel, but I'm sure she and Henry will make the journey someday."

Sylvia would be perfectly content if Henry decided to stay behind in California. "But what about the baby?" she persisted. "Either he'll leave Elm Creek Manor, or he'll stay here but be unhappy."

"Well . . ." Mama took a deep breath, sighed, and fell silent for a moment. "Well, babies can't go anywhere on their own, so we have years before that will be a concern. Even after that, perhaps he'll travel a lot, but always come home to the family." She gave herself a little shake. "Why are we even going on like this? It's a silly superstition, nothing we need to fear, and it isn't right to be so gloomy on Christmas morning. The New Year is going to bring us a new baby, and that's cause for joy, not worry."

She tickled Sylvia under her chin until Sylvia giggled, and she resolved, as her mother had so many years ago, to be happy for her little sibling, to think only of the good the superstition might visit upon the family, and not worry about dire predictions that probably would not come to pass. The very idea that any Bergstrom would not be happy at Elm Creek Manor was laughable. Perhaps her little brother would see the world, but surely he would always come home to them. The lucky colors she had stitched into the quilt would see to that.

That quiet Christmas passed and the New Year drew closer. When Mama's condition did not worsen, warm rays of hope began to illuminate the manor. When the subject of New Year's Eve came up around the dinner table, Great-Aunt Lucinda remarked that it would be a shame not to welcome in a year that was sure to be brighter than the one before, a year that was certain to bring the family much happiness. To Sylvia's delight, her father and the other adults of the family agreed.

A Sylvester Ball was out of the question, of course; the family had not celebrated with *Bleigiessen* since the New Year's Eve the leaden shapes foretold Claudia's heartbreak and Mama's death. Even though the predictions had not come true, no one could laugh at how they had been frightened and misled. By unspoken agreement, the family had decided not to peer into the future in that way again. The consequences of what they might discover could not be reduced to the triviality of a party game.

Finally they settled for a quiet family observance at home, with a supper of pork crown roast with apples, creamed potatoes with peas, and sauerkraut. Father would make his *Feuerzangenbowle* punch for the adults, Great-Aunt Lucinda would make *Pfannkuchen* for everyone, and the girls would be allowed to stay up until midnight to welcome the New Year with noisemakers and apple cider toasts.

Sylvia was so pleased by the idea of a family party that she eagerly offered to help prepare the meal. "She only wants to dip her fingers in the jelly when Great-Aunt Lucinda isn't looking," said Claudia, which made the aunts laugh and Sylvia smolder. Grandma must have believed that Sylvia's offer was sincere, however, for she tutted sympathetically and said that Sylvia could be her special helper.

As they went down to the cellar to retrieve a crock of sauerkraut Great-Aunt Lucinda had made the summer before, Grandma reminded her that the family recipe had been handed down through the years from Gerda Bergstrom, Grandpa's aunt and the finest cook in the Bergstrom family. "I didn't take to the dish at first," she confessed, her voice echoing off the cool, dark walls of the cellar. "The flavor was so sharp and pungent I thought Aunt Gerda had served it to me as a prank. I had to force myself to choke it down, but what else could I do? I was a new bride and I wanted to make a good impression."

"Didn't your mother make sauerkraut?"

"No, but we had our own traditional dishes that might

have caught the Bergstrom family by surprise." She smiled to herself and added, "I'd love to see what Lucinda would do if I set a plate of haggis before her."

Sylvia didn't like the sound of any dish that Great-Aunt Lucinda might refuse. "But didn't you eat pork and sauerkraut for the New Year?" Grandma fussed about good luck and bad more than anyone Sylvia knew. It was difficult to imagine that she would knowingly pass up an easy way to bring good luck to the household.

"That's a German tradition. My mother was a Scotswoman, which means that you're part Scot, too." Grandma gestured for Sylvia to help her lift the crock from its low shelf. "My father was Welsh, so you have some of that, as well. You're part English, from your mother's people, and there's a little Swedish on your great-grandfather's side. You're quite a little American mix, aren't you? It's a wonder you're not constantly at war with yourself."

Sylvia had never really thought about it. She was a part of the Bergstrom family, and that was all that mattered.

They carried the crock upstairs to the kitchen. There Grandma instructed Sylvia to put on her apron and help her peel potatoes. Grandma looked thoughtful as she took a potato from the burlap sack on the floor and inspected it for bad spots. "My mother called the celebration of the New Year 'Hogmanay,'" she said, setting the sharp blade of her paring knife against the dusky potato skin.

"What does that mean?" asked Sylvia. By the sound of it, it had something to do with pork, lots of it.

Grandma shrugged. "She never said. I'm not sure she knew. She had so many funny words for ordinary things that I never questioned it." She smiled as she sent potato peelings flying neatly into the trash bin. "I remember we had to clean the house thoroughly before we could give any thought to a celebration. Before midnight on New Year's Eve, the fireplaces had to be swept clean and the ashes carried outside. All debts had to be paid, too. Sometimes my mother would send one of my brothers running to a neighbor's house after supper with a coin or two to pay off a debt, even though most of our neighbors weren't Scottish and wouldn't mind if she waited another day. The purpose was to prepare yourselves and your home to begin the New Year with a fresh, clean slate, with all the problems, mistakes, and strife of the old year forgotten."

"I like that idea," said Sylvia. Her family never seemed to forget any of her mistakes. It would have been nice if a holiday obligated them to try.

"My parents followed other traditions in their homelands that they didn't carry with them to America." Grandma placed a potato in Sylvia's hands. "You can peel while you listen. That's a good girl."

Sylvia peeled the potato slowly, wary of cutting herself. "What did they do in Scotland that they couldn't do in Pennsylvania?"

"It's not that they couldn't. I suppose they could have, but some traditions are simply more enjoyable when everyone in the town joins in." Grandma smiled, remembering. "My mother told me about a tradition called First Footing, which told that the first person who crossed the threshold after the stroke of midnight would determine the luck of the household for the coming year. The year would be especially prosperous if a tall, dark-haired, handsome man was the first to enter the house on the first day of the New Year."

"Why did it have to be a handsome man?" asked Sylvia, placing her peeled potato in the bowl next to Grandma's and reaching for another. "Why not a pretty lady?"

"If the lady was expecting a child, or if she was a new bride, she was also considered to bring good luck," Grandma said. "A blond man, on the other hand, was believed to bring bad luck. My mother said that was because a dark-haired man was assumed to be a fellow Scot, but a blond could be a Viking, come to pillage and plunder. Naturally, since everyone wanted good luck and no one could stay shut up in their homes until the appropriate person came to the door, the tradition changed. Tall, dark-haired, handsome men would be enlisted to go around to the homes of their neighbors, bringing with them symbolic gifts such as coal for the fire, or salt, or a treat like fruit buns or shortbread. No one was supposed to speak to the First Footer until he entered the house, gave them the traditional gifts, and spoke a blessing: 'A good New Year to one and all and many more may you see.' After that you could speak to the guest and offer him a drink of whiskey before he departed for the next house."

"My father would be a good First Footer," said Sylvia. "He's tall, he has dark hair like mine, and he's very handsome. Everyone would be glad to see him on New Year's Eve."

Grandma laughed. "I've always thought he was very handsome, too, but he's my son, so I can't pretend to be impartial. Oh, there's something else my mother told me about that I've always wished I could see. The young men of her village would build large balls about a yard wide from chicken wire, paper, tar, and other materials that would burn. They would attach a chain, light the ball on fire, and walk through the streets of the town swinging the burning fireball around and around. It must have been a dazzling sight, all the young men out in the streets lighting up the darkness with those crackling circles of fire. When the fireballs were almost burned out, or when the young men tired of the game and wanted to celebrate with more whiskey, they would parade down to the riverside and send the fireballs sailing through the air into the water below."

Sylvia shivered with delight. It sounded terribly beautiful, and terribly dangerous. "I probably wouldn't be allowed to try that here," she said.

"Absolutely not," said Grandma. "It's a wonder those Scottish villages weren't burned to the ground, or the young men seriously injured. As much as I'd like just once to see those fireballs swinging, I suppose it's just as well that my mother's family left that tradition behind when they came to America."

"Maybe someday we can go to Scotland for the New Year and see them."

Grandma smiled at her affectionately for a moment before taking up her paring knife again. "Perhaps you will someday, my dear. I hope you travel far and wide and see many beautiful and wondrous things in your lifetime."

Sylvia bit back the impertinent question that immediately sprang to mind: Then why did Grandma fear the Wandering Foot quilt pattern so much? Wasn't what Grandma wished for her exactly what the quilt was supposed to bring?

She almost, but not quite, wished that someone had given her a Wandering Foot quilt when she was a baby. Maybe Claudia's choice wasn't so bad after all—not that Sylvia would ever tell her sister that.

Since Claudia had taken Mama her breakfast tray, Sylvia was granted the honor of serving her the special New Year's Eve dinner. Sylvia entertained her mother by retelling Grandma's stories of Scottish New Year's celebrations and imagining what would happen if she tried to make a fireball of her own. "Your father would have a fit, that's what would happen," her mother said, smiling. "Grandma would never tell you another story out of fear that you might decide to try it."

"How did you celebrate New Year's Eve when you were a little girl, Mama?"

Her mother regarded her with mild surprise, and Sylvia felt a quick flush of shame. It was true that she rarely asked her mother to share stories of her girlhood in New York. Unlike Claudia, she had little interest in descriptions of pretty dresses and fancy balls, of dance lessons and learning good manners. Her mother never spoke of mischief or play, but only of rules and restrictions. Grandfather and Grandmother Lockwood had raised her to be a proper young lady, and since this was the very sort of well-behaved child Sylvia invariably failed to emulate, her mother's stories seemed like dull morality tales. Sylvia had decided long ago that the Bergstrom family was far more interesting than the Lockwoods. Unlike Claudia, who hung on their mother's every word, Sylvia paid little attention when a distant look came into her mother's eyes as she remembered events long ago and far away.

"I really want to know," Sylvia persisted.

"We didn't eat pork and sauerkraut," said Mama. "My father believed hard work brought one good luck, and my mother put her faith in knowing the right people. My parents almost always went to a New Year's Eve ball at one of their friends' homes or somewhere else in the city. When we were older, my sister and I were allowed to go with them. The men wore elegant coats and tails, and the ladies dressed in stunning gowns and wore their finest jewelry. The orchestra played, we danced and danced, and at midnight we threw streamers and drank champagne. My sister and I were quite grown up by that time," she hastened to add.

"That sounds like fun," Sylvia said gamely.

Mama tried to hide a smile. "You might truly think so when you're older. My favorite New Year's Eve came years before I was allowed to go to fancy balls. I was ten years old in 1900, and the city was electric with anticipation for the turning of the century. My parents and sister celebrated by going to the theater and then to a party at the home of my father's biggest business rival. The men didn't get along, but they ran in the same social circle so they had to include each other in their gatherings or people would talk. They were both glad, too, for any opportunity to show off their wealth and success to the other. If my parents refused the Drurys' invitation, it would be seen as admitting they could not compete or, worse yet, rudeness."

"Your sister got to go but you didn't?" Sylvia exclaimed. "Again?"

"I was too young, and my mother thought I would catch a terrible chill if I stayed out so late on a winter's night."

"That's silly. You would have been indoors almost the whole time. You could have worn a coat."

"That's what I told them. My father and sister stuck up for me, but my mother wouldn't hear of it." Mama smiled and lifted her shoulders as if to say it had happened so long ago that it no longer mattered. "I was terribly disappointed to be left behind. After they left, I went upstairs to work on my Crazy Quilt. It was nearly finished, and stitching upon it usually lifted my spirits, but not that night. A new century was about to begin, and I would have to watch its arrival through a nursery window."

Sylvia stung from the unfairness of it all. "I would have snuck out of the house and followed them."

"The last time I had tried anything like that, I got my nanny fired," said her mother. "I loved her dearly, too, so it was a great loss to me. But after they sent her away, there was no worse punishment they could deliver, or so I thought at the time. I waited for my mother's maid to fall asleep, then I dressed in my warmest clothes and left the house."

Sylvia stared, disbelieving. "Where did you go? What did you do?"

"I walked through the city, enjoying the lights and the celebration. I had a little pocket money, so I bought myself a cup of hot chocolate and a cinnamon doughnut at a small café that my mother would never have considered worthy of her patronage. I walked a long, long time until I came to City Hall Park in lower Manhattan. I had overheard other passersby say that there would be fireworks at midnight, and I thought there could be no better way to welcome the New Year than with fireworks.

"I had never seen such a crowd, and I was thrilled to be a part of it. Everywhere, people were laughing and singing, too distracted with their own fun to notice one little girl all alone. Finally, at the stroke of midnight, City Hall went dark for just a moment, and then suddenly all the lights came on and fireworks lit up the sky. All around me people were cheering and kissing, and sometimes, above the din, I heard the bells of Trinity Church ringing in the New Year several blocks away.

"Then, suddenly, I felt a hand on my shoulder. 'Miss Lockwood?' I heard a man ask. He spun me around and I found myself looking up into an unfamiliar face, rough and incredulous.

"I gulped and spoke not a word. 'You're the younger Miss Lockwood, aren't you?' the man asked. I didn't see any point in denying it, so I nodded. He glanced around for my parents, but of course, they were nowhere to be found. 'What are you doing out here all alone?' he asked. 'This is no place for a girl like you.'

"When I offered no explanation, he shook his head and said that I must return home at once. He told me he worked on the loading docks at my father's store, and he had seen me come in just days before to pick out my Christmas present, as my sister and I were allowed to do every year. He took me firmly by the shoulder and steered me out of the crowd. Somehow he managed to hail a cab, and he gave the driver strict instructions to take me home and not to leave until he saw me safely inside. I was mortified when the man dug into his pockets and counted out change to pay my fare. I knew he couldn't possibly earn very much; the low wages of my father's store employees had been a constant source of disagreement between him and my nanny, who supported workers' rights to form unions. I wanted to apologize, but I was speechless from embarrassment. I could only nod as he warned me never to do such a dangerous thing again, shut the cab door, and waved the driver on."

"You were so naughty," breathed Sylvia.

"Oh, don't I know it, but I was lucky, too. I crept off

to bed and was sound asleep long before my parents and sister returned home."

"Did they ever find out?"

"At first, I wasn't sure." Mama finished her supper, wiped her lips, and set the tray on the nightstand. "My father stayed home from work on New Year's Day, but he kept to himself in his study and I only saw him at mealtimes. I watched my mother carefully to see if she suspected anything, but she was too busy going over every detail of the previous night's party with her maid, Harriet. My sister assured me that the play had been dull and the party afterward even worse, but I knew she was only saying so to make me think I had not missed out on anything. I didn't breathe a word of my New Year's Eve adventure even to her, and I was relieved that I had apparently gotten away with it.

"The next day my father returned to work and, as usual, did not come home until supper late that evening. My mother, sister, and I were already seated when he strode in and took his place at the head of the table. 'Did you hear about the panic at City Hall Park two nights ago?' he asked us.

" 'Of course, my dear,' my mother told him. 'I do read the papers, you know. It was all over the *Times*. Some of the worst of it happened right in front of its building.'

"I kept silent while my sister begged our father to explain. I then learned that I had unwittingly been part of a historically momentous gathering. Remember that I told you I heard the bells of Trinity Church from where I stood at City Hall Park, several blocks away? An enormous crowd had massed in the narrow strip around the church, as well, and as the night went on, both gatherings swelled to such numbers that the two crowds, thousands strong, merged on Broadway. The revelers made merry until shortly after midnight, but then chaos erupted as people set off at cross-purposes, some trying to make it to the Brooklyn Bridge, others fighting their way uptown. Families were separated, and a child was trampled underfoot as the revelers pushed against one another. It was a terrifying scene, and the police could do little to manage it.

"I had been sent home in my cab only moments before the panic started. I gaped at my father, thinking of what a narrow escape I'd had. 'Was anyone hurt?' my sister asked.

" 'One child was injured,' my father said, 'but it could have been much worse. Thankfully both of my little girls were safely far away from that midnight disaster.' And with that he raised his eyebrows at me as if daring me to disagree."

"The man from the store tattled on you," said Sylvia.

"He probably thought it was his duty to tell his employer that his little girl had put herself in great danger," said Mama. "I don't find any fault with him. That little child who was trampled could have been me. I didn't have any grown-ups around to hold my hand or pull me out of harm's way. If I had not left City Hall Park when I did, my New Year might have had a tragic beginning."

"I can't believe you left the house alone at night," marveled Sylvia. "Did your father spank you? Did he tell your mother?"

"Goodness, no. If he had, I'm sure she would have locked me in my room for a week. I received no punishment for what I had done, and in fact, my father never spoke of it again." Mother smiled, her gaze distant. "It was the most adventurous, most disobedient thing I had ever done, and would ever do, until I married your father."

"Why was marrying Father disobedient?" said Sylvia. "Didn't your parents like him?"

Her mother hesitated as if regretting the mention. "Oh, I suppose they liked him well enough, but they wanted me to marry someone else. I wanted to please them, but I loved your father, so I married him instead."

Sylvia shook her head at this new, unbelievable revelation. As difficult as it was to imagine her mother as a naughty little girl, it was impossible to believe that anyone would want Mama to marry someone other than Father. Sylvia couldn't imagine either of them loving anyone else.

"After making such a disobedient start to a new century, I resolved never again to defy my parents out of anger or jealousy," said Mama. "The New Year wasn't only a time for celebration, you see. It was also a time for reflection, and for deciding to mend one's ways and change one's life for the better." Sylvia's mother put her arms around her and kissed her on the top of the head. "You could do that, you know. Think about how you would like to improve yourself in the year ahead and make a New Year's resolution to change."

Sylvia frowned, thinking. "I'd like to run faster," she announced. "I think I'll resolve to do that."

Her mother laughed. "Very well. Deciding how to improve yourself is the first step. Now, how would you go about achieving that goal?"

"Practice? Maybe if I try to run a little faster each day, by next year I'll be lots faster."

"That sounds like the right way to do it. But practice only outside or in the nursery," Mama hastened to add. "I don't think Grandma and the aunts would like to see you running through the halls. For your first New Year's resolution, I think that's fine, but you should know that most resolutions are meant to improve one's character rather than one's athletic skills."

"You mean like . . . not fighting with your sister?"

"Exactly," said Mama. "In fact, that's a resolution most people in this house would be very happy to see you keep."

Sylvia hadn't meant that resolution for herself, but for Claudia. Still, she supposed she could keep it, too, and better than her big sister could.

Father appeared in the doorway then, so Sylvia carried her mother's dishes to the kitchen and ran off to play, thinking of New Year's resolutions and her mother's New Year's Eve adventure so long ago. If Sylvia had been in her mother's place, she would have resolved to have more exciting escapades like that one, instead of promising to be less defiant. It sounded like her mother had only been defiant that one night, so why should she have to resolve to change? It must have been unbearable to stay behind so often and watch her sister go out into the city with their parents. Grandmother and Grandfather Lockwood should have made resolutions to treat their daughters more fairly. Certain members of the Bergstrom family ought to do the same.

In fact, Sylvia thought as she climbed the stairs to the nursery where she kept paper and pencil, everyone in the family would benefit from making New Year's resolutions, and she knew exactly which ones were most necessary.

Sylvia wrote, crossed out mistakes, and copied her writing over neatly on fresh sheets of paper as night fell. She rolled the pages into fancy scrolls and tied them with ribbons, and she had just hidden them in her sewing basket when Claudia came upstairs and summoned her down to the ballroom. Great-Aunt Lucinda had set out *Pfannkuchen* and apple cider, and everyone was gathering for the New Year's Eve party. Father had spent all evening by Mama's side, looking through photo albums and reading aloud, but when Mama wanted to sleep, he joined the rest of the family downstairs by the fire. The adults of the family told jokes and stories of New Year's Eves past, remembering loved ones that Sylvia knew only through family legends. Great-Grandfather Hans and Great-Grandmother Anneke, who had come to America from Germany and founded Elm Creek Farm. Hans's sister, Gerda, who never married but had loved to read and discuss politics and cook. Sylvia drifted off to sleep to the murmur of their voices, but Grandma gently shook her awake five minutes before midnight so she could count down the last seconds of the old year with everyone else. When the mantel clock chimed midnight, she jumped up and down, blew on her tin horn, and shouted, "Happy New Year!" louder than anyone, but after that, she did not argue when her father sent her upstairs to bed.

First, though, she wanted to wish her mother Happy New Year. A light shone through the crack beneath her mother's bedroom door, so Sylvia knocked and softly called out to her. When she did not reply, Sylvia slowly pushed open the door and found her mother sleeping soundly, her book resting open on the bed.

Sylvia tiptoed across the room, bent over to kiss her mother's thin cheek, and picked up the book so her mother wouldn't roll on top of it while she slept. The envelope with the New York postmark Mama had been using as a bookmark lay on the nightstand, but the flap had been opened since Sylvia had last seen it.

She glanced at her sleeping mother, then back to the doorway where she expected her father to appear any moment, then set the book facedown on the bed and quickly slipped a single, thick page from the envelope. When she unfolded it, a newspaper clipping fluttered to the floor. Sylvia quickly scooped it up; a quick glance revealed a society page story about a Christmas ball in New York that the elegantly dressed couple in the photograph had apparently hosted. Sylvia didn't recognize the faces in the photograph or any of the names, so she turned her attention to the letter.

The message, written in firm, dark strokes on ivory writing paper edged in black, began abruptly: "Mrs. Edwin Corville enjoys every luxury, while you waste yourself on a horse farmer in the middle of godforsaken nowhere. Your wishes for a Happy New Year ring hollow, as does the news of your condition. How a strong-willed young woman like yourself can submit to the demands of a husband who clearly has no regard for the risks to your health never ceases to astonish me."

Sylvia swallowed hard and returned the letter and the clipping to the envelope, tucked them into the book, and set it on the nightstand. Mama would think Father had moved them; she would never know Sylvia had read Grandmother Lockwood's cruel words. A sudden thought struck Sylvia: Did Father know what Mama's mother thought of him? Mama had said her parents had wanted her to marry another man, and it seemed Grandmother Lockwood had never forgiven her.

Sylvia bit her lips together, turned off the lamp, and hurried from the room. She climbed into bed, sick at heart. This couldn't be the first ugly letter Grandmother Lockwood had sent, or Mama would have shown some sign of shock or remorse. All the other letters, all of Mama's stories, must have been edited for a little girl's ears. Was Mama a liar? It was unthinkable. Was she ashamed?

Sylvia drifted off to a troubled sleep.

The next morning she woke late, the letter a vague and unpleasant memory fading like a dream. She hurried downstairs just in time to stop Grandma before she set the kitchen table for breakfast. "It's a holiday. Why don't we eat in the dining room?" she asked. "I'll set the table."

Grandma blinked with surprise at her breathless suggestion, in part, perhaps, because Sylvia rarely agreed to a chore without arguing that Claudia ought to help, too. "I suppose that's fine," she said, waving Sylvia off to the task. "Use the good dishes."

Sylvia did, but not before racing up two flights to the nursery and stuffing her pockets with the ribbon-tied scrolls she had prepared the night before. Sylvia tucked one beside each plate and finished setting the table just as Great-Aunt Lydia came in carrying a platter of hot sausages. "What's this?" she asked, smiling at the sight of the scrolls. "It seems we're having a rather formal breakfast this morning, complete with place cards."

"It's a New Year's surprise," said Sylvia, fairly bouncing with excitement. She hurried off to the kitchen to help carry plates to the table. Claudia had taken a tray up to their mother, but she came down right away, disappointed, and reported that Mama was sleeping. Claudia had covered the dishes and left the tray on the nightstand.

Sylvia's thoughts flew to the book, and the letter tucked inside. She studied Claudia's face, but her expression betrayed no shock or alarm, only disappointment that she had not been able to eat New Year's Day breakfast with their mother. Claudia had not read the letter, Sylvia decided, and that was no surprise, for Claudia would never dream of sneaking glances at her mother's private letters. Sylvia wished she had been as good a daughter the night before.

Claudia took her seat as Grandma and Great-Aunt Lucinda began to pass around serving dishes piled high with scrambled eggs, juicy sausages, potatoes fried with onions and peppers, and *Pfannkuchen* left over from the night before. "What's this thing?" Claudia asked, picking up the scroll Sylvia had tucked beneath the edge of her plate.

"It's Sylvia's New Year's Day surprise," said Great-Aunt Lydia.

Great-Aunt Lucinda fingered her scroll warily. "I'm almost afraid to open it."

"Go ahead." Sylvia took a *Pfannkuchen* from the platter and set it on her plate, licking the sugar from her fingertips. "It's not scary."

"Napkin, Sylvia," her father said, untying his own scroll.

No one spoke as they read the words Sylvia had written for each of them. Sylvia ate her breakfast and looked around the table, watching their faces expectantly. With a start, she remembered that she had forgotten to make a scroll for her mother. That's all right, she decided. Mama was perfect exactly as she was.

Suddenly Claudia shrilled, "Is this supposed to be funny?"

Great-Aunt Lucinda laughed. "Mine certainly is. 'One: Bake more cookies. Two: Not just at Christmas. Three: Let Sylvia have as many turns to take the breakfast tray up to Mama as Claudia gets.' She ran out of space or I suppose I'd have more suggestions."

"I only have one," said Great-Aunt Lydia. "I must not need as much improvement as you, sister."

"Mine will be a little difficult to fulfill," said Grandma wistfully. " 'Go to Scotland to watch the swinging fireballs.' "

"The swinging what?" asked Great-Aunt Lucinda.

"That's between me and my granddaughter." Grandma rolled up her scroll, slipped the ribbon around it, and gave Sylvia a little wink.

Sylvia's father was shaking his head, his mouth twisted wryly. " 'Let Mama do whatever she wants.' Sylvia, if you think I could do otherwise, you haven't been paying attention."

"Why are you laughing?" Claudia cried. "This isn't funny!"

All the adults turned to her in surprise. "Why, Claudia, what does your scroll say?" asked Grandma.

"This ought to be good," said Great-Aunt Lucinda.

"I'm not going to read it," said Claudia. "It's mean."

"No, it isn't," protested Sylvia. "It's a resolution."

"It could still be mean," said Father, a mild note of warning in his voice. "Go ahead, Claudia. Tell us what it says."

Her eyes red, her jaw set, Claudia took a deep breath and reluctantly read her scroll aloud. " 'One: Stop being so bossy. Two: Stop hogging Mama. Three: Stop hogging everything. Four: Be nice to Sylvia.' I am nice to you, you little brat. A lot nicer than you deserve." She flung down the scroll and folded her arms. "I'm not going to read any more of these insults."

"They're not insults; they're New Year's resolutions," Sylvia explained. "They're promises you make so you can improve yourself."

"I know what a resolution is," snapped Claudia. "You're not supposed to make them for other people. You're supposed to make them for yourself."

"I did make one for myself," said Sylvia, taking the last scroll from her pocket.

Great-Aunt Lucinda's eyebrows shot up. "And what does that say?"

" 'Don't fight with your sister.' "

The adults burst into laughter. Sylvia looked around the table in puzzlement. Grandma wiped tears from her eyes; Father snorted into his handkerchief; Claudia seethed and glared. Sylvia felt like she was choking. No one had ever explicitly told her that she was supposed to make resolutions for herself alone, but now it seemed so obvious she did not know how she could have misunderstood. Of course it was rude to tell other people what they were doing wrong and how to change; it was especially rude for a child to say so to an adult. What would be worse: allowing the family to believe she was a thoughtless little girl, or to reveal the truth, that she was too stupid to know how New Year's resolutions were supposed to be made?

She decided she would rather be thought rude than ignorant, so she shrugged, stared fiercely at her plate, and willed the tears away. "I was only trying to help."

"Some help you are," snapped Claudia, shoving back her chair. "You've already broken your own New Year's resolution, and it isn't even nine o'clock!"

Miserable, Sylvia sank down in her chair as Claudia marched from the room, probably on her way up to Mama's bedroom to tell her what Sylvia had done. Sylvia wished she could run after her sister and beg her to stop, but Claudia would assume Sylvia's only concern was to avoid their mother's disapproval. Claudia didn't know about that letter from Grandmother Lockwood, and how sad their mother certainly was, no matter how well she hid it. Now Sylvia had made everything worse. The doctor said unpleasant news was not good for Mama and the baby, and because of Sylvia's thoughtlessness, Mama would wake to learn that her daughters had already spoiled the bright, fresh new start of the New Year.

From the corner of her eye, Sylvia saw her father shaking his head in exasperation, while Great-Aunt Lucinda rested her chin on her hand, ruefully watching the doorway through which Claudia had departed. Great-Aunt Lydia sighed and stirred sugar into her coffee, as if that would rid the morning of its bitter taste. Only Grandma did not seem concerned. Her eyes had a faraway look, as if she were imagining blazing fireballs swinging in brilliant arcs against a starry night sky.

Nine days later, Sylvia's mother gave birth to a robust, cheerful little boy. In the excitement and joy that surrounded his arrival, everyone forgot about Sylvia's ribbon-tied scrolls—everyone except Claudia, who never forgot a slight. Whenever the girls disagreed about whose turn it was to rock their darling baby brother to sleep or sing him a lullaby, Claudia reminded Sylvia of her resolution not to fight with her. What choice did Sylvia have then but to give in? Claudia kept a running tally of how many times Sylvia broke her resolution until spring, when she lost count as well as interest and found new ways to annoy Sylvia instead.

Although Sylvia had to share baby Richard with Claudia the way she had to share everything, she doted on him. From the start she resolved that she would make up for her mistakes as a little sister by being the loving and protective big sister he deserved. Her resolution would be no less binding for all that it came on January 10 instead of the first day of the year.

Sylvia never mentioned New Year's resolutions in her sister's presence again. In years to come, whenever Sylvia made a resolution for herself, she wrote it on a scroll of paper and tied it with a ribbon as a reminder of that unhappy morning and how she should look to her own faults and failings before trying to correct others'. Every New Year's Eve, she would untie the scroll of the year before and read over the vows she had made. Sometimes she noted with pride how she had kept her resolution and had reaped the rewards of her diligence and self-discipline; more often she looked back ruefully upon her optimism of a year ago, when the hope and promise of the New Year had made high goals seem within reach, and difficult resolutions easier to keep than they would prove to be.

With the excitement of the wedding and their sorrow over Andrew's children's disapproval, Sylvia had been too distracted to give much thought to New Year's resolutions that season. She had a few she wished Andrew's children would make, but as she had learned all too well that New Year's morning so long ago, she could not make those decisions for anyone but herself. If she ever forgot, the New Year's Reflections quilt would remind her, for she had sewn the lessons learned into the quilt. A Wandering Foot block called to mind the dangers of blindly fearing superstition, for what one person shunned as misfortune could be welcomed as a blessing by someone else. A Year's Favorite pattern honored her brother's birth, reminding her of her mother's patience and endurance, and the great happiness that was her reward. And the Resolution Square block reminded her that she could wish for positive change in another person, she could even lovingly nurture it, but ultimately, she could control no one's behavior but her own, and often that was where the real problem resided.

As the taxi pulled up in front of the theater, Sylvia imagined her mother as a little girl boldly stepping out into a festive night, welcoming the turn of the century with curiosity and excitement. She thought of her Grandma, entranced by her own mother's stories of the New Year in a faraway land, longing to see those wonders for herself but never venturing forth, so she had only her mother's stories and no memories of her own to pass down to her granddaughter. What would those two beloved women think of the turns Sylvia's life had taken, of the resolutions made and broken, of the adventures she had gladly embarked upon and those she had been drawn into unwillingly?

Andrew paid the driver and helped Sylvia from the taxi. "You were lost in thought the whole drive over," he said, escorting her into the warmth of the theater lobby.

"Adele's story was amazing, wasn't it? It's funny to think what can come of a simple New Year's resolution."

Sylvia was too ashamed of her childhood foolishness to explain the real reason for her reverie. "Adele made the right resolution at the right time for the right person," she replied instead, "and that made all the difference."

Chapter Three

THE NEXT MORNING, Sylvia and Andrew woke beneath Adele's antique quilt in the elegant four-poster bed in the Garden Room, well rested and refreshed despite their late night at the theater. After the show, they had wandered along Broadway arm in arm, stopping for dessert and coffee at My Most Favorite Dessert Company. "We can't go wrong at a place with a name like that," Andrew said, opening the door for Sylvia with a flourish.

He turned out to be right. The three-layer chocolate ganache cake Sylvia enjoyed was so rich and heavenly that she swore she wouldn't be able to eat a bite for breakfast, but in the morning, delicious aromas from Adele's kitchen beckoned her from Andrew's arms. She kissed him good morning, then folded back the beautiful quilt, gave it an affectionate pat, and hurried off to the shower. They had a full day planned, and Sylvia could not wait to begin.

The other guests were just sitting down at the table when Sylvia and Andrew arrived. As Adele and Julius served the meal, everyone introduced themselves and chatted about their excursions in New York. Most were holiday vacationers, some from overseas; Sylvia was pleased to learn that one of the couples, Karl and Erika, resided in a small village not far from Baden-Baden, Germany, the ancestral home of the Bergstrom family. "You must tell me all about it," Sylvia exclaimed, delighted.

"Have you never visited?" asked Karl.

Sylvia was embarrassed to admit that she never had. She had always meant to, but as the years passed, it had seemed increasingly unlikely that she ever would. Erika promised to act as Sylvia's own personal tour guide if she ever did make the journey, and in the meantime, she would be happy to show Sylvia the pictures of her hometown stored on her digital camera.

One couple from upstate was in town visiting relatives who did not have room in their cramped apartment for extended family. "I'd rather stay here anyway," the woman confided. "My daughter-in-law couldn't make a breakfast this tasty with four cookbooks and two days to prepare, and I know, because she's tried."

Sylvia smiled politely as the other guests chuckled, resisting the urge to point out that the woman was fortunate her daughter-in-law was willing to go to so much trouble for someone who clearly would not appreciate her efforts. One cookbook and a couple of hours was all Sylvia had ever been willing to put into a meal. But Sylvia held her tongue, unwilling to ruin the friendly mood around the table. She knew, too, that the woman had only meant to compliment their hostess—and that she herself was too easily provoked of late by any show of disapproval between in-laws.

The conversation turned to the holiday season and the upcoming New Year. Sylvia told Karl and Erika about the German traditions her family had celebrated in America—eating pork and sauerkraut to bring good luck, enjoying delicious sweets like *Pfannkuchen*, indulging in the rum punch made over the fire, and trying to glimpse the future by interpreting lead shapes in a bowl of water.

"Not so many people make *Feuerzangenbowle* anymore," said Karl with regret. "It is so much easier to open a beer."

"My uncles still make it every New Year's Eve," said Erika. "But lead pouring is out of favor. No one wants their children playing with lead near the fire, breathing in those toxic fumes! Nowadays, one uses melted candle wax, and I suppose the predictions are no more or no less accurate than they used to be."

Sylvia smiled, but her heart sank a little. She knew it was foolish, but she had always imagined the place of Great-Grandfather Hans's birth to be frozen in time, exactly as it had been when he departed for America, exactly as the family stories had preserved it. Of course it had grown and changed with the times, just as Elm Creek Manor had.

"We still enjoy the Sylvester Balls," Erika assured her, perhaps sensing her disappointment. "And dinner for one."

"That doesn't sound very festive," said Andrew. "In America, no one wants to spend New Year's Eve alone."

"Nor do we, necessarily," said Karl. "We gather together with family and friends and watch together."

The mother-in-law from upstate looked confused. "Watch what?"

"The television," said Erika. "Or video, if you have other plans and don't want to schedule everything around a broadcast."

Sylvia was utterly lost. "So . . . you eat supper alone, and later you meet to watch television?" She did not want to insult their new German friends, but she thought they would have done better to stick to *Pfannkuchen, Feuerzangenbowle,* and *Bleigiessen.*

Karl's deep laugh boomed. "No, *Dinner for One,* the television play, of course."

"Of course," echoed Andrew, but his expression of utter bewilderment told Sylvia he was no better enlightened than she.

"It wouldn't be New Year's Eve without it," said Erika. She glanced around the table at the other guests. "Surely you've seen it. It's in English, after all."

"Miss Sophie? James?" Karl added helpfully. "The same procedure as every year?"

His question met with blank stares. Incredulous, the German couple fired off other names—Sir Toby, Admiral von Schneider, Mr. Pommeroy, Mr. Winterbottom—only to learn that their native English-speaking companions did not recognize a single one. "Everyone in Germany watches *Dinner for One* on New Year's Eve," said Karl. "I myself have seen it at least fifty times."

"It's a television skit," Erika explained. "It was written in the 1920s for the British cabaret, but the version we Germans know best was filmed in the early 1960s in front of a live audience in Hamburg. It's been shown on German television every New Year's Eve since the 1970s."

"All the stations broadcast it," said Karl, searching their faces as if he still could not believe they were unaware of the tradition. "It's almost impossible to avoid seeing it on the holiday."

Not that anyone *tried* to avoid it, the German couple added. The comical black-and-white skit was as integral to a German New Year's celebration as they assumed dropping the ball in Times Square was to New Yorkers. The heroine of the story—Karl and Erika broke into fits of laughter as they explained—was Miss Sophie, an elderly British aristocrat celebrating her birthday as she did every year, with a dinner party attended by four dear old friends, blissfully ignoring the unfortunate truth that the men had passed away years ago. Rather than ruin the celebration, Miss Sophie's butler, James, not only serves the meal but also fills in for the absent gentlemen—mimicking their voices, offering birthday toasts, and draining their glasses. As each course begins, James inquires, "The same procedure as last year, Miss Sophie?" to which the lady replies, "The same procedure as every year, James." With each course and round of drinks, James becomes more and more intoxicated—stumbling about, tripping over the tiger skin rug, sending a platter of chicken flying through the air. At the end of the meal, Miss Sophie announces that the party was wonderful, but now she wishes to retire. James links his arm through hers and repeats the now-familiar refrain: "The same procedure as last year, Miss Sophie?" Miss Sophie answers, "The same procedure as *every* year, James." James steadies himself on the staircase banister, declares, "Well, I'll do my very best," and gives the unseen studio audience a broad wink before escorting Miss Sophie upstairs.

Sylvia found herself smiling, not because the broad slapstick sounded particularly funny, but because Karl and Erika's inexplicable fondness for the show was amusing to see. "It's a bit ribald at the end, isn't it?" she said.

"I don't get it," said the mother-in-law from upstate.

"I think it's probably one of those shows that gets funnier the more times you watch it," said Andrew, ever the diplomat.

"Absolutely," Erika agreed. "It's funnier with a group of friends, too. Some people watch in bars, and shout out all the lines with the characters. Others watch at home and prepare the same meal James serves Miss Sophie—Mulligatawny soup, North Sea haddock, chicken, and fruit. Still others use the show to play a drinking game, finishing a beer every time the refrain comes around, or drinking the same liquors James does as he makes each guest's toasts to Miss Sophie."

"I don't recommend that unless you want to start your New Year very, very ill," warned Karl. "Although some say the skit is most humorous when one is as drunk as James."

"Too much imbibing on New Year's Eve is an American tradition, too," said Sylvia. "I never found anything amusing about that, myself." For all that the Bergstroms had enjoyed her father's rum punch, drunkenness had been unacceptable in their family, and it was not something Sylvia tolerated in others, either. She could never have married Andrew if he had been what in their day had been called "a drinking man."

"Where are you going to watch *Dinner for One* this year?" Andrew inquired.

Karl and Erika exchanged a look. "We thought we would watch on the television in our room," said Erika, "but I suppose that won't be possible."

"We assumed everyone in the States watched it, too," said Karl, with a shrug that asked, why wouldn't you?

"I don't think that show has ever been broadcast here," said Adele. "I'll look into it and see what I can do."

"We've seen it so often that we can miss it once and still have a happy New Year," said Erika, but she did not sound convinced. "You shouldn't go to any trouble."

"It's no trouble at all," said Adele. "That would be nothing compared to last year, when a Danish family stayed with us. On the morning of December thirty-first, they suddenly absolutely had to have dishes. You know, dinner plates and such. I offered them several from our cupboard, but for some reason those wouldn't do. I assumed they wanted some to take home for souvenirs, so I offered directions to Tiffany's and Bergdorf Goodman. That wasn't what they wanted, either. Finally I directed them to the Arthritis Foundation Thrift Shop at Third and Seventy-Ninth, where they found some old dishes on sale. I had never seen anyone so happy over old dishes, and I thought it was a very odd souvenir, but of course I didn't say anything. Later that night, I learned that in Denmark, it's the custom to throw old dishes at the doors of your friends' homes on New Year's Eve. The more shards of broken dinnerware on your doorstep on January first, the more popular you are. Our Danish guests had been worried that the neighbors would think Julius and I had no friends, so they smashed all those old dishes on our front stoop. It was a mess, but I didn't want to offend them by not respecting their tradition."

"At least they said it was a Danish tradition," Julius broke in. "We wouldn't have known. They might have been playing a New Year's Eve prank on us."

"Maybe practical jokes are the real tradition," said Andrew, and the other guests laughed.

"How do you suppose we'll spend New Year's Eve?" asked Sylvia as she and Andrew returned to the Garden Room after breakfast.

"I'm not sure," said Andrew. "Amy never made a big deal out of the New Year. She loves Christmas, Thanksgiving, Easter, Halloween, Arbor Day—"

"Arbor Day?"

"She likes to plant trees," Andrew explained. "But she never got too excited about New Year's Eve."

Sylvia found it difficult to believe that someone who enjoyed holidays—including the most obscure—would be indifferent to the New Year's celebrations. "What about when Amy and Bob were young? Your family must have kept some New Year's traditions Amy has passed down to her own children."

"Well, sure, we had a few. When Amy and Bob were kids, they could never stay awake long enough to ring in the New Year at the proper time. Katy would set the grandfather clock in the hall ahead so they could hear it strike midnight, and we'd toast the New Year with apple juice at nine o'clock. That routine fell by the wayside as the kids grew up. When Amy was a teenager, she babysat for other families in the neighborhood so the parents could go out and celebrate. She and my wife used to spend New Year's Day watching home movies while Bob and I watched football, but I don't know if you'd call that a tradition. If Amy's ever made a New Year's resolution, she's kept it to herself." Andrew searched his memory for a moment, but then shook his head. "If you're looking for a big celebration, we should stay in New York and watch the ball drop in Times Square. I hope you're not disappointed."

"I won't be disappointed unless Amy leaves us standing on the front porch with our suitcases," Sylvia promised. To her dismay, Andrew snorted as if he considered that a real possibility.

Sylvia's thoughts of New Year's celebrations—and fears that she and Andrew might indeed be left outside in the snow upon their arrival in Hartford—soon faded as she and Andrew embarked upon what Sylvia was sure would be the highlight of their stay in New York.

They hailed a cab and drove through the crush of

morning traffic toward Fifth Avenue. As they rode along Central Park, snow falling lightly upon the windshield, Sylvia reached for Andrew's hand and held it tightly. She had no idea why she was so nervous. This visit to her mother's childhood home was long overdue, and why she had not at least driven past the old Lockwood house on one of her previous visits to New York, she could not say. It was not a lack of curiosity that had prevented her. Perhaps it was a sense that her mother had not been happy there, and that she would not have wanted to burden Sylvia with her unhappiness.

The cab let them out in front of a stately home facing the park. Sylvia took in the marble façade and the ornate front gate, admiring and yet uncertain. Nothing of the elegant building spoke to her of her mother, although she could not pick out any particular detail that did not fit with her mother's stories.

"Are you ready?" asked Andrew, offering her his arm as she stood rooted on the sidewalk, business people and tourists flowing past her. Sylvia managed a nod and forced herself to approach the front entrance, where Andrew rang the bell.

The woman who answered was dressed in a brilliant rose-colored sari. "You must be Sylvia and Andrew," she said, smiling and beckoning the couple indoors. "I'm Aruna Bhansali. I'm so pleased that you wished to visit. How exciting it is to meet the granddaughter of our home's first resident!"

"Thank you so much for indulging me," said Sylvia. She introduced Andrew as they removed their coats, admiring the elegant foyer. It was warmly lit and inviting, with white marble floors, vases of red calla lilies on a pair of mahogany tables flanking the entrance to a drawing room, and brightly painted carvings of Hindu gods and goddesses displayed in arched nooks. An elegant curved staircase rose gracefully to the second story, and Sylvia imagined her mother as a little girl carefully descending them, her hand raised to grasp the banister.

Aruna showed them to a parlor, where she offered them tea and asked Sylvia to tell her all about her grandparents. Sylvia hated to disappoint her hostess, but she had little information to share. It had never occurred to her that the current owners would be as curious about her family as Sylvia was to see the house where her mother had once lived. To her relief, Aruna seemed pleased with the sparse details Sylvia offered about her grandfather's famous department store, their high-society lives, and Eleanor's decision to leave it all behind to marry a horse farmer from rural Pennsylvania. "How romantic," Aruna said, sighing wistfully. "I always suspected this grand old place had an intriguing history."

"I wish I could tell you more about it," confessed Sylvia. "I couldn't tell you why my grandfather chose that marble, or why he was apparently so fond of classical architectural styles. He was a rather remote figure in my mother's life, I'm afraid, and he figures only very rarely in stories from her childhood."

Aruna smiled. "Perhaps she told you more than you know. You may remember some of those stories as we walk through the house."

Sylvia eagerly finished her tea and followed Aruna as she showed them around the first floor, through rooms that were obviously designed to entertain in high style, to Mr. Bhansali's home office, once a drawing room. The bright colors and Indian décor were nothing the Lockwoods would have chosen for themselves, and yet Sylvia could imagine the successful businessman and society wife at home there.

Upstairs, Aruna showed them bedrooms for family members and household servants, and asked if Sylvia knew which one had been her mother's. Sylvia shook her head. "All I remember is that her nanny had the room next door to hers," she said. "My mother spent most of her time in the nursery."

Aruna brightened and led them up another flight of stairs to a large room with a fireplace, dormer windows, and the smell of incense in the air. Paintings and gold-embroidered silk adorned the walls, and soft rugs and pillows invited the visitors to sit on the floor. It looked nothing like a child's playroom, and yet—

"This must be it," said Sylvia, turning around to take in every detail. How many hours had her mother passed within these walls, playing, dreaming, longing for adventure in the world beyond the front gate? Her mother had called the nursery her refuge, even after she had become a young woman. Had she written letters to her beloved nanny on that window seat? Had she watched from the window, hoping Sylvia's father would appear?

Andrew went to one window and peered outside. "There's a great view of the park."

"That's why I chose this room for my very own," said Aruna. "It's my retreat from the world, the one place in all of New York that feels most like home to me."

"I believe my mother felt very much the same," said Sylvia softly, wishing she could ask her if it was true. When she held quite still, she could imagine her mother's light footsteps on the wooden floor, her quiet laugh, her gentle kiss. When she closed her eyes, she felt her mother standing beside her, welcoming her home.

It had been far too long since Sylvia had felt the warmth of her mother's embrace. What she would not give to have even one of those days back to live again, one of those ordinary days she had taken for granted because it seemed impossible that they would not stretch on endlessly into the future.

Sylvia was ten years old when her mother died. In the years to come, she would wonder if Grandma's death in 1928 and the Great Depression had hastened her mother's decline. Surely the new hardships the family faced worried her, and she was deeply concerned for their less fortunate neighbors. But upon reflection, Sylvia always came to the same conclusion: Her mother had lived far longer than anyone had thought possible, and she had regarded every day as a gift. She loved her family so deeply that she would have clung to life longer to see them through those difficult times, if she could have. In her heart of hearts, Sylvia knew her mother regretted leaving them at a time of such uncertainty.

None of the Bergstroms could bear to celebrate Christmas of 1930, with Mama's death so recent and the wound of their grief so raw. They made their religious observances with heavy hearts and wrapped gifts for Richard, almost four years old, but as December wore on, no one could bear to decorate a tree or bake the famous Bergstrom apple strudel. The old traditions that had once brought them such joy would bring them no comfort that first Christmas without Mama.

The entire season so pained Sylvia that she could not wait for it to end so she could return to school and lose herself in books and math homework. She grieved for her loss, for her own loneliness, but she felt sorrier for Richard than for herself. She had enjoyed nine Merry Christmases with her mother, but Richard had been granted only three, and he would not remember those. Sylvia could not decide if it was a blessing or another great cruelty that he would never realize the dearth that was life in their mother's absence.

To Sylvia's surprise, Santa did not forget any of the Bergstrom children, but left presents for them beneath a small Christmas tree that had miraculously appeared in the ballroom Christmas morning. Richard whooped for joy and played with empty boxes with almost as much delight as with his new ball and toy fire truck, but most of the grown-ups sat quietly, watching the children open their gifts and mustering up smiles when Richard amused them. After the last gift was opened, Father departed swiftly and silently; Great-Aunt Lucinda watched him go, grief etched in the lines of her face, but no one interfered. Sylvia wanted to run after him because wherever he was headed had to be better than the ballroom, where they went through the motions of the holiday when no one felt like celebrating, where the once-festive manor echoed with her mother's absence. The quiet of the snowy woods, the muskiness of the barn, the warmth of the stable—any place would do, anywhere but here.

Christmas passed like a breath held too long, relief welling up to fill the emptiness it left behind. The family resumed the routine of ordinary days. Father and the uncles tended the horses. Great-Aunt Lucinda, Great-Aunt Lydia, and Uncle William's wife kept the household running almost as smoothly as ever, in proud defiance of their dwindling resources. Great-Aunt Lucinda often reminded the children how fortunate they were to have the farm, to be self-sufficient when so many others were out of work or in debt. Although they had lost nearly all of their savings when the Waterford Bank failed after the stock market crash, they would never be forced from their lands, even if Bergstrom Thoroughbreds never earned another dime. Business had declined precipitously, but the Bergstrom family had built its fortune raising their prized Thoroughbreds, and someday, when the Depression ended, their once wealthy customers would return. That was what Sylvia's father said, and Sylvia believed him.

Still, the family could not make or grow everything they needed—shoes for growing children, farm implements and tools—so for the first time in Sylvia's memory, her father took on work away from Elm Creek Manor. In the months following his wife's death, Sylvia's father had begun accepting invitations to lecture at agricultural colleges across the state. Sometimes he would leave the farm in Uncle William's care for days at a time, traveling from one college to another, earning modest fees for sharing what he knew about regional cultivars, animal husbandry, and fireblight. Sylvia missed him terribly while he was gone and wished he would invite her to accompany him, but the solitude of travel seemed to do him good. Each homecoming seemed to remind him that although the greatest love of his life had departed forever, there was still much love awaiting him at home, people who cared for him, children who depended upon him, reasons to go on. The money he earned, though it flowed out almost as quickly as he could draw it in, allowed them to feel as if they were regaining their footing little by little, that they would manage until their customers returned.

Sylvia's father often returned home with stories of hard times in the towns and cities beyond the Elm Creek Valley, of bread lines and soup kitchens, of bankrupt farms and closed factories. With each tale, Sylvia felt the desperation and fear of the outside world creeping closer until it seemed as if Elm Creek Manor stood alone, apart, bathed in sunlight in the tightening eye of a storm.

Once, in late autumn, Father returned home from a trip to Philadelphia, his demeanor quiet and pensive. Long after she was supposed to be in bed, Sylvia stood outside the library door and listened as her father told Great-Aunt Lucinda and Uncle William about a strange encounter with a man at the train station.

"He knew my name, although I had never seen him before in my life," said Sylvia's father. "His shoes and his fine topcoat told me he was no farmer, and although I didn't recognize him from my lecture, he seemed to know a lot about me. He followed me onto the platform, questioning me with direct intent about Elm Creek Manor. Right before my train was due to arrive, he got to the point. 'I don't think there's much market for Thoroughbreds in these hard times,' he said. 'It's a good thing you have all that land.'

"'Not a single acre is for sale,'" I told him.

"He told me he was glad to hear it because he worked for certain men in the city—he didn't offer their names—who wanted to hire a farmer to grow particular crops for them. In exchange for growing, harvesting, and delivery, they would pay ten dollars a bushel over the most recent market value."

"Good heavens," said Great-Aunt Lucinda. "What crop could anyone possibly want so badly?"

"Barley and hops."

Uncle William gave a low whistle. "Who do you think he was? Mickey Duffy? One of the Lanzetti brothers?"

"Could have been," Sylvia's father replied. "He kept his hat brim pulled down and stayed out of the lamplight."

"You should have asked for his autograph just in case."

"The joke seems to be on those unsavory characters," said Great-Aunt Lucinda. "They pinned their hopes on an honest man. You've never broken a law in your life, Fred—as far as I know. Why would they ask you, of all people, to get involved in one of their schemes?"

"He didn't say, but I can guess," said Sylvia's father. "Elm Creek Manor is remote, but still accessible to the city. I'm traveling around giving lectures for peanuts, so it's obvious I could use the money. The point is they did ask me, and we have to decide how to answer."

Great-Aunt Lucinda's gasp made Sylvia jump. "You mean you didn't turn him down right then and there?"

"It's a family farm, so it's a family decision."

"Well, my answer is no," declared Great-Aunt Lucinda. "Absolutely not. We should have no dealings whatsoever with bootleggers and moonshiners. Ties to organized crime won't bring us anything but trouble."

"It's good money," said Uncle William. "We could sow the north field with half corn for feed, half hops, easy. Think of the money we could earn. It would make up for all our lost income."

"My soul is not for sale at any price," Great-Aunt Lucinda shot back. "If your conscience wouldn't bother you, think of the consequences if we were found out."

"It's not against the law to grow barley and hops," said Sylvia's father.

Great-Aunt Lucinda spoke no further, but Sylvia could imagine her withering glare in reply.

"Then the answer is no," said Sylvia's father. She thought she detected a note of relief in his voice.

"But you said you didn't know the man," said Great-Aunt Lucinda. "How will you contact him?"

"He said he would be in touch."

Uneasiness swept over Sylvia, but Great-Aunt Lucinda held steady: "Perhaps we'll never hear from him. Let's hope he finds someone else to be his patsy."

Autumn turned into winter, and if the man from Philadelphia ever contacted her father, Sylvia did not hear of it. As time passed, she stopped waiting for an unfamiliar car to circle the front drive, stopped fearing a sinister figure at the front door. Although she longed to know for certain whether the gangsters had lost interest in the Bergstrom farm, she could not ask her father without revealing that she had eavesdropped. Nor could she breathe a word to Claudia.

The day after Christmas, Sylvia escaped the lonely confines of the manor, her coat pockets full of apples for her favorite horses. Apples the Bergstroms had in abundance, for the orchards had flourished in glorious indifference to the hard times all around them, to their loss and their grief. Her boots crunched through the icy crust on the snow as she made her way to the stable, holding her hood closed tightly with one mittened hand to keep out the sharp wind.

Suddenly, a few yards ahead of her, a shadow broke away from the stable wall. Too startled to scream, Sylvia froze in her tracks and stared as the unfamiliar figure of a man shuffled toward her. She took a stumbling step backward, her thoughts flying to the gangster from Philadelphia.

"Don't be scared, miss," the man said gruffly, taking a hesitant step forward, his palms raised. "I didn't mean to scare you. I was just trying to find someplace to wait out the storm is all."

She took in his threadbare layers of clothes, dark stubble on a haggard face, and knew at once that he could not possibly be the man from the train station. "You can't go in the stable," she said, her voice high and thin. "You'll scare the horses."

"All right." He ducked his head and stepped back. "I hear you, miss. I don't want any trouble. I'm just trying to keep warm."

He turned around and headed for the bridge over Elm Creek, back into the woods. "Wait," Sylvia called, then turned and ran to the house without waiting to see if the man obeyed. She burst through the back door and raced through the house until she found her father upstairs in the library, his ledger lying open on the oak desk before him. "There's a man outside," she said breathlessly. "I don't think he's the gangster. I think he's a hobo."

"I wasn't aware that you were acquainted with either," her father said, as she seized his hand and pulled him to his feet. In another moment they were at the back door, pulling on coats and boots. They found the man just outside, sitting on the back steps.

"Good afternoon," Sylvia's father said, addressing the man with utmost respect.

"Afternoon, sir." The man removed his hat despite the cold wind. "I'll work for a meal. I can clean out stables, milk cows, whatever you need."

"The cows won't need to be milked again until tonight," Sylvia's father said, and Sylvia knew he was thinking that anyone who didn't know the proper times to milk a cow could not have much experience with farm life. "Can you handle a shovel?"

"I have a strong back."

"All right, then." Father opened the door wider. "Come inside to the kitchen and get a bite to eat. Afterwards I'll show you around the stables."

The man came inside—quickly, before Father could change his mind—and tugged off his boots. Sylvia recoiled at the smell and backed off down the hallway, wrinkling her nose. She knew it was rude, but she couldn't help it.

She peeked through the doorway as the man wolfed down everything Great-Aunt Lucinda set before him—eggs and ham, bread, coffee, tomato and corn relish, dried apple pie. He ate every crumb, including a few that fell into his lap or the folds of his grimy scarf. When he finished, he thanked Great-Aunt Lucinda politely and followed Sylvia's father back outdoors.

At supper Father reported that the man had put in a good day's work and might make a decent farmhand even though his last steady job had been as a shoe salesman.

"We can't hire him on," said Uncle William, anticipating his brother's unspoken suggestion.

"We could use the help," Sylvia's father pointed out.

"But we can't afford his wages," said Great-Aunt Lucinda. "It would be wrong to expect him to work only for room and board."

Sylvia thought the hobo would gladly accept such an offer, but the children were expected to stay out of business discussions, so she kept her thoughts to herself. She stole a glance at her sister, who looked horrified at the prospect of that filthy man joining them at their table every day.

"We know nothing about him," said Lydia, glancing nervously out the window to the barn, where Sylvia's father had told the man he could spend the night. "He says he's a shoe salesman, but what proof do we have of that? He could be on the run from the law. What's a hobo doing this far from the train, anyway? Don't they ride the rails?"

Father fell silent, his gaze shifting to Sylvia, Claudia, and Richard. He studied them for a moment as if weighing a heavy burden. "I think he's just a man fallen on hard times, but you're right, we don't know for certain. I'll let him work for his meals and a place to sleep in the barn as long as he likes, but he stays out of the house and away from the children."

Claudia looked relieved, but Sylvia felt a wave of disappointment. She had never met a real hobo before, and she wanted to hear about riding the rails.

The man left the next morning, after breakfast. Two days later, another man knocked on the back door. He had heard, he said, that a kindly family there would give a man a hot meal and a place to sleep in exchange for chores. Father found work for him in the barn, Great-Aunt Lucinda fed him ham and eggs, and the man spent the night in the hayloft.

"We're not a hotel," Claudia muttered as she and Sylvia spied on the man through the kitchen window. "We never should have helped that first hobo. Now he's told all his hobo friends about us and they'll never leave us alone."

"Father could never send a man away with an empty stomach," Sylvia replied.

After a day, the second hobo left, and when two days passed with no strangers at the back door, Sylvia began to think their visits had ended. But late in the morning on the last day of the year, a knock sounded as she was helping Great-Aunt Lucinda cut up carrots for soup.

"I'll get it," Sylvia sang out, wiping her hands on her apron and hurrying to the back door before anyone could warn her to keep her distance. On the back steps stood two boys not much older than she and Claudia, huddling together for warmth.

She was too surprised to do anything but stare at them.

"We can do chores," the elder boy said. The younger nodded, his face streaked with dirt.

Sylvia didn't wait for permission. "Come in."

The boys exchanged a glance and followed her to the kitchen. Great-Aunt Lucinda quickly hid her surprise and invited the boys to wash up before sitting down at the table. She sent Sylvia to the cellar for butter and apples, and she quickly put together a meal of bread-and-butter sandwiches, cheese, cold bacon left over from breakfast, milk, and apples. The boys devoured the hasty lunch as if it were a feast.

When they had eaten every bite, Great-Aunt Lucinda instructed the younger boy to sweep out the cellar and sent his older brother outside to scrape ice from the back stairs. They were hard at work when the rest of the family came to the kitchen for lunch.

"Runaways?" Uncle William asked his aunt.

Sylvia, who had chatted with the boys, peeling carrots while they ate, piped up, "Not on purpose. Their dad sent them away."

"Why?" said Claudia. "What did they do?"

"Nothing," said Sylvia. "I think they didn't have enough food at their house, so their parents kept the little kids and sent the big ones away."

"What is this world coming to," said Great-Aunt Lucinda, "when families have to send their children out to fend for themselves? We should take them home at once."

"Who's to say their parents won't turn them out again?" said Sylvia's father.

Great-Aunt Lucinda, unaccustomed to helplessness, fluttered her hands and made no reply.

Sylvia's father frowned thoughtfully. "We can't have them stay in the barn."

"Heavens, no," said Great-Aunt Lucinda.

"But we can't take them in," said Uncle William.

"Why not?" said Sylvia. "We have enough room."

"Ample space isn't the problem," said Great-Aunt Lucinda, as if the admission pained her.

At once, Sylvia understood. With the business all but defunct, they could not afford two additional mouths to feed. How that must have pained her father, who had always generously shared his family's abundance. How her mother's heart would have broken to turn away someone in need.

"We could take them to the Children's Home in Grangerville," said Great-Aunt Lydia. "The good sisters will see that they have warm beds and enough to eat, and they'll be able to go to school."

"It's the best we can do," said Uncle William.

One by one, the adults at the table nodded their assent.

After lunch, Great-Aunt Lucinda sent the brothers off to take a bath; they obeyed reluctantly, sensing, perhaps, that their fates had taken a sudden turn. Sylvia and Claudia searched the attic for warm winter clothing Uncle William had outgrown, and before long the boys were clean and clad in sturdy wool trousers and soft flannel shirts. There was even a pair of boots for the younger boy.

Uncle William cleared his throat as he gave each boy a dime "for emergencies." Great-Aunt Lucinda wrapped cookies in napkins and tucked them into the boys' pockets. She kissed them each on the brow and quickly disappeared into the kitchen. The boys shifted uneasily, throwing anxious glances at the door as Sylvia's father explained where he was taking them. To prove that everything was all right, he asked Sylvia to accompany them on the drive to Grangerville.

The brothers spoke very little as they traveled along the country road winding through the Elm Creek Valley. Sylvia tried to lift their spirits with cheerful accounts of the sights they passed—downtown Waterford, the Four Brothers Mountains, the swirling waters at Widow's Pining where children were not allowed to swim, the forest where old Indian trails could still be followed for miles from one end of the valley to the other.

She had run out of things to say by the time they passed the first sign for Grangerville. Soon afterward, her father pulled up in front of a stately three-story red brick building not far from the center of town. The younger boy let out a sound that might have been a whimper, but his brother quickly hushed him.

Inside, a gray-haired nun in a stiff black-and-white habit welcomed the boys and took down their names and ages. Sylvia, longing for signs of happy children, heard footsteps and laughter overhead. Two girls ran past in simple pinafores, their hair neatly braided. At the sight of the sister, they slowed to a walk, pausing to nod a welcome to the boys.

Sylvia's father pressed a crisp bill into the nun's hand. "For anything they might need," he said. "Write to me if they require more."

The nun nodded and thanked him graciously. Sylvia's father squeezed her shoulder and led her back outside to the car.

"Do you think they'll be happy there?" Sylvia asked as they drove back to Waterford.

"I hope so," her father said. "I hope they'll stay long enough to give the place a fair chance. They could run off again and find themselves in serious trouble."

As uncertain as Sylvia felt about an orphanage, she knew it was a far better place for the boys than haylofts and boxcars. She hoped the boys would think so, too. She hoped they would find the food as delicious as Great-Aunt Lucinda's and the beds as warm and comfortable as those where she and her sister slept.

"Your mother would have been proud of you today," her father said suddenly. "Those boys were frightened, but you helped them to be brave."

"All I did was talk to them."

"That was precisely what they needed," he said. "Sylvia—" He hesitated. "Sylvia, your mother made the most of her time on this earth. Her kindness and generosity live on. It makes me very happy to see that you are going to be exactly like her in that regard."

He reached over and ruffled her hair, yet what had she done to deserve such praise? Mama would have taken the brothers in. She would have found them rooms with soft beds and warm quilts, and she would have seen that they never went hungry. Mama always found a way.

Sylvia wished she were more like her mother. She knew she was not.

But perhaps she could try to be. On that New Year's Eve before Richard was born, her mother had told her that the New Year presented an opportunity to reflect and to improve oneself. Why shouldn't she resolve to be more like her mother?

When they returned home, Sylvia retrieved her sewing box from the nursery and asked Great-Aunt Lucinda if she could borrow from the aunts' scrap bag. "What are you making?" her great-aunt asked, kneeling on the braided rug and pulling out the bag from behind the old treadle sewing machine Great-Grandma Anneke had brought over from Germany. No one used it anymore, preferring the newer electric model Sylvia's father had bought for her mother, but it remained in a place of honor in the west sitting room as a proud memento of their thrifty, industrious ancestor.

"I want to make some quilts to give to the orphans at the Children's Home," Sylvia answered.

Great-Aunt Lucinda sat back on her heels. "Why, Sylvia, that's a lovely idea. It's also quite a task for one girl to take on all by herself. Would you like some help?"

Sylvia gladly accepted her offer, for Great-Aunt Lucinda could sew twice as fast as she could. The more quilts they made, the more comfortable and snug the orphanage would be, and the more likely the brothers would stay.

As they sorted through their fabrics, Great-Aunt Lucinda found a paper sack full of leftover blocks from various projects dating back years. "I had almost forgotten about these," she said, holding them up for Sylvia to admire. "The quilters of this family hate to throw anything away. Fabric was so difficult to come by when the Bergstroms first came to America that we learned to save every scrap. My mother and Aunt Gerda would no more discard a pieced block than they would leave a sewing machine outside in a rainstorm. 'Waste not, want not,' they always said—and today I'm inclined to believe that was a very good lesson."

Since the pretty blocks brought them much closer to their goal, Sylvia was inclined to believe it, too. After laying the blocks out on the floor and debating the possibilities, she and her great-aunt decided that with the addition of a few more blocks, they would have enough to make four quilts just the right size for a child's bed.

They chose simple blocks—Four-Patches, Pinwheels, Bright Hopes—and cut triangles and squares from the brightest, most cheerful fabrics in the scrap bag. As they sewed the pieces together, Great-Aunt Lucinda told her stories of New Year's holidays from long ago. Most of the tales Sylvia had heard several times before, but her great-aunt always remembered new details with each retelling, so that even familiar stories taught her something new about the first Bergstroms to come to Pennsylvania.

They had been hard at work for an hour when Great-Aunt Lydia, with Richard in tow, came looking for her sister. When told about their project, she offered to join in, and soon several rows of blocks were draped over the back of the sofa, waiting to be sewn together with the older women's quick, deft stitches and Sylvia's steady, careful ones.

Claudia must have wondered where everyone was, for eventually she made her way to the west sitting room, drawn by the sound of their voices in laughter. After they explained their task, Claudia regarded Sylvia skeptically, not quite believing her little sister had come up with the idea on her own. "You'll never be able to make enough quilts for every orphan who needs one," she said, lingering in the doorway.

"That doesn't mean she shouldn't do what she can," said Great-Aunt Lucinda, before Sylvia could think of a retort. "Even if she makes only one quilt, that's one more child who will feel warm and loved."

"With our help, she'll make more than one," added Great-Aunt Lydia. "I'm quite proud of our efforts, if I do say so myself. From blocks that were abandoned and forgotten, we are creating objects of beauty, warmth, and comfort. I wish I had resolved to be more frugal and charitable in the coming year, because that's a New Year's resolution I'm already keeping."

She and Lucinda laughed merrily together, as only fond sisters can. Sylvia watched them enviously, not daring to look at Claudia, certain they would never get along so well.

"You may join us if you like," said Great-Aunt Lucinda, but Claudia replied that she would much rather help Aunt Nellie make supper. After she left, Lucinda said, "It's not too late, you know."

"It's not?" said Sylvia.

"Of course not. It's only New Year's Eve. We can still resolve to be more frugal and charitable in the year ahead."

"Oh." Sylvia frowned at her quilting, disappointed. She had assumed Great-Aunt Lucinda meant it was not too late to befriend Claudia, to become as close as sisters were meant to be, as Lucinda and Lydia were.

Lucinda grimaced and paused in her work to flex her fingers. Her arthritis bothered her in cold weather, and although warm compresses helped, she complained that she couldn't get anything done with her hands wrapped in steaming dishcloths. "I don't see how we can be any more thrifty than we have been," she said, taking up her needle again.

"We could use tea leaves twice, like Bitsy always wanted us to," said Lydia, smiling. Sylvia remembered how Grandma used to urge everyone to squeeze every last drop of tea from the leaves in the strainer, and how Great-Aunt Lucinda, who loved a strong brew, had always added new leaves when Grandma wasn't watching. Suddenly Sylvia felt a pang of remorse so sharp that she had to put down her sewing. Grandma had never made the journey to her mother's homeland, as Sylvia had resolved for her years before. Except in her imagination, she never saw those blazing fireballs light up the New Year's night sky.

"I miss Grandma," she said.

"We do, too," said Great-Aunt Lydia softly, and Great-Aunt Lucinda nodded.

Great-Aunt Lucinda sat lost in thought for a moment, but then she smiled, tied a knot in her thread, and cut it with a quick snip. "I remember stories Bitsy used to tell us about New Year's Eves her father celebrated," she said. "When she first married our brother, she was homesick for her own family's traditions, and telling us about them helped bring her parents closer. They had quite a raucous time, to hear her tell about it."

"I know," said Sylvia. "Swinging fireballs in Scotland. She told me all about it."

"Those are the stories from her mother's side of the family," said Great-Aunt Lydia. "Her father—your great-grandfather—was born in Wales."

Sylvia was instantly captivated. She had heard many stories of Great-Grandfather Hans, founder of Elm Creek

Manor, but she could not remember ever hearing about a Welsh great-grandfather.

"Some of the traditions your great-grandfather celebrated in Wales were similar to those your great-grandmother enjoyed," said Great-Aunt Lucinda. "All debts were to be paid, for example, but in Wales there was another twist: If the debtor failed to repay those he owed, he would be fated to be in debt for the rest of the year. It was also considered very bad luck to lend anything on New Year's Day, even something as simple as an egg or a penny."

"I suppose there would be ways around that, to help someone in need," remarked Great-Aunt Lydia, rising to add a completed block to the communal pile on the sofa. "Just call it a gift. If you have no intention of being repaid, that should divert the bad luck."

"You sound just like Bitsy, trying to untangle a knot of superstitions," Great-Aunt Lucinda declared, laughing. To Sylvia, she added, "Debts had to be paid and homes had to be cleaned because your behavior on New Year's Day foretold how you would act throughout the year. If you rose early and got right to work on the first morning of the New Year, you would be industrious for the next twelve months. If you fought with your sister, well, you would probably be argumentative the whole year through."

"That would explain a lot," said Great-Aunt Lydia, with a sidelong glance at Sylvia. "Perhaps we should consider keeping the girls apart on New Year's Day from now on, Lucinda. What do you think?"

"It's worth a try."

Sylvia ignored the banter. "Did my great-grandfather's family eat anything special for good luck?"

"Not that I know of," said Great-Aunt Lucinda, "but they did follow another interesting custom called Letting In. It claimed that the first visitor of the New Year brought luck into the house, good or bad."

"I've heard of that," said Sylvia. "Grandma said that in Scotland it's called First Footing. A tall, dark-haired, handsome man like my father brought the best luck of all, but ladies expecting babies or new brides were good, too."

"Not in Wales, they weren't," said Great-Aunt Lucinda. "Oh, a handsome dark-haired man would be welcome, but a woman was the last person you wanted as your first visitor of the New Year. She might be a witch, and a group of young boys would have to run through every room of the house to break her spell, just in case."

Sylvia felt vaguely affronted. "What if the woman is your neighbor, and she just came over to wish you a Happy New Year, and you know she definitely isn't a witch? What if she's your cousin, coming to visit for the holidays? Couldn't that be good luck, too?"

"Not according to the tradition, I'm afraid," said Great-Aunt Lydia.

"It doesn't seem fair."

"It's not fair," said Great-Aunt Lucinda. "The Welsh tradition on the day after Christmas is even worse. Young men and boys were permitted to take holly branches and slash the arms and legs of their female servants until they bled. Can you imagine being a maid or a cook's helper in those days? Christmas would be a day of dread because of what was in store the day after."

"The grown-ups let them do that?"

"I suppose most of them did, or the custom wouldn't have endured so long."

"That's terrible," said Sylvia. She couldn't believe

such naughtiness would be tolerated in children. "I hope my great-grandfather didn't hurt anyone like that."

"I think it's highly unlikely that our branch of the family had any servants to torment," said Great-Aunt Lydia. "They were more likely to be on the receiving end."

"Maybe that's why they came to America," said Sylvia.

Her great-aunts laughed. "There was probably more to their decision than fearing injury on the day after Christmas," said Great-Aunt Lucinda. "But I suppose the inequality and tolerance of ill treatment of the lower classes by the wealthy might have played a part."

"My sister, the philosopher," said Great-Aunt Lydia fondly. "You take after Great-Aunt Gerda."

"If only my apple strudel was as good as hers."

"No one's apple strudel will ever be as good as Great-Aunt Gerda's, but don't let that stop you from trying. We'll be happy to eat your attempts."

Both sisters broke into laughter. Richard looked up at them from his toys, grinning happily, certain that he was responsible for their mirth. He usually was, but this time Sylvia knew the great-aunts' joy came from the shared bond of sisterhood and from the satisfaction of knowing they were doing good work in the company of loved ones. Although they had experienced losses and disappointment in past years, they did not despair, but faced the future with courage and hope.

Suddenly Sylvia decided on her own New Year's resolution. "Didn't Grandma say that when she was a girl, their custom was to clean the house so that the New Year would offer a fresh, new start?" said Sylvia. "From now on, every New Year's Eve, I'm going to clean out my sewing basket and my scraps and I'm going to make at least one useful thing to give to someone else."

Her aunts praised her resolution and promised to do all they could to help her keep it, that year and every year she lived at Elm Creek Manor.

"You'll be able to help me a long, long time," promised Sylvia. "I'm never leaving home."

The great-aunts exchanged a smile. "What if you meet a nice young man and decide to marry?" asked Great-Aunt Lydia.

Sylvia was surprised they had to ask. When she married, she would bring her husband home to live at Elm Creek Manor with the rest of the family, just as her father did when he married her mother. Elm Creek Manor was the home of her heart, the only home she would ever love. Any man she married would have to understand that.

Since they had no party planned for the evening, no Sylvester Ball to attend, no sugar cone for *Feuerzangenbowle,* and no confectioners' sugar for *Pfannkuchen,* Sylvia and her family had a sewing bee instead. Richard played with toys on the floor or climbed from one lap to another, begging for stories and cuddles. They paused only for supper, and when the great-aunts told Sylvia's father about her New Year's resolution and her plans to make quilts for the Children's Home, he ruffled her hair as he had earlier that day and said, "We'll take the quilts over as soon as you finish." Knowing how he used the automobile as little as possible to conserve gasoline, Sylvia glowed with pride, recognizing his offer as a sign of his approval.

After that, Claudia could not hang back while the others joined in to help. They moved the quilting bee to the ballroom, the site of so many happier New Year's celebrations of days gone by, and sat by the fireside sewing, telling stories, and reminiscing. Not wanting to be excluded from the impromptu party, the men kept the women company, popping corn over the fire, telling jokes, and making outlandish resolutions for the year ahead. "I'll sell one hundred horses," Uncle William promised. "I'll grow two hundred bushels of hops and another two hundred of barley." Everyone laughed as Lucinda feigned outrage and swatted him with a quilt block, but Sylvia wondered how many of them understood the reference.

Settling beside her father on the sofa, Sylvia told him what she had learned about her Welsh ancestors. "Your Grandma told me those stories when I was a boy," he said, and Sylvia realized that just as she had lost a mother and a grandma, so had her father lost his own mother and the wife he loved beyond all others. She had thought only of her own grief, forgetting his. Since her death, only upon Richard would he bestow a rare smile.

At Christmas, he had been too overcome by painful memories of happier days to endure a celebration. But he chose to pass New Year's Eve by the fireside with his family, amending the great-aunts' stories of Sylvia's great-grandfather and revealing a tradition called Calennig. Very early on New Year's morning, Sylvia's great-grandfather and other young boys would procure a fresh evergreen twig and a pail of water. From dawn until noon the boys traversed the village, dipping the twig into the water and sprinkling the faces of neighbors out and about. In return, they would be rewarded with Calennig, or "small gifts" of coins or fruit. If they came to a house where the occupants were still asleep, they sprinkled the doorways instead, singing songs or reciting chants that welcomed the New Year.

"They got treats for splashing grown-ups with cold water in the middle of winter?" asked Claudia, dubious.

"What about the girls?" said Sylvia. "You said the boys went through the villages. You meant boys *and* girls, right?"

Her father shook his head. "My mother said young boys, not boys and girls. I guess little girls weren't interested in mischief. They probably preferred to stay home and help their mothers cook breakfast."

Sylvia caught the look that passed between the great-aunts, the knowing gaze heavenward that said they doubted the little girls' preferences had anything to do with it, and that they didn't expect a man to understand. But then her father's eyes twinkled knowingly. Sylvia smothered a giggle, but her heart welled over with happiness. If her father could joke and tease, perhaps one day he would laugh again.

The family sewed and talked and remembered bygone days and departed loved ones until the clock struck midnight. The New Year had begun, offering a fresh start, a new beginning. Sylvia said a silent prayer that the year ahead would be kinder to them than the one before, that the family would know prosperity and peace, and that time would ease the ache in their hearts.

The next day they ate pork and sauerkraut and the women quilted from morning until nightfall. By the time Sylvia went to bed, two hours past her usual bedtime, the Bergstrom women had finished four quilts, each just the right size to comfort a child.

True to his word, the next day Sylvia's father drove her to the Children's Home in Grangerville. Sylvia presented the quilts to the supervising nun and promised to make more quilts, as many as they needed, though it might take her a few years. When her father asked about the two brothers, Sylvia held her breath, afraid that the nun would shake her head sadly and say that the boys were unhappy, or worse yet, that they had run away. But instead she reported that they were settling in fine; they got along well with the other children, followed the rules, and did their chores. She had written to their parents in care of the post office in the boys' hometown, but she was not hopeful of a reply. "Sometimes the parents have moved on by the time their children make their way to us," she explained, with a gentle turn of her hand that suggested both loss and forgiveness. "Other times, I imagine, they are too fearful or ashamed to write back, or they don't know how to read or write. That's if they ever receive the letters we send. I'm sure some of our children are not entirely honest when they tell us where they came from. Far too many have good reason to fear their parents' finding them."

The nun kept her eyes firmly on Sylvia's father's, not sparing a glance of misgivings for Sylvia as adults often did when they forgot themselves and spoke of adult concerns in front of children.

"I would give the boys a home if I could," her father said. "My wife passed on a few months ago, and my business is failing. I have three children of my own. It—it wouldn't be possible for me to take in two more."

The nun lowered her gaze and nodded. "Of course. I understand."

He dug into his overcoat pocket and pulled out a folded bill. "For the boys," he said, pressing it into her hand. "When I can do more, I will."

"You've already done a great deal." This time, the nun turned her smile upon Sylvia and gave the folded quilts a pat. "Both of you. God bless for your generosity. I know you won't forget our children."

Sylvia's father took her by the hand and led her back out to the car. As they left Grangerville, Sylvia summoned her courage. "Father?"

"Yes, Sylvia?"

"You said the business is failing." She bit the inside of her lip to keep from crying. "Is it?"

Her father was silent for a long moment. "It hasn't failed yet."

Sylvia never forgot the boys they left behind that day, or the other lost and abandoned children, or the nuns who watched over them. As the Great Depression wore on, whenever she felt sorry for herself, frustrated by made-over hand-me-down clothes, disappointed by the lack of treats and pleasures that had filled her early years with delight, she swallowed her complaints and forced herself to imagine how much worse off she could have it, if not for the family who loved her, if not for the farm.

Years later, after the nation climbed back on to its feet and their wealthy customers returned as her father had always promised they would, still she kept her New Year's resolution. Every winter she made several quilts for the Children's Home; every year her father drove her to deliver them and to check in on the boys. One year they arrived to find a different nun running the orphanage, for her predecessor had died. Another time they learned that the younger brother showed great aptitude for carpentry and had been apprenticed to a local craftsman; a year later, they discovered that the older boy had run off to join the army.

Long after she left Elm Creek Manor, when it became a more practical matter to send checks rather than quilts,

Sylvia continued to think of the brothers and wonder what had become of them. On New Year's Eve, when she brought out her UFOs and made at least one useful thing to give to someone in need, she imagined them healthy and happy, with families of their own and all the joys of home that had been denied them as children.

After Aruna had taken Sylvia and Andrew through the entire house, the newlyweds thanked her and departed. Sylvia took Andrew's arm as they strolled through Central Park, lifting her face to the gray sky as snowflakes danced lightly against her eyelashes. This year, the New Year's Reflections quilt would become the one useful thing she made for someone else. Had she known, somehow, that she was not making the quilt for herself when she had cut the first pieces? Had she sewn the Four-Patch, Pinwheel, and Bright Hopes into the centers of the Mother's Favorite blocks as a reminder of her childhood resolution? Sylvia still believed Great-Aunt Lucinda's plainspoken truth that one should do whatever one could to bring comfort and hope to others in need, even if, as Claudia had bluntly pointed out, one person's efforts would not be enough to set everything to rights. The New Year was the perfect time to look outward as well as inward, for resolutions did not have to be about self-improvement alone. They could very well reflect a wish to make the world a better place—even if in small ways, even if for only one person.

If Sylvia could reach Amy, if her peace offering could persuade her stepdaughter to let go of her anger and reconcile with her father, it would be the greatest gift of happiness Sylvia could give Andrew. And to Amy, who did not know that her stubbornness would hurt more people than her father. Anger and misunderstanding could destroy a family from the inside out, as conflict forced everyone to take sides. Even refusing to favor one side over the other would be seen as taking a position, until even the unwilling were drawn into the conflict. Sylvia had seen this happen to her own family, and she would not let it happen to Andrew if she could help it, if she could show Amy another way.

When Sylvia and Andrew returned to the 1863 House, Sylvia's emotions swirled as she told Adele about the visit to the old Lockwood home. Even the physical experience of the place had done little to evoke the elusive sense of connection to her mother's past.

"Except in the nursery," she said. "I could imagine my mother sitting on the window seat, embroidering her Crazy Quilt, gazing out at Central Park and longing for . . . something. Or someone. I don't know."

Adele's smile was full of compassionate understanding. "Maybe since you have such indelible memories of your mother at Elm Creek Manor, it's difficult for you to sense her anywhere else."

"I suppose so."

"We found one of the Colcrafts' quilts when we bought this house," Adele reminded her. "Did your mother leave behind any of her quilts in the Lockwood home?"

"I didn't see any." Her mother's patchwork certainly would have stood out among the Indian décor. "I'm sure Aruna would have mentioned it. I didn't expect to find any of my mother's possessions there. The Bergstroms couldn't even hold on to her quilts. I spent the last few months searching for several my sister sold off decades ago."

"Did you find them?"

"I found her Crazy Quilt in excellent condition for its age, and the new owner sold it to me for what she had paid—plus a week at quilt camp for her daughter-in-law. The quilt my mother had made to celebrate my parents' anniversary had been cut up to make quilted jackets. Andrew bought the last one for me at an art shop in Sewickley." The jacket was pretty in its own way, but the quilt had been a masterpiece. Sylvia could not understand what could have possessed the woman who cut it up. "Just a few days ago, Andrew and I tracked down my mother's long-lost wedding quilt to a traveling exhibit from the New England Quilt Museum. We had searched quilt shops and museums across the country and had tracked down leads from the Internet, and in the end, it was a tip from a quilter staying at our last bed and breakfast that led us to the right place."

"Think of the odds against finding a single quilt after so many years," Adele marveled. "Did you bring the wedding quilt with you?"

"Why, no," said Sylvia. "Even though my mother made the quilt, it isn't mine anymore. My sister sold it long ago. I don't know exactly how it ended up in the hands of the museum, but I can't simply take it from them."

"You could buy it."

"If the museum is willing to sell it, I suppose I could." How wonderful it would be to take the New York Beauty quilt home to Elm Creek Manor. Sylvia would cherish it always as a memento of her mother, and she would display it for all the quilt camp's guests to enjoy. But should she? As a part of the museum's collection, her mother's wedding quilt would be seen and enjoyed by many more people. It would be properly cared for and preserved for generations to come. Perhaps taking it home for the enjoyment of a relative few was selfish, and offering it freely to the world was what her mother would have wanted.

"I'll have to think about it," said Sylvia.

Adele reached for her purse. "While you're thinking, I know a place that might provide some inspiration. You're sure to meet several quilters eager to offer their opinions whether you want them or not."

While Andrew relaxed in front of the fire with a copy of Adele's manuscript, Sylvia and Adele took a cab to the City Quilter, a quilt shop in Chelsea that Adele promised was the best in New York. Sylvia was inclined to agree; she had visited the shop once, when it first opened, and she had been delighted by the fabric selections and courteous service. To her surprise, when she and Adele entered the shop, salespeople and customers alike greeted her as something of a celebrity. "I loved your quilt *Sewickley Sunrise,"* gushed one woman, her arms overloaded with shopping bags. "I think it's your best work."

"Thank you," said Sylvia, concealing a wince. She knew the woman didn't mean any harm. *Sewickley Sunrise* had won Sylvia many ribbons and now belonged to the Museum of the American Quilter's Society's permanent collection, so it was undoubtedly her best-known quilt. Still, she had made it so long ago that it pained her whenever anyone told her it was her finest creation. Did they honestly believe she had shown no improvement since then, no growth as an artist? *Sewickley Sunrise* would always remain one of her favorite quilts, but she preferred to believe that her most recent work was far superior and that the best was yet to come.

Sylvia and Adele browsed through the rainbow of

fabric bolts displayed on the shop walls, and after their selections were cut and folded, Sylvia searched the display case for a spool of thread in a suitable shade of blue. When she brought the New Year's Reflections quilt from her tote bag to match the thread color to the binding fabric, several onlookers quickly clustered around to catch a glimpse of her work-in-progress. When the quilt shop owner suggested she drape the quilt over a table in the classroom so that everyone could have a better look, Sylvia was happy to comply. She hoped Amy would respond to the quilt as warmly as those quilters did, admiring her adaptation of the Mother's Favorite design, the harmonious colors, and the precise piecing. When one customer asked how she had decided which patterns to include in the center of each larger Mother's Favorite block, Sylvia said only that each one reminded her of a New Year of her past—resolutions made and abandoned, opportunities for new beginnings gladly accepted or stubbornly ignored.

As the quilters bent over the quilt, Adele drew close to Sylvia to murmur in her ear. "Your points are so perfect no one would ever know that you'd had a stroke. You should be proud. I know it wasn't easy."

With a jolt, Sylvia suddenly wondered if that was why she had felt compelled to give this particular quilt to Amy, out of the many she could have chosen. Had she subconsciously hoped it would prove to her new stepdaughter that she was perfectly sound, that she had completely recovered from her stroke and would not be a burden to Andrew? Sylvia hoped not, or at least she hoped that Amy would not think so, because that would diminish the beauty of her gift.

Besides, she had stitched most of those blocks long before her stroke, so as proof of her current dexterity and mental acuity, it was flimsy evidence indeed.

Sylvia smiled so that Adele would not realize that the generous praise troubled her. She folded up the quilt and returned it to her tote bag, thanking the onlookers for their kind words and reminding them to visit the Elm Creek Quilt Camp website for more information about the upcoming season of quilt camp. "I hope to see you next summer," she said as she and Adele made their way to the cash register. Several customers called out that she could count on it.

Outside, the sun had come out from behind the clouds, and although the wind was still brisk, Sylvia assured Adele that she felt quite comfortable walking. "Good," said Adele. "I have something to show you."

Mystified, Sylvia strolled along with her friend, up Fifth Avenue back toward Midtown. Surely Adele did not mean to show her the Empire State Building or Rockefeller Center or any of the other obvious tourist stops, which Adele pointed out only in passing. Just as Sylvia's curiosity could bear it no longer, Adele stopped at the corner of a large building in a busy shopping district. "We're here."

Sylvia glanced around, uncertain what distinguished that place from any other in the city. The elegance of the classical architecture was striking, but in that it was not unlike many other buildings they had passed along the way. "Where's here, exactly?"

Adele gestured toward the marble cornerstone. "You might not recognize it, but I think your mother would."

Her heart quickening, Sylvia drew closer to read the bold engraving on the stone. "The Lockwood Building.

1878." She gasped and turned to her friend. "Do you mean—"

"This was the site of your grandfather's store," Adele confirmed. "Lockwood's took up the entire block, once upon a time. The interior has been subdivided and resold many times over since then, but the exterior hasn't been changed since your grandfather's day except for repairs and maintenance."

"I almost can't believe it really exists." Sylvia traced the engraving with a fingertip. "Lockwood's always seemed like nothing more than a setting from a story to me, just like . . ."

"Just like your mother's childhood home?"

Sylvia nodded. "Until this morning, anyway." She stepped back and gazed skyward to take in the entire building her grandfather had built, not caring if she looked like a wide-eyed tourist to the more sophisticated passersby. "One of my mother's favorite memories of this time of year was coming to the store with her father and being allowed to pick out any toy she wanted for Christmas."

"Perhaps this photo was taken on one of those occasions." Adele reached into her bag and pulled out a large padded envelope. "Here's the second part of your surprise. Merry Christmas, a little late. Happy New Year, a little early."

Sylvia pressed a hand to her lips before setting her shopping bags on the sidewalk dusted with snow and accepting the envelope with a trembling hand. She lifted the flap and spied the edge of a photograph, protected between two sturdy pieces of cardboard. Carefully she withdrew a black-and-white photograph of a New York street scene in what appeared to be the early 1900s. A man and woman dressed in turn-of-the-century coats and hats stood with two girls in front of a storefront window emblazoned LOCKWOOD'S DEPARTMENT STORE in elegant script. The elder girl, who looked to be around twelve years old, held her father's hand and beamed into the camera as if caught by surprise, a delightful surprise. The mother stood somewhat apart from her husband at the front of the group, while the younger brought up the rear, peering curiously at the photographer. She wore a dark coat with fur trim around the collar and carried a white fur muff, and her thin legs were clad in heavy black stockings.

Sylvia studied the younger girl's face. In her delicate features, she saw the woman her mother would become. "I have no photographs of my mother as a child," she said. "None except this."

"Not even one?" asked Adele. "I would have assumed the Lockwood family had their photographs taken often. They were considered celebrities in their day."

Perhaps the family had once had many photographs, but Sylvia's mother had brought none with her to Elm Creek Manor. Sylvia was beginning to suspect there was more to her mother's story of her decision to marry Sylvia's father than had been revealed. "Where on earth did you find this picture?"

"In the archives of *The New York Times.* I have a friend on staff. This picture appeared in the society column. I included a printout of the newspaper page in the envelope, if you can tear yourself away from the photo long enough to look."

Sylvia gazed at her mother's family, her voice catching in her throat. "Adele, I don't know how to thank you."

"It's just a reprint, not the original," Adele said, almost apologetically. "They wouldn't part with that. But since it isn't the authentic photo, you don't have to worry about it disintegrating before you can get it home. You also won't have to treat it like a museum piece, with archival matting and protective glass."

Sylvia might not have to, but she would. Reprint or not, this photo of the Lockwood family was the only one she possessed, and she would not trade it for a dozen museum pieces.

Chapter Four

THE NEXT MORNING at breakfast, the resourceful Adele reported that she had found *Dinner for One* on the Internet. Pleased, the German couple invited the other guests to join them around the computer on New Year's Eve. Only Sylvia and Andrew declined, with some regret, because they would be leaving New York later that day.

They bade their fellow guests good-bye and Happy New Year; they parted from Adele and Julius with warm embraces and promises to get together again soon. They enjoyed a morning of exploring museums, shopping, and savoring a delicious lunch, then they packed up the Elm Creek Quilts minivan and continued on to Amy's home in Hartford, Connecticut.

As Andrew drove, Sylvia once again took up her needle to finish sewing the binding on Amy's quilt. She had not made as much progress during their stay in New York as she had planned, but she hoped to make up for it on the two and a half hour drive.

"Do you think you'll finish it by New Year's Eve?" Andrew asked as they pulled on to I-95.

"I'll take until New Year's Day if necessary," she said, "but I hope I won't offend anyone if I sneak away from family gatherings now and then to work on it."

Amy might prefer, in fact, for Sylvia to leave the family to themselves. It was difficult not to be hurt by the younger woman's sudden disapproval. Amy had liked Sylvia well enough when she and Andrew were dating; Amy had been a gracious hostess whenever the couple visited and she had even asked Sylvia to teach her to quilt. But Amy's friendliness had evaporated the moment she heard of their engagement. Andrew had anticipated this and had decided to break the news to his children in person. First the couple had driven to his son's home in southern California, where Bob and his wife had taken the news with surprise and concern. Although the visit had ended badly, Bob had agreed to say nothing to his sister so that Andrew could be the one to tell her. Andrew had forgotten to secure that promise from Bob's wife, however, so when Sylvia and Andrew returned to Elm Creek Manor, they had found Amy waiting for them.

Andrew frowned and flexed his fingers around the steering wheel. "That's fine with me as long as you're only sneaking off to quilt, and not because anyone has made you feel unwelcome."

"I'm not expecting a warm welcome," Sylvia said. "Please don't feel you have to rush to my defense over the tiniest slights as you did in California."

"You're my wife, and I expect my children to treat you with respect."

"They're more likely to do so if you let them do it on their own terms, and not because you've scolded them into it."

"I guess you're right. Maybe." Andrew tapped the steering wheel thoughtfully. "Maybe we should make a plan. How should we break the news?"

"I don't think we need to worry about how Daniel will take it." Amy's husband had approved of their engagement from the beginning. Sylvia and Andrew were counting on him to help bring Amy around. "I think it's best to tell her right away, but delicately. We should be sensitive to her feelings, but at the same time she needs to know that there's no longer any point in trying to convince us to cancel our plans to marry."

"It's too late for that," said Andrew, reaching for her left hand and pressing it to his lips. Her thimble fell into his lap, and she laughed as she retrieved it. Andrew's smile faded into a sigh. "I don't understand these kids. Why shouldn't they want us to get married? We love each other. They ought to be happy for us."

"They should be," said Sylvia. "Unfortunately, in my experience, people in love almost always stumble over objections thrown in their path by one side of the family or another. 'The course of true love never did run smooth,' as the poet said."

"I wouldn't say 'almost always,' " said Andrew. "Do you really believe that?"

"Almost every marriage I know of has offended someone," said Sylvia. "And I'm not talking about envious former sweethearts, but friends and family who ought to have the couple's best interests at heart. Sarah and Matt McClure, for example."

Andrew shrugged in acknowledgment. Sarah's mother's antipathy for her son-in-law was as infamous in Elm Creek Quilts circles as it was perplexing, for Matt was a fine young man. "All right, that's one."

"My parents," said Sylvia. "Agnes and my brother."

"Who objected to their marriage?"

"Her parents," said Sylvia. "Don't you remember? And . . . I admit I did, too."

Andrew grinned. "That's because you didn't want to share your baby brother with anyone."

"That's not the reason. They were too young."

"Richard was about to be shipped out," Andrew protested. "It was wartime. Lots of young couples rushed off to get married back then."

"Fair enough." Sylvia knew he was right, and if Agnes and Richard had not seized that moment, they never would have married. "John Colcraft and Harriet Beals."

"Who?"

"The couple who built the 1863 House."

Andrew laughed. "Okay, that's three, spanning two centuries. I can't call that a trend."

"My cousin Elizabeth and Henry Nelson." Sylvia couldn't admit that she was the only person who had objected to that pairing, but Andrew had heard enough of her childhood stories to figure that out for himself. "My sister and Harold Midden."

Andrew scowled, for he had good reason to dislike Harold. He had been outraged to learn that Claudia had married him. "Sometimes it's right to object to a marriage."

"Your son and daughter think this is one of those times."

"They're wrong."

"I know that, dear. You're preaching to the choir."

Andrew fell silent, lost in thought, and Sylvia returned her attention to the New Year's Reflections quilt. Even if Andrew couldn't detect a trend, Sylvia could, and she couldn't ignore it. It seemed that nearly all married couples of her acquaintance had encountered some disapproval of their marriage, and sometimes Sylvia herself had been the source. She would never change her mind regarding Harold Midden's unsuitability, but in hindsight, she wished she had been more generous to Agnes and Richard and to Elizabeth and Henry. She could not help wondering if her resolute lack of acceptance then had come around to haunt her now.

She might have believed it, except for one thing. Out of all the couples she had known throughout her life, one had been blessed with a marriage welcomed with unabated joy on both sides of the family.

The fortunate couple had been Sylvia herself and her first husband, James.

They had met at the State Fair when Sylvia was sixteen and James eighteen. Although James's father was her father's business rival, the men shared a mutual respect and approved when James began courting Sylvia. When they married and James came to Elm Creek Manor to live, as Sylvia had planned since childhood, Mr. Compson celebrated their happiness even though it meant that his son had joined the family business of his chief competitor. The Compson family never failed to treat Sylvia as a beloved daughter and sister, and the Bergstroms extended the same love and acceptance to James.

The first years of their marriage were as blissful as any young couple could have hoped for, the only unfulfilled promise the absence of children. But they had plenty of time, they told each other, years and years in which the blessing of a baby might be granted to them.

Then the war came. Richard and Andrew, whom in those days Sylvia thought of only as her brother's friend, left school and enlisted. In hopes of looking after them, James promptly enlisted, as did Harold, Claudia's longtime suitor, perhaps bowing to pressure from his fiancée. Within weeks of the men's deployment to the South Pacific, Sylvia learned that she was pregnant.

Sylvia, Claudia, and Agnes waited out the lonely, anxious months together at Elm Creek Manor. Sylvia and her father, who had all but retired from Bergstrom

Thoroughbreds after teaching James all he knew, held together the family business as best they could. Winter came, and although it was difficult with their loved ones facing unimaginable dangers so far away, those left behind managed to find joy and hope in the Christmas season and faced the New Year with resolve. Nineteen forty-five would be the year the war ended and the boys came home, they told one another as they toasted the New Year, but their voices were wistful. Nineteen forty-five was the year Sylvia's child would be born and Claudia would marry. Their only resolutions were to keep up their courage, to pray for peace, to make any sacrifice they could to speed the end of the brutal war.

But 1945 saw the destruction of all their hopes. A few months after Christmas, James died attempting to save Richard's life after a horrific attack on a beach in the South Pacific. The shock of the news sent Sylvia into premature labor. Her daughter succumbed after struggling for life for three days. Unable to bear the shock of so much loss, her father collapsed from a stroke.

Sylvia remembered little of those dark days. Devastated by grief, she remembered lying in a hospital bed, holding her baby's small, still body and weeping. She recalled begging the doctors to release her so she might attend her father's funeral. She remembered calling out for James and when he did not come, screaming at Agnes until her sister-in-law wept.

Eventually Sylvia was released from the hospital. At first, the numbness of shock protected her, but all too soon it receded, to be replaced by the most unbearable pain. Her beloved James was gone, and she still did not know how he had died. Her daughter was gone. She would never hold her again. Her darling little brother was gone. Her father was gone. The litany repeated itself relentlessly in her mind until she believed she would go mad.

The war ended. Andrew went home to family in Philadelphia, while Harold returned to Elm Creek Manor thinner, more anxious, and aged beyond the months he had spent in the service. As if to cast off the grief and sorrow shrouding the home, Claudia threw herself into their wedding plans. As her maid of honor, Sylvia was expected to help, but although she wanted to please her sister, she often forgot the tasks Claudia assigned to her. Sylvia's heart was not in the celebration. She had lost her heart when she lost James and her daughter.

A few weeks before the wedding, Andrew paid an unexpected visit on his way from Philadelphia to a new job in Detroit. Sylvia was glad to see him. Like Harold, Andrew had changed. He walked with a limp and sat stiffly in his chair as if maintaining army regulations. He was kind and compassionate to the grieving women, but he coldly shunned Harold, who seemed all too willing to avoid Andrew in turn. Though Sylvia would have thought the men unified by wartime experiences, perhaps, she decided, seeing each other dredged up unbearable memories.

It fell to Andrew to tell Sylvia how her brother and husband had died, although he warned her she would find no comfort in the truth. Haltingly, every word paining him, he described the terrible scene he had witnessed from a bluff overlooking the beach, how Richard had come under friendly fire, how James had raced to his rescue, how he would have succeeded with the help of one more man, how Harold had hidden himself rather than risk his own life.

Andrew begged for her forgiveness. He had run straight down the bluff to the beach where his friends lay dying, knowing that he would never make it in time. Sylvia held him as he wept, the heart she thought she had lost hardening to cold stone within her. She told Andrew she forgave him for his sake, but there was nothing to forgive. The blame was not his. Andrew had tried to save her brother and husband. He had risked his own life despite knowing that he would likely fail. Harold had not even tried.

Andrew left Elm Creek Manor the next morning, and Sylvia brooded over the burden of Harold's secret. As the days passed and the plans for the wedding progressed, Sylvia eventually realized that she could not possibly allow her sister to marry Harold unaware of his role in James's and Richard's deaths. But to Sylvia's astonishment, Claudia accused Sylvia of lying out of jealous spite and insisted that the wedding would go on. Sylvia left Elm Creek Manor that day, unable to bear the sight of the man who had allowed her husband and brother to die, unable to live with a sister who embraced a lie.

Into two suitcases she packed all she could carry—photographs, letters from Richard and James, the sewing basket she had received for Christmas the year before her mother died. Everything else she left behind—beloved childhood treasures, favorite books, unfinished quilts. Everything except memories and grief.

She left the manor not knowing where she would go. She walked miles to the bus station in Waterford, where she purchased a ticket to Harrisburg. She spent the night at Aunt Millie and Uncle George's hotel, conscious of their surprise at her unexpected appearance and their concern for her fragile state. She burned with rage and grief, but she told them nothing of Andrew's devastating account of Harold's betrayal of the Bergstrom family, the family he did not deserve to join.

Mercifully, her aunt and uncle were satisfied with her explanation that she needed time away from the manor, and they did not inquire too insistently about her itinerary. Instead they shared recent letters from Elizabeth, cheerful accounts of Henry and the children and Triumph Ranch. The bright sunshine and warm breezes of southern California seemed impossible in a world without Richard and James and her daughter and father.

As she drifted off to sleep that night, Sylvia considered taking a train west as Elizabeth had done so many years before. Her cousin would take her in. Sylvia could work herself into exhaustion on the ranch and drop off to a dreamless sleep every night. Love for her young niece and nephews could fill the void in her heart. But when she woke in the morning, Sylvia knew she could not find refuge with any Bergstrom, even one as far away as Elizabeth. A Bergstrom would send word to Claudia and urge her to return home, and that Sylvia could not bear.

The next day she thanked her aunt and uncle for their kindness and bought a train ticket to Baltimore.

She had phoned ahead, so her mother-in-law was waiting for her on the platform, dressed in black, clutching her handbag anxiously. Sylvia disembarked and almost fell into her arms. "There, there, dear," Mrs. Compson murmured, patting her on the back. "It's all right. Don't worry about anything. We'll take you home."

James's father was waiting in the car, but he leaped out to help her with her luggage. Her throat constricted at the sight of him, so like her James, tall and dark-haired, with blue eyes and a smile that warmed her to her very core. Mr. Compson did not smile now and his face was haggard with grief. She had not seen her in-laws since the funeral. They seemed to have aged decades in a few months.

Mrs. Compson sat beside Sylvia in the back seat of the Packard as Mr. Compson drove them to their horse farm on the Chesapeake Bay about twenty-five miles southeast of the city. "We've fixed up Mary's room for you," she said. "We hope you'll be comfortable there."

Sylvia's sister-in-law had graduated from the University of Maryland a few months after the attack on Pearl Harbor. While her brothers were at war, she had married a congressman and moved to Washington. At James's funeral she had grieved silently, clutching her husband's arm and staring into the distance.

"I'm sure I will be." Sylvia's voice sounded hollow, unfamiliar. On her last visit to the Compson farm, she and James had stayed in his old room. She was grateful Mrs. Compson had known not to put her there.

Not once did the Compsons ask her why she had come or how long she planned to stay. When the white fences and green pastures of the farm came into view, Sylvia felt a gentle whisper of peace upon her soul, a promise that one day she would be able to remember James's smile or his touch upon her skin without feeling as if her life had ended with his.

Compson's Resolution, six hundred acres of neatly fenced pasture, rolling forested hills, and cultivated farmland, had been in the Compson family since the eighteenth century. The name of the farm came from the settlement of a border dispute with the farmer who owned the acres to the northwest of the Compson property. The Compsons still lived in the two-hundred-year-old brown stone farmhouse with a Gambrel roof that their first ancestor in Maryland had built. Unlike the Bergstroms, who had added an entire wing to the original homestead farmhouse as the family prospered, the Compsons had brought modern conveniences to the interior but kept the footprint of the house essentially unchanged.

Sylvia was accustomed to life on a horse farm, and she soon fell into the rhythm of the Compson household. She rose early to help Mrs. Compson prepare breakfast for the family and the hired hands; she washed clothes and cleaned house; she fed chickens and pigs and tended the kitchen garden. Her mother-in-law appreciated Sylvia's help, for in Mary's absence, the housework had fallen on her shoulders alone. "I'm happier still for your company," she said, pressing a soft, plump hand to Sylvia's cheek. Her kindness brought tears to Sylvia's eyes. How could Mrs. Compson, wracked with grief for the loss of James and her grandchild, bustle about with such brisk, cheerful authority? Perhaps knowing that two of her sons had returned safely home from the war in Europe and that Mary was expecting a child gave her purpose.

Without James, without Elm Creek Manor, Sylvia felt adrift, her only tether to this world the love and kindness of James's parents.

She was most content out of doors, helping Mr. Compson with the horses. Although he and the stable hands would have managed fine without her, whenever Sylvia appeared at the corral, her father-in-law invariably found a horse that needed to be exercised. Riding alone on the trails that criss-crossed Compson's Resolution, resting by the old farm wharf to watch ships on the Chesapeake, Sylvia let go of her grief and soaked in the beauty of a swift horse and blue water and fertile land. But at night she would dream of James and wake up sobbing. Another day without him had begun.

Autumn brought golden hues and crisp sunrises to the farm. Every morning Sylvia wept less; each day she felt less likely to break at the slightest touch. One afternoon, as she and Mrs. Compson peeled apples for a pie, Sylvia reflected upon the apple orchard at Elm Creek Manor and wondered how Claudia and Harold had managed the harvest.

She did not realize she had spoken aloud until Mrs. Compson gently said, "You could return home and find out."

"I can't." Sylvia shook her head. "I can't ever go back. You don't understand."

"I might," Mrs. Compson said, "if you told me why you left."

Sylvia hesitated. Would it be cruel to burden James's mother with the truth of her son's unnecessary death? Mrs. Compson had embraced her with kindness and unconditional acceptance. Sylvia could not bear to bring her any more pain.

Mrs. Compson set down her paring knife and took Sylvia's hand in her own. Her grip was firm and steady. "Nothing you could possibly tell me about James could be worse than losing him," she said. "If I survived that, I can withstand hearing whatever is so terrible it drove you from the home you love."

Sylvia closed her eyes as she retold Andrew's story, but that did not shut out the images seared into her memory as if she, too, had witnessed the terrible scene.

Then she explained how she had confronted Claudia, and how her sister had chosen Harold over her family, and why Sylvia could never return as long as they lived in the home where she had known so much happiness with the men Harold had been unwilling to save.

When every word had drained from her, Mrs. Compson groped for the kitchen stool and sank down upon it, weeping twin rivulets of tears without making a sound. Suddenly she took a deep, shuddering breath. "You have only Andrew's account of what happened that day."

"I've known Andrew since childhood," Sylvia responded. "He loved Richard like a brother. He would have no reason to lie, and I trust him implicitly."

Mrs. Compson studied her hands in her lap for a long moment in silence. "You don't know that Harold could have saved them," she said. "You don't know for certain that James would have been able to rescue Richard if Harold had only helped him. Harold might have gone to their aid only to be caught by the second explosion, as my son was."

"Andrew told me what James shouted to Harold before he was killed." Sylvia's voice trembled. "James thought he could save Richard with Harold's help. Andrew thought so, too. But you're right, we'll never know for certain because Harold didn't even try."

"He might have known it would have been in vain," said Mrs. Compson. "He might have seen that second plane coming and known that coming out from cover would be suicide. We can't possibly know what was in his heart."

"How can you excuse what he did?" said Sylvia. "And what he didn't do? Your son is dead because of Harold's cowardice."

Mrs. Compson's shoulders slumped, weary to her soul. "It might not have been cowardice. And my son might have died anyway."

Sylvia could not believe what she was hearing. "How can you not be angry? How can you not hate him?"

"Because it would do me no good." Mrs. Compson looked up at her, a new fierceness in her eyes. "It would not change what happened. Hatred and anger will not bring my son back. They would only destroy me, the way they're clearly destroying you."

Sylvia shook her head, unable to reply. Mrs. Compson was a good woman, too good, perhaps, to understand how wrong she was. Harold deserved Sylvia's hatred, and anger was the only thing that kept her on her feet.

Though Sylvia had told her mother-in-law she would never return to Elm Creek Manor, Mrs. Compson must have thought she heard a quiet note of longing for home in her voice. A few days after Sylvia told her Andrew's story, Mrs. Compson began slipping reminders of Elm Creek Manor into their conversations, whereas she had always avoided the topic before. As they canned tomatoes, she inquired about the Bergstroms' favorite varieties and preparation methods. When Mr. Compson sold a prized yearling, she wondered aloud if the Bergstroms would have demanded a higher price. Sylvia usually offered simple answers, but Bergstrom Thoroughbreds and Elm Creek Manor had been a part of her life for too long for her to feign indifference to them now. She found herself wishing for news of the family business and the estate she once believed would be her home forever, but curiosity could not compel her to write to Claudia. She knew she could not speak to her sister without hurling accusations of betrayal. The very thought of Harold sleeping beneath the roof of Elm Creek Manor while James, Richard, her father, and her daughter slept forever so filled her with revulsion that she was not even tempted to pick up a pen.

All through that beautiful autumn, Sylvia worked alongside the Compson family. Gradually she found contentment in the routine, in the company, in the rhythm of the days and the satisfaction of the harvest. Then one day, Mrs. Compson declared that she and Sylvia deserved a holiday, and she invited Sylvia to accompany her to a luncheon at a friend's home in Baltimore. "You'll have a lovely time," Mrs. Compson persisted when Sylvia was reluctant to leave the peaceful sanctuary of Compson's Resolution. "My friends are delightful company, and our hostess has some family heirlooms I know you'll find very interesting."

In spite of herself, Sylvia was intrigued, so she agreed to the outing. A Wednesday morning in early November found her beside Mrs. Compson in the black Packard driving northwest into the city. Her friend, Mrs. Cass, had invited several ladies to gather at her grand house in what Sylvia surmised was one of Baltimore's most fashionable neighborhoods. The women welcomed Mrs. Compson and Sylvia warmly and offered Sylvia their condolences in murmurs, as if her grief were a carefully concealed secret. Sylvia was the youngest present by decades, and the only widow among the wives of doctors, lawyers, and businessmen.

Sylvia grew increasingly ill at ease as the other women discussed their husbands and children and household conflicts, for she had lost her husband and had never raised a child and had abandoned her home. She tried to nod and murmur appropriate phrases when an answer was required, but through no fault of their own, the other women made Sylvia feel like an indulged child sent to dancing school in a starched dress to learn how to mimic the mannerisms of grown-ups. The leek soup was flavorful, the crab cakes a new and unexpected pleasure, but although Sylvia smiled and conversed and hid her discomfort as well as she knew how, she could not wait for the luncheon to end. She longed for the sanctuary of the Compson stables, of the wooded riding trails, of the comforting presences of lighthouses overlooking the Chesapeake Bay.

After the meal, Mrs. Cass led her guests into a parlor for coffee and more chat. Sylvia longed for a moment alone with Mrs. Compson so she could beg to be taken home, but she knew that Mrs. Compson would kindly but firmly refuse. Her impeccable manners would not permit her to slight their hostess, and she was convinced a change of scene would do Sylvia good. A new riding trail on the Compson estate was all the change of scene Sylvia wanted. The sympathetic gazes and gentle words of the Baltimore ladies were excruciating.

In the parlor, Mrs. Cass spoke a word to her maid, who disappeared and quickly returned with a bundle wrapped in a muslin sheet. "Your mother-in-law tells me you know a great deal about quilts, Sylvia," Mrs. Cass said as she thanked the maid and took the bundle.

"My mother taught me when I was very young," Sylvia replied. "I grew up watching her and my aunts and grandma quilt together."

"I'm afraid quilting is a lost art among the women of my family," said Mrs. Cass, "but I am fortunate to have several fine examples of my ancestors' handiwork.

Although I don't like to brag, I think it's fair to call this quilt a masterpiece."

Sylvia and two other ladies helped Mrs. Cass unfold the bundle. A murmur of appreciation rippled through the room as everyone gathered around to view the quilt. It was a masterpiece, indeed—twenty-five different appliqué blocks depicting bouquets of spring blossoms gathered in three-looped bows, bowls of fruit with embroidered seeds, symmetrical Turkey red flowers with green stems and leaves, and scenes of eighteenth-century life reproduced in such painstaking detail that they must have been drawn from the quilter's own observations.

"You wouldn't recognize these landmarks, Sylvia, since this is your first visit to Baltimore." Mrs. Cass gestured to several blocks in turn. "This is a famous clipper ship that sailed in the Chesapeake Bay in the 1840s. This is a train from the Baltimore and Ohio Railroad, and this is the Baltimore Basilica on Mulberry and Cathedral streets."

"This is the Peale Museum in its glory days," said another guest, indicating another block. "Before all that dreadful stucco was added."

"It's a truly wonderful quilt," said Sylvia. She had seen quilts made in this style before, but the Bergstrom women had never made any like them as far as she knew. She came closer for a better look. "It looks like the blocks were signed in brown ink and the handwriting . . . yes, a different hand signed each block. Could this be a group quilt?"

"That's what the family stories say," said Mrs. Cass. "My grandmother once told me that this was a Freedom Quilt, made by the women of the family for one of my long-distant great-uncles when he turned twenty-one. For generations we assumed that each block was signed by the quilter who made it, but I've discovered that the record in our family Bible disputes those claims." She gestured to a block in the bottom row. "Hettie Cass would have been only five years old when the quilt was made, and I don't know any child that age who could sew a lyre and floral spray as perfectly as those in her block."

"Is it possible that an older relative didn't want Hettie to be left out of such an important family project, so she made the block on the little girl's behalf?" asked Sylvia.

"I suppose so," said Mrs. Cass thoughtfully. "It seems like the sort of thing a mother or aunt would do."

"I have a similar quilt among my own family heirlooms," said another guest. "The blocks aren't identical to these, of course, but the style is very similar. I like to imagine that our great-grandmothers were friends, and that they quilted together." She smiled at Mrs. Cass.

"Can you imagine how many hours these women must have spent on their masterpieces?" said another guest. "How did they have time to do anything else?"

The other women laughed, and Mrs. Cass said, "They didn't have the amusements and distractions we have today. Quilting with friends might have been the only entertainment available to them."

The implication that women quilted only because they had nothing more interesting to do bothered Sylvia. "Whoever made this quilt was a true artist. I imagine she looked forward to working on it whenever she could slip away from her household chores. I wouldn't be surprised if she turned down invitations just so she could be alone with her fabric and needle."

"It's a pity no one makes quilts like this anymore," said another lady with a sigh.

"Some people do," said Sylvia, surprised that the woman did not know. "Perhaps not in this style, exactly, but intricate and beautiful in their own right."

"I suppose they do, on the farm," another guest acknowledged. "Here in the city, we're much too busy to quilt, and we have so many fine stores where you can buy well-made coverlets at very reasonable prices."

"I don't believe city women are any busier than farm women," said Mrs. Cass, with an amused smile.

"Even in the Elm Creek Valley, the stores carry blankets," said Sylvia. "If all that mattered was keeping warm, we would buy our coverlets, too. The women of my family quilt—they quilted—as a matter of choice, not necessity. We each had our own style, our own favorite colors and patterns, our own unique way of arranging the pieces—even if two of us chose the same pattern and traced the same templates, the quilts we made would be as unique to us as our faces and our voices. My mother's quilts say 'home' to me in a way no blanket from a store ever could."

"I don't know if my daughters could say something so heartfelt about anything I've ever given them," said Mrs. Cass.

"When you put it that way," said the woman who owned a similar quilt, "it sounds like a lovely pastime. I only wish my grandmother had taught me how to quilt."

"I could teach you," said Sylvia.

For the first time, the women regarded her with genuine interest instead of pity. "Could you?" asked one of the guests, a doctor's wife. "It seems so terribly difficult."

"We wouldn't have to begin with a quilt as challenging as this," said Sylvia, indicating Mrs. Cass's heirloom. "We could begin with something simple—a sampler made up of several different blocks in increasing complexity. Working on each block would help you master a particular quilting skill, so that by the time your sampler is finished, you'll be able to approach other patterns on your own with confidence."

The ladies peppered her with eager questions, but Mrs. Cass's voice rose above the chorus: "And how often would you be willing to return to Baltimore to teach us?"

Sylvia threw a questioning glance to Mrs. Compson, who gazed back at Sylvia from beneath raised brows, as curious as the others. She was not going to answer on Sylvia's behalf, so Sylvia took a deep breath and said, "Twice a month, if it's all right with Mrs. Compson."

"Oh, it will be fine with her," said the most outspoken of the ladies. "Isn't it, Josephine?"

"I suppose I can spare her," said Mrs. Compson, smiling. "I believe I'd like to join the quilting bee, too."

Sylvia and the women decided to meet every other Wednesday for lunch and quilting lessons, with each woman taking a turn as hostess. Sylvia advised her new pupils on the supplies they would need to collect for the first lesson, and the room buzzed as they made plans for shopping expeditions.

Everyone bade Sylvia a cheerful farewell as they parted on Mrs. Cass's front walk. As Mrs. Compson turned the Packard toward home, Sylvia's thoughts ran with block patterns and lesson plans. It was a pity they couldn't meet more frequently. Perhaps she could begin each class by introducing a new quilting skill, which the ladies would practice together as a group. She could also leave them with the pattern to another, more advanced block that would reinforce what they had learned in class. Her students would be instructed to finish both blocks before the next class, where Sylvia would inspect them and offer constructive criticism before presenting a new quilting technique.

Suddenly a thought occurred to Sylvia. "Mrs. Cass's friends were nice, but did you notice how they only thought of me as poor Mrs. Compson's widowed daughter-in-law until Mrs. Cass brought out her quilt?"

Mrs. Compson's smile was both amused and knowing. "Did you notice that until Mrs. Cass brought out her quilt, you behaved as nothing more than poor Mrs. Compson's widowed daughter-in-law?"

Sylvia sat back against her seat, chagrined. It was true that she had not really made an effort to get to know any of the ladies, not even Mrs. Cass. Their kind-hearted sympathy had been so unbearable that her only aim had been to get through the afternoon. She had not even bothered to learn any of their names. She could not fault them for not seeing the person behind the grief.

Somewhere deep inside her, a spark of realization kindled and burned, a small but steady light. There was still a person behind the grief. Until that moment, she had forgotten.

Sylvia spent the next week planning her lessons and preparing patterns. She had tried to teach quilting only once before, when Agnes admired the quilts her sisters-in-law had made and wanted to make a wedding quilt for her and Richard. Sylvia tried to steer her toward basic patterns, but Agnes insisted upon making a Double Wedding Ring, with disastrous results.

Agnes finished only one lopsided ring of her quilt

before word came that her new husband had died. Sylvia doubted she would ever make another.

Sylvia wondered what would become of Agnes. After Richard's death, she had stayed on at Elm Creek Manor instead of returning home to her parents, who had not approved of her hasty marriage. Now that Sylvia had left, would Agnes remain at Elm Creek Manor with Claudia and Harold? Sylvia could not imagine the young widow finding any happiness in that arrangement—but she quickly drove her concerns from her thoughts. Agnes was free to make her own decisions. It was none of Sylvia's business whether she stayed to help look after the Bergstrom legacy or if she departed forever as Sylvia had done. Agnes had been a Bergstrom less than a year. She would likely put her girlhood romance behind her and marry again, with, Sylvia hoped, a much happier ending.

The next Wednesday, Sylvia and Mrs. Compson returned to Baltimore and met the aspiring quilters at the home of the doctor's wife. After another delicious lunch, Sylvia demonstrated how to make a simple Nine-Patch block, starting with making templates from cardboard, tracing the shapes on the wrong side of the fabric, cutting and pinning, and sewing the pieces together with a running stitch. Sylvia heard herself echoing the advice and warnings she had heard since childhood from the Bergstrom women: trace the templates with a sharp pencil, make the stitches small and even, mind the seam allowances, don't stretch the fabric out of shape. The Baltimore ladies took eagerly to her lesson, and each finished a twelve-inch block by the end of the afternoon. Sylvia left them with patterns and instructions for a Sawtooth Star block and promised to see them two weeks hence.

The following session, each lady had completed a Sawtooth Star, with the quality ranging from acceptable to expert. Sylvia hesitated as she examined one woman's block, uncertain what to say. While her color choices were among the best in the group, her stitches were uneven and seam allowances almost nonexistent. A child in the Bergstrom family would have been instructed to pick out the stitches and try again. A Bergstrom woman might have passed the block around the quilting circle for a laugh, but then she would have known to start over, perhaps after seeking advice from more experienced quilters in the family.

"What do you think?" asked Mrs. Simmons, after Sylvia studied the block in silence for much longer than it had taken her to evaluate the other women's work.

"You have a wonderful eye for color," said Sylvia.

"Thank you, dear, but what about the sewing?" When Sylvia hesitated, Mrs. Simmons said, "I'm prepared for your honest opinion."

"Well," Sylvia said, "what do you think of your work when you compare your block to what your friends have done?"

"Oh, tell the truth, Doris," teased another lady, a Mrs. Cook. "She knows you didn't do your best but she's too well-mannered to say so."

When the other ladies laughed, Mrs. Simmons gave Sylvia a guilty smile. "I was a bit pressed for time at the end."

"She starting working on the block last night, while the rest of us began the day after our last lesson," another woman called out. "She finished the last seam in the car on the way over."

"Tattletale," retorted Mrs. Simmons, giggling. To Sylvia she added, "I had hoped no one would notice."

Her hastiness certainly explained her results, and Sylvia couldn't help feeling disappointed in her pupil. "I'm sure you see the problems with your block as readily as I do," she said as kindly as she could. "If you put more effort into your next blocks, I'll be able to evaluate your skills more accurately and offer you better guidance next time."

Mrs. Simmons went back to her seat perfectly content, so Sylvia suspected she felt worse about her first student failure than the student herself. Still, she figured everyone deserved a second chance after one bad decision, so she moved on to the next part of the class and introduced the LeMoyne Star block, one of her favorites. This block would be more challenging than the first two because it required the quilter to "set in" pieces, or sew a piece into an angle between two other pieces.

As the rich colors of autumn faded into the snowy white of winter, the Baltimore Quilting Circle, as the ladies had dubbed themselves, made progress on their quilts. Sylvia made progress of her own, improving her patterns and teaching methods. She learned that good humor could make a difficult evaluation more tolerable, and that students were more likely to take her advice if she brought them around with encouragement instead of demanding they do what she knew was right. Her newfound wisdom came too late to help her when it would have done the most good for her personally, such as in countless childhood conflicts with her sister. It was too late to unsnarl the tangled threads of sibling antipathy now.

The quilting class continued, with mixed results. Mrs.

Simmons dropped out of the group after Thanksgiving, but the others assured Sylvia that her decision had nothing to do with Sylvia's teaching. Sylvia believed them, but other students' offhand remarks suggested that they never intended to make another quilt after completing their first. To them, their expedition into quilting was a lark, not a pastime they were eager to pursue after this one enjoyable outing with friends. Most disheartening of all, the class was evenly divided between those who considered quilting to be an art form and those who considered it to be merely an enjoyable hobby.

Sylvia tried to persuade them that a quilt could be just as much a work of art as a painting or a sculpture. One woman finally relented, saying, "Perhaps quilts are art, dear—folk art." The other ladies were satisfied to see the debate end with that, but Sylvia thought it was a grudging compromise on their part, a nice, safe label that put quilting in a quaint little box but that ignored its true value. When she protested that on the day they first met at Mrs. Cass's house, they had admired her ancestor's masterpiece and declared it a true work of art, they considered her point briefly before concluding that antique quilts made generations ago could be called art, but that none of the quilts made in their day and age deserved that approbation.

Sylvia gave up in frustration. Even if only half of her class believed quilting was an art, that was six more people who believed it than before the class began. She would have to be content with that.

Christmas approached, and because the ladies of the Baltimore Quilting Circle were busy with holiday preparations and family gatherings, they agreed not to meet again until after the New Year.

Sylvia braced herself for the approaching holidays. Memories of Christmas mornings and hopeful New Year's Days at Elm Creek Manor filled her thoughts as she helped Mrs. Compson prepare the household for a bittersweet observation of the season. Mary and her husband were coming in from Washington, and with James's brothers and their sweethearts, as well as cousins and aunts and uncles from the city, the farmhouse would be full to the rafters with relatives by marriage Sylvia scarcely knew. James's absence from the family circle would be conspicuous.

As they baked Christmas cookies and pies, Mrs. Compson told stories of holidays when her children were young. Sylvia was both amused and pained to hear her tales of James as a young boy. She craved any memory of her husband's life, even those that did not belong to her, because she would not be able to make new memories of life with him. And yet each story tore at her heart because that little boy and the good, loving man he had become were gone.

She remembered their first Christmas together as husband and wife, when in accordance with Bergstrom family tradition as the most recently married couple they had ventured out into the snowy woods to find the family Christmas tree. She thought back upon another, lonelier holiday when the men were at war, and she, Claudia, and Agnes had found strength and courage in their love for one another and in the simple joy and hope of the season. Those feelings should have sustained them when tragedy struck, but Claudia had betrayed them and Sylvia could never face her again.

When the time came to decorate the farmhouse at Compson's Resolution, Mrs. Compson sent her husband

and sons into the wooded hills to bring home six small fir trees. Sylvia was jolted by a sudden memory of walking in the woods with James. They towed the toboggan behind them, James carried the ax, and he smiled as he told her about boyhood Christmases at his parents' house. "My father always wanted a floor-to-ceiling tree," he told her, "but my mother preferred a small one to stand on a tabletop. She said that was the way her family had always done it, and to please her, my father went along with it. Over the years they collected too many ornaments to fit on one small tree, but instead of getting a larger one, they chose two small trees and kept them in different rooms. By the time I was in school, we had small trees on tabletops in almost every room of the house. When visitors came, my next-oldest sister and I would lead tours to make sure they didn't miss any of them."

Sylvia had smiled then, entranced by the image of her beloved husband as a boy on Christmas morning. Now the memory of his voice in the snowy woods made her ache with grief and longing.

Christmas Day came, a day she expected to be unable to endure, but although the family had not forgotten their sorrow, they found happiness in one another and in hope for the future. The war was over and more prosperous times seemed on the horizon. Mary's child was due within a month. Although Sylvia missed Elm Creek Manor more that day than she had since her departure, the love and acceptance the Compson family offered her helped her to feel the simple hope and joy of the season anew. She felt James's presence in the midst of his family, and she knew that his love for her remained, and that one day she would know love again.

The feeling of enduring love lingered until three days after Christmas, when Mrs. Compson approached Sylvia hesitantly, a letter in her hand. Sylvia knew at once who had sent it.

"Claudia heard from your Aunt Millie and Uncle George that you bought a train ticket to Baltimore," Mrs. Compson told her, when Sylvia refused to take the letter, which was addressed to her in-laws. "She asks if you're here with us, or if we know your whereabouts."

"Don't tell her I'm here."

"I have to tell her something," Mrs. Compson pointed out. "She'll think her letter went astray and send another, or she'll come to us herself."

Sylvia felt faint as a vision of a resentful Claudia at the farmhouse door crowded out her anger. "Tell her I stayed with you for a month, and left without telling you where I was going."

"You're asking me to lie?"

"Yes, I am."

"She sounds worried."

"She probably wants to gloat about her beautiful wedding." Claudia and Harold were the most recently married couple in the family now. They would have brought home the family Christmas tree that season as Sylvia and James had done, but there were few Bergstroms left at Elm Creek Manor to enjoy it. "She no doubt also wants to scold me for not attending. Does she offer anything in the way of an apology?"

Mrs. Compson scanned the letter. "No," she said, reluctantly, "but the letter is addressed to me and Charles. She didn't know you would be here to read it. If she had known, I'm sure she would have said how sorry she is that you two had a falling out."

"It was much more than a falling out, and I'm equally sure that she would not have apologized."

"You'll never know unless you return home."

The thought of wandering through Elm Creek Manor, hearing the voices of her lost loved ones whispering in the empty halls, catching glimpses of them in the corner of her eye, made Sylvia recoil in pain. "I can't."

Mrs. Compson regarded her for a long moment in silence before returning the letter to the envelope. "Very well. I'll do as you ask, but I hope someday soon you'll see how you've set up an insurmountable hurdle for your sister."

"What do you mean?"

"You want her to apologize, and yet you refuse to read her letter or go see her. How can she apologize if you won't listen? How can she ask for forgiveness if she can't find you?"

"I know my sister," said Sylvia. "She's never apologized to me for anything, not once in her life. She isn't about to start now."

Mrs. Compson tapped the envelope against the palm of her hand. "Why is she searching for you, then?"

Sylvia could not answer.

Mrs. Compson sighed. "Sylvia, dear, Charles and I are very happy to have you here with us, but eventually you're going to have to move on with your life. I believe your place is at Elm Creek Manor, but if you don't feel you can go home under these circumstances—well, only you can make that choice. But you must choose something. You can't continue to go through the motions of living. You have to truly live. You're still a young woman. You could marry again, have children—"

"No," said Sylvia. "I could never love anyone else the way I loved James."

"Perhaps not," admitted Mrs. Compson. "But I know one thing for certain: James loved you. Don't choose a life of endless grieving for his sake. You are not honoring his memory by harboring anger in your heart. That is not what my son would have wanted for you."

Sylvia's gaze fell, unable to bear the weight of Mrs. Compson's compassion. She knotted her fingers together in her lap, her throat tightening. "I'm not ready to face my sister," she choked out. "I can't see her with Harold, not yet, not without hating her."

Mrs. Compson clasped Sylvia's hands in her own. "Think of the name of this farm, Compson's Resolution," she said. "A resolution is also the settlement of a dispute. Perhaps, with the New Year approaching, you will find the strength to make a resolution that will allow you to go home."

Sylvia closed her eyes against tears. She could not bear the thought of leaving the Compson farm. She felt safe here, hidden away, protected. But if Claudia suspected Sylvia was living on the farm, it could not shelter her forever.

New Year's Eve came. The Compson family stayed up until midnight reminiscing about bygone years and making hopeful predictions about the year ahead. Sylvia tried not to think about how Claudia, Harold, and Agnes were marking the holiday back home in Pennsylvania.

At midnight, to the strains of "Auld Lang Syne" on the radio broadcast of the Lombardo New Year's Eve Party, Sylvia and the Compsons toasted the New Year. "May the New Year bring us peace, contentment, and hope," said Mrs. Compson, raising her glass. "May each of us find the courage we need to overcome our sorrows and achieve the happiness we deserve."

Sylvia's eyes met hers over the rim of her glass, and she knew Mrs. Compson's wish was meant especially for her.

The next morning, Sylvia helped Mrs. Compson prepare breakfast for the family, missing Great-Aunt Lucinda's *Pfannkuchen*. She thought ruefully of the battered cookbook in the kitchen back home, stuffed full of recipes jotted down on index cards and the backs of envelopes in the handwriting of generations of Bergstrom women. She wished she had thought to take it with her when she fled Elm Creek Manor, even though the best family recipes would not be found there for they had never been written down. She longed for the aromas of pork roasting with apples, of sauerkraut, of her father's *Feuerzangenbowle*. It hardly felt like the New Year had begun without them.

She found herself telling her mother-in-law about all the old Bergstrom traditions, about lead pouring and unreliable predictions, of blazing fireballs and unfulfilled dreams. Mrs. Compson listened, almost forgetting the sausages frying on the stove. "And what about your dreams?" she asked when Sylvia finished. "Surely you must have a few left that you can still fulfill."

"I do." Sylvia had given her dreams a great deal of thought since Claudia's letter arrived. And after Mrs. Compson's New Year's Eve toast, she had determined to do something about them.

As the Compson sisters and brothers, cousins and uncles exchanged New Year's Day greetings, Sylvia thought of the generations past who had sat at that heirloom trestle table, glad to put the sorrows of the past year behind them, facing the year ahead with courage or with trepidation. Her story was a part of their history now, and although she would always long for James and for home, she found hope in knowing that for all that she had lost, she had also gained a second family. No matter where the year ahead took her, she would never truly be alone as long as she kept the memory of those she loved and those who loved her alive in her heart.

The conversation turned to New Year's resolutions. One aunt resolved to respond more promptly to friends' letters. James's sister, due to deliver her first baby any day, resolved to regain her slim figure by spring, which earned her a round of laughter from other mothers around the table.

"What about you, Sylvia?" prompted Mr. Compson. "Do you have any resolutions for the New Year?"

All eyes turned to her. Sylvia could imagine what the more distant relations saw when they looked at her: a poor curiosity, a fragile young widow overwhelmed by grief, inexplicably in flight from her family and the home she had always loved. Though they would never say anything to suggest she was not welcome among them, they probably wondered why she did not simply go home.

"I've made one resolution," Sylvia said. This was not how she had planned to tell them, but she plunged ahead. "I've decided to return to college."

An exclamation of surprise and delight went up from those gathered around the table. "Why, Sylvia, that's a wonderful idea," said Mrs. Compson. She knew that Sylvia had left school after two years at Waterford College to marry James. "I'm sure a business degree will help you run Bergstrom Thoroughbreds."

"Perhaps I should be worried about the competition," remarked Mr. Compson, but he looked pleased.

"I'm not seeking a business degree," said Sylvia. "I want to become an art teacher." When Mrs. Compson's smile faded into confusion, Sylvia quickly added, "I've enjoyed teaching the Baltimore Quilting Circle ladies how to quilt, and I think I've discovered that I have a talent for teaching. I also want to show people how quiltmaking is a true art form. The more I learn about art, the more I'll be able to make that argument and back it up with critical thinking."

"Then—" Mr. Compson cleared his throat. "Then you have no intention of returning to Bergstrom Thoroughbreds?"

Sylvia laughed shakily. "I don't think a horse farm has much need for an art teacher on staff."

Some of the family members who did not know the story of Sylvia's self-imposed exile laughed, but James's parents and siblings looked stricken. "You do intend to resume your studies at Waterford College, though, don't you?" asked Mrs. Compson, her joy of moments ago all but vanished.

Sylvia had no intention of returning to the Elm Creek Valley, but she could not bear to admit to it and ruin her mother-in-law's New Year's Day. "I haven't thought that far ahead. I don't know if Waterford College would take me back after so many years, and I don't know if my credits would transfer if I were accepted somewhere else. Perhaps . . . perhaps I shouldn't have made a resolution without looking into it first."

Several people quickly assured her that her resolution was quite all right; she had set a goal for herself and that was the important thing. The rest could be sorted out later. Sylvia thanked them, but as the conversation moved on to others' resolutions, she glanced at Mrs. Compson and saw her exchange a look of dismay with her husband. When Sylvia had announced her resolution, Mrs. Compson had surely assumed that Sylvia would be returning to Elm Creek Manor and attending Waterford College only a few miles away. As much as Mrs. Compson wanted Sylvia to find the courage to fulfill her dreams, she would prefer for those dreams to set her on the road toward home.

Sylvia stayed on at Compson's Resolution while she planned her future. Winter ended and spring came to the farm. On Sylvia's birthday, Claudia sent another letter to the Compsons asking if they had heard from her. With a disapproving frown for her daughter-in-law, Mrs. Compson penned the reply Sylvia implored her to make: They were unaware of Sylvia's whereabouts, but if Sylvia contacted them, they would urge her to get in touch with Claudia. "That much is true," grumbled Mrs. Compson as she sealed the envelope. Not a week passed that she did not beg Sylvia to write to her sister.

A few days after the anniversary of James's death, the Compsons received an unexpected letter from Andrew. From his new home in Michigan, he wrote that he had been thinking of them and that he hoped they had friends and family nearby to see them through that difficult day. He shared memories of his friendship with James, of James's courage on the battlefield, of his reassuring confidence, his humor that helped them forget where they were, if only for moments. James had spoken of his family and Compson's Resolution often, Andrew wrote, and his descriptions of his boyhood home were so vivid that Andrew almost felt as if he had walked the wooded trails himself. "I know he loved you and Sylvia very much," he wrote. "He spoke of you often and he was looking forward to seeing you again. I want you to know that he saved my life more than once, and if I can live my life with half the courage, honor, and decency he demonstrated every day, I will consider myself a successful man."

Sylvia was in tears by the end of the letter. She wondered if Andrew had sent a similar letter to her at Elm Creek Manor. He would not know that she was not there to receive it.

By the end of summer, Sylvia had made her decision and could no longer conceal it from Mr. and Mrs. Compson. For months they had observed her preparing applications and checking the mail for information from prospective colleges. When the time came to break the news, however, she was unprepared for the depths of their disappointment. Upon hearing that she intended to enroll at Carnegie Mellon, Mrs. Compson became uncharacteristically tearful. "If Waterford College is out of the question, why not attend the University of Maryland?" she implored. "Mary received a wonderful education there, and you'd be close enough to come home for visits now and then. I know you applied; I know you were accepted. I've seen the postmarks."

Sylvia was touched by Mrs. Compson's heartfelt plea, especially because she had instinctively referred to Compson's Resolution and not Elm Creek Manor as Sylvia's home. But Carnegie Mellon suited her interests best, and a lingering fear remained that if she stayed too close to the Compsons, eventually Claudia would come looking for her.

On the morning she departed for Pittsburgh, she

embraced her in-laws and thanked them for taking her into their home. "You're James's wife," her father-in-law said. "You'll always have a place here with us."

Sylvia promised to come visit them often, and she did, at first. On school holidays and summer vacations, she took the train east to Baltimore, gazing out the windows as they chugged south of the mountains surrounding the Elm Creek Valley, pressing her hand against the cool glass and longing for a glimpse of the land beyond the mountain passes.

After Sylvia graduated and began teaching in the Allegheny Valley School District, her visits to Compson's Resolution became less frequent. Mrs. Compson honored her promise not to disclose her whereabouts to Claudia, and eventually Claudia's letters stopped coming.

Whatever word the Compsons received of Elm Creek Manor or Bergstrom Thoroughbreds, they passed along to Sylvia. There were glad tidings for Agnes, Sylvia's former sister-in-law, for she had married a history professor from Waterford College. Darker rumors swirled that Bergstrom Thoroughbreds was failing, but Sylvia could not believe that even Claudia and Harold would allow the family business to falter so completely and so suddenly. Over time, news from Elm Creek Manor slowed to a trickle, and with Mr. and Mrs. Compson's passing, it stopped altogether.

As she grew older, Sylvia built lasting friendships with fellow quilters and neighbors near her redbrick house on Camp Meeting Road in Sewickley, Pennsylvania. She offered her love for quilting to anyone who wanted to learn, and she was passionate about quilting as a traditional art form even before the "quilting renaissance" began in the 1970s. On every New Year's Eve, whether she celebrated alone or with friends, Sylvia reflected upon her mother-in-law's toast at Compson's Resolution. Had Sylvia found peace, contentment, and hope at long last, so far from home? Had she found the courage to overcome her sorrows and seek happiness?

Sylvia thought that she had. This was not the life she had expected, but it was rewarding, and she was thankful.

Fifty years after leaving Elm Creek Manor, she received a phone call from a lawyer, the son of a man she had known as a classmate in Waterford. She was stunned when he told her Claudia had died. "How?" she stammered, shaken. Of course Claudia had aged as she herself had aged, although in her mind's eye Claudia had been frozen in time exactly as she had been in 1945. People their age died every day, and others called it natural causes.

Harold had preceded Claudia in death and they had no children, so the estate was Sylvia's. She was not sure she wanted it. She had made a life for herself in Sewickley, and she could not imagine rattling around the manor alone, not at her age, not when none of her friends remained nearby. She hired a private detective to find a more suitable heir—a distant relation, anyone. When the quest proved fruitless—so promptly that Sylvia wondered if the detective had searched as thoroughly as his fees merited—Sylvia returned to Elm Creek Manor as the sole heir of the Bergstrom estate.

It was late September when she made the trip through the rolling hills of central Pennsylvania to the Elm Creek Valley. She almost could not breathe as she turned off the main highway onto the narrow, gravel road that led through a wood encircling the Bergstrom property, ablaze with the hues of autumn. Her heart was in her throat as the taxi rambled over the old stone bridge crossing Elm Creek, curious, but fearing what she would see upon emerging from the woods. The broad, dry front lawn was overgrown, but the gray stone walls of the manor stood proudly above it. The Bergstrom legacy seemed as strong and resilient as ever until the cab pulled to a stop in the circular driveway and Sylvia beheld peeling paint, broken windowpanes, and crumbling mortar.

The lawyer's warnings had not adequately prepared her for what she discovered inside. Claudia had sold off many family heirlooms to make ends meet after the business failed, but the empty spaces once occupied by valuable antique furniture and fine art startled her at every turn. As if to make up for ridding the manor of its treasures, Claudia had stuffed rooms full of worthless clutter—junk mail, yellowing newspapers, meat trays from the supermarket, burned out lightbulbs, quart jars that had once held spaghetti sauce. Sylvia could not fathom why her sister had hoarded so much useless rubbish. What had she intended to do with it all? How many empty mason jars did one woman need, especially a woman who had let the garden run wild and had nothing to can? Was it nothing more than one last spiteful jab at her estranged sister, whom Claudia must have suspected would be responsible for cleaning up the mess?

Sylvia tackled the kitchen first, but hours of labor made little headway. Exhausted, she made up a bed on the sofa in the west sitting room, for the thought of spending the night in the room she and James had once shared was unbearable. When she woke the next morning in the empty house, she felt pinned to the bed by the sheer weight of the enormous task awaiting her. The manor was hers, now, as well as the remaining lands that Claudia had failed to or forgotten to sell off. She had to meet with the lawyer and pay her sister's debts. Every room had to be cleared, the rubbish sorted from items worth keeping. There were details and entanglements to sort out, papers to sign, accounts to close. It would take her at least a month, and she had packed for only a few days. She would have to make a trip into Waterford for groceries and pray that the old stove and icebox still worked.

Waterford had changed since she had seen it last—progress, she supposed some people would call it—and it seemed both familiar and strange. The college had expanded; a few buildings downtown had been demolished and replaced. There was a new quilt shop on Main Street, so she stopped in to browse for a while and chatted with the friendly owner. At least if she was forced to extend her stay, she needn't fear running out of quilting supplies.

Spending a solitary Christmas at Elm Creek Manor was out of the question. Bygone seasons of warmth and laughter now seemed shrouded in perpetual mourning. Every room, every possession reminded her of faces she would never see again, voices she would never hear. She closed up the old house and returned to Sewickley to spend the holiday in the company of friends. As dear as they were to her, they knew little of her past before she came to Sewickley as a young widow. Some believed she had lived all her life in Sewickley and were surprised to learn of a long-lost sister and family estate in the Elm Creek Valley. They offered condolences for her loss and assistance in tying up the loose ends of Claudia's estate, but Sylvia knew the task was hers alone—and a more arduous task than they suspected. Not wanting to boast, she had not been completely honest about the size of the estate or its former elegance. She certainly hadn't referred to it as a "manor."

"You won't be leaving us for your old family home in the country, will you, Sylvia?" asked one friend, half in worry, half in jest.

"There's little chance of that," said Sylvia. "I left home fifty years ago. Nothing remains for me there."

Later, another friend took Sylvia aside and urged her not to make any hasty decisions. "When my husband died last year, I couldn't bear to see any of his things," Alice confided. "I told my sons to take anything they wanted, and I gave everything else to Goodwill. I saved only photographs, his war medals, and his wedding ring. Now my house is clean and tidy, and there are days when I miss him so much I want nothing more than to slip into one of his old flannel shirts and read a book by the fire and pretend he's there with me. And I can't."

"Oh, Alice." Sylvia embraced her. "I'm so sorry."

"Who would have thought that what I'd miss most would turn out to be his favorite flannel shirt?" said Alice wistfully. "If I had waited another month for the weather to turn colder, I'm sure I would have known. Sylvia, I understand you can't sit on that old place forever, especially since it's so far away, but please don't make my mistake. Don't get rid of everything until you've had time to carefully reflect upon what it might mean to you later. I can guess that you and your sister didn't get along, but there must be a few mementos you'd like to keep. If not your sister's belongings, then perhaps your parents'." Alice pressed her arm. "There's no rush. Promise yourself you won't do anything you can't undo."

Sylvia thanked Alice for her wise advice and promised to take heed.

Two days after Christmas, she returned to Elm Creek Manor with a renewed sense of purpose. The details of Claudia's estate were nearly resolved, and a decision loomed before her. As she deliberated over the fate of the manor, she chose a precious few family keepsakes to treasure always. Her friends assumed she would follow the most sensible course—sell the property and return to Sewickley. Still, Sylvia had been away from the manor so long that she didn't care to hasten her final leavetaking. It troubled her, too, to think of selling the estate to a stranger when it had belonged to the Bergstroms since the day Hans, Anneke, and Gerda Bergstrom had set the cornerstone in place.

In the kitchen she discovered her Great-Aunt Lucinda's cookie cutters. She set those aside in the west sitting room, along with photograph albums and her father's watch. She wanted one of her mother's quilts, perhaps her New York Beauty wedding quilt or the Elms and Lilacs anniversary quilt, but she did not find either spread on any of the beds. They were such exquisite quilts that very likely they had been put away for safekeeping, so she decided to continue her search for them later. To her surprise she found a Featherweight sewing machine in the parlor; Agnes or Claudia must have purchased it after Sylvia's departure.

Suddenly Sylvia remembered Great-Grandmother Anneke's sewing machine in the west sitting room. Sylvia spent part of every day there, and it was strange she had not thought of it before. When she reached the doorway, she understood why: It had been pushed into the corner away from its customary spot and draped with a graying bedsheet.

"Customary spot," Sylvia said with a derisive sniff.

More than fifty years had passed since she had known what was "customary" around Elm Creek Manor.

She tugged off the sheet and sneezed as a cloud of dust encircled her. Waving the motes away, Sylvia blinked her watering eyes and sighed with relief at the sight of the priceless treadle sewing machine Anneke had brought with her to America. Family stories handed down through the generations claimed that she had helped support the family by taking in sewing from a dressmaker in town. Her skills with a needle and thread were as legendary as Gerda's reputation as a cook.

Then Sylvia peered closer. Wedged between the foot pedal and the sewing machine cabinet were two overstuffed laundry bags. Curious, Sylvia carefully extricated them from their hiding spot and untied the drawstrings of one of the bags. Inside, she discovered the Bergstrom women's scrap collection, as well as folded yardage of more recent acquisitions.

Sylvia settled down on the floor, her heart pounding with anticipation. Gazing into the bag, she quickly recognized strips of bright calico her Great-Aunt Lucinda had cut for cousin Elizabeth's Chimneys and Cornerstones quilt. She found pretty florals from which she and Claudia had carefully cut squares for the Nine-Patch quilt they had sewn for a newborn cousin. Pastel scraps left over from her mother's Elms and Lilacs anniversary quilt mingled with red patches from Agnes's failed attempt to make a Double Wedding Ring quilt for Richard. Fabrics familiar and unknown kept a jumbled account of landmark moments in the Bergstrom women's lives, occasions they had marked with the creation of a quilt. Births and celebrations, times of learning and times of teaching others—Sylvia could find a memento of each within the soft cotton scraps so long forgotten.

Blue and yellow had always been her lucky colors. As if she could feel the Bergstrom women gathering nearby, urging her on, Sylvia searched through the bags and withdrew all the blue and yellow-gold scraps she could find.

It was New Year's Eve, the time for reflection. As Sylvia cut fabric and traced templates, she thought back upon all the New Year's Eves she had spent sheltered within the gray stone walls of the manor and within the even stronger circle of love of her family. As she sewed a Good Fortune block into the center of a Mother's Favorite pattern, memories of decades of New Years greeted far from home cast melancholy shadows upon the seasons past, but she did not flinch. If she were to take an honest look at her life and her choices, she could not pick and choose what to remember. The New Year had not always fulfilled its promise of good fortune, and when it had not, it had been up to her to make the most of what was given, to learn and to grow, and in so doing, to turn ill fortune into good. In the stillness of her heart, she knew she had sometimes stumbled along the way, had allowed fear or anger or resentment to prevent her from living as fully as she could have. She could not change the mistakes of the past, but she could learn from them.

Sylvia worked on her New Year's Reflections quilt, adding a Peace and Plenty block in tribute to Josephine Compson and the New Year's blessing she had bestowed upon her family so many years before. She pieced a Memory Chain block so she would never forget the hard lessons learned from the unexpected course her life had taken. She sewed, lost in thought, until the clock struck midnight. There were no noisemakers, no champagne toasts, no kisses and cries of "Happy New Year" ringing through the halls, but this New Year's Day would mark a new beginning for Sylvia, for she had resolved what course to pursue in the year ahead.

She would clear the manor of Claudia's detritus, bringing in a forklift if necessary. She would hire workers to make repairs and get the grounds in decent shape. Then, when the manor was no longer an embarrassment to the Bergstrom name, she would sell it and return to her home and friends in Sewickley.

For as much as she wanted to blame her sister for the manor's disrepair, she knew that she was at least as much at fault. She had abandoned home, family, and business, knowing that Claudia and Harold were not fit stewards of the Bergstrom legacy. What had befallen Elm Creek Manor was as much her responsibility as Claudia's, perhaps more.

Sylvia resolved that although she would sell the manor, she would not entrust the Bergstrom estate to just anyone. As long as it took, she would wait for a buyer who would restore the manor to its former glory, who would fill the halls with love and laughter once more. She had no idea who could possibly fit the bill, but she would wait until that person came along. She had mishandled the Bergstrom legacy once, but she would not fail her family a second time.

As long as she lived, the New Year's Reflections quilt would remind her of her resolution.

As Sylvia made small, neat stitches to secure the binding to the back of the quilt, she smiled when she thought of the resolution she had made in the first minutes of that New Year and the unexpected way she had kept it.

The following summer, she had hired a young woman

named Sarah McClure to help her clean out the manor and prepare it for sale. One prospective buyer had spoken of turning the manor into a residence hall for students of Waterford College, and Sylvia had been tempted to accept his offer. No one else with a more attractive plan had appeared in all the months the estate had been on the market, and as a retired teacher, Sylvia liked the idea of offering students such a beautiful place to live. To Sylvia's everlasting gratitude, Sarah became suspicious of the developer's plans and secretly investigated his company. When Sarah learned that the developer intended to raze Elm Creek Manor and build condos on the property, Sylvia immediately broke off negotiations. At a loss for what to do next, she asked Sarah to help her find a way to bring the manor back to life. Sarah's ingenious and unlikely suggestion was to turn Elm Creek Manor into a retreat for quilters, a place for them to stay, to learn, to find inspiration, and to enjoy the companionship of other quilters. The new owners she had resolved to find turned out to be herself, Sarah, and a group of local quilters who became the first staff members of Elm Creek Quilt Camp.

Thank heavens Sylvia had accepted Sarah's proposal, or her beloved home would now be rubble in a demolition landfill. What a blessing it was that Elm Creek Quilts had prospered, or Sylvia might have been forced to sell the manor anyway, and she would have been a hundred miles distant when Andrew pulled up in his motor home for the surprise visit of a lifetime. She had thought he had forgotten her long ago, and she had been delighted to resume their friendship. She never would have guessed that their feelings would grow deeper and that they would fall in love.

The New Year's wish Mrs. Compson had made for her so many years ago had come true at last.

As they drove through Hartford, Sylvia smiled up at Andrew, her heart full of joy and affection. "I'm so glad you came back to Elm Creek Manor," she told him. "I'm thankful I was there when you came."

"Not half as thankful as I am," he said.

She realized, then, that no matter what Amy decided, whether she chose the wise course of reconciliation or resolved to close her heart to her father, Sylvia and Andrew would be all right. Their love and their gratitude for the blessing of that love would help them endure whatever difficulties came their way.

They turned onto a broad, tree-lined street, recently cleared after what must have been a heavy snowfall. A few houses sported snowmen in the front yards, others impressive snow forts where children in snowsuits and mittens pelted one another with snowballs.

Andrew pulled into the driveway of a sage-green Victorian home with a broad front porch and an octagonal turret on the southeast corner. Evergreen boughs wrapped with small, gold Christmas lights graced the front porch railing and a wreath of fresh holly adorned the front door.

He shut down the engine and paused with his hand on the keys as if tempted to start the car and tear back down the driveway. But Andrew never lacked for courage, so instead he pocketed the keys and gave Sylvia what he probably thought was an encouraging grin. "We're here."

Sylvia was seized by a sudden fear. "Please tell me they're expecting us."

"I called from the 1863 House," he assured her, peering up at the house's darkened windows. Small, icy crystals of snow fell upon the windshield, gently threatening to obscure the view. "But . . . that doesn't mean they're here."

"Perhaps they left town when they heard we were on our way."

Andrew snorted, but the question was promptly settled when the front door opened and Amy stepped out on the front porch, unsmiling, folding her arms over her chest against the cold.

Chapter Five

AMY DISAPPEARED INTO the house but returned to the porch dressed in a coat and boots just as Andrew and Sylvia finished unloading their suitcases from the Elm Creek Quilts minivan. "Here, Dad, let me help you with that," Amy said, hurrying down the front steps.

"I think I can handle two suitcases," said Andrew.

Sylvia had to fight the urge to roll her eyes. Already it had begun. "If she wants to help, let her," she murmured, but Andrew pretended not to hear. He carried both suitcases into the house, with Amy and Sylvia trailing after.

Daniel and the three lanky teenagers—grandsons Gus and Sam, granddaughter Caitlin—welcomed them in the foyer with warm hugs and cheerful smiles. Only Amy seemed ill at ease. The grandchildren, thankfully, seemed unaware of any conflict between the adults, which Sylvia took as a hopeful sign.

"I have pot roast in the oven," Amy announced, taking their coats and hanging them on a mahogany coat tree in a corner near the door. "It'll be ready in a half hour, so please, come on inside and make yourselves at home."

It was certainly a much warmer welcome than Sylvia had anticipated. She prayed that Andrew would not spoil it by blurting out a wedding announcement.

Amy led them into the living room and offered them hot beverages. Sylvia gladly accepted a cup of peppermint tea and settled down on the comfortable sofa. In the fireplace, blazing pine logs crackled cheerfully and gave off steady warmth. In front of the picture window stood a stately Norway pine, festooned with small white lights. Blown glass figurines hung amidst glittering silver tinsel, candy canes, and ornaments the children must have made in school many years before. Every fragrant bough offered a glimpse of a family as it grew and changed, from the crystal swans engraved with the year Amy and Daniel married, to the gilt frames bearing school photographs, to keepsake ornaments revealing the children's favorite sports and cartoon characters. Sylvia's gaze fell upon a pair of delicate white snowflakes, embroidered with pale blue silk threads and as intricate as lace. "How lovely."

"My mother made those," said Amy. "She didn't have much time for crafts, but she loved Hardanger embroidery. One year when Bob and I were still in elementary school, the women of the neighborhood had a Christmas ornament exchange party. My mom made dozens of these, and I begged her to let me have these two. She was surprised that I wanted them but I think she was flattered, too. I've placed them on my Christmas tree every year since." She gazed at the feathery snowflakes and smiled wistfully. "I miss her so much at this time of year. The holidays just aren't the same without her."

Andrew put his arm around her and she briefly rested her head on his shoulder. Sylvia's heart lightened as she witnessed the silent exchange between father and daughter. Despite their recent disagreements, they surely loved each other too much to allow Andrew's remarriage to divide them forever. If Amy's pride and Andrew's stubbornness did not get in the way, surely they would choose reconciliation over estrangement.

When supper was ready, the family gathered in the dining room, where a centerpiece of candles and poinsettias gave the antique cherry dining table a festive air. The roast and potatoes made for a hearty meal, perfect for a snowy winter evening. Sylvia found it encouraging that although Amy had set out the good china, she had chosen a homey, comforting meal one would serve at a gathering of friends and family rather than a stuffy, formal menu meant to impress a not-entirely-welcome guest. Two hours into the visit, all was going well—so well that Sylvia wished she and Andrew had agreed to wait until the morning to make their announcement.

"Do you have any plans for New Year's Eve?" Sylvia asked. "Our family kept many German-American traditions that don't seem to be followed in the Old Country anymore. At our bed and breakfast in New York, we met a charming couple from Germany who told us that everyone in their country—and they did emphasize *everyone*—watches a particular television program that sounded a little unusual to me."

"New Year's Rockin' Eve from Berlin with David Hasselhoff?" guessed Gus.

Sylvia laughed and explained about *Dinner for One*, knowing that she was telling the story not only to amuse her listeners, but also to postpone their announcement. She wished she could have a moment alone with Andrew so she could ask him to wait, but perhaps it was just as well. It had been her idea, after all, to reveal the truth early in their visit. As much as she dreaded Amy's reaction, they ought to get it over with and hope for the best.

Andrew held off breaking the news until after supper. The grandchildren cleared the table as Amy brought out coffee, but before the youngsters could return to their video games and IM chat rooms, or whatever it was that so absorbed them on the computer, he asked them to take their seats again.

As the teenagers seated themselves, exchanging curious smiles, Amy grew very still at the foot of the table. Sylvia said a silent prayer for peace and wished for just a moment that Andrew had broken the news over the phone.

"What is it, Dad?" Amy asked. "You're not . . . ill, are you?"

"No, no," said Andrew. "I've never felt better, and part of the reason is that I am now the proud husband of this lovely woman right here."

With that, he laced his fingers through Sylvia's, smiled at her reassuringly, and raised her hand to his lips.

The grandchildren cheered, and Daniel smiled broadly. "Congratulations," he said, clapping his father-in-law on the back. He rose and came around to Sylvia to kiss her on the cheek.

Amy sat wide-eyed and still, her gaze fixed on her father. "You mean you're her *fiancé*," she said. "You said husband."

"I didn't misspeak," said Andrew. "Sylvia and I married on Christmas Eve."

Amy stared at him, slowly comprehending. "Are you trying to say that you eloped?"

"We had a lovely wedding at Elm Creek Manor," said Sylvia. "It's true that we caught most of our friends by surprise, but we don't consider that eloping."

"Not that anything's wrong with that," said Sam. "Congratulations, Grandpa. You want to play Xbox with us? We have four controllers." His older brother nudged him. "What? What did I say?"

Crushed, Caitlin wailed, "You mean we missed everything?"

"We wanted you to be there," Andrew said. His gaze shifted from Daniel to Amy. "You and Bob and Kathy and their kids and the whole family. Now you understand why we were so eager for you to come for Christmas."

"If we had known you were going to get married, we would have made the trip," said Amy.

"Why, so you could stop us? You told us you couldn't come for Christmas, but we were supposed to know that you could suddenly become available if a wedding was involved?"

"Andrew, this isn't the way," murmured Sylvia.

"The wedding was a surprise," Daniel said to his wife. "They couldn't tell us or they'd spoil it."

"Why did it have to be a surprise?" said Amy, her voice rising. "Wasn't the engagement surprise enough? The wedding has to be a shock, too?"

"Let's all just take a deep breath and settle down," said Sylvia.

"Seriously, like, peace out, people," said Caitlin, folding her arms and shaking her head at her mother and grandfather.

Amy glared at her daughter. "I don't appreciate your tone, and was that even a sentence?"

Caitlin rolled her eyes.

"If you had really wanted us at your wedding, you would have told us," said Amy, turning to her father. "Do you think I'm stupid? I know what happened. You knew we didn't approve, so you invited us just so that you could say you tried, and then you snuck your wedding in under the radar."

"Would you have come if you had known?" said Andrew. "Would you have supported us, or would you have stood up and thrown a tantrum when the judge asked if anyone had any reason to object to the marriage? Maybe it's just as well that you didn't come."

Amy pushed her chair back from the table, but Sylvia quickly placed a hand on her arm. "Please stay. Let's work this out."

"What's to work out?" snapped Amy, but she stayed in her seat.

Sylvia clasped her hands together in her lap. "Perhaps we should have handled things better, and if we've offended you, I'm sincerely sorry. What's important now is that we are married, and we're hoping that you can find it in your heart to be happy for us. If happiness is out of the question at this particular moment—and I can understand why it might be—we ask instead for your acceptance."

Amy refused to look at her. "How can we offer you our acceptance when you gave us no say in the matter?"

"Because you don't deserve any say in the matter," said Andrew, incredulous. "It was never up to you whether I married, or whom, or when, or how. This was between Sylvia and me. It was never a group decision."

"Nothing around here is ever a group decision," muttered Caitlin.

"That's enough out of you, young lady," snapped Amy.

Caitlin sniffed in disdain, rose deliberately from her chair, and left the room. Her brothers exchanged quick, wary looks and decided to follow her example.

Daniel planted his elbows on the table and cradled his head in his hands. "Just for the record, I think you two make a great couple and I wish you both years of happiness."

"Daniel," gasped Amy.

"Oh, come on, honey, you know where I stand."

"Yes, against me, apparently."

"This isn't about you." Daniel gestured to the newlyweds. "It's about them. It's about their happiness. Sylvia's right. What's done is done. It's time for us to come together as a family."

"They're flaunting their wedding in my face and I'm supposed to act happy about it?"

"That would be better than acting like a spoiled brat," said Andrew.

In a gesture reminiscent of her daughter's, Amy gave him a steady, wordless look before rising from her chair and striding from the room.

"I'm sorry," Daniel told the newlyweds.

"It's not your fault," Sylvia assured him as he hurried after his wife.

"I should have known this would happen," muttered Andrew when they were alone.

"It was bound to happen," said Sylvia. "You walked in here with a chip on your shoulder daring Amy to disapprove of us. Honestly, Andrew, you could have handled this much better."

"You're blaming me?"

"Oh, there's plenty of blame to go around." She reached for his hand. "We both knew she would take the news badly. If only you had responded with more compassion instead of losing your temper—"

"I know," said Andrew, chagrined. "I know. I should have behaved myself, but Sylvia, when she started in on you—"

"I've told you before, dear, it takes more than angry words to bring me to my knees." Sylvia shook her head. Everything had gone so wrong so quickly. "She's being unreasonable, you're overreacting, and I'm afraid we're much worse off than we were before."

Andrew frowned and rubbed at his jaw. "What do we do now?"

"I think there's only one thing we can do."

"What's that?"

"Give her what she's asked for."

Breakfast the next morning was a tense affair. Amy hardly spoke, and she was clearly just as angry with her husband as with Sylvia and her father. The grandkids tried to lighten the mood with jokes and amusing stories, but they grew discouraged when their listeners barely smiled. Caitlin persisted long after her brothers gave up, peppering Sylvia with questions about the wedding. Mindful of Amy who was studiously ignoring the conversation, Sylvia provided an understated description of the candlelight ceremony in the ballroom of the manor, restored to its former elegance thanks to the attention of Sarah McClure's husband, Matt, who had become the full-time gardener and caretaker of the estate.

"Have you told Bob and Kathy yet?" Daniel asked Andrew, referring to Andrew's son and daughter-in-law.

"Not yet," Andrew replied.

"Don't expect a shower of rose petals," said Amy shortly. "I doubt they'll welcome the news any more than we did. The girls wanted to be bridesmaids, as I'm sure you recall."

Andrew peered at her curiously. "Are you angry now because we got married or because we got married without you? I've lost track."

Sylvia frowned. Why must Andrew rise to the bait every time Amy spoke?

"I wanted to be a bridesmaid, too, but you don't see me whining," said Caitlin. "My cousins will get over it. The important thing is that you got married the way you wanted to."

"Not entirely the way we wanted," said Sylvia. "We wanted all of you to be there. Truly, we did."

Caitlin shrugged and made a face to suggest it didn't matter. "What should we call you now, anyway? Mrs. Cooper?"

"No, I've decided not to change my last name. I've been Sylvia Compson so long that I don't think I'd remember to answer to anything else."

"But it's not like you're keeping your maiden name," Amy pointed out. "You're actually keeping your first husband's name instead of taking my father's. Some people might think that suggests a lack of commitment."

Andrew loaded scrambled eggs onto a piece of buttered toast. "If it doesn't bother me, it shouldn't bother you."

Caitlin threw her mother a brief scowl before returning her attention to Sylvia. "Should we call you Grandma?"

Amy slammed her palm on the table. "She is not your grandmother."

"We can't call her 'Step-Grandma,' " said Sam. "That's so lame."

"Lame or not, like it or not, that's all she is."

Andrew glowered. "All right, now, I've had just about enough—"

"We've all had just about enough." Sylvia rose. "I can't bear to think that I've divided this family. Amy, you're right. You win." She turned to Andrew and steeled herself. "I'm sorry, dear. Our marriage was a mistake. When we return to Elm Creek Manor, I'm going to file for an annulment."

Andrew looked up at her, pain in his eyes. "Sylvia—"

Sylvia managed a tender smile, blinked back her tears, and hurried from the room.

Upstairs in the guest room, Sylvia rolled Andrew's suitcase into the hallway and shut the door. If she wasn't going to stay married to a man, she couldn't share a bedroom with him.

She arranged pillows into a comfortable seat on the bed and retrieved the New Year's Reflections quilt from her tote bag. She spread the quilt over her lap and gazed upon it, her heart momentarily lifted by the soothing colors and the intricate patterns. Threading a needle, she got to work, wondering if Amy would still be willing to accept her gift or if all her efforts had been in vain.

Through the closed door she heard the muffled sounds of heated debate as she mitered the last of the four corners. Voices rose and fell as she turned her attention to the last edge of the quilt. She couldn't hear the details of the argument, but she could imagine the way things were going. Five minutes of silence told her they had reached an impasse, and sure enough, before long she heard footsteps approaching from the far end of the hallway.

The door swung open and Andrew leaned inside. He gestured to the suitcase at his feet. "You're throwing me out?"

She raised her eyebrows at him over the rims of her glasses. "It wouldn't be proper to do otherwise."

Andrew frowned, but he could hardly disagree. "You're not going to stay locked up here until the New Year, are you?"

Sylvia considered. "As tempting as that might be, I don't think so. Now that Amy has had her own way, I imagine it will be much more pleasant downstairs now that we've made her so happy."

"Oh, you'll see how happy she is," Andrew said scornfully as Sylvia returned quilt and notions to her tote bag.

The grandkids had made themselves scarce, and Sylvia couldn't blame them. In the kitchen, Amy and Daniel were rinsing the breakfast dishes and loading the dishwasher. "May I help?" asked Sylvia.

"No," said Amy. "We've got it, thanks."

She did not look in Sylvia's direction, but it was obvious she had been crying. Sylvia pretended not to notice, sat down at the kitchen table, and idly paged through the newspaper.

Andrew pulled out a chair beside her. "Is there anything I can do to change your mind?"

"I'm afraid not, dear." Sylvia passed him the sports section, but he ignored it. "This is best for everyone."

"How can you say that?"

"With me out of the picture, you and your children can—" She waved a hand, searching for the appropriate phrase. "Go back to normal."

"As if nothing ever happened? That's not possible. I'll always remember that they were responsible for driving you away. It'll be impossible to forgive them. Our divorce would divide the family more than our marriage ever could."

Sylvia saw Amy and Daniel exchange an anxious look. "Perhaps this is a discussion better made in private," Sylvia said, lowering her voice a fraction. "We have a long drive home. We can save it for then."

Andrew threw up his hands in exasperation. "And when we get 'home,' what then?"

"Oh, dear. You're right. I hadn't thought of that."

Amy couldn't restrain her curiosity. "Thought of what?"

"I can't very well live with Sylvia after we divorce, can I?" said Andrew. "Elm Creek Manor has been my home for years, but not anymore. Where am I supposed to go?"

"Didn't Bob and Kathy ask you to live with them?" Amy asked in a small voice.

"That's crazy talk. You know how small those southern California tract houses are. We'll be tripping over each other. And I sure can't sleep on their fold-out sofa for the rest of my life, not with my back."

"Well . . . there's your RV, for the immediate future. You can even park it at Elm Creek Manor through the winter, if you like. But—" Sylvia threw an imploring look to Amy and Daniel. "I don't think anyone would expect you to live in the RV forever."

"You can move in with us," said Daniel, placing an arm around his wife's shoulders. "It's the least we can do, since we're responsible for Sylvia's decision."

"Wait." Amy shrugged off her husband's arm and held up her hands. "Maybe we're being too hasty here."

"Do you have a VFW in town?" Andrew asked Daniel. "Can I park the RV in your driveway or would it be better on the street in front of the house?"

Sylvia beamed at Amy. "You're such a generous daughter, opening your home to your father, especially with the children going off to college in a few years. Taking on all that cooking and laundry and chauffeuring just when you were probably looking forward to more time to yourself—well, I don't think one daughter in ten would be so generous."

"I hope you didn't have any other plans for that guest room," said Andrew.

Amy shook her head, looking faintly ill. "I was thinking about turning it into a sewing room, but—"

"Oh, dear," exclaimed Sylvia. "I suppose we won't be able to continue your quilting lessons, since this will surely be my last visit."

"Can I redecorate?" asked Andrew. "No offense, but that room's awfully lacy and frilly. I'd like to hang up my fishing trophies."

"Dead trout on a varnished plank, that's what I always called them," Sylvia confided.

"Maybe the kids can drive me around town when you're too busy," Andrew mused. "They all have their licenses by now, right? I don't think I should take the RV around on errands unless you have very forgiving neighbors. These streets are so narrow I might knock over a few mailboxes."

Sylvia, Andrew, and Daniel all began talking at once, their voices a babble of redecorating suggestions and driving tips. In the center of it all, Amy clutched her head in her hands, her gaze flicking around the room as if desperate to find an escape.

Before long Amy had clearly heard enough. "All right, all right!" When the others fell silent, she closed her eyes and inhaled deeply. "Dad, Daniel, will you excuse Sylvia and me for a minute?"

"Why?" said Daniel, wary.

Amy looked as if another word might cause her to explode. "Just go. Please."

Daniel nudged his father-in-law and gestured toward the door. Andrew struggled to hide a grin as they left the kitchen. Sylvia knew he was thinking that this would be his moment of triumph. This was Amy's cue to beg Sylvia not to divorce him.

Sylvia wasn't so sure that was what Amy had in mind, but she pushed the newspaper aside and composed herself as Amy pulled up a chair on the other side of the table. "I take it you want to speak to me alone?"

"My father would just waste time proclaiming his

innocence, but I doubt you will," said Amy. "You can let the curtain fall on the drama now. Please."

"I beg your pardon?"

"The breaking up with my father act. I know what you're doing, and I think I know why."

Sylvia sighed. "How did you know? Was our acting really that bad?"

"My father loves you," Amy said. "If he believed you really intended to divorce him, he wouldn't be talking about parking spaces for his RV and hanging dead fish on the walls. He would be brokenhearted. He would be devastated. And I think you would be, too."

Reluctantly, Sylvia admitted, "I suppose the lack of tears and pleading was a dead giveaway."

"And also, yes, your acting really was that bad."

"It couldn't have been," said Sylvia. "You were genuinely alarmed for a few minutes. I saw it in your eyes when visions of cleaning up after your father and losing your sewing room flashed before your eyes."

"I might have had a nervous moment or two."

"Your father hoped to drag this out for at least another day," said Sylvia. "He thought that given a taste of how his life and yours would be affected if we were no longer together, you'd give our marriage your heartiest endorsement."

Amy managed a small smile. "That's ridiculous."

"We had to try something. Reasoning with you wasn't working. Arguing made matters worse." Sylvia laced her fingers together and rested them on the table. "Frankly, Amy, I'm at a loss. You've said you're concerned because I had a stroke. My doctor and I agree that I've fully recovered and that I'm in excellent health, but even if you're right and we're wrong, I have sufficient resources that you needn't fear your father will exhaust himself caring for me."

"It's not just that. I'm thinking of the emotional toll if he loses you. You didn't see what he went through, tending my mother in her last years, mourning her when she died."

"Your father already loves me, so if I do pass on before he does, he will mourn me whether I'm his friend or his wife. I could lose him. You could lose Daniel. That can't stop us from loving." Sylvia shook her head, knowing nothing she said would persuade Amy to see reason. "We've told you all this before, dear, and not once have you disagreed. You accept our premises but not our conclusions, so I can't help thinking there's something else behind your disapproval."

Amy studied her for a long moment in silence. "There is."

"I thought so." Sylvia reached for her hand. "Amy, dear, you're not betraying your mother's memory by accepting my marriage to your father."

Amy said nothing, but her eyes filled with unshed tears.

"I could never replace your mother," said Sylvia. "I would never try. Your father found love a second time. That doesn't mean he's forgotten your mother or that his love for her wasn't strong and true."

"He knew you first," Amy choked out, snatching her hand away. "But you were married to another man. Was that the only reason he married my mother? Was she his second choice, and all these long years he was putting on an act, pining away for you?"

Aghast, Sylvia sat back in her chair. "Amy—"

"If that's true, then everything I ever learned about love since I was a child has been a lie."

"Oh, Amy, you couldn't be more wrong." Sylvia hardly knew where to begin. "What has your father told you about his time in the service?"

"Very little," said Amy with a bitter laugh. "You know what men of his generation are like. They don't complain; they don't brag. They just do what needs to be done—whether that's winning a war or keeping a marriage vow even when your heart longs to be with someone else."

Sylvia silently promised herself to prevail upon Andrew to clear away Amy's misunderstandings. She deserved to know what a fine man he was, even if that forced him to boast. "There's so much to say and it's your father's place to say it," she said. "For now, you need to know that your mother was indeed your father's first choice. She always was his true love."

"We'll never know for sure."

"On the contrary, we do know," said Sylvia. "My husband was killed during the war. When your father came home after his service ended, he came to see me at Elm Creek Manor. If he had wanted to declare his love for me, he had the perfect opportunity."

"He wouldn't have considered that an appropriate time," said Amy, with such certainty that Sylvia decided that perhaps she knew her father well after all. "You had just lost your husband. He wouldn't have made a move on a grieving widow."

"Perhaps not," said Sylvia, amused in spite of everything at the thought of the gentlemanly Andrew "making a move" on anyone. "But he surely would have stayed nearby, so that when the time was right, he would be in the right place. Instead he took a job hundreds of miles away where he met your mother and fell in love." Sylvia forced herself to confess her own guilty secret. "There are days, I admit, when I wish he had been in love with me back then, and that he had stayed in Waterford, courted me, and asked me to marry him while we were still young. If he had, I would have been spared years of loneliness. I almost certainly would have remained at Elm Creek Manor. I could have reconciled with my sister, kept the family business thriving, and saved myself a lot of trouble restoring the manor fifty years later. I might have had children. But if all of those things had happened, you and Bob, your children and your nieces never would have existed. Elm Creek Quilts never would have been founded. And your father would not have loved your mother, in which case I know he would not be the fine man he is today."

A tear ran down Amy's face, and she ducked her head to hide it. "I don't like change," she said. "I prefer to hold on, to keep things as they are."

"You're fighting a losing battle in that case, dear," said Sylvia. She glanced around the room at the antique furniture, the years-old children's crafts decorating end tables and shelves, and suddenly she felt as if she were truly seeing Amy for the first time. It wasn't Sylvia that Amy disliked, but the unknown future. "Life is all about change, but you don't have to face the future with fear."

"I love Christmas but hate the New Year," said Amy, forcing a laugh as if she expected Sylvia to think she was a fool. "I don't like sweeping away the old year and welcoming in the new. Those moments of the past twelve months that I cherished so much are gone and they'll never come again. To me, that's a loss."

Sylvia suddenly understood why Andrew's love for her had turned Amy's world upside down. Amy thought the past was fixed, immutable, safe. Andrew's engagement to Sylvia had not only called into question her father's love for her mother, but also threatened her very way of understanding the world.

"Is something seriously wrong with me?" Amy's voice broke. "On New Year's Eve, everyone else parties and celebrates and counts down the minutes until midnight as if they can't wait to see the year end, and all the while I'm holding on to it with both fists. I'd push the ball in Times Square back up to the top of the flagpole if they'd let me."

"There's nothing wrong with you that a little perspective wouldn't cure," said Sylvia. "You aren't the only one who feels a little bit of sadness to see the old year go. After all, what's the most popular song on New Year's Eve but 'Auld Lang Syne'? Even Robert Burns felt melancholy reflecting upon days gone by, upon friends no longer near. We can't hold on to the past, it's true, but we can keep the best part of the days of 'Auld Lang Syne' in our hearts and in our memories, and we can look forward to the future with hope and resolve."

"I suppose that's all we can do," said Amy softly.

Sylvia smiled. "It's not as bad as all that. I've learned to think of the New Year as a gift. It's a blank page and you can write upon it as you wish. Sometimes we make a pledge to improve ourselves in the year ahead. My mother taught me that it's also wise to make the world a better place for someone else, even if it's only in small ways." She remembered Mrs. Compson's wise counsel. Sylvia had not taken heed in time to reconcile with her sister, but she would not make that mistake again. "A resolution is also the settlement of a dispute. Perhaps you and I and your father can make a resolution today. We're a few days shy of the New Year, but this resolution is too important to delay."

"It's not too early," said Amy. "I'm thankful that it's not too late. Besides, with three kids, I always feel like the New Year starts in September with the first day of school."

"Then let's not wait until New Year's Eve to resolve our differences." Sylvia rose and took her stepdaughter by the hand. "Come with me. I have something to show you."

Sylvia led Amy upstairs to the guest room, where she removed the New Year's Reflections quilt from her tote bag and spread it upon the bed. "I wanted this to be a New Year's Day gift," she said, "but a day or two sooner doesn't matter. It's not quite finished, so mind the pins in the binding."

As Amy looked on, Sylvia shared the story of the New Year's Reflections quilt, from the discovery of the long-forgotten fabric stash of the Bergstrom women and the loneliness that inspired her to cut the first pieces to the unexpected path she had followed in keeping the resolution she had made that night. She described the blocks she had chosen and how each one preserved a memory of a New Year of long ago. A True Lover's Knot for Sylvia's belated acceptance of Elizabeth's marriage to Henry, and an Orange Peel for the sweetness of life she hoped they found in California. A Hatchet to mark the lead figure Claudia had found in the bowl of water by the fireside, foretelling her unhappiness in love and the severing of ties between sisters. A Wandering Foot block, a fond remembrance of her dear brother and her mother's gift for finding hope and courage in the face of uncertainty and fear. Simple patterns like those she had sewn together to make quilts for the Orphan's Home, and complex patterns to trace the tangled relationships of family united by love and chance and divided by tragedy. The Resolution Square for promises made, and Memory Chain for lessons learned. Every New Year's Eve of nostalgic farewells and each New Year's Day full of anticipation and new beginnings had been recorded in the patchwork mosaic of memories.

Sylvia would need years to tell Amy every story, every lesson she had sewn into the quilt, but for the first time since she and Andrew had announced their engagement, she believed Amy would grant her that time.

Sylvia was not the only one who shared New Year's memories from days gone by. At Sylvia's prompting, Amy recalled New Year's Eve parties in her childhood home, snowball fights and ice skating on the pond on New Year's morning, gathering around the table for a traditional meal of ham and sweet potatoes, and curling up beside her father on the sofa to watch the Rose Bowl on television. Packing up the holiday decorations on the last day of Winter Break and hauling the Christmas tree out to the curb. Settling into the New Year until it was no longer the future but the familiar present.

They lingered so long that eventually Andrew and Daniel came looking for them. The apprehension on the men's faces when Andrew tentatively pushed open the door made both women burst out laughing. Sylvia's heart soared when Amy threw her arms around her father and murmured something in his ear. The words were meant for him alone and Sylvia would not pry, but the look of sheer happiness that lit up Andrew's face at that moment told her all would be well.

Over the next two days, Sylvia finished the New Year's Reflections quilt, often sitting in front of the fire while

Amy hand-pieced a simple block nearby. As they sewed, they shared memories of New Years past, of years welcomed with excitement or with trepidation, of years that were too lovely to forget and others too sorrowful to dwell upon. Sylvia almost felt as if she were back at Elm Creek Manor, gathered together with the Bergstrom women she missed so dearly. Sylvia knew only time would allow the true bond of family to grow between her and her one-time reluctant stepdaughter, but she would resolve to be patient, to give Amy the time she needed. It was the season for hope, for joy, and for new beginnings, and Sylvia prayed she, Amy, and Andrew would be mindful of how quickly years could pass, and how unwise it was to waste a single moment in enmity.

Sylvia put the last stitch into the binding on the morning of New Year's Day, and when she presented it to Amy, it was with a heartfelt prayer that they would make the most of the fresh start the New Year offered. She knew there was no better time to reflect upon the past—mistakes and triumphs, happiness and sorrow—and look for lessons that would guide her into the future. She trusted Amy and Andrew would do the same.

Sylvia did not pretend to know what the year ahead would bring. The road before them passed through sunshine and shadow, and she could not see far beyond the first bend. But with loved ones by her side and loving memories of those who had gone before in her heart, she would move into the future with courage and hope that the best was yet to be, if she did her part to make it so.